MW00426558

HEARTWOOD

A novel by

PJ Piccirillo

This is a publication of Middleton Books
832 Dana Drive, Coatesville, PA 19320
USA
www.middletonbooks.com

ISBN 978-09716611-2-7
Printed in the United States of America

I may there discover the wondrous power
which attracts the needle

Mary Shelly, *Frankenstein*

For Laurie, without whom...

and for Mum

Many years ago, on a bleak December day as snow fell across the rolling tableland of northern Pennsylvania, a man murderously exacted vengeance in a woodlot. This man was acting on regret for having been made to bear blame for someone else's misdeed. But he'd been terribly mistaken in the circumstances, caught within the braided story of two childhood friends and the woman they each came to love. This is that story.

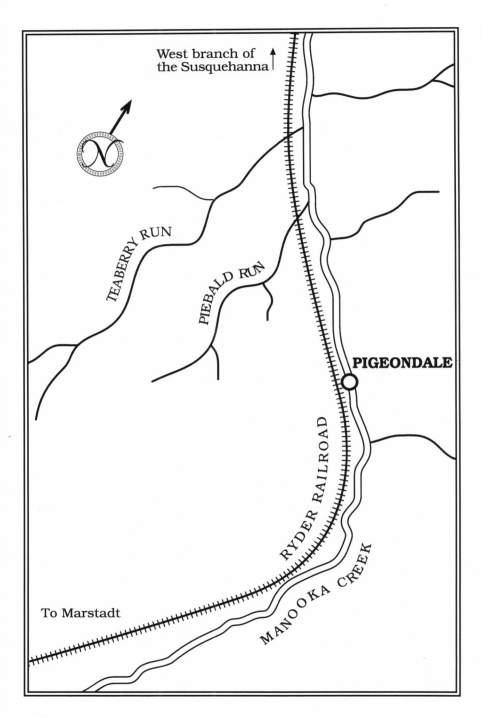

West branch of
the Susquehanna

TEABERRY RUN

PIEBALD RUN

RYDER RAILROAD

MANOOKA CREEK

PIGEONDALE

To Marstadt

Prologue

The Willys pickup grinded as he geared to slow for the turn off of the macadam and onto the gravel road. Tree-by-tree the woods dawned as he drove farther into the hollow, the place waking with the color and chill of wet canvas. Out the passenger window, past his grandfather's steady stare, past the two-fingered hand on the door panel, rushed the sliver of creek he loved. He was one of few who could believe that such tiny waters held wild trout, and he felt lucky for that.

When they crossed onto the posted land he glanced out his own window at the paper no-trespassing signs tacked to the square backboards trailing into the hardwoods, boards his grandfather had put up for the company years ago, signs his grandfather detested—something about how, of anything in this world, these hollows were for everyone.

Wherever the stream wound close to the road, swelling in the congestion of an arc, his eyes—of their own—looked over, enticed by the dark mystery of deeper pools. But his grandfather stared on, the crippled hand bracing him steady against the puddle-pocked road.

By the pond, where the creek was dammed for the lodge, he parked his grandfather's truck among the broad pines and poplars left long ago to shade the Piebald camp, gone now sixty years.

His grandfather took his big western from his lap, perched it on his head, and unlatched the door. It swung as he turned and leaned his shoulders out, giving himself momentum to slide off the seat.

They each went around to a side of the truck bed, his grandfather taking up his wicker creel with its crisp leather trim, chafed away where his elbow had rubbed all those years he'd walked these streams.

The young man looked up at the lodge. "It's a shame the old place doesn't get more use."

His grandfather did not turn to the creek-stone porch piers or the mossy tar shingles hung now where pine shakes and pitch had capped the place on his honeymoon so many years back—the building he—steward of this land—had never since entered.

The young man put his elbows on the bed rail and regarded his grandfather there in relief against that cobblestone lodge. "This is my last semester of school," he said. "And Grandma wants me to start full-time in the carbon plant."

His grandfather had writhed into the strap of his creel and was sifting now in a coffee can of dirt and worms. "What does your mother say to that?"

"She says that by rights it would be mine to run someday. That I'm all there is to keep it in the family."

"And what do you think?"

"Something tells me that's not what I want." The young man looked uphollow, then down. "Crazy as it sounds, sometimes I feel like I need to be out here. Have a home in little old Pigeondale. Like you. Work out of doors the way you did." He nodded over his grandfather's shoulder. "Maybe run the lodge or manage the landholdings. But then I think that's ridiculous in modern times like this, times when the carbon plant's making parts for rockets. Rockets that might even put men on the moon."

His grandfather's patient regard made him uneasy, made him feel he should say more. "I don't know, I guess I'm caught again between two halves pulling—one like you, one like Grandma." He thought for the right way to put it. "I think of hers as the conventional way, yours as the less sure one."

He looked into the bed of the truck, at his grandfather's two-fingered hand dropping maggots one by one into a matchbox, at his own vest with its pockets of fishing flies. "It's like the two halves will never settle terms, never come together. No more than you two ever did."

His grandfather looked up Piebald Run, past the pond where there was no road. With his neck turned, some of the vigor that had stemmed from his shoulders still showed, still sign of a stallion's neck, or the broad trunk of a tree, strong. Same as those big hands, his steady will.

"One or the other is right for you," his grandfather said. "And you know it." He turned and looked up at the lodge now. "You'll need to brace up and face that." And when he looked back, his grandson saw his mouth pinched straight, as if held against the chance of a lament.

His grandfather finally said, "I thought once too, that an old-fashioned way didn't stand to reason—or I let myself be told. Make sure whose reasoning you go by." Then his face un-tautened, and he said, "You'll know where you're a part of something. Where you see all the pieces and how you fit."

He watched his grandfather stuff wax-papered sandwiches into his creel, then take up his three pieces of bamboo pole, that heirloom twelve-footer handed down by his father.

"Why don't you fish downstream," his grandfather said. "And I'll go up."

"You're serious? You don't want to leapfrog hole-to-hole, like usual?"

His grandfather shook his head and pointed the sections of fishing pole downhollow, below the pond. "You can fish brown trout down there. They're bigger than the little brookies uphollow."

"You know I like to fish for brookies, Grampa." He flicked his thumb over his shoulder, downstream. "Stocked brownies are bigger because they eat the natives—they're defenseless against those invaders. Let me go along. I like to fish brook trout with you."

"Not today," his grandfather said. "You fish for stocked trout below the pond." He'd fitted up the three pieces of fishing rod. He set the butt on the ground and walked to the tip.

The young man shook his head. "It's not just the brown trout. I think it's best if I stay with you."

His grandfather had started dragging his rod. He stopped and shrugged, but did not look back. "What's the worry?" he said.

"Grampa, you're eighty years old."

His grandfather held still a moment. "When you fish," he said, "age goes away." Then he moved along.

Chapter 1

He wanted to leap without being coaxed. Tobias Meier crouched lower as his father trotted alongside the flatbed railcar and shouted against its wailing wheels. "Don't weigh it, do it."

Tobias reached for his father and forced his legs to spring. All the world of Manooka Valley paused, as if he dove into water, the clatter of the log train fizzing away until he had hold of his father's shoulders.

"Why do you hold back?" Herbert Meier said, setting Tobias on his feet. "The world won't wait for you to size everything up."

Tobias stayed while his father backtracked to find the feed sack of creels, sandwiches and bamboo poles he'd thrown before jumping. The boy watched the rear cars—mere platforms of rough timbers on wheels—sway off the main tracks toward a cleft in the valley, then worm into a break in the brush. The fireman, who'd been waiting by the split in the rails, threw the switch and chased the train.

Shouldering their gear, Herbert moved past Tobias, his stride set to every second crosstie of the spur line. Tobias stepped fast to keep up, counting off each adze-hewn log.

A staircase stream had whittled away the side valley; deep and narrow, it was more a gorge, a hollow. Like all hollows thereabouts, it took its name from legend or landmark. This was Piebald Hollow, old haunt of a patch-coat deer which, by some long-ago encounter with a hunter, had cast the tint of itself on that narrows, would remain forever gracing its falling waters with the name Piebald Run.

Tobias looked over his shoulder toward the wider valley. "Pop, why don't we ever fish the big crick?"

"Because there's nothing in there but eels, suckers and carp, and we'd rather have trout on our plates."

Tobias thought about this for twenty crossties. "Why don't trout live in the big crick?"

"Don't take to it," his father said. He slung the sack over his other shoulder, grasping together the sections of fishing pole that poked from its neck.

"Then how'd the trout get to the little cricks?" Tobias knew his father was rolling his eyes at what he called *unshakable interest in nonsense*.

"Tobias, that's just where they were put. They didn't get anywhere." Herbert shooed the matter with his hand. "Besides, some things is just for us to know, not wonder how."

Tobias took back to counting. He thought there must be a rule that a thing temporary, like the spur line, be built to look accidental. The crossties lay at jagged angles with uneven spacing; he could feel this in his stuttering steps. They were hewn of beech, but barely squared. And unlike on the permanent railroads, the ties hadn't been dried or creosoted, so under the iron rails they'd twisted like roots.

That's the way things were in hollows—raw and coarse-grained, right down to the woodhicks who felled their timbers. But Tobias looked to loggers with awe, men godlike somehow in their earthiness. Woodhicks, like that old piebald deer, were parts of these places, and woodhicks, he suspected, were somewhere ahead.

Blades of light were just slicing through the pole timber rimming the ridgeline, still winter-gray. But the valley trees that had survived axe and saw had already softened overhead, a peach and cream veil of woods blossoms. Tobias liked the humble colors of May better than fall's; a person had to look for them hiding high in the branches.

Herbert led his son from the tracks to a streamside sandstone, table-tall, and shook out the contents of the sack. They assembled home-cut poles of bamboo—a two-piecer for Tobias, a three-piecer for his father. Each slipped a billfold of snelled hooks and fork-tine sinkers between his shirt buttons, and put leek and lard sandwiches into his wicker creel.

Tobias studied the pencil scrawlings on their matchboxes of bait. "Pop, should we fish worms or salted minnies? Or maggots?"

"How about I start with maggots, you start with worms?"

Tobias dumped half the bait from each box into a tin can and laced his belt through its wire bail. His father stuffed their coats into the sack and nestled it where a brim jutted from the boulder like the spout of a gravy boat. Then they were on their way, businesslike, but content with this

5

business, moving silently on a mold of winter-flattened leaves, which in the distance looked drab as potato skin against the new dogwood blooms white-peppering the under-woods.

The stream flowed mighty bold, so narrow even a boy could leap across it in places, as he could most runs of the plateauland. But by late summer, the bed would lie dry between pools. Even so, the waters spawned swarms of flying insects and surged with crayfish and minnows and trout.

Tobias loved these backwoods places of brook trout. He connected here with time gone by, as when he unearthed a fossil. Fishing was an isthmus from a part of himself tangled with that history—soaked in the terrestrial, compressed and ancient, like shale itself. And with fishing there was that new mystery at each hole, where a nod of nature might let him lure it out.

"Tobias, you've fished that hole long enough."

His line traced an invisible eddy at the end of a pool. The worm surfaced where the water riffled away to the hole his father fished. Tobias didn't want to move on. He'd seen a silver flash near his bait, and the mechanical motion of trying, trying for the secrets below the surface had put him where time happened apart from him.

He waited for his father to walk far upstream, then tossed his bait to let it drift through just one more time. Something across Piebald Run drew his eye—a bird alighting on a dogwood at the foot of the hollow's slope. This tree hadn't blossomed yet, remaining inconspicuous in the early spring understory. The bird preened a wing and went still, still as the woods. It was dove-shaped, but with a long blade of a tail feather. Had it not been for the bird's deep colors, Tobias might have guessed the kind that roosted about the cupola on the rail shop in Marstadt. No, not one of them. This one's neck bore a patch of pink, and its breast was as golden as the meat of a peach. The bird did not fit the story of those woods as Tobias knew it. And that, he sensed, accounted for the fear, or maybe sad uncertainty, in the ruby eye.

Tobias stared until he knew his father had gotten well ahead. He moved on, looking back on the bird for as long as he could pick it out of the web of tree limbs.

When he caught up to his father, Tobias was careful not to step on any of the twelve feet of bamboo Herbert dragged. The length of his fishing pole further declared his belief in the wiliness of trout: *If a trout sees you, the ruse is up.* Its length never encumbered him. Between holes, Herbert simply dropped the butt end to the ground and moved along with the rod sliding through his hand until he could pull it by its tip.

"Tobias," he said, nodding to where the water chuted between sister sandstones into a frothy tempest. "Sneak up on that hole and give it a few tries. Then move on. If a fish doesn't bite straightways, it ain't meant for you to catch."

Tobias raked his fingers through his bait can for a fresh worm and watched his father move upstream. He was built unlike any other man Tobias knew. Most wore their greatest girth just above their pants or at their shoulders. But Herbert Meier's body, an inverted kite, tapered from his hips. Men in the mill yard joked that Herbert Meier would have to go feet-to-the-fore-end in his coffin. His hands could hold four pears each, and they hung low—below his pockets—where they hardly swung when he walked, his wide hips affording such balance.

Tobias fished his worm through the chute. On his fourth try—one more than his father would have made—the convulsion ran through his fishing pole to his shoulder. He lifted his rod and out came his reward, a red-speckled brook trout, arcing this way and that against the hook. On the ground, the brookie flopped and flailed while Tobias's hand chased it, the fish matting itself in shards of last year's leaves until Tobias gripped behind its gills. He dislodged the hook from the upper lip and peeled pieces of leaf. He stroked the fish, then dropped it through a square in his wicker creel where it shook among the butcher-papered sandwiches.

Upstream he moved, past his father to the next hole, following their leapfrog pattern.

By late morning they'd covered half the distance to the head of Piebald Hollow. At a place where the bottomland broadened and a rillet of spring water tumbled down a sharp side-hollow, there stood a logging camp. The living quarters was a long barn of a building—rough-cut planks weathered to the hues of a molting rabbit jacket. Outbuildings leaned here and there. Not a soul about. Tobias would have given anything to look inside, sit at the big feed tables, peek at the sleeping quarters. Not within memory had he wanted anything more than to be a woodhick. Someday.

The hollow narrowed, and the grade steepened, the fishing holes crowding one another as the water tumbled over hydro-sculpted sandstones and tangles of driftwood. For the bed of the railroad to pass especially tight stretches, man and horse had cut arcing shelves into the hollow's flank; so narrow were these that were it not for the tracks, they might have been mule trails.

Each time Tobias moved away from the falling waters, he caught locomotive chugs breaking the din. Following his father, he spoke across the twelve feet of bamboo, lowly though, since trout scare to voices easy. "Pop, do you think barkpeelers are spudding up ahead, it being Saturday?" Now he could hear the dull iron-on-iron of the engine coupling loaded cars.

His father stopped and sniffed the air, and Tobias had to throw his weight to his shoulders to avoid stepping on the butt of the fishing pole.

"I suppose they are, Tobias."

So his father hadn't yet regarded the fresh tang of hemlock flesh. Tobias tried to quiet his urge to ask about the bird—just one more thing to dismiss.

In spite of fingers fat and stiff like hog legs, his father nimbly impaled maggots onto his hook. The woods were somehow fuller of light now that sunrays weren't leaning in, and Tobias guessed it was because there were no shadows—popcorn clouds had packed together over the infant leaves and the boughs of leftover hemlock. Against the clouds, a gliding black cruciform folded into the shaggy flap of a raven.

Some of Tobias's trout still shifted in his wicker creel. He walked to the stream and took out his jackknife. With his own nimbleness he slit each blaze-flanked belly, knife up, vent to throat. He scooped and pulled away viscera. "Here coon," he whispered with each string of gut and gill he tossed into Piebald Run. Just how had these plucky little fish forged their way clear to the birth of waters, here where all else was raw land? A lonely stream like Piebald Run had to be a finger severed from some great body.

Tobias moved along. The raven had turned, cruising downhollow. Up there, its keen eyes could tell for sure how frail that silver thread was, could see what Tobias had heard of the Allegheny Plateau: it was not the mountain country it seemed, rather a rolling tableland fissured by water-cut valleys and hollows that tentacled from their common trunk, the west branch of the Susquehanna. The ridges exaggerated their height by their steepness, masqueraded as the spines of hills—at least to someone looking from the bottom. He'd seen how they dropped on one side only, so dangerously sheer they seemed endless from up there.

And here in the reaches of those tentacles, the brook trout held to their own hollows, fending as clans cut off by ridge and tableland. Forever. No wonder people called them natives.

That got to what bothered Tobias. He knew being cut off. He related to the brook trout's wobbly straits, sensed a threat to his little town in the changes people whispered about.

"Pop," he said, catching up to him. "Do I think too hard on—" A glance from his father choked off the rest, this despite Herbert Meier's eyes never telling his thoughts; they were constant with surrender, eyes made sad by puckered eyelids that wilted downward at the far ends.

"You think too much on most anything."

Tobias knew he did not expect an explanation. Still, he went on. "It's just that if I can figure out why something fits, I can figure it out."

"What do you mean, 'figure it out'?"

Tobias thought a moment as he stroked the fresh leather trim of his creel. "Figure out how it's important, I guess." He tripped on a root, nearly fell.

"You talking people-important? Like President Cleveland?" Herbert kept moving.

"Important like a piece of a story—how it makes it come out so." Tobias looked to a ridge. "Like you've shown me—paper birch grow on the tops, sycamores in the bottoms. What's the reason, I wonder."

"You mean belonging?"

"I don't know," Tobias said.

"Tobias, being important depends on who's deciding." He stopped, just long enough to glance up. "Maybe you're getting at being useful."

"No. That's not it. I know there's words for it, I just can't pull them up, roots and all."

Now Herbert turned to his son. Everything on Herbert's face was overdrawn thick and wide—jowls, nose, even his mustaches—so much that his lip showed only when he spoke. "Tobias, it's one thing to be a curious boy. It's another to be wondering beyond your situation. Don't think into things too much. Just do." He reached for his baited hook and patted its tip, checking the sharpness. "Reasons will find you and you'll act by them."

Herbert pulled the butt of his pole to himself and stepped toward the stream. Tobias left it at that, troubled mostly that his father said it so matter-of-factly. He moved on, concentrating less on fishing, stopping only a moment at each pocket, until he realized he was well ahead of his father.

As he tossed his line into a deep channel clogged with rhododendron root, Tobias got the notion he was being watched. He looked upstream where the bottomland leveled and widened for a stretch. At the base of a ravine that a spring seep had whittled into the hollow, the locomotive had spotted a stake-sided bark car on a side rail. A boy scuttled busy as a squirrel over the cargo of hemlock bark, spreading out the pieces fleshy-side-down. But it wasn't the boy who watched Tobias.

Snaking up the ravine, a v-shaped trough of boards standing on legs made of tree limbs led Tobias's eye. He always marveled at inventions of backwoods ingenuity, especially these—bark slides. Tobias thought of them as processions of praying mantises or forever centipedes on stilts meandering among the felled hemlocks.

The peeling crew had built up piles of bark along the slide. Near one, a pair of spudders—as peelers were known—stared down at Tobias. They were thin and dirtied to the same dun as the understory; Tobias wouldn't have readily picked them out of the remaining trees had the slide not pulled his eyes there. They'd stripped their top shirts, and even their sweaty union suits had drawn the color of the woods. Halted mid-motion, the pair held sheaves of bark they were about to line onto the slide. He could tell they were young, even from a distance, one a beardless teenager, the other a little older, taller, still as an alert doe, along with her fawn awaiting her cue.

Aware again he had a fishing pole in hand, Tobias raised the tip. The hook had snagged. He began yanking while he looked to the spudders. A wide-rimmed hat shifted, the brim of a derby tipped up to it, and the pair passed words. Then their lean arms went back to tossing bark onto the slide, sometimes reaching to push it along its course. But by turns, they turned cool faces to Tobias.

In his attempts to free his line, Tobias finally broke it. He walked to a rock toward the bark car, sat, and took from his billfold a snelled hook. He unraveled the leader, watching the boy stack hemlock bark; he still hadn't noticed Tobias. The boy had serious, poking eyes—walleyes, like on the crazed-looking, scaly fish that mill workers from Canada brought back from fishing expeditions. Boys know boys, and the way this one scurried over his layers of work, pigheaded and pouty, told Tobias he scorned this business of loading bark. Then it came to Tobias he'd seen him somewhere.

Local boys often worked with spudders through early July, when hemlock bark tightened and couldn't be peeled with the spoon-like chisels crews used to pry sections they scored with axes—boys of even eleven or twelve, especially brothers of woodhicks. But this one was at most a year older than Tobias.

Tobias wrapped a strip of sinker to his leader and tied it to the spool at the tip of his rod—country fishermen reeled their lines merely by rotating the bamboo. He looked up to see the boy flinch as he spotted Tobias—an annoyed rousing, as if a fly alighted on his cheek. They locked eyes until Tobias finally turned. But each time Tobias glanced back, the boy still glared, and Tobias felt obligated to make some greeting.

He smiled. But the boy narrowed his jutting eyes, as though staked railcars were pens for lions, and fishing poles were goads to harass them.

"Johnny." A yell from one of the spudders cut through the murmur of Piebald Run. The lion lost its fierceness; the walleyes widened. "Quit playing with the little fisherman. Bring water."

"Now," hollered the other. And laughter pattered down the slope.

The boy dropped an armload of bark and jumped from sight beyond the railcar. Then he was running for the creek with a silver-gray bucket, a ladle sighing along the lip like a farrier's rasp. He tipped the mouth into a pool and tugged against the bail as the water of Piebald Run took it down.

He hoisted the bucket with two hands, and with eyes turned from Tobias, wobbled away. Leaves of water lapped to the ground as his knees brushed the side, the ladle tapping the rim softer and softer as he approached the steep of the hollow. And the spudders leaned luxuriously against the bark slide.

As the boy inched up the incline, shrugging and waddling against his load, Tobias tried to remember where he'd encountered him. He was too young to be an acquaintance of Tobias's sister, and Tobias had never seen him at school.

The boy set the bucket before the older spudder, who nodded in Tobias's direction. They looked, laughter trailing down to Tobias. Then they became quiet, and the boy turned back.

With midday nigh and the clouds cracking open, the sun shone directly into the snug hollow. A breeze lifted with the warming air and smoked silent through the bare trees, carrying away whatever comment accompanied a turn of the big-brimmed hat toward the trim derby. But what happened next needed no words.

Big brim rested the toe of his boot against the lip of the pail. He paused, then tipped it onto its side, and the bark peelers' hats jittered with their laughter. Then the boy, head down, took the bucket and dipper, and started away. He never looked in the direction of Tobias, just fixed his gaze on Piebald Run.

A worm of regret un-balled and inched around Tobias's heart. He knew he added to the boy's shame, giving the gag an audience. But Tobias couldn't look away from this boy whose walleyes now had a determination beyond their years.

Tobias strained to spark recognition as the boy stooped at the water where the railcar hid him from the spudders. But now this was a stranger. The face earlier had been a child's set with scorn. Now it was fixed with ugly ambition he'd seen only in men.

One of the pair cupped his hands to his mouth and yelled against the breeze. Tobias couldn't make sense of it all, but in the terminus he heard a threat: "…if you ever tell your father." Then the spudders returned to their work.

The boy did not react. Yanking his bucket out of the pool, he looked at Tobias, face flushed, eyes jutting mad—in both meanings of the word.

Then, his stare still on Tobias, the boy tilted his head over the bucket, opened his mouth and drooled all the spit he'd mustered in his anger. And even after he stopped, he stared, mouth agape, as though it was Tobias's bucket he spit into.

Not until the boy rounded the bark car did Tobias notice that Herbert Meier had approached and watched from the rail bed. The breeze had trailed off, and laughter and taunting from the spudders rolled down the hollow with the slaps of the bark they threw onto the slide.

"Tobias, do you have everything you need to rig that pole?" Herbert nodded at the tip of the rod on Tobias's knee.

"Yeah, Pop." He didn't look down at the leader, eyeing again the boy's course as he trudged up the incline, slower, surer this time. "Pop, do you know who that is?"

"I believe I do." Herbert's words quaked, so light with bewilderment they would have wafted away had the breeze not ebbed.

"Is he from Pigeondale?"

"Yes. He belongs to Warren P. Ryder's new woods superintendent, Josiah Blesh."

That explained why the boy seemed so proud. Warren P. Ryder held reign over most everyone on that part of the plateau, whether through his railroads or mills, his tanneries or timber. A personal connection to him, even once removed through a father, was a distinction.

"His name's Johnny?" Tobias looked over at his father. "That Blesh boy?"

Herbert cocked his head, tracing the bark slide to where the boy had arrived to slake the spudders. "Yes, though I've heard him spoken of as John." He held the absorbed gaze he'd wear untying a knot. "Just can't figure why he'd be working on a bark crew, bein' such a young fella. 'Specially bein' Blesh's boy."

Tobias turned back. The older spudder beckoned the boy nearer, then reached for the dipper. And in the time between his hat bobbing with another outburst and it finally reaching Tobias in that ghoulish burbling of distant laughter, the spudder drank. Then he passed the ladle to his partner in the derby hat.

Tobias glanced at his father. And at that moment, for whatever reason, he knew he would never ask him about the peculiar bird with the peach flesh breast.

Chapter 2

At nine o'clock every Saturday morning in Marstadt, Pennsylvania, Celia Ryder set out for the Erhart Brothers Steam Laundry with a basket of her father's field clothes.

The Erharts lived upstairs of their false-fronted, clapboard laundry along the pine-plank sidewalk of Station Street, a strip of mud leading from the town square to the new Ryder Tannery, just beyond the Ryder Railroad depot. Sharpened by the caustic fume of tannin leaching from the milled bark of hemlock, a stagnant stench from the innards of the tannery pooled along the tracks and Station Street. In the dark stalls of the tannery's barn-sided buildings, which crouched end-to-end like a train of enormous chicken coops, men sloshed and soaked maggoty hides in tubs of lime solution and the manure of fowl, then scraped and softened, stretched and stripped, a by-hand process that stung lungs and made raw meat of arms.

The stink did not rise uphill to Celia Ryder as she descended from her home where it spired above Station Street, a lone house with twin turrets of the same leather-beige brick as the tannery's smokestack—bricks baked in the kilns of the Ryder Clay Company. For opposite her, an open slope rose west, and on it Warren P. Ryder had his yard crew stack hemlock bark to dry in rows like sod barracks rearing out of the landscape, their pitched tops as tall and slanted as shed roofs. The bark bouqueted the air above Marstadt, and when a breeze wafted down onto the tannery yard, even Station Street basked in that musk made by spudders in the springtime woods, the same scent of hemlock flesh that would spice the air out in Piebald Hollow twelve years later, that day when Tobias Meier encountered John Blesh.

In constant view of that smokestack, which bore her surname in bricks blocked out in blue, official Ryder blue, Celia moved along the boardwalk with her basket. She passed skinny stilts propping the second-tier porches of tenant houses, the bakery that fed tannery workers, and finally the spawn of the station—the hotel, saloon and barbershop—the supply for the demand that overtook that side of Marstadt when Saturday trains delivered woodhicks from Ryder lumbering operations.

Raising a knee to support her basket, Celia pushed open the laundry door—slowly, so she'd have her poise when it swung wide—and she stepped through. But when she closed the door behind her, no vacuum of damp air sucked from the washroom carrying nips of kerosene and chloride of lime. And there was silence.

No sears from the iron machine, no creaks and stomps from its foot pedal. No spit-on-a-coal-stove hiss from the leaky steam boiler. No Erhart whisking a garment stain. The pursed lips of the mangle looked tame not gnawing stockings. She walked to the counter, set her basket on it, listened for any sound from the boiler room. Nothing.

The lack of activity laid bare the feeling she'd come to associate with this place: ease, a weekly break from being Marstadt's most noticed eighteen-year-old, one whose father forbade her to realize the potential in that. But however much the stillness revealed, Celia was most attentive to the absence of J. Hadley Erhart.

She moved around the counter, straining for some noise upstairs. She stopped at a garment-folding table, traced a J in a smattering of starch, then wiped the finger with a scrap of tissue torn from between shirt folds. She stepped to the spotting table, strummed the bristles of the brush Hadley used to work solution into stains.

Celia started toward the back where the day's damp grayness reached through a window and swabbed buttons and needles and thread on the sewing counter. But she bumped a scrub board she hadn't seen resting over a suds tub. At the rasp and clang, she watched the stairs against the wall.

She'd never known J. Hadley Erhart to remain upstairs with his brother and mother after opening time. With all that had befallen the Erharts, and considering the leisureliness that doom takes in shadowing certain households, she knew something might be wrong. Still, a thought gnawed obstinately as a toothache: Doesn't he, too, look forward to Saturdays?

She was about to leave when J. Hadley Erhart opened the door at the top of the stairs.

Celia always liked how his cool self possession stood against the heat of his looks; he was a man tinged with red: cheeks, hands and forearms chafed from the chemicals and soaps of a steam laundry; forehead always flushed; red tints to his sandy hair. The brows, tipped crimson and flared at the temples, gave him a cordial look, where they would have made for a scowl on a man less composed. This morning, though, they were splayed wing-like across his forehead.

As he reached the bottom stair, Hadley saw the laundry basket. He turned and winced at the sight of Celia. "You can't be here today."

She heard pain and coughed out what she feared. "Not your mother?"

"This time it's Monroe—gone." He gestured around the room. "Celia, it's dangerous. He died just last night."

Composure already. She saw him trying to regain himself, calculate. He'd probably come down to sort the chaos that accompanied losing another brother, work out the problems from the logical side of the pain. Erhart industriousness—already planning for what might next happen to unlucky souls. And in this, she couldn't help a trickle of irritation, for it meant he'd come to the laundry on a Saturday morning without giving her a thought.

"But he was well just last week," Celia said. Monroe had been one of three remaining brothers of six. She shook her head, hand to cheek. This sickness made no sense. She started toward Hadley. But he held up his palms.

"Celia, no. Consumption is contagious. It's a fact now. Please, just leave."

She was already to the counter, a step from him. "Had, I'm very, very sorry. So much lost, so quickly."

His brows bundled with that problem-solving stare he gave new stains in the clothes she brought. "Why is this happening?" Though he whispered, it was as offhanded as if he asked about the stain.

But his eyes implored so openly she could see into his aching, and it was so raw she couldn't find the pluck to confront it. "Your mother, how is she?"

"She can't bear it. It's been just three years since the young ones. Then we come here and Madison dies. Now Monroe. She has no one left but

Hap in Harrisburg, and me. And she can't take being here any more than down there, where the boys and Father are buried."

"Had, I've never, ever heard that consumption is contagious." She closed the step, reached for his hand. He didn't stop her. She stroked the mitt of his palm, rough from cranking machines and brushing spots.

"It's true, Celia. We've been passing it around like leprosy. It's a germ, seen under microscopes." He slipped his hand away, slowly, as from a mitten. "I've read it in the newspapers Hap sends from Harrisburg."

"Had, sit with me." She took his hand firmly now. "Please?"

He followed her to a chair at a table used as a desk. Celia dragged another chair from the sewing area. Sitting, she pushed papers and an inkwell away. Elbows on the table, she took his hands, and with her powdered cheeks buffed those knuckles made raw by washboards.

Three things were getting in the way of Celia shoring his pain. Foremost, she couldn't summon enough imagination to offer him some fresh hope; death had become a routine for this family. Second, just where was Monroe? The idea of a corpse overhead was making her corset very tight. And through all that, a thought kept surfacing: How would year after year of grief affect Hadley from here on?

"Had, where is your brother's body?"

"Upstairs. And it has to stay up there for the moment." He pulled his hands away. "Even the undertaker knows now consumption can be caught." He turned, took in the laundry. "We have no place proper to pay respects. But this time he won't take the body to a parlor, like he did Madison. Mother and I are to close him into his pine box. And then it's straight to the grave." She followed his gaze to the ceiling plaster, cracked with gray drip marks where the daily assault of iron steam leached tannin out of the lattice. "They want to keep the disease in those damned walls up there," he said. "Now do you see that you shouldn't be here?"

Celia mulled helping Hadley and his mother—who was probably hysterical—and she apprehended something that scared her: seeing his mother together with the body of Monroe. Pathological terms that even she'd heard—contagious and bacillus—did not phase her. A kiss from J. Hadley Erhart could be a death sentence? Those were just words. But being in the same room as a corpse and a grieving mother, one who'd already been wild with the pain of losing her husband and two young boys before fleeing with Hadley hundreds of miles to the laundry of her eldest boys, that held her tongue. This was a woman who'd hoped to escape pollution and diseases, only to then lose those two older sons. And now she was left with a laundry that had taken them to run, and a young son to do it. Her two youngest, dead; her two oldest, dead; her husband, dead. Strangely, that held Celia's compassion fast. And it led her mind to new fears.

"Had," she whispered, "I know it's sudden, but have you thought about what you'll do? Will you keep the business?"

His eyes were on her, but they were limp and turned in on some deep burrow where his grief gnawed.

Celia narrowed her eyelids to say *look at me*. She'd learned early the strength of those mocha dots, so dark for a girl of Anglo extraction, a novelty in that settlement where Bavarians reined over a few Danes and Swedes. Hardly eyes at all. Only abysses between the mystery of her thoughts and what a person guessed on the other side. Lodestone eddies that could suck a man into speaking his heart compliantly as sands shoal with river currents.

Hadley drew a breath and held it a moment before exhaling. "Well—" He stopped short, then continued, his tone rationalizing now. "My first concern, of course, is Mother. Too many new ghosts here. It's better to send her off to Harrisburg—to the old ones." He tilted his chair away from the table. Celia reached for him but stopped herself midway.

"As for me," he said, "I don't know if I can keep the business going. But," he paused, looked to the ceiling, "maybe that's what Madison and Monroe would want."

Celia reflexively leaned ahead. One of her mother-of-pearl buttons, which pulled in a tight slash across her heron-blue day dress—puff-shouldered and a bit smart for a laundry delivery—tapped the table edge and turned his eyes back to her. "Had," she whispered, "my father can help you."

"What do you mean, 'help' me?"

"I mean he'll loan whatever you need to keep the business going." She motioned with her hand, sweeping from a rack of suit jackets to the tins of starch at the rear. "I've mentioned to my father—" she paused— "us being friends." She tilted her head, the ostrich plumes on the small toque she'd pinned among her black curls twitching into view. "I know your pain is deep and fresh, Had. But there are decisions you'll soon have to make. I just want you to know all your options."

"Celia, you're kind. I just don't know if I want that kind of help right now—or even need it."

She sifted through the gathered skirt folds of her dress and found its fan pocket—the air felt humid, and this conversation was spiking her discomfort. Celia was deft at withdrawing and spanning her fan in one motion. She set it flickering at the tip of her chin. "You have to know what means are available to you, Had. You could run off not knowing if that's best for the long run." She fanned faster. "Or for us." This slipped, and she attributed it to the stuffiness.

At that second, rain pattered the planks of the walk like a flush of starlings, then it crescendoed with a cloudburst into the solid slaps of wings taking off across water. The sound seemed to waken Hadley to the larger room, and he peered around as if he'd never seen it. He stood and moved past the counter to the narrow front window, four flat panes, rain-speckled and dull-slate against the outer murk. He leaned his forehead against the frame.

Celia stopped fanning. She told herself that her little shiver came of the strain of the moment, not from looking where Hadley's back splayed abruptly from the waist of his trousers, its sharp angles pronounced by his braces, which un-tautened as he rested his elbows to each side of the window.

"Five years," he said, "five deaths. Five times my mother failed."

"Failed?" Celia said it not so much out of wanting to know as to bring Hadley back to the table.

"Failed to nurse health to husband and child. Win back life she'd given. She lost, then suffered seeing lids nailed to coffins."

"Had, stop."

He turned. "This time she's to endure *us* putting nails in the coffin, us carrying it to the street to be picked up like some damned ransom."

"Had—"

"So you can understand that her comfort comes first."

Celia thought of going to him, but she feared if she so much as stood he'd move away—like trying to sweep a feather.

"Then comes the good name of this family, Celia. It's all up to me to preserve it."

That was her hole in his fence. "The good name of your family is painted on that sign outside." She pointed to the door and at the same time tapped the toe of her shoe. "The Erhart name is established in Marstadt, and leaving it to go back to Harrisburg, where your brother is already doing just fine raising a family and running a—what does he run?"

"He's a banker. Like our father was."

"Exactly. Going back there would simply destroy half of what your family's done." This, she saw, gave him something to think about, but she needed to keep it from going awash in his pain. "This business is what you know. This town is a place where Erharts have put down roots. Don't give up, Had."

"Maybe it just comes down to practical considerations for Mother."

Celia cut him off. "Sit down." She folded her fan onto the table, stood and went around to his chair, turning it to face him. Hadley came and sat, and she rubbed his shoulders with her palms while she took in the room. Neckerchiefs and corsets were draped over irons; starched collars and cuffs hung from wheeled hanger racks. Her father would not accept her living in a laundry where the air boiled like a hot spring. In fact, under his irrational standards of piety, she was beginning to wonder if he'd ever accept the idea of a suitor. He'd certainly object if he knew she—instead of an errand boy—delivered his soiled field clothes to her "friend," Hadley. But he would approve of the spirit that fueled this place, and between him and her, they could hand that spirit over to some worthy enterprise. That she knew, and that she could set forth. After all, she herself wouldn't live this life.

But this was not the moment to start. She needed Hadley to stay where, with time, he could realize his opportunities.

"Had, you'll get through this and see clearly what to do." She bent close to his ear. "Give it time and just know this—if there is one thing I can do for you, it is help the Erhart name prosper—in ways you won't find elsewhere."

When she felt his shoulders relax, Celia wrapped her fingers around them, waiting.

"Celia, I've seen how unpredictable life is. No one's in a bigger hurry to do some good in the name of father and brothers." He shook his head up and down. "You'll see."

The rain came in pelts, cackling against the clapboards. The occasional sloppy stomps of horses passing in the mud disappeared against the din, the squeaks and creaks of the Saturday wagons they led from farms and groceries, coal piles and icehouses, drenched to silence. So when horseshoes throbbed close enough to the front door to be heard, slowing and stopping as wagon wheels scudded the walk, Celia straightened and looked to the door. A moment later, heels thudded the wooden planks, and two passing figures in wide-brimmed hats and mackintosh overcoats broke the gray of the window. Hadley did not move, but the ruddiness of his forehead and cheeks spread all the way to his neck. When the footsteps stopped, there came a fast hollow rasp like a saucer sliding over a cupboard shelf, then the drum thump of an empty box against the wooden walk. And with this, Hadley jolted. For the first time, Celia heard a sound from the apartment above, a wail, flat in pitch, beginning to end, achieving its screaming peak across its duration—inhuman, it lasted so long. Just one wail and nothing else from upstairs.

Celia nudged Hadley's shoulder, leaned over him. "What could that be on a Saturday?" This interruption of their discussion annoyed her. "Are you expecting some delivery?" He sat expressionless as a puppet in a closet.

When there came a single knock against the door, Celia took her hands from Hadley's shoulders, expecting him to rise. But almost immediately a man snapped, "Git, git," and in two steps the horse was in a trot that faded into the slough.

Hadley's voice was unanimated, as if the puppet in the closet spoke on its own. "That, Celia, was the undertaker delivering my brother's box." There came a slight *I told you so* to his tone. "And now I have to get it to my brother. Or him to it."

"So those damned fools really are afraid of consumption." She shook her head. "Well, I believe, as Mother says, Fate's hand brushes us in the womb."

"No. Fate's hand is our own. We just don't like to admit responsibility."

"You think you and your brothers brought this on? How could you deserve such hell?"

He was silent, just looked at the door. Celia crossed her arms against a new chill, the dampening air as spongy now as on a work day.

"All right," Hadley said, "there are things we can't help. But what is in our power is to live life like that's us next. That's how you spite your so-called fate."

"So you just have a different way of saying that something else controls your life. I'll be damned if I'll live with urgency in the face of that." Celia nodded toward the door.

"And I'll be damned if I won't."

"So that you can set yourself up with more to lose? You're just egging on fate."

"Are you suggesting I not aspire, Celia?" He waved a hand around the laundry.

She did not respond. And the place seemed to tighten, as it might pressed through the rollers of the mangle, and Celia could no longer keep out the thought of Monroe's body waiting upstairs.

In the silence of the room, with the rain in the background steady now as a stage effect, and in their unnatural poses—Hadley stiff in the chair, and Celia propped against it—she felt as removed from the moment as she would from a theatre set. Even her voice sounded scripted as she forced her words; she heard herself offering help, ashamed that she hoped he would refuse. And he did refuse. But on grounds that she'd been exposed to Monroe, she resisted, already growing nauseated from the looming smell of sickness and death and the sobbing grunts his mother would be choking back throughout the undertaking. She would do it. Lift the body and haul the box, if only because no one else would be allowed upstairs, if only to tend the tide she'd set in motion.

Chapter 3

At thirteen, John Blesh wore the extra year he had on Tobias Meier sure as a holstered gun. Tobias knew that if John wanted to spend a Saturday morning in October sitting on an apple crate in his father's one-room office building, that's what he'd have to do—if he was going to be John's pal. John was, after all, the son of the man who hired woodhicks, the superintendent of Ryder Lumber's Pigeondale operation. Besides, not every boy in Pigeondale had a chance to listen in on logging talk. Those were boasting rights well worth the risk of being put to some task at the mill, which would happen if Josiah Blesh broke from his concerns long enough to consider the loiterers by the stove.

Tobias was thinking that today the risk paid a bonus. Blesh had company, and there was serious business at hand.

"How much hardwood?" Josiah Blesh said.

"Fifteen percent, tops." Emory Sundae leaned down and put his hands on the edge of Blesh's desk. "Maple. Birch. Beech. And some decent chestnut on the ridges." He was the top woodsman in the Ryder empire: an expert surveyor, mapmaker, log scaler and timber estimator, all rolled into one. Sundae was legendary for figuring how much lumber a tract would yield, almost to the board foot of each kind of tree. Tobias liked how he always wore a distant stare, watchful, as if he looked out from a fire tower. And his name, too—it gave a lonely feeling, but in a nice way. Every boy in town tried to make friends with Emory Sundae. He spent so much time cruising timber and locating routes for logging trains, day and night well beyond rail lines and skid roads, Sundae was always good for the whereabouts of a bear's den or beaver dam. He told some tales, too, about hoop snakes that coiled in rings and rolled down hills, and black panthers that followed boys through the woods at night.

"Trams?" Blesh said, leaning back in his chair and thumbing his braces through the armholes of his waistcoat. For a big man who seemed to dispatch his authority from his waist, his voice whispered along like a tin can sliding across slate.

"Easy." Sundae pointed at a map on the desk. "We follow the course of Teaberry Run three miles—only four crossings before we reach the end of the company's tract. Then along this side-hollow we run three switchbacks to the top of the north ridge. Only a two-percent grade—max."

Tobias could just see the map by stretching his neck. Hand-drawn with the standard stenciled border: "Ryder Lumber Company—Quality Rough and Dressed Lumber, Staves, Lath, Shingles and other Finished Goods."

Sundae's finger traced the side-hollow—spikes in the rows of lines that marked the grade of Teaberry Hollow's northern ridge. The spikes pointed to a rumpled oval that defined the edge of tableland. From the precise alignment of dashes that called out boundaries, to the complex waverings of the contour lines, to the way the penned lettering of landmarks appeared typeset, the map showed why Ryder Lumber trusted the accuracy of Sundae's calculations of elevation gradients. In fact, after a map for a timbered tract was decommissioned, Warren P. Ryder had it framed for the respective superintendent's office. On the pine plank wall behind Blesh's desk, there hung four.

"Everything on the flats above that side of Teaberry Hollow, we can skid to the track that we run up there," Sundae said.

"The southern ridge?" Blesh said.

"We'll have to skid that timber to log slides."

The boys sat facing the stove in the front corner of the office, keeping quiet, arms folded. Tobias mulled the matter. Anything involving new tracts was serious business, and anyone in Pigeondale would pay admission to hear this conversation. Logging towns were portable, and their anchorage was a supply of feasible timber. An operation had to carefully weigh the costs of reaching out to new land versus its expected yield. There was always the chance Ryder would move where trees were easier to get to. In the four-year span in which Tobias had known John Blesh, he'd spent enough Saturday mornings here to understand that the company was figuring the trouble of reaching farther out. As always, the mill town was on the line.

The day they'd met four years earlier had been just after Tobias encountered John in the woods. Boys whiled away their evenings along the muddy trough that was Pigeondale's main street, looking for woodhicks in from the woods, hicks as they were known. When Tobias saw John, the woods encounter gave him the sense they already knew one another. So he nodded familiarly, and John Blesh did the same. John's nod was a little too eager, like he was intent on meeting up with Tobias, whom he must have recognized in the woods. All the time since, that day never came up. But it made Tobias uncomfortable—not for his part, rather because he could feel it was on Blesh's mind, always—something about his attitude with Tobias.

Josiah Blesh gave signals that today was a special meeting. He paused between his questions, the usual bossy offhandedness gone. That likely meant a decision would be run up the next rung. Blesh stood and leaned over the map, pushing down its edges with pudgy-boy thumbs. His eyes darted all over the paper.

"How do we get the teams up to the southern ridge to skid?"

"Easiest way," Sundae said, "is to walk them up the head of the hollow and then back the ridge. It's a steep sonofabitch otherwise."

"So we'd have to cross a Williamsporter's tract."

"Yep."

"Shit."

Tobias mulled *Williamsporters*. Everybody hated them. Even though no operation as far into the headwaters as Pigeondale floated logs to Williamsport anymore, its big-money mills were buying up the last available tracts. And they weren't even full, nine-hundred-acre warrants. Everyone said the Williamsporters believed that the knotty wood of hemlock would go up, and they had the money to sit on all the land they wanted. When the time was right, they'd send in their own crews and rail the lumber clear to their mills a hundred miles away. Now they held ground that blocked local operators like Ryder from extending their lines, and that was pushing Ryder to move operations out of these reaches of the Susquehanna watershed, which before had been safely beyond the Williamsporters' direct lumbering; during the days of the big river drives, they had timbered farther downstream and bought off the river from other outfits what extra logs they needed for their mills.

"Shit," Blesh said again. "I hate kissing their prim city asses."

Sundae glanced over his shoulder at the boys. They turned their heads away as though an appearance of no interest would keep Blesh—if he looked too—from noticing them.

"How much track altogether?" Blesh said.

"Five miles."

Blesh sat again. The boys had turned back, and they and Sundae watched Blesh gaze at the map, eyes narrowed. "I need to know—to the day," he said, "how soon we could have the track out of Piebald Hollow. That's the rail we'd use in Teaberry. If we go there."

"But that's the closest track we've got to the big hardwoods up on Fiddlers Flats. Ryder may want them."

Blesh frowned, his bald pate stretching and sheening with the pull of his brows. He continued staring at the map, tugging his beard. Tobias knew that the frown told Sundae to hush.

He also knew enough about a lumber baron's course with the land to understand that a decision against logging Teaberry Hollow could drive the mill right out of Pigeondale—farther from the Williamsporters, somewhere in the upper-Allegheny watershed. And the scales were weighted on the relocating side. Tobias had learned from hicks in town that the denuded plateau and hollows that stretched farther from Pigeondale by the year— that seeming moonscape of creeping vegetation quilled here and there by a nude column of dead timber—weren't as worthless as they appeared. There was still sapling timber to be salvaged behind the felling of the great pines and hemlocks and scattered hardwoods, though the hicks denounced the work, said it couldn't be real lumbering if it was as safe as swinging in a schoolyard, and paid so poorly. There were companies that looked to wood only for its heat and ashes, and others for mushy pulp. What was chaff to the lumber barons, stave wood at best, was to the chemical plants acetate of lime, and to the paper mills, raw material. A railroad grade into a valley of saplings and a steam-leaking locomotive with a few stake cars, a row of crumbling company houses and a transfer point on a mainline railroad, that was as good to a chemical plant or paper mill as a river of saw logs to a lumber baron.

Quick, the boys looked back at the stove as Josiah glanced from the map to the window across the room. Coming off the plateau from the direction of Marstadt, a locomotive shrilled as it put out steam. Tobias tilted his head to see Emory Sundae roll the map and tie it with twine, then turn to listen for the train. Sundae stayed that solemn gaze where Tobias peered back. Thirty working winters in the woods had chiseled deep lines around Sundae's eyes. But unlike the old hardtack hicks who boarded in town, he remained beardless and young looking. Sundae winked.

Intervals of steam from the locomotive became distinct, fluting like the first rush of well-water into a wash bucket. Emory Sundae walked to the front window and looked down the plank walk that separated the office from the rails. In addition to a sidewalk, it served as a platform for trains to and from the mill yard or points beyond. Pigeondale had no depot, just that stretch of pine boards that spanned from the small engine shed to the outbuildings of the railroad and mills, a place to debark or to hail the train as it huffed through. That branch of the Ryder Railroad may have served Pigeondale and a few farms in the valley before it connected with the main line, but that was incidental to its purpose of pulling logs, lumber and bark. Some said passenger service was mainly to justify a common carrier charter. Especially since on their jaunts to the woods for picnics, berries or trout, or when hicks went off Saturday nights to Marstadt, they had no luxury of a passenger car. If the crowd was small enough, they made do in the engineer's cab; otherwise they rode the coal tender, even the tops of logs or lumber. A real passenger car to Pigeondale meant something big was doing, usually company business. So the rail line was both Pigeondale's lifeline and its leash.

Josiah Blesh had gone right back to work, oblivious to the others in the room as he arranged papers where the map had been.

"Here comes Number One," Sundae said. He leaned his forehead until it nearly touched the window glass, watching in the direction of the coal crib and the engine shed. Number One was the first return from Marstadt, back with empties and mail and maybe goods for the company store. When the train went outbound, it would leave the Pigeondale mill yard for Marstadt pulling lumber, lath and barrel staves. And bark when it was in season.

"Looks like she's got a passenger car," Sundae said.

Josiah Blesh had already taken notice, cocking an ear to the way the locomotive was slowing for a passenger stop—unusual for the first inbound on a Saturday. He pressed his chest to his desk, raised chin saying *tell me more.*

"Hell, it's Ryder's personal car." Sundae still looked down the tracks while the polished black boiler, full of hisses and squeals, stomped past the window. Framed in the cockpit, an apologetic-looking engineer peered into the office from under his thin hat brim. One leather-gloved hand braced the panel where *Ryder Railroad* was gilded onto the cab. With the other, he reached for the iron ring strung to the brass bell atop the boiler.

"Is it Ryder?" Blesh arranged papers into one stack at a corner of his desk.

Sundae responded slowly, as if he wondered the same thing. "Can't tell yet."

The engineer dinged the bell three times as the stakes of a log car passed the window. Tobias and John stretched their necks to see around Sundae. Now they looked at the still casements of a passenger car, the railroad name under them in gold.

"I'll be damned," Sundae said, looking toward the back of the car.

"What—what?" Blesh smoothed the bunting of hair at each side of his head.

"It's not Ryder. It's his son-in-law, J. Hadley Erhart."

Blesh stared around the office, face blank.

"Damn," Sundae said.

"What is it now?"

"I've never seen Ryder's personal car. It's a regular Pullman. Even has a conductor—blue waistcoat and all." Sundae laughed.

Josiah Blesh pointed at him and went to speak, but then Sundae said "damn" again.

"Now what?"

"He's got a lady with him."

"A what?"

Sundae turned to Blesh, eyes stretched and head tucked. Even the boys, trying extra hard to be invisible—what with this double bonus—couldn't help looking at Josiah Blesh.

"A lady as in a woman," Sundae said.

"I know what the hell you mean." Blesh looked at the boys hard and went to speak, but approaching heels on the wooden walk turned everyone's attention.

The door swung open. Her head high, eyes indifferent, Celia Erhart took the room.

Her husband, secretary and operations officer of Ryder Lumber Company, looked over her shoulder, his face getting ruddier as he spread his grin around the office. And from that moment, Tobias liked that smile, true as a lantern beam. Under the pluming brows, Erhart's eyes, too, swept the place, and he didn't overlook the boys. Rather he met their stares. Tobias looked quickly back to the lady.

Erhart stepped to her side. "Gentlemen," he said. "This is my wife, Celia. Her first visit to Pigeondale." His voice was deep with raspy roots, as if it came up from a well, but one with a grate at the bottom. He wore a dark jacket tapered back from his waist and buttoned almost to his collar, which had the tiniest butterfly folds. His red tie and scuffed cheeks softened the dark suit. The way Erhart was dressed, he could have been a dandy that boys and hicks made fun of by the Post Office, except he had that strong voice and solid frame. And he didn't wear those clothes stiffly like some local show-off just returned from a trip to the city. Tobias had never known that a person could look like a man in such clothes.

As Erhart put a hand to his hat, he gave a personal nod to everyone in the room, and included grins and winks for the boys. The hat alone could have told Tobias the Company was in town; only hats that spent their days on racks stayed crisp as J. Hadley Erhart's: a crown-creased fedora with a pearl-gray ribbon. Its brim sloped up at his temples in the same sweep as his brushy brows.

Josiah Blesh was across the room in time to snatch Erhart's hat, then shake his hand. But Blesh's eyes were on Celia the whole time, and even as he pumped Erhart's hand, he said, "Mrs. Erhart, I don't believe I've seen you since your wedding. And that's been how many years?"

"Fifteen," her husband said, chuckling.

"Doesn't seem possible." Blesh's voice was pillow-soft now. "And it's been twenty-five that I've been with your father, Mrs. Erhart, working my way up to superintendent. Right back to the beginning of it all." Everyone knew that Blesh reported directly to the man in front of him, but even Tobias understood he didn't like it.

Shutting the door behind the couple and hanging Erhart's hat on a nail, Blesh introduced Celia to Emory Sundae, and asked what precipitated her unexpected but fortunate visit.

Erhart spoke up. "Really nothing to it, Josiah. We had the day, and I thought I'd call on the operation directly instead of send a message."

"A message?"

"Let's have a chair and I'll explain."

Tobias went to offer up his apple crate, wishing he didn't have to make himself conspicuous. But he was saved when Blesh dragged two chairs from the opposite wall to the front of his desk, mumbling apologies for not offering seats.

Emory Sundae was leaning next to the window, arms crossed, taking it all in. "Will you need me around, Mr. Erhart?"

Josiah Blesh turned to Erhart expectantly.

"No, Emory, my business won't require an expert mapmaker. At least I hope it won't." He grinned at Celia as he tilted the back of a chair, inviting her to sit.

As Blesh watched Sundae make his way for the door, he took note of Tobias and John. "You two get outta here. Go down the mill and bag sawdust."

Erhart walked to them at the woodstove. "No, let them stay, Josiah. My idea may call for two boys." He put a hand out to John, the tops of Erhart's fingers chafed red like the tips of his cheeks, but not raw like the laundry hands everyone knew they'd been sixteen years ago. "I believe you are Master John Blesh."

John shook Erhart's hand, looking at the floor, his face pouty.

"Speak up," his father said.

"Yessir, Mr. Erhart." John still looked at the floor.

Tobias was so eager to shake the hand of J. Hadley Erhart, he could hardly keep from jumping up. And when Erhart moved around the stove, he did.

"And who is your stove-tending partner?" Erhart said.

"Tobias Meier," John said.

The way John eyed Tobias made him feel awkward for standing. But taking hold of Erhart's hand and saying, "Nice meeting you, sir," felt as natural as it had to get up. Erhart gave the whitest tobacco-free smile Tobias had ever seen on a man—frank, even though it was from an adult to a boy. And Erhart's "It's my pleasure, Tobias Meier," was genuine. Tobias felt the contagiousness in enthusiasm and was ripe for it; he'd been wanting for a long time to trust what tried to bubble up out of him.

"How old are you, Master Meier?" Erhart said.

"He's twelve," John said, "a year younger than me."

"Well, listen close," Erhart said. "I may have a business proposition for a couple of boys twelve and thirteen."

As Erhart stepped away, he winked, and Tobias noted it was on the sly, as if to say his plans were going to be their fun, too.

The boys turned their wooden crates toward the desk. Celia Erhart had taken the nearest chair, in profile to them, her back rigid. But her husband turned his seat just enough to make the boys feel included in the discussion, though they sat eight paces away. Tobias had never seen Josiah Blesh smile; it was funny watching him try so hard.

"Josiah," Erhart said. "Two weeks from Wednesday I intend to return to Pigeondale." Josiah nodded. "But I'll only be passing through." Josiah smiled. "Celia's father and I—" Erhart glanced at Celia— "will use the old Piebald lumber camp while we do some hunting. A fellow named Andy Hoehn will be with us."

Tobias wondered if John, too, was already scheming a way to be around the office two weeks from Wednesday. Tobias had only seen Erhart's father-in-law, Warren P. Ryder, from a distance, always through windows, either in his Pullman car or at the mills when word had gotten around that he'd come for a visit. And this Hoehn fellow, what could that be about? With the state of the Pigeondale operations, mere mention of a stranger was enough to raise suspicion.

When Josiah Blesh finally spoke, it came out as if he'd been holding his breath. "I'm not sure what kind of shape that old camp's in. We haven't cut up there since just after I took over here. That's four years."

"I suspected that. And I figured you'd need some notice to have the place looked over and opened up—break camp, so to speak." He said the last with a chuckle, which he shared with the room.

Blesh just nodded.

"It should be cleaned up and checked that all's airtight," Erhart said. "We'll need a good stove put in." He glanced at the boys and nodded, as if asking for their consensus. Tobias shook his head—yes, yes, yes.

"Just clean up enough space for three of us," Erhart said. "Plus quarters for a cook and an all-around helper. I'll have provisions sent. Say two days ahead?"

"Well, sure," Blesh said.

"I'm not looking for the luxuries of home, but it should be made comfortable." His wife glanced at him. "Well, certainly not too comfortable.

This is a hunting trip after all." Erhart grinned when his wife dipped her head as if saying, *but of course.*

"Just remember that Mr. Ryder will be along," Erhart said. "An exacting man."

"We all benefit from Mr. Ryder's high standards." Blesh smiled at Celia, then looked back at her husband. "So how long will you be at the camp?"

"No less than three days. I suspect until Sunday morning." Erhart leaned ahead and raised a brow, confidentially. "This outing involves business." He leaned back. "But it's the cooperation of grouse and deer that will determine its duration." Then he smiled and spoke a little louder. "I'd also like to enlist some hands to fetch spring water and split wood. Keep the fire burning. A couple stove tenders, let's say. Do you have any idea, Josiah, where I might find two young fellows willing to take on that assignment?"

"We'd do it, sir." The words just came out of Tobias, and Erhart pretended utter surprise. But Tobias caught John Blesh glaring with a scowl that reminded him that John was, after all, the senior of the two, whose privilege it was to do all volunteering of services.

"Well, Tobias Meier," Erhart said, "an eager young man is what I'm looking for. But you haven't heard the terms."

Josiah Blesh watched, looking confused, and Tobias guessed that he was grappling with whether this outburst had been improper or if his son should have made it. Well, Tobias had given up to that vigor that swelled from his bones, and for once it felt right, so why not keep going.

"Doesn't matter, sir, we're your pair. I can split and stack as quick as my pop. And John here, his first job was fetching water for spudders."

He looked to John, thinking he'd get some support by now. But John's eyes had narrowed with a look Tobias hadn't seen in four years. These words too, had just come out, seemed natural since everyone knew that Josiah Blesh had put his boy to work at nine years old to make sure that the son of the superintendent would never be coddled by his community. But Tobias saw straightaway that John Blesh wasn't in favor of being thought of as a water boy.

"I assure you," Josiah Blesh said, "they'll work hard as any two men. And they'll be outta your way while they do it." He cocked his head with due respect to Celia Erhart. "Just as much as I can assure you, Mrs. Erhart, that we'll make that camp most livable for your father and Hadley. And, oh," he looked at Erhart, "for this Mr.—did you say Hoehn? Can't place that name."

"Yes, it's Hoehn." Erhart still hadn't looked away from the boys. "Can you boys skin a buck?"

"Yessir." They said it together, but now John Blesh spoke louder than Tobias. Erhart's smile broadened, the wings of his brows tilting straight for the ceiling.

"Can you oil guns?"

Again, two yessirs.

"Suppose we need a couple wily boys to climb to a ridge, then zigzag to hunters through slashings and thick tangles of mountain laurel." He still smiled, though his tone had become businesslike.

"I know I can do it," John said.

"We're the ones," Tobias said.

"Are you familiar with Piebald Hollow?"

"Fished and hunted it since I could hold a pole," Tobias said.

"I know it," John said, with no reference to his days working there.

"The woods beyond?" Erhart said. "Wouldn't want anybody getting lost."

"Yep," they said. And Tobias added, "Even drove deer there."

"Then it sounds like two young men will earn fair pay. And all the camp vittles they want. Josiah, add to my list sleeping spaces for two more. They'll join us that Thursday morning."

Tobias beamed Erhart's smile right back while John looked to his father, who said, "You boys do as you're asked."

Tobias was awash in visions. It was one thing to stoke a fire in Josiah Blesh's office, another to do it in a hunting camp for Warren P. Ryder and J. Hadley Erhart. To care for their gear and chase deer, to sit at the breakfast table and hear their plans and tales. The light sifting in from the pearly-cloud sky turned from dreary to that glow of possibility a boy felt at dawn on a day in the woods.

But his father's view of all this tried to break through. Tobias pushed that back, and with the confidence gained by his prospects, he dared to get a better glimpse of Celia Erhart. He had been gnawingly aware of her, and now that he'd had a serious conversation with J. Hadley Erhart, it seemed all right to look. Tobias had seen ladies in Marstadt dressed like this, but never here in Pigeondale. She wore what was called a walking dress—

which differentiated it from what, he'd always wondered—the color of a daisy eye, thin-waisted and dignified with wide shoulders and drape folds, like bells, hanging at her hem. The squeeze of her corset bulged her breasts.

The room was quiet; it seemed Erhart held the next part of the conversation in his smile. But Josiah Blesh spoke, disappointing Tobias by changing the subject, even irritating him; Blesh had used the silence to take the conversation his way.

"How is your daughter, Mrs. Erhart? The last I saw her, she was in your father's office in Marstadt. Just coming from school—couldn't have been prettier. Or better behaved." Celia didn't answer, just nodded expressionless, so she seemed to acknowledge the fact of it more than the compliment. Her dark hair shifted slightly where it was gathered under the back of her hat in the figure eight of a pompadour twist. Tobias looked at her neck long enough for it to be called staring. The tall autumn collar left a hint of skin, light mocha, exotic to a boy who'd thought of all the women of Marstadt as fair Bavarians. And he'd never seen such deep smoky eyes or shadows of dusky skin, except on Italians who worked the section crews.

But J. Hadley Erhart beamed all the more. "I recall the day, Josiah. She was waiting for me while you and I met. And since then, Cassandra has not only grown *up,* but out of her cocoon. She's less at rest than a butterfly."

"How old is she now?

"Twelve."

"Well, that's just a year younger than John." He nodded toward his son.

Tobias tried to envision a miniature Celia Erhart. Celia Erhart, his own age. But no image came. It was impossible to scale down that air her mother carried. So he pictured himself as an older Tobias, meeting a Celia Erhart. That was a daring thought, a world of possibilities. But then a vague shifty bearing came into the scene, huffing up out of a corner of his mind, a thing roused disagreeably from where it lurked. His father.

"I wanted to bring her along today," Erhart said, "but Celia thought it best we didn't."

"Well, I don't blame you, Mrs. Erhart." Blesh patted a spot on his desk between him and Celia. "A lumbertown's no place for a young girl, especially with that damp chill we've got today." He nodded at the front window and frowned.

Tobias wondered how air in Pigeondale could have more chill than air in Marstadt. The only difference he knew was the smell; in Pigeondale there was always that blend he loved—fresh-cut lumber, machine oil, the sulfury coal smoke of steam engines. Marstadt just smelled like a town. Except down by the tannery.

Tobias had followed Josiah Blesh's nod and caught John rubbing the sole of his shoe against a stove leg. How could he have lost interest already?

With the Pullman car gone now, the front window framed the tin roof of a tool stable across the tracks. Just then, Emory Sundae appeared. He leaned close to the glass, then stepped away toward the door.

The everyday whine and zing from the saw at the lumber mill had become invisible in its familiarity. But when Sundae swung the door open, the spike of it turned everyone's attention—even Celia shifted in her chair. Sundae removed his hat and nodded face to face, bashful and apologetic. Tobias wouldn't have taken a new pocketknife for all the fortune coming his way; he could tell Sundae had news.

"Knowing you're in town, Mr. Erhart, I thought I'd let you know we've got the picture-taker here for the woods operations like you asked. I'm taking him out to Brandy Run Hollow to make pictures of the Wade boys' teams. Saturday's the only day the hosses aren't lathered too much." He glanced at Celia, then at the floor a second. "He just unloaded his things off a boxcar from your train down at the lumber mill. I didn't know if there's something else you might want pictured."

When the company put on a new, heavy-boomed log loader or when a train lost its footing on a steep ridge and spilled its cars and crew like snow from eaves, a photographer was called in. Sometimes the order was just to capture a pageant of curried horses in their necklaces of ivory rings, stern teamsters thumbing the bridles, other times an especially long trestle over a backwoods gully. Tobias had seen such photographs at the stave mill, and though Ryder commissioned them to boast what his company conquered, Tobias saw a greater magnificence hiding in the bony-faced grit and long-mustached pride of the woodhicks. Not thrust chests, just the calm that beams with hardiness.

Erhart closed his eyes and tilted his head toward the floor a moment. He looked up. "Why *this* is an event to remember." Then to his wife: "It's your first visit to a company town. I think a photograph of you, me and Josiah is in order." He turned to Blesh who looked at Celia for a response. She made no sign, just stared at her husband.

Sundae began explaining himself. "I didn't mean to confuse matters, I just thought I'd mention—" Josiah Blesh cut him off with the snap of a scowl.

"We'll hang the photograph here in the office," Erhart said. "It'll give Josiah a company·emblem more personal than those block letters on the mill stack."

Celia's eyes widened as she looked around the room.

Sundae must have interpreted this as asking, *Where do you propose we stand for this picture?* "You'd have to do it out on the plank," he said, using the Pigeondale term for wooden walks.

"Well then," Erhart said. "We'll have the camera looking toward the mills, with the slopes of Manooka Valley framing us."

Erhart stood. Decision made. He winked at the boys and held Celia's chair as she rose. No wonder she sat so stiffly. Bustles, it was said, had fallen from fashion with the soon-to-change century, but really it seemed they had just fallen into the length of an even longer skirt, which Celia wore looped up at her behind. With the dress folds jutting primly from the back of her nothing-waist, Tobias couldn't help but stare. She wears a duck's ass, he thought, and does it with grace. His heart took a few quicker beats.

Erhart still watched the boys, grinning. "I think our new hires should be part of the picture, too," he said.

Now the tempo of Tobias's heart picked up and stayed that way. He'd nearly jumped at the prospect of seeing a photographer. To actually be in a photograph was as lucky as going grouse hunting and finding a spaniel on the way.

Most of his life he had never seen a photograph—illustrations in a primer, sure, but when he finally saw *real pictures,* as he said, he lost himself to them. Saturdays his sister took him to the stave mill where their father worked—the one day he got a fresh lunch. Tobias was too young to walk with his sister through the saw room to the mill yard where Herbert Meier bundled keg staves and loaded them onto railcars for a cooperage in some city where people had never heard of a Pigeondale, Pennsylvania. So Tobias paced outside, scuffing dirt to the zip-sap buzz of the cylinder saws skimming staves off bolts of oak. He'd daydream of working in the woods, a hick, an important player in some side-hollow operation.

With every visit, Tobias dared himself closer to the stave mill door, always opened, where down a hallway he saw men pushing logs across rollers. The hallway was a gallery of sorts, a place to tack scratched and saw-dusty prints from calotypes—unframed, edges arcing. The more he looked, the more they seemed to call. So eventually Tobias gained the nerve to pile castaway slabs and step up to look into those worlds. Five pictures, and he came to know every gray shade.

First, a string of three log cars, each bearing a section from a sixty-inch white-oak bole, its diameter chalked across the butt end. Next, a sweeping view of a denuded hollow, varicose rails winding through jumbles of bucked logs that matted the walls of the valley like the settled quills of a porcupine. Then a mannequin shot of managers and shareholders visiting a cutting crew in the woods, two token hicks off to the side.

Next was the stave mill itself, the crew squatting in the dust where Tobias shuffled his feet, his father as nameless in his contrived pose as the others.

Tobias liked best the picture nearest the mill floor—a teamster with his Percherons hitched to a lóg, one horse black, the other mottled gray and white, ears pricked and eyes on the camera—you could hear the photographer clucking his tongue. As if for inspection, a pair of sawyers held their crosscutter across the log, scythes, axes and cant hooks propped against it. The teamsters and sawyers stared with a humble pride he'd never seen, nakedly truer than the air of the company officers. The bony faces betokened bodies lean—not from a lack of good meals, but because they spent them working daylong. To Tobias, those men were the heroes of their time, and maybe no one outside that hallway would ever see that. Unless by the slow truth of time they'd someday gleam again, like pebbles under a stump.

But what got Tobias most was the eye of that teamster—it sent a wave through him so warm he was sure it stirred from his heart. He'd have crawled into that picture if he fit. And if he could help seeing his father grab him by the pants, for there was no escaping his constant matter-of-fact nagging that a mill-town boy dare not plan his path, woods work or not.

Emory Sundae started for the door. "I'll go fix the picture-taker with a mule from the mill yard," he said. "He'll need one to pack all those cases." Tobias figured that Sundae, who carried only a satchel of parchment and pencils, thought it was a lot of equipment to illustrate something on paper.

Tobias couldn't wait to see that equipment. He knew that a photo came from a box with an aperture, a blinking eye socket. Even everyday people in Marstadt spoke of buying cameras now, small ones that saved pictures on film they sent away for prints.

The men went for their hats, and when Celia walked toward the door, Tobias perked to the rustle of her silk underthings and a breath of her floral-fragrant talc.

On the plank, J. Hadley Erhart arranged the group cattycornered from the edge, the roofs of track-side sheds and the smokestack, lettered *Ryder Lumber Company,* all that broke the background cupped within Manooka Valley. Above it all, the clouds held a glowing haze like a sheet over a window. Erhart shuffled Celia left and right by an elbow while she stared ahead, stiff-necked. When Erhart finally finished, Josiah Blesh stepped tight to her, face sour. His son, standing before him, followed the cue, as if any moment he'd roll his eyes and exhale a deep breath. Tobias sidled in front of Celia, trying to imagine himself as one of the hicks in the pictures at the stave mill. What went through their minds while they stood for a two-second shutter?

While Erhart framed the scene with two hands, Tobias tried the hicks' grave and noble glare. But the silence of the other posers left an atmosphere of bored impatience, which made Erhart look a little ridiculous, even to Tobias. He tried for his photo-face all the harder, and wondered if Erhart could tell. What he'd do for a mirror.

On the other side of the tracks, the photographer led his mule along the muddy road, corrugated by wagon wheels and pocked and pimpled by the hoofs and dung of horses. He stepped warily.

Erhart jumped from the plank to meet him. Tobias couldn't believe that a man of that standing would lend a hand. The photographer ignored the help though, mumbling oaths for being rushed and juggled like a toy. So Erhart hitched the mule to one of the plank's piles while the photographer untied the legs of a wooden tripod and pulled canvas sacks from the saddlebags. Out came the camera, which he unfurled like an accordion. Instead of the new box type, his was some old style, as wide as the pictures it would make. The photographer tightened wing nuts on the mahogany frame and screwed the camera onto the tripod. He lifted it and stood it on the plank, and looked around for steps.

Erhart braced himself and leaped up, quick as a cat. He held out a hand. "Lift your foot to the edge. I'll pull you up." But the photographer ignored him, stepping onto a rail and mounting the plank as he would the mule, nearly rolling off as he got his balance.

After Erhart took his place, the photographer moved the camera back and forth to frame the group, waving the boys apart for a better view of Celia where she stood silent between Blesh and her husband.

Tobias glanced back at her; she'd been the incessant presence of a ticking clock. She concentrated entirely on the camera now, face beaming straight on, upper body turned askew, stiff and erect, fierce; she seemed taller. Tobias kept watching. Her change from indifferent to intense made her a new person, even more stately. She tucked her chin and cocked her head, but just a flinch, enough to angle her hat brim smartly over a brow—a black fedora, like her husband's, but a miniature of it, an Alpine, with a jeweled brooch on a crushed silk ribbon. Wooing that camera, she settled into a composure as surefooted as the valley behind her. Completely solemn, yet charged. Tobias was lost in this private extravagance.

In Celia Erhart's disdain for anything but that lens, Tobias saw the prerogative of gentle-blood his father tried to make him understand. He was looking over a rift he'd been warned to keep his back to. It chilled Tobias. But at the same time, he couldn't take his eyes from her. She so suggested some far world, she might have been undressing.

Everyone knew a camera's power to lay bare something of a person. Yet as much as Tobias was willing to offer himself up to this picture, Celia Erhart was determined to alter herself for it—for that far world. That was plain untruthful.

The photographer called everyone's attention to the pinwheel eye of his camera. He peered over the mahogany box, grabbed the rubber shutter bulb.

What would this picture say, Tobias wondered, if he could look into it over the years, as he did those at the stave mill—what would come of these people?

The photographer squeezed the rubber bulb. In the lapse between the aperture opening and closing with its faint sound of rubbing quarters, the dizzy thrill of the day faded, and a thought slid into Tobias's mind: What would Pop think of being put on paper with such company?

Chapter 4

"I don't suppose your father still wants us to bag sawdust?" Tobias watched the bundle of Celia Erhart's dress waddle along the plank toward the mill.

"Don't care. I ain't," John said.

Tobias grinned. "I can't hardly believe Mr. Erhart asked us to the camp with him. And with Warren P. Ryder, to boot."

Instead of watching the Erharts, John was facing his father's office. He tucked his hands into the high pockets of his britches where they buttoned to his shirt waist. "Listen here, big mouth." His voice carried the menacing edge boys use before a punch.

Tobias watched him closely.

"I wouldn't get too excited until we find what's in it for us. We never heard what pay we'd make."

"Pay? There isn't a hick in the valley who'd get a chance to be right there with them."

John regarded Tobias as though he'd thrown a rock at Josiah's window. "First, big mouth, you ain't a hick. And what do I care what kind of work hicks get?" He took a step toward Tobias, lifted his chin in the direction the Erharts walked. "You think this is big because you're not used to being around that type. They're not so great." A half step closer. "They'll look like hobos next to me someday."

Tobias had heard John Blesh make a lot of oaths. But this time he picked up on determination way beyond John's years; he might as well have grown whiskers. And then came those stabbing adult eyes John showed in Piebald Hollow four years ago.

"And get it straight," John said. "I do the negotiating." He put a finger on Tobias's flannel.

"I think I'm going home now." Tobias narrowed his eyes so it wouldn't show that John scared him. And he really did want to hurry off to his father to have the telling over with.

He leapt from the plank and crossed the mulch of hemlock bark and engine grease between the rails, their inner edges sheening away, out of town—gossamer polished by the flanged wheels of railcars. That was the only thing in Pigeondale not covered in coal dust, cinders or wood ash. Locomotives contributed some; the rest came from coal burned by the town's few businesses—a cheap, filthy grade from close to the surface where it could be mined and peddled by nearby farmers—or from the free fuel wood of the mill's castoffs, punky boards whose jaundiced smoke spewed from every home's stovepipe.

Tobias hopped onto another scaffold walk, which faced the only commercial street in Pigeondale. Not accommodating railcars, this plank was squat to the ground, though it lifted, tottered and fell by sections, like stone slabs over tree roots. The cleats of hicks' boots pocked the pine boards.

Change. Tobias saw its reflection as he passed the big panes of the barbershop and the Seneca House Hotel. His body was stretching; he was bound to be lanky. But he moved as one who'd mastered those bones too grown for a twelve-year-old. Past doorway leaners and crate sitters, busy wives and kids, he carried every limb in that forward grace of the trotting giraffes that came with the circus to Marstadt. And a boy always off to the woods held the quietness in his walk of sneaking along trout pools, of easing through brakes to flush rabbits.

He drifted under the balconies of falsely squared buildings—the post office, the livery, the Ryder Company Store where the wagons of the valley's few farmers were backed to the plank, cabbages, potatoes and pumpkins stuffed between their sideboards.

Inconspicuous as a breeze.

And without slowing to look across for what was doing at the boarding house, he moved between the iron arches of the Manooka Creek bridge, over its loose boards, a few still nailed, all warped and always cantankerous at the weight of horses and wagon wheels. An awareness was sinking in, as a fog at dawn descends to hint a damp day—he was rushing from one sour face only to give his prospects up to another. He looked down at the shallow sheen trembling over eggs of river stone. Water always lightened him.

He stepped onto another plank, this one spanning Company Row Two: ten houses leading up to the slope of the valley, identical down to the unpainted barn walls and tin-topped porches, each one tethered to the plank by its own walk. But they weren't tethered too tightly; Ryder Lumber Company rented its houses at four dollars a month and could have any one of them dismantled and shipped away in the day it took to build it. Two-storied, facing the street lengthwise with kitchen rooms projecting to the back, they wore their long, rear roof slopes like longshoremen's hats.

Tobias turned onto the plank to his house. It was a good location, facing a hand well.

Ten years earlier, Herbert Meier had worked his way there from Germany by route of four year's section jobs on the Philadelphia and Erie. He'd sledged his way up the Susquehanna and along its West Branch, only to land in a headwaters like the place he'd left: dark and steep with looming trees and its own kind of feudal work. Somewhere along the way, near a cleft in the wall of the West Branch river valley where it gave way to a tributary, Tobias was born in a shack that squatted on some sandy strip between river and rail grade, same as his sister was wherever the crew had been planted down-line two years prior.

In the steely waters of the little tributary, Herbert Meier baptized his son, witnessed by skinny sectioners whose common language was an English of necessary utterances. All of Tobias's life, valleys of the West Susquehanna watershed made their imprint on him, as much as they etched the broad face of the Allegheny Plateau. He grew up learning every shade of the side-hollows of Manooka Valley, wore their ridges as bodily as his shoulders. And he came to understand how that place was too fragmented, sliced out of the tableland too sharply, to be of interest to humans for more than what it could give up, an interest as temporary and detached as company houses. Or as seasonal as hunting grounds, white man's or red's.

His ten years in Pigeondale had traced its sputtering ebb from a full-bodied lumber boomtown to this frail skeleton whose lifespan wavered day to day. The musk of tree flesh that once leached from the mills, heavy as the stink of a wet cat, had waned in proportion to the increasing distance of timber. Now, with the big mill running only one saw, the air of the valley had an innocent whiff more like damp paper.

*   *   *

"Hey you," his sister said as he hurried across the rag rug of the front room.

"Mom," Tobias said, not stopping, "I saw J. Hadley Erhart today. And Mrs. Erhart, too."

By the look Edna Meier gave where she stood at the table grating cabbage, Tobias could have announced President McKinley had arrived on a railcar. "In Pigeondale with his wife?" She set aside the grating board and scooped the cabbage with her hands into a kraut crock on the floor.

Tobias told her about his invitation to work at the Piebald camp. "And guess what," he said.

Edna tugged a sleeve where she'd rolled it to her elbow. She wore a patternless white wrapper with no collar, soft and plain as a muslin underskirt. It hung loose, but still showed her lankiness.

"What?" said Tobias's sister, Frieda. She stepped to the table and spooned salt into the crock.

"Mr. Warren P. Ryder is going. And another man that even John's dad never heard of."

Tobias's mother carried a little look of wonder as a matter of course— under bristles of wiry charcoal hair, her face was round as a pumpkin and propped like a lollipop on her long and thin neck. But she flared with real surprise now, then a frown. "Why would men like that want two boys in the way?"

Tobias picked up on her suspicion. "Mr. Erhart came right out and said he needed help, and—"

"And you volunteered?"

"Myself and John. But Mr. Erhart would have asked us anyways."

So she asked for particulars, and while Tobias related them, the brightness of his prospects caught in the eyes of his mother and sister.

Frieda gestured toward the kitchen window, beyond which the roof of the privy towered over their mother's dominion where she kept a cow, garden and hens. "Let's hurry down to the mill," she said, "so we can tell Pop you saw the Erharts."

Their mother watched the air come out of Tobias. She wiped her hands and touched his shoulder, and it seemed to Tobias a too-late motherly gesture to plug boy-hopes from leaking out. Mothers: seal in what's left, stopper the opening before something bad breaks in.

It must have hit her that things find a way in anyway. "Tobias," she said, "don't get your mind set on going out there."

"You don't think he'll like it?"

The three of them stared at the same spot on the floor.

"It's just that he won't see the sense of it," his mother said.

"And he won't like it," Frieda said.

* * *

Only five years older than Tobias, Pigeondale was ancient for a logging town. Seventeen years. It dated to the end of the era when the first wave of loggers felled alleys of trees just to clear way for soaring white pines, days when logs weren't milled locally, but floated to the Susquehanna, and then to shipyards on the Chesapeake. Next, the broad-waisted hemlock became king, but only for its hide, so the great boles were left to rot like potatoes, and tanneries came to be as common as train depots in the new boroughs scattered across the tier. Ryder Lumber Company branched its railroad from Marstadt to establish mill towns like Pigeondale as the bases of logging operations. Crews reached into draws and side-hollows to feed bark to Ryder's tannery, and hardwoods to the mills—beech, chestnut; strong oak for lathe and staves. They timbered what pine was left, and then even sent hemlock to the mill; round nails, becoming widely available, proved not to split that twisted white flesh.

Tobias toted his father's lunch pail, still warm under a tea towel. He and his sister crossed the bridge, and in a male rite required in the presence of a girl, he slowed and looked over at the boarding house to see what was doing. The place had for boys the naughty allure of a brothel. But to Tobias, it was a temple—hicks lived there.

It was the largest building in Pigeondale—a square of three hulking stories, the only painted clapboards in town—lime white, so white they stood out against a snowfall, and accounted for the place being called the Whitehouse. Great roofed porches spanned the first two tiers, replete with railings, the posts turned in lathes even. The third floor watched out through dormers that jutted from a tarpapered mansard roof.

Besides a few unmarried mill workers, the Whitehouse boarded hicks between jobs, or crews working close to town. There lived hard men who could drive their bodies like mules for work, and wallow like hogs for pleasure. Young men on their way up, until their bodies couldn't pull saw and swing axe eleven-straight. Or a few old hicks still working, said to be on their way down. Some believed though, that hanging on proved the old ones were bred to the temperament, that woods work ran in their veins—men who'd shunned town jobs and families, somehow made a life passing from crew to crew. And now they did the lighter work, maybe oiling slides or scaling; only teamsters or engineers could stretch a career out of one logging occupation.

So the Whitehouse was a melting pot of storied drifters who'd worked all along the tier, some local, some with roots in New England, maritime Canada, even Scandinavia. After dinner, smoke time, the old-timers reigned on the long porches. And while town boys squeezed faces between the tobacco-stained rail posts, white pine grew taller, runaway locomotives faster, and rattlesnakes fatter. But there were truths between the tales, memories of Saturday night fights and whoring, and Sunday hangovers on slow railcars back to camp—teeth missing and the cold rain a-soaking. It was a place mill town mothers marked off limits, which made it all the more alluring.

But it was too early, even on a Saturday, for any loafers. Just the chambermaid shaking bed tickings from the balcony porch.

"Come on, Tobias. It's near lunchtime."

"Just making sure nothing's doin' at the Whitehouse." As if on hire to keep watch of the place.

Frieda slowed to let him catch up. "You're lucky to stay at a logging camp with Mr. Erhart and Warren P. Ryder." Frieda pronounced Ryder's name as everyone did in his company's domain—as if announcing it to an audience, the whole handle rising to and falling from the apex P.

"Yep."

"I'll want to hear all about what goes on when men like that are together."

"Nope."

When they got to the end of the main street, the company's raspy whistle hooted lunchtime for the mills. The pair trotted across the road of soupy mud and horse dung. They forwent the plank, stepping with the rail ties, past equipment shacks and the mill pond, upon which the pole-toting pondsman sorted logs and birled them clean.

The pair were in sight of the little stave mill now, tucked up close to the big mill with its knotty up-and-down slats. The big mill was not so tall as its name; it just carried an air in its high stack and long cupola, which spanned the spine of its roof. It was big in its length, though, a county's worth of barns teamed end-to-end.

Tobias stepped out ahead of his sister so she couldn't insist they keep to the main track. He cut along a siding between cribs of lumber.

While the pond staged logs to feed the mill, the yard took what she discharged. It was a shadowy maze of stacked lumber arranged in hulking cubes tall as houses, their centers left open to vent the boards as they dried.

Tobias zigzagged toward the stave mill, following a sense of direction he'd discovered while orienteering brushlands and woods—a swooning momentum he could feel in his breast, something in him aligning to his destination, drawing him as a leash.

Frieda yelled over the noise of the big mill. "Tobias, we're not supposed to be in the yard."

Lunchtime or not, the big mill's innards whine-groaned, whine-groaned with the circular saw, and thumped and thrummed with the belts, pulleys and steam engine that powered it. Along with the complaints of machinery—rhythmic almost to the point of sense—hemlock timbers wailed as they birthed off boards.

Tobias didn't answer his sister—he could keep his pace by her carping. He dodged this way and that until finally, veering between stacks in the last row, he stepped into the shipping yard of the Ryder Stave Mill. He looked across the soggy clay square to the pavilion where his father loaded railcars. No sign of him. Tobias turned to the stave mill. There his father sat on a stone step, watching toward the rail line for his Saturday lunch.

Frieda plucked the bucket from Tobias. "We're in for it now. You're doubly in for it."

"How'd I know he'd be watching for us," Tobias said.

The fume of green hemlock drafting out of the lumber piles had spumed thickly against the dampness that hung over the valley, snapping the roof of Tobias's mouth harsh as horseradish. But where he followed his sister into the yard, the muskiness washed brackish into the vanilla that came from the sawing of oak staves. A few steps farther, that taste held in the air tight as a cask, as if the staves were already seething their flavor into a Kentucky bourbon.

As they approached, their father just stared on. He let out a deep breath, his boughs of squat cheeks settling into the same wilt as his mustaches.

"Sorry we're late, Pop." Frieda set the bucket beside Herbert Meier's crossed legs. His arms were folded and his hat pulled tight to his eyes. The only shine to the man was on the buttons fastening the braces of his sawdusty overalls.

"You know to stay out of the mill yard," he said.

"I just wanted to make up time," Tobias said.

"We have a good reason for being late," Frieda said, still panting, the cranberry flush of her face extending into the pencil-straight part of her hair—wiry black just like her mother's. "Tobias had a big morning."

Tobias frowned at his sister. He'd rather have brought it up his own way. Ease it in as no big deal.

Herbert tilted his head back to see past the narrow brim of his tall, khaki-colored thimble hat. His look was not that of someone who liked news.

"Why don't you go ahead and eat, Pop," Tobias said, turning to his sister. "What did we bring him?"

"There's buckwheat cakes with apple butter and jam. Salt pork, a tin of steamed prunes, and an apple." She sat on the square of stone, beside her father. "And I shucked nuts for you this morning. Hickory and chestnut."

Herbert moved the tea towel from over the bucket and took out the cakes she'd folded in newspaper. Then he looked back to his son, hefting a brow. Tobias remained mum.

"Tobias met up with J. Hadley Erhart," Frieda said. "And his wife. He even made a photograph with them."

Herbert stopped unwrapping the newspaper. "You in Marstadt?"

"No, Pop," Tobias said. "Mr. and Mrs. Erhart came to Mr. Blesh's office this morning."

"And you and the Blesh boy invited yourselves in."

"We were already in there."

Herbert finished unwrapping his buckwheat cakes, a stack of three. He held them up at Tobias as he would a finger. "I told you before. You got no business around Josiah Blesh. And you sure as hell got no place bothering the Erharts."

"But Pop," Frieda said, "don't you want to know what they were doing out here?"

Herbert took a bite from his buckwheat cakes, his caramel eyes glaring at Tobias. "That's no more my business than his." His mustaches twitched with his chews.

"It's John that wanted to be in the office," Tobias said. "And his dad didn't know the Erharts were coming, so he paid no mind to us being there."

Herbert set down his cakes and reached into his bucket. His broad hand hid an apple as he bit into its flesh, the crack muffled under his mustaches.

With his shoe, Tobias troweled ashes, tossed there from the mill's boiler. He withdrew into the buzz and zap of the cylinder saw skimming staves, then back to the days he shuffled on the other side of the mill, waiting for Frieda. He relaxed into the stories he'd read in the pictures in the hallway. Then he thought of the allure of Celia Erhart's indifference to all but a camera, the prick of shame in how far he was from a world that dressed and perfumed and painted women like that. The two very different memories frothed in his breast. He looked at his father. And into it all unfurled the usual cloud of warning: Don't step over boundaries.

Frieda tugged her sweater sleeves. "Oh Pop, Mr. Erhart was just out to plan a hunting trip and Tobias and John got hired to do the chores. That's all."

Herbert threw the remainder of his apple into the mill yard. "Why in the devil would you offer up to do that?"

"I didn't. Mr. Erhart was already looking for a couple of boys to keep the wood split and shag deer at the old Piebald camp." Tobias shifted from shoe to shoe. "So he asked us." As Tobias said it, he realized he was lying. Erhart never got a chance to ask them, not directly.

"Well, he ain't going to find his help in Tobias Meier," Herbert said. "Tobias Meier doesn't belong among Erharts and Ryders."

"But Pop," Tobias said, "it's just chores."

"Don't matter," Herbert said. "You belong there as much as I belong in the mill office." He reached into his lunch bucket and took out his salt pork. "There's a difference between you and that Blesh boy. Know your station."

Tobias cocked his head and frowned, begging an explanation.

Herbert shook his head and glanced away, across the yard. "A boy shouldn't put himself someplace he won't ever belong. He'll likely expect things."

"How's John Blesh belong working among Ryders and Erharts more than me?"

Herbert worked a mouthful of salt pork he'd taken. He slowly looked to Tobias, jowls pulsing. "Because Tobias Meier's place ain't to ask what. You ask how, and don't think about it. Those with a station to ask what—like the Bleshes—they work straight for the Ryders and the Erharts. Those without one, they stay to their place and be what the Bleshes will have them be."

Tobias hadn't feared a no so much as what always came up: how he should see his future. He knew where he wanted to go. And it fit his father's idea. But his father's reason to go there—no, there was more—the getting there, the narrow and sure path he wanted him to take—that was confusing. Inside of Tobias was a vane aligning to a wind that veered from his father's course in spite of the same destination. It was a way that allowed questions and glances, while his father's was safe with narrow walls.

Herbert turned to Frieda, and his mustaches flinched with a brief grin—the world was thus fixed. And Tobias decided at that moment he would, no matter what Herbert Meier said, go to the Piebald camp come two weeks from Thursday.

Chapter 5

In the thick black of predawn, Tobias leaned against a pier of the plank near Josiah Blesh's office, and waited.

Finally, late but in no hurry, John Blesh trudged across the tracks.

"Figured you'd chicken out," John said.

"Wouldn't miss it," Tobias said.

"D'you tell your pop you're going?"

"Nope."

"So he thinks you're at school again."

"A-huh."

With October edging toward November, it had been reasonable for Tobias to start back to school earlier that week, to endure the tedium of learning tables, the long hike over a ridge and out a farming valley to the schoolhouse. For one thing, he had the season on his side—late fall and winter were the time of erudition. Starting in spring, farm work and bark peeling occupied most every boy old enough to jump a train. Then there was berry picking or fishing, or odd jobs around the mill, which Tobias, at twelve, had already taken up: most recently, shaving shingles from unsound logs.

Besides, he'd want to get his nose into the cloth-covered primers and readers. Evenings, by dusk or lamplight, he read all he could, but the scarce books in Pigeondale were shared like cropland. Each time Twain's tales or Cooper's leatherstockings made rounds, more pages were missing. And the only books the Meiers owned were a history text that was history itself, an annual copy of a farmer's almanac, and a dictionary which Tobias browsed when literature was real scarce. Between books, he could fill his mind only with his latest issue of *Grit* or stories and stale news from the week-old *County Gazettes* his mother received compliments of the company store and pasted with buckwheat to bedroom wallboards, layer upon layer to soften the drafts. Mornings, he'd read some new addition of the yellowing type, one column telling of the county's town-to-town visitors, the next the glory of the Rough Riders taking San Juan Hill. Another day he'd wonder at illustrations of automobiles, consider accounts of western loggers recruiting Pennsylvania woodhicks, or of local timbers used in buildings ten stories tall.

So neither Herbert nor Edna Meier had suspected him, though he knew his sister had. But she could be trusted.

"We better hurry," Tobias said. We need to be there before daybreak."

John put his hands in his coat pockets. "Too bad you can't stay the night. That'll be the best part." It was straightforward and true, but soaked in gloat.

"I've got till dinnertime to get back," Tobias said.

"Sure you do. But the good storytelling doesn't start till later. There'll be card games and lie swapping, tall tales and business deals."

*   *   *

Down the main line to where rails split off to Piebald Hollow, the boys made no sound. But on the spur track, their bootlegs whisked the crisp ragweeds and asters rooted now where steam engines once tramped. Tobias whisked louder, for he wore his pant legs stuffed into his boots, as hicks did.

Alongside the tracks, clumps of beech saplings emerged in the twilight. The little winds that flutter here and there before daybreak frisked their sere cornucopia leaves. The breezes smelled of damp earth and worms, the way they do on the other side of winter.

"Beech trees never shuck their leaves," John said when a shrubby sapling jittered at his elbow.

"Just the little ones," Tobias said. "They shed when the new buds come."

"How do you know?"

"Remember the big beech where we turned into the hollow? You could just make it out. Not a leaf. Just like the ones out behind the smitty shop."

"I doubt that was a beech back there. Anyways, they'da cut it if it was." John pointed his chin uphollow as if to remind Tobias that in that darkness, all was denuded.

"It's too twisted and knotty," Tobias said. "Hicks call them lightning bolts. They get struck if they cut them." Tobias spoke as offhandedly as possible, careful to not insult John, easy as it was. "Leaving them makes seed so hicks always have work somewhere."

"Hogwash," John said.

"Well the tree's there, plainer than a wart."

"Not the tree, the believing all that crap."

Tobias shrugged off his coat—a canvas-lined, worsted hand-me-down sized for a man. He draped it over his shoulder where the collar of his checkerboard shirt splayed broad as a beagle ear, then he hooked his thumb to a suspender. John wore a thick wool shirt too, but plain gray, as was his open coat—no emulation of a woodhick.

Then there was Tobias's hat.

Most boys, including John, wore slouchy ones that melted around their crowns in the Scottish golf style. But not Tobias, who knew hicks and the combinations of hat style and color from which each created a brand, then trademarked it with trappings of bands and pins, and by shape of brim and crown. A hick knew how to make his hat one in a million, as distinct as a name, an epigraph for the man.

Tobias knew, though, that his hat looked more like an epigraph he wanted to grow into, as tall as a Texas Ranger's, and deep-brown as peat. He wore the brim sombrero-flat, except for a slight crescent bent downward at his forehead. A plaited thong of raw leather lassoed the base of the crown, and he'd knocked four dimples into the upper gallon. Despite the hat's immenseness, Tobias had seen in mirrors that it didn't so much make him look smaller as thinner, wider-eyed.

It was a five-dollar hat he could not have afforded—given in exchange by the landlord of the Whitehouse for a week of wood splitting. Its origin made it most authentic to Tobias. Past property of a real hick: a Downeaster, said to have been beaten with the handle of a cant hook on a Saturday night in Marstadt. After he'd abandoned the hat in flight, hicks from the Whitehouse returned home with it so the rest could scoff at the sin of a man leaving his hat.

The deeper the boys penetrated the narrowing hollow, the thicker its air became—a tang of earth and debarked hemlocks left to decay. Saplings, though, sweetened the mix with a hint of birch beer.

The tangle of brush along the ridges took shape with dawn, and a coon gave its last gut-chuckle before sunrise. Tobias caught in it a rapid approximation of Piebald Run's slaps and gurgles. A pair of ravens cruising their remnant haunts croaked and tocked like large old men, casual and confidential. Tobias imagined they remarked on the state of their clear-cut ridges and hollows—such long-lived birds would be uncommonly intimate with the place. John did not seem to heed any of it, though, jutting eyeballs fixed on the iron rails ahead. All this world to him, Tobias guessed, was a flat and boring canvas where, as John once said, a bird's of no use if you can't eat it.

But anything Tobias set eye or ear to, picked up or smelled, sparked thoughts—what it did, what it fit together with. Talk of beech leaves had sent his mind to seasons and soils and nuts. Then birds.

"Pop says Pigeondale got its name from passenger pigeons that came for beechnuts. When section gangs worked to the mouth of Manooka Valley, beech covered all these bottoms, and hemlocks grew on the edges 'so thick you couldn't shoot a treed bear's ass at noon.'"

"Hogwash."

"The passenger pigeons came in springtime, so many they made clouds in the sky. They'd roost in the hemlocks and fly down to the beech groves to feed at first light." Tobias squinted around, imagining the dawning bottomland crowded with elephant-skin beech trees. "When Pop worked down-line on a repair gang, the old-timers—ones who'd laid rail up this way years before—they'd say 'pigeon feathers' whenever someone farted."

John's mouth twitched with a grin, though his face still held the pout of a boy bored.

"Those old sectioners would say, 'The pigeons flying off the roost up in the hollows off Manooka Valley, they'd alight loud as a group fart in a choir loft.'"

"Beech trees?" John held out a hand to halt Tobias. "I thought just apple trees grew in groves."

The rail bed there had been embanked over a marsh of willow switches, Piebald Run oozing through the middle. Tobias knew by an old mound of breastwork beyond the stream that this was the drained remnant of a splash dam, left by an earlier generation of loggers who'd floated lowland pine timbers in the spring rush. In every sign of men having shaped these hollows, Tobias saw the message of an old stone fence—stubborn and enduring, sure, proud even, but the woods would grow back to where you wouldn't know the side of the farmer's field.

"Apple trees grow in orchards," Tobias said. "A grove's any bunch of trees."

John shook his head back and forth. "You sure do know lots of useless stuff." He nodded that they could move on.

Tobias pointed up a ridge. "Those birds would take over whole hollows. Rail crews called them pigeon cities. I think they swarmed here as much for all the hemlocks to nest in as for the beechnuts." He tipped back his big hat brim to picture hemlocks rearing from the slopes of the hollow, arm in arm and shifting in the wind. But the image fell of its own into heaps of rusty-needled tree toppings. Up wafted an acrid draft of tannic bark fallen from trains bound for Marstadt.

"If they even ate beechnuts like you say," John said.

"Oh, they ate them all right. They churned through here like rows of armies, back rows leapfrogging to the front to sweep new leaves for beechnuts, and maybe a chestnut or ack-corn. Probably rolled like ocean waves through this hollow right here. And on the driest days, instead of raking, they just beat their wings to winnow leaves from the nuts."

John had been looking about, whistling. But he stopped and turned to Tobias. "What do you know about ocean waves?"

"What I've seen in pictures and heard from Italian sectioners."

"Not me," John said. "I only take for fact what I see. Besides, all I ever heard about those pigeons was how dumb they were. That old gimp-legged farmer up Manooka valley—one they call Cap'n and always sets there counting pig potatoes on his cart at the company store—from what he told me, he'd be rich if he'd had more time with them."

"Say?"

"Said he could get maybe a hundred when they flew through. He did it from an old scaffold on the point above Whippoorwill Hollow. Said he'd know the birds were due late winter when he'd see a few early-comers peck around his yard with the chickens."

Tobias held up a hand. "Those would have been the scouts." He'd read about the pigeons, re-created their cycles in his mind. "When the flock started north in spring, a group went ahead to find nesting places where the most beech would go to nut that year. They'd go back and meet the flock, lead them."

"Those birds were too dumb to know grit from shit, let alone find a flying flock. Anyway—" John drew out the word while he cast a sidelong glance that reminded Tobias he'd interrupted his story. "Every day in late winter, an hour before supper, one of Cap'n's boys—there must be eight of them still around here, grown now—would wait up on that scaffold looking south. The way he told it, sooner or later you'd see a swelling over a far-off ridge." John glanced skyward.

"The boy'd holler like hell and up would come the old man, his old lady, the other boys. They'd be toting big sticks with shakes nailed to the ends while their old mutts followed along quivering like they'd been fed porcupines whole. The boys would climb trees to the tops while that gimpy Cap'n and his old lady would crawl onto that scaffold. You see—" John kicked an iron rail and grinned— "dumb as flying moles, those birds barely cleared the trees up on the ridges. So Cap'n and crew would swat them down easy as apples."

Tobias was all for taking birds—no challenge matched pulling on a grouse as it thundered out of a brush tangle. But it was in keeping with the way of the land, as Pop said, for the score to be always in the bird's favor. And he said so to John who shuffled his boot soles rail tie to rail tie, boring head-first as if pulled by a string on his nose.

"I suppose the score *was* in the birds' favor," John said. "No matter how dumb they were, there were enough to handle the casualties."

"Then where are they now?"

"That's on account of the guns and trappers," John said.

"The whats?"

"According to Cap'n, pretty soon anyone from here to Buffalo that could load shot into a muzzle came hunting. They'd sneak under the pigeons' roosts barefoot in the dark, and ambush them at daybreak. Then trappers from out West moved in. They'd set nets where the birds fed, and snag a bushel at a time."

Tobias looked across the timbered hollow and tried to picture this. "You sure know a lot about it for someone that takes for fact only what he sees."

"Either what I see or what's given by a reliable source. Not a bunch of dago sectioners lying about an ocean when all they've seen's the bilge of a ship.

"What's a bilge?"

John rolled his eyes. "Anyways, by the time the trappers showed up, the railroad passed the mouth of Manooka Valley. Cap'n said trains would haul pigeons by the carload down to Harrisburg. Says that with every potato he digs, he thinks about all the good eating that went down the line. And all the money he could have made if he'd have thought of trapping."

"Pop tells me," Tobias said, "that after the railroads went through, the Indians quit hunting the birds."

"Yep. Cap'n says the one good thing about the birds dying off was those Indians not coming after them anymore, bunches of them camping in the hollows around here. You couldn't even leave the dogs out at night."

"They were harmless," Tobias said. "They just came down from the reservation to follow an old way of life. And they didn't take so many they could fill a train car."

"Well, according to Cap'n, there ain't such a thing as a tame Indian. And he knows through seeing." He pointed to an eye.

"Like there ain't a tame panther that's still a panther."

Tobias would have liked telling what he knew of those descendents of Chief Cornplanter, of their following an urge every year as natural as the pigeons'. For tradition's sake, some had kept on even after the great flocks—despite roads and rails—pursuing other game, until most of Cornplanter's Indians too, disappeared. And not so long ago that Tobias couldn't remember their stops in town.

From what he'd read and heard of passenger pigeons, he'd pieced together a scene: *a hemlock rearing from the base of a hollow, two birds brooding their nestlings in a sparse halo-littering of twigs. Dawn sifts weak and gray through heavy boughs. The male flies off and the female moves a wing to tent her brood. Below, something moves up the hemlock trunk. But the pigeon watches only straightaway, purrs. A boy's copper-skinned arm hugs the tree above her, and she pecks and wing-slaps at his hand reaching into the nest. He's naked except for a sinew headband gartering his hair into a shock from which plume three striped feathers of turkey wing, and he shoulders a sling of bobcat gut holding a sack made of elk bladder. The bird flushes and flutters around him in downy orbits, croaking while the boy snatches two fistfuls of warm nestling for his sack. He diminishes down the tree, and the forest is new with daylight, and fewer unfledged pigeons.*

Tobias didn't see it as plundering. There was something perfect in it, a clean and fair taking.

"Being wild," John said, "sure didn't keep Indians from dying out. No more than it did your pretty passenger pigeons."

"Passenger pigeons might not be died out. And there's still Indians up in the reservation."

"Unless there's a reservation for passenger pigeons, there ain't any."

"There might be." Tobias tried to step up the pace; at this rate they'd miss out if the men decided to hunt today.

"What makes you think so?"

"First, there's still laws against shooting them."

"A little too late," John said, stopping. He looked up, then ducked to the rail bed, as if a sky frescoed with pigeons fell on them.

Tobias watched him laugh. "I got the rest of my information from my eyes."

"Yeah, while they were shut."

"No," Tobias said. "In full daylight four years ago. Pop and me were fishing right here on Piebald Run."

John started along, but slowly, against Tobias's hurry.

"I was throwing my line when a bird across the crick took roost in a dogwood. Eyes red as trout speckles. Claws just as bright. And its whole breast was like the meat of a peach." Tobias shook his head back and forth. "Something about that bird told you it was supposed to be in a bunch." He looked at John. "You ever seen anything like that?"

John just kept his slow pace, looking straight on.

"I hope he wasn't the last one, come back looking for the rest that will never show."

The hollow was a narrow furrow here, no more than two barns wide. Straight ahead it opened enough to let in the full light of morning. Tobias could feel in the damp air one of those October days when the sky would change only in shades of gray. "That was the same day I saw you," he said, and then couldn't keep himself from stepping out ahead of John, for Tobias knew the old Piebald logging camp lay there in the widening hollow.

"All hogwash," he heard John say.

*   *   *

A feeder spring poured in to merge with Piebald Run there in an oasis of old pine and poplar, giants spared for their shade. All the camp's buildings were of warped and gray-weathered planks. Shacks that once housed horses, tools and a blacksmith leaned along the rail line, and another, an engine stall, stood over a siding of track. A log car was backed into it, decked with trunks, crates and flour sacks. The main camp, that long barn of a building that whetted Tobias's desire every time he fished here, stood by the slope of the hollow. The boys headed where the cook's quarters and kitchen slanted off the closer end, a smudge of smoke jittering from a stub of stovepipe. Tobias breathed the smell of fried bacon and caught the bobs and wags of three draft horses hitched alongside the twenty-stall stable. He thought aloud: "Funny to see those logging hosses saddled to ride, not harnessed to skid."

"Do you think someone like Warren P. Ryder would climb himself out of this hollow, with it steeper than those horses' muzzles?"

"I just figured that if they were hunting, they'd be walking."

"Those horses will do that," John said.

Near the kitchen, a pair of setters with red-peppered faces jigged around the boys as they picked their way through cast crates and casks, bent crosscut blades, tar paper, and a keeled stove with a crack in its belly. Looks more like they left the job yesterday, Tobias thought, not two years now.

All the windows were above their heads, and the only door on their side was to the kitchen. So they knocked; any mill-town boy knew not to barge into the domain of a camp cook, off-limits even to hicks.

Swinging on leather hinges, the door squawked across the floorboards. The kitchen's oily steam slapped solid as a lard paddle.

The cook wore drooping mustaches, thick and rusty-gray as fox fur. He was hatless, a wisp of bacon-greasy hair pasted across his forehead. "What do you want?" he said, as if this were one in a string of interruptions.

Tobias forgot the rule that John was to speak first. "We're here at Mr. Erhart's asking."

John stared at him as hard as the cook, who pulled a rag from his shoulders and worked it between his hands. His shirt was but the uppers of his union suit, stained yellow from pits to trousers, which were hefted so high by his suspenders that he didn't have to button his waist.

"Ah, the wood splitters. Go round to the dining hall. And remember, this isn't a way in." The door shut. "Or out."

Tobias followed John to the other side, then into the near-empty hall. He strained to sort the three faces at the table across the room.

"Mr. Erhart," John said, "it's John Blesh and Tobias Meier come to do chores."

"Come on over, boys."

Tobias was keen to his boot heels scraping the gritty floor planks as he walked to where the men sat near the door to the kitchen. He knew enough that the pine table and its benches would have once been among dozens parked in two rows across the room.

J. Hadley Erhart was closest to the boys, grinning. But an older man beside him watched schoolmaster fashion, hard and superior, and it made Tobias aware of every fray in his shirt. He pictured his father watching this, shaking his head of heavy jowls. For Tobias knew this was Warren P. Ryder, father-in-law of J. Hadley Erhart, and founder and sovereign of mills, railroads, tanneries, towns; a man with a hand in every venture within seventy-five miles of Marstadt.

Ryder was prominent in figure, too. Though he was not much taller than his son-in-law or the other man, his canvas field coat hung from his shoulders as it would from an ox yoke. A powerful stoutness resisted his effort of turning on the bench while he regarded the boys. The rest of him appeared as he offered it in photographs: righteous eyes, small lips holding a permanent smirk. His pug snout however, showed more nostril in real life.

Tobias reached up and thumbed his hat brim, wondering if he should leave it on or hold it. The men's hats lay on the table beside their breakfast plates—two large outbacks, and Ryder's black bowler with a silk ribbon.

J. Hadley Erhart gestured at the boys, his big brows flaring like squirrel tails. "Gentlemen, meet Masters John Blesh and Tobias Meier, Pigeondale recruits to split and pile wood, chase and shag game. They'll stoke and bank the fires, and—we hope—clean and skin the prize."

He remembered my name, Tobias thought.

Ryder regarded them up and down, cocked his head and said, "Very well." Then he turned his frame back square to the table. Erhart nodded his way. "My father-in-law, Warren P. Ryder." Then he motioned across the table. "And this is our guest from afar, Andy Hoehn."

The stranger gave each boy a nod and a wink.

"Mr. Hoehn is a city fellow. But a great admirer of our parts."

Tobias could tell the man's young looks lied his age. He guessed forty, but his puffed and chalky features, and the rigid black waves of his hair, made a boy of him, an eager-looking one with a hearty grin.

"He hails from our state's industrial jewel," Erhart said. "Pittsburgh." Erhart lifted his chin to Tobias and John. "Andy, these are local boys."

Tobias heard solemn assurance in the words, telling him Hoehn regarded the people of the big woods as a novelty. Part of him felt gawked upon. But a little pride floated through. He saw in the boy-gumption his same respect for the forbidding shapes and shades of the plateau. Tobias glanced at John. As he'd expected. John had creased his eyes; he disliked being tagged a local.

"What do you want us to do?" John said.

Erhart ignored the question. "John is the son of Josiah Blesh, superintendent of the Pigeondale operations. He's already been to work in the woods and helped out around the mill." Erhart leaned back for Hoehn to get a better look.

"Soon to work, sure to heaven," Warren P. Ryder said.

Erhart swung around on his bench to face the boys fully. He wore a checkerboard shirt, blue instead of the red or green preferred by hicks. Official Ryder blue. Even with snug beige suspenders and in a dimly lit dining hall, J. Hadley Erhart could never look the part of a woodhick; a man like him showed anywhere he was meant to inherit an empire.

Elbows to his knees, Erhart addressed the boys at their level. "Today we're going to have a look around—get bearings for where to hunt. But there's plenty for you to do until we get back."

Tobias nodded.

"First, get your fill of breakfast. And mind that tomorrow morning we eat at four-thirty, sharp."

Tobias realized how hungry he was. But a worse pang came from knowing he'd have to leave home tomorrow before three a.m. And it wasn't forgoing sleep that troubled him—he could handle that.

"Help the cook clean up," Erhart said. "Then you'll find a pile of slabs out back. Cut and split them to fit that stove." He pointed past the boys to where a squat box-stove stood beside a cask of kindling sticks and boards, edges rounded and bark on them. "There are hatchets and saws in an outbuilding in front. Old Snyder is around here somewhere. He'll help you find them."

"Crosscutters, sir?" Tobias said. It sent Erhart and Hoehn into laughter, and Warren P. Ryder to shaking his head back and forth.

"No, Tobias," Erhart said, "the trees have already been felled. "We just need the slabs cut to fit the stove. Use a bucksaw."

John rolled his eyes while Erhart watched Tobias. "Tobias," he said, "it sounds that you aspire to fell trees."

"Yessir, I most want to work in the woods."

"That's what it takes to be a hick. Desire. They're hard workers—from sawyers to spudders to teamsters."

"I can see why, sir," Tobias said. "They have big jobs. Important ones, at the head of the operation."

John wheezed through his nose.

Erhart looked now at John. "Don't you doubt it, Tobias. And every job relies on the other, the whole way through. The operation on them all."

"If you can keep them from the whiskey," Warren P. Ryder said, without turning.

His son-in-law just smiled. "Can you boys put an edge on a knife?"

"Yessir," John said, taking out a jackknife and opening it as he handed it to Erhart.

Erhart raked his thumb across the blade. "Handy work. Old Snyder can find you an oilstone. We'll leave our hunting knives here." He returned the knife to John, pulled his own from a back pocket and set it on the table. It was hidden in its sheath, but Tobias bet it was a hefty, bolstered piece of forged carbon steel. He thought he could stand right there—talk about logging and hunting and good knives—until his legs went numb.

"There's a springhouse out back," Erhart said. Fill buckets as the cook needs them, and help with the supper settings. But—" he held up a finger and paused— "stay out of his way. That's a camp rule."

The boys nodded.

"We'll be back at dark. So be sure to light all these lamps." He motioned around the room. "There are more in the barn and up in the bunkhouse."

"See Old Snyder for oil?" Tobias said.

"Exactly." Erhart regarded Tobias a moment. "And while you're upstairs, each of you take your pick of a bunk. Find yourselves blankets and sheets for your ticks in the trunks on the log car."

"We'll only need one bunk," John said.

Erhart laughed. "You can have your own bunks. There's no crew of hicks here."

"What I'm saying is that Tobias won't be staying nights. He has to go home."

"It's not that I want to, sir." Tobias looked at his boots. "I've got work at home."

"Then it's hardly necessary to come back," Erhart said.

Tobias looked up. "I've counted on it, sir, so I know I can do it."

If Erhart doubted the story, it did not show, though Tobias guessed the word school had crossed his mind. "Then we can let you take a horse," Erhart said.

"No please, sir. It's no trouble." His panic weakened his voice now, and Erhart must have heard this. He arched his great brows and nodded. His father-in-law gulped the last of his coffee and tossed the tin cup onto his plate. He set out his hunting knife, tugged at his watch chain, and looked to Erhart.

The men rose from the table. The stranger, Andy Hoehn, put out his own knife, and nearly tripping on the heels of his hosts, gave Tobias and John a lopsided, boyish grin.

*   *   *

Tobias carried plates and cups to the kitchen where the cook smoked in a maple rocker beside the stove. Near a window stood a lone cupboard and a counter shelf, above which hung pots and a family of frying pans. In the middle of the room, an enormous slice of tree trunk lay end-up, a cleaver planted into it alongside a flank of bacon, a meat saw hanging from a hook in a rafter above. Crates and barrels had been stacked in the far corner. Otherwise, the kitchen yawned empty expanses where, Tobias guessed, once spanned shelves and countertops.

Later, seated before a kettle of coffee and tiers of thick-cut bacon and cornbread, heaps of fried apple wedges, eggs and potatoes, Tobias imagined himself a hungry hick in a working camp. But the dining hall's sparseness seemed to rear against this, and he couldn't keep hold of the picture. It fled farther and farther away, and the latest street rumors grumbled out of the emptiness between—the days of woodhicks in these hollows were numbered.

Out back, the boys sized their pile of slabs, then sought Old Snyder. In what had been the saw filer's shack—a dirt-floored stall littered with rusty saw teeth and filings—they found him at a bench, drawing wicks into lamps. He was a stiff man, seemingly immobile of features, neck, torso—all but his arms, which occasionally sent his hands reaching for an odd pipe that had a walnut-colored bowl and a metal stem as thick as a man's thumb.

The thing about old Snyder was that he wasn't old—just acted it. Tobias figured him to be about the age of foremen at the mill. As the boys went to him later for the whereabouts of a dipper or a sharpening stone, he'd stop in fitting a wick or cleaning a globe and not move a cell, including his eyes. Then he'd take out his pipe, hold it for a pause, and answer as if struck with something he'd been trying to remember. "Why, there's still some extra stones 'round the old smitty's shop." He always followed what he said with a stare and a statue-grasping of his pipe until all at once his body jerked, and he picked back up on the task at hand.

He had the long and narrow face of the Bavarians in Marstadt, but his skin was tea-tinted, as if steeped in the caramel die that renders from the innards of walnut husks.

Each boy took a turn using his backside to steady a slab across a three-legged sawhorse while the other bucksawed. Then they split any boards too wide for the stove door, stopping only to dip from the springhouse, which jutted like a dormer from the side of the hollow. By the time the waning day's chill began nipping through their shirtsleeves, and the sour tang of hardwood flesh drenched the air, a pile of firewood humped its back right to the windowsill.

Inside, in the last of the window light, the boys sat at the feed table and whetted the knives. J. Hadley Erhart hadn't disappointed Tobias; his was one of the new Cases, a stag-stocked piece with a broad bolster, its heft potent and reassuring in the hand. Hoehn's was a jackknife, common and well-used. But Ryder's, a lock-blade, was of shiny German steel. It had a rosewood handle set with a gold emblem the size of a thumbnail and inscribed with his initials. Tobias shaved each knife across the stone, over and over, until the cook roused the boys from the table, grunting from his great mustaches that they'd scuffed the black oilcloth.

The camp air sharpened as the nickel sky molted black. The boys made trips for armloads of slabs and stacked them by the stove. Old Snyder already had lamps lit in the barn, so each boy set to an indoor task. Tobias knelt and opened the stove door and made a teepee of kindling around crumpled butcher wrap while John kicked an apple crate lamp-to-lamp to reach and light the wicks.

"Don't forget the ones in the sleeping quarters," Tobias said.

"I don't need you to remind me."

Tobias struck a match to the butcher wrap. He shut his eyes. When he opened them, the wall lamps tinted the room in warm copper. He heard John walk up the stairs, and again he closed his eyes, squeezing them this time, picturing how the lamplight in the sleeping quarters would cast onto grinning men and great hanging frock coats, the walnut stocks and blued barrels of scatter guns and carbines where they leaned in the corners, the sheen of beeswaxed knee boots. He heard bouts of laughter, jesting insults and one-ups. He smelled sweet pipe tobacco and the musky smoke of damp firewood. He suspected those rare moments that matched daring expectations.

Later, hours after it had been dimmed, that same lamplight would touch up to a day of watching and searching and chasing in the big woods.

The kindling was crackling. He piled slabs on the fire, shut the stove door, and went out to the darkness of Piebald Hollow.

Chapter 6

The instant Tobias saw his sister's face, he knew he'd been found out, but he could tell, too, he had an ally. All through his nighttime walk, he hadn't thought on whether he'd again use artifice or try honesty to stay the next night at camp. He'd just resolved to be there. But he'd expected different circumstances when he'd stepped into the Meier sitting room.

Frieda sat at the sofa, leaning against its arm of bare birch wood. The girl who seemed made of smiles and bristle-curls wore wide warning eyes he read easy as a barber pole. From an end table beside Frieda, a lamp shone dull white onto the profile of their father at his high-backed rocker, broad hips wedged so tight he might take it with him if he stood.

"You been to school?"

"No." Tobias pushed the door closed and leaned back against it.

"So you went where I forbade."

"I went to work for Mr. Erhart at the Piebald camp."

Herbert's face flushed. He glanced at his daughter, then at his hands. "A pine peg doesn't fit an oak knothole." He spoke it decisively, as if from a Bible on his lap.

"I know I did wrong, Pop."

"The medicine's in your hide." Herbert had yet to look at his son. Frieda rocked her head side to side, silent.

"I ought to be out there right now," Tobias said. "I'm going back tomorrow." He gripped the doorknob. "And I'll be needing to stay the night. So you better double up on this lashing."

Turning to his son, Herbert's words rose one upon the other toward a yell. "I'll more than double it to keep you quiet and in your place."

"Pop," Frieda said. Her father kept his eyes on Tobias. "Pop, you always say Tobias is too old for school. And he's making money at that camp. Why can't he go if it's for work?"

Edna Meier spoke from the kitchen: "In one way or another, everyone in this valley works for J. Hadley Erhart and Warren P. Ryder. Including you, Herbert."

"Me working *for* them and him working *with* them is different."

Herbert typically dispensed words as frugally as nickels; Tobias had stirred something of his creed. He looked back at his father more boldly than he should have. It made no sense, how a man whose world was thus fixed could set out from Germany in the first place. Yes, he said he could not live freely or comfortably there. But it hardly seemed worth leaving for so little life beyond a wage.

"It's just for these few days," Tobias said. He looked away. "The point ain't that I'm working for Mr. Erhart, it's the things I'm getting to do." He wanted his father to explain what was wrong with his notions. But the world to Herbert Meier was drawn out on a chalkboard, and his job was to stand in front of it and make sure nothing was marked upon or erased from it.

So his father responded by not responding, which meant that until Tobias led him to the outhouse and braced himself against its planks in presentation of his backside, the conversation would proceed one-sided.

Outside, Tobias took it almost eagerly, for he saw the double lashing as the price to return to Piebald Hollow. And that night he lay under his quilt broken in every quarter except one. The part that had to know how his notions were wrong.

* * *

Pre-dawn next day, the air's pedigree was cousin to water, the kind of spongy dampness that registered colder through the body than norther winds—a day when a fast walk couldn't stave the chill off even a boy.

Tobias had left earlier than three in hopes of arriving before the hunters awakened. But reaching the camp, he saw that Old Snyder had cressets of pine knots already burning in the engine shed and the stable.

Tobias peeked in the camp door. Lamps above the table cast a sheen across the oilcloth. He smelled only the sulfur of coal oil—breakfast hadn't been started. John Blesh slogged from the kitchen with a stack of plates, his forefingers hooking wreaths of tin coffee cups.

"John, I'm here," Tobias hiss-whispered across the room.

"Then help me unload these plates." John's eyes moved blindly as he searched where Tobias's head poked through the doorway. "And stoke that fire. It's clammy as riverstone in here."

Tobias ran for the plates while John dropped the cups onto the table.

"Easy and quiet," the cook growled as he appeared and disappeared in the kitchen doorway.

"So, how was last night?" Tobias said. He knelt and opened the stove door with a poker, his lashed backside smarting at the chafing of his wool union suit. "Card games and stories? Talk of lumbering?"

"Some of it all."

"What about the hunting today? Birds? Deer?"

"They didn't decide. That stranger—the Hoehn fellow—he kept them on the business talk. And when he wanted to talk hunting, Ryder said he needed to get to bed."

From the kitchen came hisses and the balm of potatoes in hot lard.

"Hoehn's a lumberman?" Tobias used the tier's term for the principal of any outfit that felled or milled trees, a word pronounced quickly, as in the plural *lumbermen*.

"No. He does factory work. A kind he thinks could work in Marstadt." John leaned against the end of the table. "Must be from Harrisburg because he keeps talking about the capital."

Tobias poked the coals. "Mr. Erhart said yesterday he's from down around Pittsburgh."

"Well if you know so much, why bother me asking if Hoehn's a lumberman?"

"Because I don't understand why he'd be talking business to Ryder and Erhart."

Tobias fed fresh slabs to the flames he'd conjured out of the embers. He stood and caught the cook in the doorway surveying the settings. His mustaches twitched as he mumbled. "Unless you want to serve Warren P. Ryder oatmeal on the tablecloth, set up bowls, butter and wares."

After the boys put out pots of coffee and pitchers of milk, the cook handed off pans of cornbread, bowls of molasses, and platters of fried potatoes and sausage links. Then came stirrings from the quarters above.

J. Hadley Erhart descended the stairs in black boots, twelve eyelets high, his olive-wool pants stuffed into the necks of gray socks. He wore a khaki soldier's hat cocked to one side, its brim edges rolled in the style recently popularized by heroes on San Juan Hill. Just like Colonel Roosevelt's, Tobias thought, picturing the newspaper illustrations on his bedroom wall.

Andy Hoehn was on Erhart's heels, a drab bush hat slouched over his brow, a grin on his face.

"True to his promise," Erhart said as he passed Tobias, patting his shoulder, "Master Meier has returned to the wilds of Piebald Hollow."

Warren P. Ryder plodded to the table, his overcoat—a black caped mackintosh—draped from his ox-yoke shoulders, a black bowler perched atop his head. He mumbled that more lamps should be burning. Tobias ran for matches and an apple crate. As he lit each remaining wick, another section of knotted hemlock wall flickered alive, from gray to reddish-brown, and Tobias wished he could take hold and slow the moments of this day.

At breakfast he sat across from Old Snyder who put aside his odd, metal-stemmed pipe. Erhart and Hoehn relived their previous day's scouting, occasionally consulting Old Snyder as they would a compass for bearings to crevices and flats that had shown signs of game. Old Snyder mesmerized Tobias, participating only when called upon. After Erhart and Hoehn debated sneaking for deer leeward or windward along a ridge rimed with mountain laurel, or the likeliness that creek bottom hemlocks held grouse, they would patiently tilt their ears toward Old Snyder while he paused statuesque, milled the discussion, then jerked to, replying in his tone of having suddenly remembered: "Why yeah, the birds hold to them evergreens on a dank day such as this."

Tobias had Old Snyder figured out, a native seethed in the moods of the plateau, probably a first generation of Marstadt pioneers. His livelihood came in stints for timber operations, roustabouting and marking out rail grades and log slides. For the likes of mapmaking Emory Sundae, he was that sixth sense surveyors of old had sought in Indians. Between jobs, Old Snyder's kind honed their feel for the land hunting and trapping it, fishing its waters.

It was five o'clock, and the decision on what and where the men would hunt took on the urgency of the hour.

"I'd like to find me a top-heavy stag," Andy Hoehn said, then took a long dram from his cooling coffee.

Old Snyder's eyes went to the milk pitcher. Tobias saw him weighing something deeper than what was inside. "Odds would be better," Old Snyder said, "if you set your thoughts on a bottom-heavy borie."

Immediately all eyes were on him, everyone awaiting his next words. Talk of bears did that to hunters, for despite its unlikelihood, the slight chance of shooting a bear had more allure than a herd of bucks.

Old Snyder didn't return their stares; his denim eyes just kept gazing at the milk pitcher. Tobias had an urge to move it just to speed his thoughts.

"Thrice now," Old Snyder said, "I've spotted a big he-bear gorging himself of chestnuts and ack-corns around the Fiddlers Flats."

Tobias knew the place, one of the last stands of old chestnut and white oak to hold to the tablelands. The white pines surrounding Fiddlers Flats had been cut and sledged years ago, but the hardwood market hadn't justified such expensive means of moving chestnuts and oaks.

Warren P. Ryder still wanted a better price before he'd build a spur from the idle rails in Piebald Run he'd left for the purpose of reaching those remote trees. But with the tracts feeding the Pigeondale mills thinning of timber fast, Ryder couldn't wait much longer before he'd have to agree with Josiah Blesh that to keep the mill saws running full speed, they'd have to move the Piebald rails to Teaberry Hollow, the last vast, un-timbered stretch the Pigeondale mills could affordably reach. Unless, that was, Ryder sent those tracks up North to an even bigger tract that would feed some other operation.

Tobias had gathered chestnuts on Fiddlers Flats many a fall afternoon. It was a grand piece of tableland, its trees true Titans.

"Do you suppose he's still going there to feed by day?" Erhart said, his intensity such that his words came out hoarse.

But for eating, the compact smirk of Warren P. Ryder had remained pursed, hardly a flinch of his face acknowledging the conversation, though whoever spoke seemed to regard him in his periphery. He said at last, "He's gorging as the devil urges him. A bear in the fall is a gluttonous beast driven by carnal compulsion."

"Yeah, and good to eat hisself," chimed in Hoehn.

"Andy," Ryder said, "a bear is a meat-eating predator and scavenger. From Proverbs: *Consort not with winebibbers, nor those who eat meat to excess.*" He dabbed at an egg yoke with his cornbread, then deposited it in his mouth. Tobias thought about what he said, then of the privy chickens out back of the company houses, picking among scant scrub grass and weeds for worms and grubs.

"Damned good eating," Old Snyder said. "And I suppose Mr. Ryder's right. That bear's likely to up and snack any time. But in any direction. So fellas would best waylay for him all around where he holes up."

Andy Hoehn turned to Old Snyder beside him. "But how do we know where that is?"

"We don't exactly," Old Snyder finally said. "All we know is that the laurels and deadfalls that touch on the edges of the flats are thick—cover bears like to lay in." He paused, then carried on in his way of remembering aloud. "Put that together with me thrice seeing him in the vicinity. Not to mention once last summer when he was shimmied half way up a dead oak with his nose in a hole. He had a paw full of honey and an ass full of bees." No smile crossed his face, but his head bobbed as it would in a chuckle.

Erhart spoke up, staying Tobias's hand just as he was about to take a forkful of potatoes. "How better might we hunt him—that's a big area?"

Old Snyder thought especially long this time. "Considering you've got these young fellas, you might profit having them shag those thickets. Might rout him past you, so long as you post yourselves where you can see into all the places he'd sneak."

The prospect ignited in Tobias. He laid his fork on his plate. Nothing so fiercely set a boy's inners afire as putting on a chase for hunters, especially bear hunters.

The plan set, Tobias and John cleared the table while the men went for their gear and Old Snyder saddlebagged the horses.

Warren P. Ryder came back looking hardly the hunter. He wore under the caped mackintosh a dog-eared collar and silk scarf. He had not stuffed his pant legs into his boots.

Tobias had never seen the likes of his gun, a lever action like the popular Winchester and Marlin carbines. But it had no hammer. Nor a tube magazine under the barrel. Every other part of the gun—stock, breech, fore-end—tapered toward that barrel as if it were a lance as well. Ryder propped the rifle against the wall near the woodstove. Under the pretense of stoking the fire, Tobias got close enough to read its birthright on the sheening blue steel. Even the name suggested the form of the thing. Savage. Model '95.

Ryder brought to mind the gentlemen hunters that hicks at the Whitehouse laughed about: lawyers, politicians and industrialists from Philadelphia or Harrisburg who arranged with lumbermen to hitch sleeping cars to log trains. They'd side the sleepers at the heads of hollows and hunt the plateau from draft horses while they had cases of beefsteaks, brandy and cigars railed in. Eventually they'd pay locals to take them to deer licks where, from scaffolds, the men jacklighted heavy-horned stags.

Watching Warren P. Ryder pull on fawn-skin riding gloves, Tobias feared he was taking part in some such arrangement. His backside smarted, and he realized he was regarding Ryder as less than the lion he was supposed to see there.

Then J. Hadley Erhart and Andy Hoehn descended the stairs. In his coat of maroon-plaid mackinaw, Erhart managed to look well-placed. He winked at Tobias as he passed, his gun slung over his shoulder and his hands buried under the great flaps of his pockets where he chimed brass rifle shells. Andy Hoehn was dressed similarly except that from knee to ankle, he wore canvas gaiters, and his coat had a flapping lapel with buttons big as silver dollars.

Hoehn carried the muzzle of his gun as he would the handle of a beer stein. He propped it where Erhart had leaned his in a corner. Tobias knew Hoehn's immediately: the venerable Winchester '94, chambered for the new smokeless 30-30. Already it was ascending to its reign as deerslayer, and down along the border beginning its other destiny—replacing range-worn '66s which had just won the West. This was the treinta-y-treinta of American cowboys and Mexican vaqueros.

But Erhart's rifle was the prize, an Adler, the handiwork of a Marstadt machinist who'd prevailed over Winchester itself with a design that required only two motions to load and fire, not three. Adler's piece was unknown outside the tier, a still-born child of small town ingenuity.

Tobias had read of Adlers in the *County Gazette,* seen them propped behind the wares counter at the company store. He was thankful for men like J. Hadley Erhart, whose pride made them prefer things novel and native, would dip at the swill barrel to grip an Adler's for-end, to press his cheek to its walnut stock.

John called from the kitchen door. "We need to help Old Snyder." But first Tobias took a closer look, saw that Erhart gave the gun even more dignity by not coddling it as a museum piece. It was well used, pewter-colored in the places of his grip.

The boys hauled gear through the kitchen to Old Snyder and helped him pack the saddlebags he'd draped over the Percherons' hips. As Tobias stowed a moleskin pouch, he felt papers crumple. Supposing maps by Emory Sundae, Tobias made sure to push them to the bottom, lest they get wet—he expected the morning mist would turn to drops.

The cook set more goods before the stone step. The boys lifted them to Old Snyder where he'd mounted, rearward, the last horse to be packed— gunny sacks smelling of ham and warm biscuits, canvas-covered canteens sloshing and plopping. John was no gentler with cookies wrapped in butcher paper than he was with a slumping sack of salt he tossed onto the saddle. Old Snyder called his rashness. "You ain't curing the hide in the woods. Put that in the engine shed where you'll skin the bear. God willing."

It was still dark when they moved out, the boys and Old Snyder on foot, each with a rein in hand. Leaning into the grade of a skid trail that zigzagged up a fold in the flank of Piebald Hollow, Tobias imagined himself heading out to team logs on a woods crew, the picture feeling so real and fated he heard the pant of saws in the blowing of the horses.

They reached Fiddlers Flats by daybreak. And until midday, the boys weaved through the lace of greenbrier, brush and laurel that had reclaimed as a crown of thorns the perimeter of that primeval oak and chestnut. Chase after chase, Old Snyder sent them toward the next hidden swale or stretch of old skid road where he'd posted the hunters to watch for the bruin. Then they'd regroup on the flats, and Old Snyder would kick away a circle of leaf mold and trace, in the black humus of the aged trees' leaves, the next scheme.

As off and on as the boys put on chase, drizzles fell. That was common in autumn when clouds sagged and stalled over the plateau. But Tobias, a sponge, couldn't tell the rain from the droplets his clothes lapped from the brush. Between drives, he shook with chills.

The later they chased, the more Tobias sensed Old Snyder was working a larger plan, each drive mounting the next to bring this to a head. Tobias's bearings told him they were coming round the flats to where they'd started. He confirmed this by reference to the lighter sky—they were heading northeast. Old Snyder, Tobias believed, had been moving them such that their short drives and no headwind would hold the bear to moving slowly and by pieces through the thickest tangles. Sure, there was a chance they'd catch sight of him if the boys pushed harder, but a shot was most likely if they could flush him eventually into terrain shaped more in the hunters' favor. And there was something Tobias was picking up in Old Snyder's mood; it had grown from casual to alert, making the first half of the day seem like a warm-up. By midday, eating lunch where the horses were hitched under the chestnuts and oaks, Old Snyder had become quiet, had kept away from the men's speculation about the bear. And now, as he rounded the hunters up after each chase, he wasn't asking what they'd seen or heard. He knew something.

The northern reach of the flats was split by a gulch where on the other side they had started that morning. The gulch yawned into a hollow of its own right, its walls dropping so steep and blue-green with laurels that from the edges, it looked like a great fold of moss. The plan was for the boys to go well out the rim of this hollow, drop down its flank, and disturb the laurel as they moved back toward the head. A hunter would be posted on each side where he could see into the hollow while the third one waited near the tip, in case the bear sneaked past the other men and up the funnel.

Headed out, Old Snyder halted the men. Tobias noticed he'd stopped where his whisper couldn't be heard in the hollow. "This will be our last shag. If we rousted him outta the skirts of the flats, he'd a come around and holed up in that hollow." He aimed his thumb over his shoulder. "West wind's come up like usual. He won't spook around the flats any farther, for the blow would be to his ass." Tobias caught that he'd shifted to speaking as if the bear had indeed sneaked ahead of them. "Only risk now," Old Snyder said, "is his turning on the drivers."

"He's in there, isn't he?" J. Hadley Erhart whispered.

Old Snyder was packing his pipe; it would be the first he smoked all day. He turned and started out of the hardwoods slow and quiet, toward the hollow where he would post the hunters.

Tobias and John were to keep away from the hollow's edge and not drop down until they were a quarter mile from the head. So it took more than a half hour to get to the bottom. Even that far along its course, the hollow was a wedge, so steep and tangled with the writhing branches of laurels that the pair crawled as often as walked toward the head, each boy to a slope. Checked constantly by thickets, Tobias hoped they'd get to the hunters while there was light enough for shooting, safe shooting; the depths of the crevice had already paled.

They hadn't gone far when Tobias heard crashing—just on the other side of a tangle too thick to see through. He'd chased in laurels for deer, and though they held tight in such cover, Tobias had never known one to spring so close, nor to disturb such a wide path of laurel tops as it plowed away. Whatever this was stopped, but Tobias could not tell where, for he'd lost sight of the course. Old Snyder had told the boys to pursue quietly, not talk to each other. If they gently prodded a jumped bear, it would sneak ahead slowly, offering a better shot. But Tobias couldn't resist coming out with, "Psst."

Nothing.

"John." His voice was half whisper, half shout.

Nothing. And Tobias felt strength in that. He liked being places where if he cried for help there'd be no one to hear him—it made him feel the most alive. Even with the darkening sky telling him to step it up, something about the extra tension slowed his pace. He had an urge to stop and look for tracks.

The chase and the likelihood of a bear ahead, the exercise, tuned his mind and senses and knitted them to the hunt, keen as a cat on a mouse. He'd been on the go since before three o'clock that morning but held his exhaustion in reins. Something had come up in him, old and animal. It fit an order of environs he didn't sense back in the world of people.

An opening allowed Tobias a glimpse of two hunters ahead, each one watching from a ridge. The plan was for them to move with Tobias and John once the hunters saw them. Looking up at one silhouette, Tobias waved. The man's bowler hat twitched with his acknowledgement. Then Tobias caught, below the figure, leaves moving along the flank of the hollow. He watched ahead and saw in an opening that it was John. Tobias crouched and moved on, losing sight of the hunters, glad one had seen him so they could stay in step by his sound and movement, know he wasn't a bear.

When it happened, etiquette paralyzed Tobias's reflexes. He'd crawled through a web of laurel branches to a rocky opening. Getting to his feet, he checked the ridgeline for a bearing, spotted a hunter next to a tree trunk, and balked, every muscle in his body faltering while he sorted what to do—a gun was aimed at him. The man lowered it, finally recognizing a boy, not a bear in the brush. But he'd had the bead of that rifle on Tobias.

The matter of who held the gun had baffled Tobias's instinct to duck—a man in a narrow-brimmed hat, broad mackinaw cape. The chill of the day broke through as Tobias realized he'd feared a person's air more than a bullet, that he'd been tamed enough to let certain men aim before they identified their quarry.

He took a step, eager for the cover of laurel, stung by the quandary. He could spite his father by leaving home, but he couldn't keep Herbert Meier from posing him in front of that gun.

A rifle fired. Muscles put in check a moment ago went limp, and Tobias collapsed, his face catching something hard and sharp. The blood at his temples and at the tips of his fingers and toes pumped in hot, snapping sparks. He lurched from his side to his back, realizing that the bullet, having hit rock beyond him, might have traveled his flesh. Pain pounded into his jaw as if a millstone squeezed his head. But no sear of pierced flesh, rather the echoing throbs and fizzes of a solid slam.

The blow sharpened his reasoning. Warren P. Ryder hadn't moved the safety back when he'd lowered that lance of a rifle. He'd sloppily left a finger on the trigger. And in Ryder's own trembling at the thing he'd done, the gun had fired. This time impulse had won, and as Tobias had fallen, his head slammed stone. If a boy could feel dead, as Tobias thought he had when Ryder looked down his gun barrel, he felt more dead lying there.

Tobias reached and felt where his jaw joined. He opened his mouth. It moved well enough, but the pain doubled. From up the hollow came voices, and he heard the word bear.

"I missed him," Ryder hollered back. And he scanned the labyrinth of laurels to see Tobias move.

*   *   *

As Tobias finished the day shagging the rest of Fiddlers draw for a bear no one would see, it struck him how the thickest laurel tangles grew in the steepest and rockiest of places. And he regarded people like Warren P. Ryder with new caution—even more than he'd need up close to a bear. The thing to trust least in that hollow, maybe anywhere, was human. So Tobias vowed he'd never again let a man's status confuse his gut. He wondered how many people gave up their lives failing at that.

Chapter 7

"Damn, the timber has a reach up on that flat." Warren P. Ryder sat at the dining hall table, a snifter of flaxen-colored brandy in his hand. "Hadley, maybe we should go ahead and take it now." Ryder sipped his brandy and touched a napkin to his lips. "If man doesn't get it soon, God will beat him to it with fire. Or the damned chestnut blight."

Tobias and John flanked Erhart where he sat across from his father-in-law and Andy Hoehn. Erhart arched his great brows and reached for his own snifter. Everyone was recovering from a hunter's supper of pork sausage and sauerkraut, dried corn pudding, fresh apple butter on piping hot biscuits, and a dessert of wild-grape jelly cake. Old Snyder leaned against the wall, metal-stemmed pipe in and out of his mouth, denim eyes straight-on staring at the floor. Every so often he'd reach for the pipe and jerk it out with the look of just remembering a shanty door he'd left opened. He'd hold still a second and put the pipe back.

Tobias wondered what was going through Old Snyder's mind. During dinner, he kept out of talk of the bear hunt. But Tobias felt his eyes every time the subject came up; Old Snyder, he believed, had read what happened, had pieced together the gunshot and Ryder's vague recounting of the size of bear he'd missed, was wary of how Ryder finally made it clear he didn't want to discuss it. And Tobias had caught Old Snyder studying the lump on his cheek, weighing it against Tobias's story of tripping in the laurel—which is how he told it when J. Hadley Erhart ran to him, seeing the swelling as Tobias broke from the head of Fiddlers draw.

Even the cook, with a thick wrap of cigar jutting from his mustaches, sat with the men and boys where he'd pulled his wobbly wooden rocker into the dining hall. As much as Tobias expected any minute an order to clear the table and wash the dishes, he hoped it would be a while. He wanted to hear J. Hadley Erhart and Warren P. Ryder talk lumbering. And find out what the "proposition" was this Hoehn kept nagging about. Though events had doubled his uneasiness for men like Ryder, he'd washed some of it away with the shot of whiskey Erhart had given for his jaw pain so he could chew dinner. Ryder rarely looked at him anyway.

"Warren," Erhart said, "there's a big difference between a pure stand of heavy hardwood and the smatterings we mix with hemlock." He bellowed a deep breath as he let the brandy he'd just swallowed take its second effect. "It makes heavier payload. We need to wait for the price to justify steel cars with air brakes and iron stakes."

Tobias reached for his tin cup of buttermilk as he followed Erhart's gesture toward Piebald's train rails. "Besides, I'm worried that old track wouldn't handle the weight."

Ryder tilted his head and held his compact smirk as he regarded his son-in-law. "So we'd take smaller loads. At least we'd have a full tract to cut in the off-season instead of picking around hemlock while the bark's tight."

"Gentlemen," Andy Hoehn said, his eager boy energy pent up now in some urgent message. "This adds to what I've been saying—you've reached the point for change." In splotches, his chalky face took on a liver color. "Look at hemlock. What's left is farther and farther from your mills, adding to costs. Yet you can't run your tannery without it." He looked Erhart in the eye, then turned and did the same to Ryder, and Tobias thought him brave. He'd never have guessed a business mind in boy-faced Andy Hoehn. He became all the more a stranger.

The quiet that ensued seemed to emanate from Ryder. When he spoke, there was space between his words. "We are lumbermen." He looked to his son-in-law, who looked to Hoehn.

Then Erhart added, "We're primarily hemlock lumbermen."

Hoehn was like a bud about to bloom. "I'll dispute that narrow view of your company. You are not lumbermen, hemlock or otherwise. You are businessmen." He turned and looked at Ryder, who was unmoved. Hoehn gathered himself fuller. "Pardon my borrowing a phrase, but it fits so well: You can't see the forest for the trees. And it matters not if those trees are hemlocks full of tannin or chestnuts bordering blight—the forest is becoming a barren place for you to put your capital."

Capital, Tobias thought, that's what John said kept coming up last night. The kind of capital they meant had nothing to do with Harrisburg.

"Well, we can't just quit supplying our tannery," Erhart said. Tobias could tell he was challenging Hoehn for more. It surprised him how much Erhart's personality came through. Not the part he'd come to know and like—the man with a ready ear for even a boy—but a human side just the same. He'd taken for granted that in business talk, men shut out that side. Erhart made this world seem at least on Tobias's plane, though a distance across it. People must feel threatened by these men because the Warren P. Ryder type—who as far as Tobias saw didn't have a personality—were more likely to be businessmen. He dared wonder if men such as these differed only in dress and speech. Until came his father's disproving scowl.

"There are ways to feed your tannery without running low-profit lumber operations. Free the capital they're eating before it's gone. Diversify. It's a year to the new century after all. The age of industrialism isn't waiting for you."

Warren P. Ryder shook his head. "I've built this business on timber, and no kind of timber ever got in my way. And that is because I *have* diversified. If there's hardwood with the hemlock and my mills can take it, I cut it. With the stave mill, we've made better use of oak. There is only one criteria for cutting: whether your mills and tannery can take it." He huffed and stared one by one into the eyes of everyone in the room, including the boys. "Even scrap wood that we don't burn in the boilers gets bundled and shipped to the cities for kindling. Don't tell me I'm not diversified." He slapped the table, then pointed at Hoehn. "If I've got capital to spend, I should spend it in timbering. It's what I know."

Andy Hoehn held up a hand. "But your money could be doing more. As a factory man, I see inefficiencies in your operations that you don't."

Ryder stared at the hand, and Hoehn put it gently on the table.

J. Hadley Erhart cocked a grin at Andy, which Tobias could hear come right through his voice. "Sure we can get cheaper bark from the new operations up North, but we can't meet demand without the little that remains here."

"Contract the extra bark to smaller outfits. And as other operations wane like Pigeondale, contract more. You'll stop maintaining old equipment. Then you can concentrate your money in new ventures with a lot greater return."

Erhart raised a brow. "Maybe he's got a point, Warren. Should we cut costly timber just to stay in lumbering?"

The cook re-focused his gaze from the floor to Tobias and John. He pushed himself up from his chair and pointed to the table, indicating cleanup. Tobias right away jumped to stacking plates so John would be the one to take them to the kitchen. Old Snyder made for the door across the room, taking a lamp from the wall.

Ryder leaned away from the knocking of dishes and cups. "I've jobbed out bark peeling before. It taught me that the only way to control costs is doing it myself. It's simply unreliable."

Andy Hoehn ran a hand over his mat of hair. "You can negotiate among competitive suppliers—some may have cut excess bark and need to dump it. Or you deal to lock in prices and let the contractor suffer fluctuations in costs." He shrugged. "With today's common carrier railroads, you can buy bark from jobbers anywhere."

"Bullshit," Ryder bellowed. "The big railroads are nothing but monopolists. I've built mills up North on the eighty dollars a day I saved in the hostage fees they charge to move logs."

"Those were dedicated trains," Hoehn said. "You'd be dealing with carload freight, transferred to your tannery from regular, scheduled trains. That's how we get our factory's raw material."

The boys had finished clearing the table, and Tobias tarried by the kitchen door while John scraped scraps into a barrel. J. Hadley Erhart leaned forward on his bench. "Let's pick this back up over cards."

"I'll wipe down the table, sir," Tobias said. "And I'll bring the deck of cards." He'd seen them on the sideboard.

"Thatta boy, Tobias."

Next, Tobias took two buckets to the springhouse and returned to the kitchen as fast as he could without sloshing water on the floor. "I'm going to bring in more wood," he said to John.

"They need cups for whiskey," John said. So along the way, Tobias set a tin cup beside each man's brandy snifter.

When Tobias returned, cradling wood, J. Hadley Erhart was shuffling cards into the palm of his left hand. John was nowhere to be seen, so Tobias arranged slabs to sit on by the stove under the pretense of fire stoker.

Erhart stopped shuffling, shifted on the bench, and creased his eyes at Hoehn. "I think it's understood we're not contracting for bark, Andy.

So this Pigeondale operation will milk the timber within reach. I think Warren agrees though, that we shouldn't risk buying new equipment to go after the hardwoods on Fiddlers Flats." He looked from man to man. When neither spoke, Erhart set down the cards, leaned forward and rested his forearms on the table's edge. "I will not abandon Marstadt. Nor our holdings out here. This is no stop on a train where I rake the land and people like the opportunists who are going to suck the tier dry if someone doesn't invest long-term." He paused and tipped a whiskey bottle to his tin cup, drank. "Sure, our counterparts are keeping their money in lumbering. But not here—this place to them is nothing but a revenue stream, and they see a drought a-coming. So off to Mississippi or Maryland or Oregon they go, while in the wake they leave swaths of saplings as tinder, and people pulling up roots."

Erhart had the room—even his father-in-law's face was tipped down with the look of meditation people wear at church sermons. The cook leaned against the kitchen doorway, ear cocked. Tobias knew these words were about his people, his place. His hopes.

"But Andy is right." Erhart held his tin cup to Hoehn. "We are vulnerable right now. And Warren is right, too. We are what we are because of lumbering. Or I should say, *because of the land*. That's what we hold. And I've an inkling that to last, we must always remember where you started, Warren—must maintain an interest in the land, no matter how far we think we're moving from it. If we listen to it, watch it, I dare say give it the respect any patron deserves, we'll be farsighted in our decisions. I'm looking to the land for lessons." He paused and nodded. "That's what will separate us from the ones who forever chase rainbows of trade.

"I want it both ways," Erhart continued, holding up a finger. "To be a viable company." He held up a second finger. "Yet remain loyal to this place and people. So, I propose we open our eyes to the future while we keep a grip on our legacy. I do believe we have to put our capital to work, and we've no choice but to do it outside of logging, if for anything, to keep the very land we log—for the bounty she's given, and I believe, will continue to give."

Everyone turned to Warren P. Ryder, but he made no response.

"I think it's good reasoning," Andy Hoehn said. "I still maintain you should look elsewhere for bark, but at least you're in a mindset to start spreading your capital." He looked down at the cards Erhart was dealing, his face puffing as he again gathered himself. "Now can we address my proposition?"

"Ante up," Ryder said. The three men slid chips to the middle of the table.

The cook stepped through the doorway and sat in his rocker, John still absent. So long as Tobias stayed put, close to the men, John wouldn't try to boss him up to the bunkhouse for bed when he showed. What was about to be decided here, Tobias suspected, would impact people and places well beyond the wilds of Pigeondale.

Without a trace of regret, Andy Hoehn folded his hand early. He looked toward a window. "I'd do whatever it takes to live up here, away from the crowds and cannibalism of the Smoky City. So I'm saying it again—I can arrange the expertise and equipment for us to make the best carbon products in the world."

Erhart laid out his cards and laughed. "You may escape the crowds here, but business is cannibalism anywhere."

Warren P. Ryder tapped the table with his knuckle. "Is that the only reason you want to start this business—to get out of Pittsburgh?"

"Of course not," Hoehn said. "Marstadt lends itself to carbon. Take natural gas for the ovens. The area is bursting with it. And hell, it's cheap as air up here."

"So cheap," Erhart said, glancing at his father-in-law, "that we keep the street lamps burning all day rather than hire a man to snuff and light them." He pushed his losing hand to Hoehn for his deal while Ryder swept the pot to his pile.

Hoehn shuffled the cards. "Petroleum coke makes the purest carbon in the world. We can get all we need from the oil distillers up in Bradford. So even if I didn't love this neck of woods, even without Marstadt's great workers, I'd look to start a factory up here somewhere."

"Warren," Erhart said, "it may be just the thing to keep our men working while the tannery business flattens. Those Bavarians are sharp machinists. That alone would let any industry thrive there, much less one that fits all these other ways."

Hoehn dealt while Warren P. Ryder regarded him, lips puckered, head reared so his eyes looked down on him. "What makes you sure these carbon products will be in such demand?"

Hoehn spoke right up with an answer he could have rehearsed. "Electricity is lighting the nation, the world." He pointed to one of the lanterns on the wall. "Carbon arc lights are fast replacing lamps. Motors with generators are doing the work of water, horses, even steam engines. And they all require brushes—made of carbon. There's a new craze for portable lights that run on batteries, which—" he paused, looking from face to face, "are made with carbon. It's the electrical age, gentlemen, and carbon products are its keystone." He took a hard swallow from his tin of whiskey, grinned behind his hand of cards.

In the shadow cast by this unfamiliar carbon talk, Tobias was again figuring his prospects as a hick in the waning Pigeondale operations. It would be at least three years before he could go to work in a lumber camp. Taking a job on some distant operation—if even those would last—instead of in these hollows that his feet seemed to grow right out of, would feel as foreign and awkward as a neighbor's privy. Somehow this carbon business was figuring in on that—it was just too far from him to see if it was in his favor. It sure didn't feel it.

Ryder looked at his son-in-law. "Before we make rash decisions, we need to talk specifics. Just what does Andy want from us?"

Hoehn was about to deal the draw, but set down the cards. "I need capital for the factory. And up-front cash for raw material and labor. I can design the building and ovens, and find all the mixing and grinding equipment."

Erhart turned up the palm of a hand. "We've got everything we need to build the plant—materials from the mills and brickworks, equipment from the railroad."

Hoehn grinned and dealt the draw while Ryder turned to the kitchen door and shouted, "Whiskey." Tobias had seen the empty bottle on the table, but hadn't dared get another while John might be around. Tobias opened the woodstove and loaded slabs, seeing out of the corner of his eye John come with a full bottle. John looked his way and nodded toward the kitchen. But Tobias sat again.

The men picked up their cards, and Andy Hoehn, without looking at his own, leaned into the table and spoke, some of the enthusiasm in his voice faltering. "There is one key ingredient that I need your trust in."

Ryder peered over his cards; Erhart stopped mid-motion while arranging his hand.

"The quality of each product we make—battery cylinders, generator brushes, arc lights, new things the future holds—depends not only on its composition of carbon, oils and binding agents, but how those are handled—the procedure and baking temperature—altogether what we call in the industry a formula. No matter how pure the constituents, we'll only be as good as our formulas. Great ones take a knack."

Ryder cocked his head. "What are you getting at?"

"The carbon business is peculiar." Hoehn nodded at the bourbon. "It's like distilling whiskey." He picked up the bottle and held it toward a lamp, the glow lighting the amber spirits. "Two distillers could work from the same mash, but one will always make a smoother whiskey. You never discount the human element in making a good thing." He shook the bottle at them and set it down. "We need a winner of a formula for every grade of every product, and only some people have the knack."

"Expertise is made, not born," Ryder said.

"Mr. Ryder, there is something different about the carbon business. These formula makers are artists. And because they keep their formulas here—" he tapped his temple— "they're well protected by their companies."

"So you're suggesting that to start this business, we bait away a formula maker?"

Erhart arched his brows. "Warren, you make it sound like pilfering."

"Give me a better word."

"Gentlemen," Hoehn said. "It's not like that at all." He gave a peddler's reassuring grin. "I just happen to know a talented man at the carbon factory where I work in Pittsburgh. He mixes test compounds for the current formula maker." Hoehn set down his cards. "He has a knack about it, and the product keeps improving because of things he's doing. Seeing that got me thinking about striking out on my own." He looked at Ryder. "Long before the day I met Hadley up here hunting."

"Then why would he leave the company?" Ryder said.

Hoehn looked around, as if to check for eavesdroppers. "For the opportunities we can give him. See, he can tell where a mix is weak just by testing the end product, but his boss the formula maker won't let him do the refining. So he makes adjustments on his own—does other tests, takes notes, then reworks batches." Hoehn leaned ahead and whispered, "He's not taken seriously."

"Why not?" Ryder said.

"He's—" Hoehn looked to be groping for the right word— "different. Plus, he's got no formal education."

"Different?" Ryder said.

"Set in his ways. Some think he's odd, weird. But aren't all geniuses?"

Ryder rolled his eyes.

"Seems to fit our situation perfectly," Erhart said.

This stranger, Hoehn, introducing a new stranger, had Tobias on the edge of his wood-slab seat. He grinned at J. Hadley Erhart's comment— just like him to give a person a fair shot.

Ryder addressed his son-in-law. "There's no wisdom investing where a reputation is pinned to one man."

"Exactly," Hoehn said. "That's why I'd handle our formulas differently."

Without betting, the men showed their hands, and Erhart took the pot. "You've thought the problem out," he said.

"Absolutely. Our formula maker would have an apprentice. He'd work at our man's side developing formulas, procedures and all, not just mixing them. He'd know everything—a second source in case our man defected." Hoehn shook his head. "It's always amazed me that other companies don't do it, just pin backup plans on their formula men's reports, which are nothing but lists of ingredients and temperatures. And by the way—" he held up a finger— "a youngster would give us a next-generation formula maker."

"So you concede," Ryder said, "that such men are made, not born?"

"No, but the formulas themselves that come of a knack can surely be taught. It may stop at the existing ones if your man defects, but that's better than nothing.

"And how will your man receive this?" Ryder said.

"Very well. I know his weaknesses."

Erhart looked at his father-in-law, and in their silence, Tobias glanced at the kitchen doorway. Just inside, John's legs showed where he sat on the floor against the wall.

"I'm to invest," Ryder said, "in a venture whose destiny rests on a decided crazy man? One who experiments behind his boss's back? And my safeguard is an inferior apprentice who could just as easily defect?"

Everyone turned when the door opened and Old Snyder stepped in. He looked toward Tobias by the stove. "Pardon me," Old Snyder said. "Just checking on the wood supplies."

Duty overtook desire, and Tobias went to help Old Snyder carry in slabs, disappointed in the timing. After three trips to the woodpile, Tobias found the men still at it. Taking his seat on the slabs, he knew by their tone they were finishing.

"We'll have to take risks regardless," Erhart said. "Why not in an industry made for this place?" Tobias could tell by Erhart's grin that he was just bubbling out added rationale for the decision he knew his father-in-law was coming around to.

"Two conditions," Ryder said. "I'm making provisions for my daughter's future."

"Whatever you require," said Andy Hoehn.

Ryder's gaze did not leave his son-in-law. "First, no Ryder lands are to be used to secure this business. I, like you, Hadley, want to keep our lands. Except my reason differs—maybe someday we'll realize the outrageous taxes we pay. The cutover hollows and ridges can't go anywhere but up in value." He turned to Andy Hoehn. "That is called a reasonable risk."

"Second," Ryder said, still watching Hoehn, "the company is to be called Erhart Carbon."

The liver splotches returned to Hoehn's face. "Well, absolutely. That's what I expected. Or *Ryder* Carbon, of course."

Ryder rolled his eyes. "Part of my reason," he said, "has to do with my daughter's future." He looked to Erhart. "We'll sort out the financials later. You'll serve as president and partner in ownership with me. Mr. Hoehn will be general manager. He becomes vice president only when a profit is turned. At that time we'll establish a board." He leaned back. "Now, let's call it a game."

After they counted their chips, Erhart swung around on his bench and stretched his legs. He winked and raised his squirrel-tail brows at Tobias. "For someone who hasn't staked an inch in this claim, Tobias, you're wide-eyed and on the ready."

Tobias tried to relax. He took his elbows from his knees, leaned back.

Erhart's smile mellowed. "Come over here, Tobias."

When Tobias got to him, Erhart put a finger to Tobias's chin and turned his head. "Tell me the pain isn't as big as the bruise."

"It's fine, sir. Doesn't hurt so much now." It hurt plenty, and he knew it would be worse through the night.

"Tobias, you're an eager young fellow, that's easy enough to see."

Tobias didn't respond, trying to tell whether Erhart thought this was good or bad.

"Keep that always." The crimson tips of Erhart's brows sank. "But be wary, Tobias Meier. Be careful of first impressions. Don't let them drive that spunk of yours." Erhart put his elbows on his knees, leaning closer, eye to eye with Tobias. "Do you know what I mean?"

All Tobias knew for sure was that J. Hadley Erhart was giving him advice, and that in itself was worth heeding. "Not exactly, sir."

Erhart studied the floor a second. "Before you board a train, it's best to check with the conductor where it's headed, not take just anybody's word it's going your way. Right?"

"Yessir."

"When you step up to anything in life, make sure its direction matches your inclination. Double check what other people say."

He must have seen fear in the way Tobias's twelve-year-old eyes looked out at the future, for Erhart shook his head and groaned a frustrated and apologetic "Aah," then gave Tobias the smile he so liked. "Just be on your guard, Tobias. Don't let anything but you take charge of that enthusiasm, for it's fast becoming what the world most preys upon."

"I'd better go to the kitchen to see what help John needs," Tobias said.

* * *

He found John still sitting against the wall near the doorway. Tobias crouched beside him, thinking of Erhart's words.

"Did you hear all that talk?" John said.

"You saw me sitting there," Tobias said.

"Did you understand?"

"I take it they're going to build a factory in Marstadt," Tobias said. "To make things out of carbon."

"Can you believe the power of those three men." John looked at Tobias. "They started a whole company over a card game."

Tobias shrugged.

"Just one card game, and a company's made." John crossed his arms and shook his head, looking much older than thirteen.

"But it's what they do," Tobias said. "I liked just hearing them do what they do."

"And what they do is throw their power around like nickel antes."

Tobias considered. "I don't see them even thinking it's power when they talk like that."

"They're using power, all right." John was quiet a second. "I'm going to be part of that deal."

"How?"

"I'm going to work in that place. Things are going to happen there. Big. You'd do the same if you wanted a chance."

"At what?" Tobias said.

"At being something—like them."

"But I ain't like them," Tobias said.

"You get like them."

Tobias weighed it, Erhart's words still sounding in his thoughts. "I don't care to go there."

"You're crazy. This'll be something."

Tobias shrugged.

"You mean you'd rather stay out here and be a woodhick?"

"What's the matter with that?" Tobias said. "I've always been here."

"Not me. I'm gonna make my own lot with this." John pointed at Tobias. "You oughta be thinking about where you oughta be going."

Chapter 8

Moody March finally swooned into a temperate April, and not soon enough for Tobias, the year he turned fifteen. Manooka Valley buzzed with signals of spring. Oases of grass surfaced at every water seep. Here and there in the woods, the first fiddlehead ferns periscoped out of the red shards of moldering stumps. Down by Manooka Creek, peepers squawked, mad as the water's swollen rush. The air was soggy with the smell of leeks.

Tobias's mind was abuzz with signals, too, and his sleep as restless as a late winter bear's. He might as well have been a bear, for loosening tree bark called them both. Under it, on dead trees, hid the larvae of the bear's first meals. And as winter had loosened its grip, so had the tannic hide of the living hemlock. That meant it was bark season, the busy time when lumbermen took on new hicks. And Herbert Meier had deemed his son old enough to work in the woods.

Beside the yellow flicker of a lantern flame, Tobias sat at the Meier's little kitchen table.

"Don't be so quick to go that I can't make you breakfast," Edna Meier said, coming into the kitchen, narrowing her eyes against the new light of the lamp.

Tobias was crisp as a peanut shell in his fresh woodhick clothes. He'd ordered his Ryder-blue Richie at the Whitehouse from the traveling Woolrich man who circled the camps and towns of the tier on a stiff-legged nag he called Sheep Shears. Leather-trimmed suspenders tugged at gray worsted pants, promoted to work wear from Tobias's only suit. He'd tucked his pant legs into thick socks, ring-necked with bright red stripes. From there down was the serious business: new AA Cutter boots, black with twelve sets of eyelets and rows of logger's corks, sharp as nails, lining the soles. He rested an ankle over his knee and strummed the corks as if they purred back. The air was foul with neat's-foot oil.

"I'll just have some coffee and yesterday's biscuits," Tobias said. He watched where the lamp flame licked at the shine of his boot. Edna stared down on her son. Tobias understood the wary look, the apprehension of seeing her boy off from her little company house into a world rumored to mill-town mothers by Whitehouse chambermaids.

She went to the woodstove where coffee sizzled at the seams in the kettle. "Think about mill work, Tobias. It's safer. And those hicks live so hard."

"Mom, more men get killed working the mill than the woods."

"But Twila Guth's son—"

"Yes, I know. Garland got his legs crushed by a falling timber. But Silas Horton got caught in the grinding hog at the mill. At least Garland came away with a head intact and not half his body mixed with wood chips for the boiler."

"But the men." She handed him a tin cup of coffee.

"Mom, hicks are as tamed by the work as their hosses. Half those Whitehouse hellions everyone talks about work in the mill anyway." He grinned to show he knew where she got her information.

"But at least you could live at home if you worked at the mill."

Tobias moved his boot to the floor and picked up his coffee. "But I'm not working at the mill." He lifted the cup. "And I'll be living in a lumber camp."

Herbert Meier stepped into the kitchen, his braces dangling from his wide hips. His great jowls churned out his words. "So he goes to work in the woods. What does it matter—the woods, the mill, what does it matter?" He sat at the table and stared around triumphant when no one answered.

Tobias lasted as long as his biscuit and molasses. He went to the front door for a farewell, took his hat from its hook, and hoisted the rope he'd tied around the neck of a feed satchel, underdrawers and week-old newspapers inside. Frieda came downstairs and smiled encouragement.

His father stayed in the kitchen, but his mother and sister held the door after him. "Tobias, you come home once a week and bathe," his mother said. Frieda simply held up a hand, and the door shut.

Against the pre-dawn darkness, he moved along the plank, his steps as sure as the break of day. Gripping the four dimples of his hat's upper gallon, he lodged the big western: past property of a real hick, back on a real hick. He tugged the brim so it leaned forward, as was his style.

For the first time in his life, Tobias didn't slow in front of the Whitehouse; now that his soles bore logger's corks, he was too lost in their tacky slaps against the plank.

At the other end of town, he turned down the tracks, and by knack, set his pace to the spacing of the ties. Across the elevated plank, no lamp yet lit the superintendent's office window.

Only yesterday he'd taken his work orders in that little plank building. Since his birthday in March, he'd inquired every morning about being "put on," as the hicks said.

No matter how early Tobias arrived, Josiah Blesh would be into a day's paperwork. Morning in, morning out, Tobias would step past the cold stove, hat in hand, holding still as he could while Josiah squinted at his work, his smooth crown buffed by the lamplight.

Tobias had to speak before Blesh would acknowledge him. "Sir?"

"We're not putting anyone on yet, Tobias," Josiah would say to his papers.

Then Tobias would ask about John, who'd become scarcer lately. Being a year older, John had been long occupied working on his "route to a big break," and doing all he could to convince Tobias that woods work was a trap that would waste his body and spare his mind. But Tobias thought that the hard work of sawing and spudding, the heaving and hauling against the resistance of steep grades and mighty trees, would make his body an efficient machine led by a quick mind. "Bad as millwork," John said, assuring Tobias the repetitiveness would render his mind as mechanized as the mill itself. Tobias, on the other hand, actually hoped for stretches of rhythmic, mindless toil in the woods; they'd give the workings of his mind a stretch, let him arrange thoughts he'd spent a boyhood gathering, maybe bring cloudy things to light.

"He still takes a train to town every day," Josiah Blesh would say. "Hangs around the new factory pestering for a job." Only when he stressed the word "pestering" would he look up. But Tobias would already be calculating what time to make the next day's visit—no telling when somebody else might come prospecting.

Then he'd dally toward the door, slowly as he dared. For above it hung his consolation prize: the gaze of Celia Erhart beaming down from the photograph taken out on the plank two years and a winter ago. Her stare drew his eyes to the exclusion of everyone else in the picture. To Tobias, she alone was the subject—that he was in it was important only to his having some claim. How she leaned out from the image, directing her poise at the camera. She was tugging on a tendency men wore like a leash, that pulled them to accomplish things. Seeing that every day roused him to know more of such powers.

Then he'd gotten his break—the day before, the first time Josiah Blesh looked up as Tobias entered the office.

"We need a hick out on the Teaberry operation," Blesh said. "Someone to bump knots. Et cetera." He bunched his brows and furrowed his bare pate, as if disgusted that Tobias was late. "Take the train from the mill tomorrow. Find the foreman when you get to camp. Name's Austin Fritz." He looked to his desk.

Tobias started toward the door, glancing up at Celia Erhart, this time a second longer and with a faint wish for her take on the assignment. It was the first anyone referred to him as a hick.

"By the way," Josiah Blesh said. "Things are slowing down—if you haven't noticed. Teaberry's our last big tract."

Tobias looked back and nodded.

"No telling how much longer this operation will justify a mill. Don't get too comfortable." Blesh looked away to where dawn's downy grayness brushed the window, then he closed his eyes a moment.

But a boss's foreboding couldn't cloud Tobias's spirits this morning with the springtime timber rush taking hold of his logging town. The mill's one saw at least ran two-shifts-strong, early crews already making the air musky with the smell of sawdust, the tempo of the blade racing the clap and chug of the shingle splitter below the mill floor, and the zip-zap cutting of staves. The swollen cadence pulled Tobias's feet as if they fit the rails he followed.

The nearer day drew, the darker pre-dawn bore on the valley, especially where the great cubes of drying lumber crowded the tracks. Tobias took a siding toward the mill, and the track eventually banked along the wooden ramp where logs were rolled to the pond. There he found his string of empty log cars.

Tobias hopped onto the lip of the ramp and cat-clawed his corks across it. The electric light shining onto the pond from the mill was lost against the locomotive's blackness, but the gold lettering of *Ryder Lumber Company* singed the steel jacket of the engineer's cockpit. Empty. He groped for the grab-pipe and climbed onto the gangway between the cockpit and tender, then to the bed of coal, the pond light catching on the chunk's flat spots as if they were diamonds. He kicked up a pile of big pieces, then sat as he awaited the crew.

The water farthest from the pond light drew the mortar color seeping now from the wedge of the eastern valley, the surface blemished here and there by the spine of a floating log. Between the sounding of the saw, and against the peepers' constant squawking from the new sedges down in the muddy places, Tobias could hear the pondsman out there sorting timbers, his humming and the splash of his pole wavering over the water gently as the strokes of an oar.

It was well past the six o'clock whistle when the crew approached by lantern. "Hobo, you ain't gonna get far on that train," said the engineer as he lifted the lamp toward the gangway ladder. He sounded unalarmed and casual, a big man, tall enough to need special-order overalls, the left suspender of which he tugged with his thumb. He wore his requisite neckerchief and a watch rope looped from his belly pocket. His sickle-brimmed cap rode upward, ready to fall from where it hung at the back of his head, big too, and shaped like a prize blackberry. Must not be able to special order those hats, Tobias thought.

"I'm not jumpin' this train, sir," he said.

As the engineer drew back his lamp, Tobias saw the face of his fireman. He was the typical bakehead—a near-twenty, eager apprentice to the engineer, red-faced from the smiting firebox he fed. His leather gauntlets reached his elbows, one holding a long-spouted oil can. His scowl showed he didn't share his boss's tolerance for this stranger in his tender.

"I've been put on with the Teaberry crew," Tobias said. "Mr. Blesh told me to take this train out. I'll help brake or fire if you want." He smiled at the fireman, who just looked at Tobias.

The engineer nodded. "There's two shovels. You help Barney coal the firebox, and you'll earn your fare."

Not even on the job yet, Tobias thought, and I'm helping fire an engine.

But he got only shrugs as he asked Barney how and when to use the foot-operated butterfly door that opened and closed like a theatre curtain to the boiler's bowels. Finally he stopped trying and settled onto the coal pile, watching the yellow ball from the engine's lantern nuzzle the mist of dawn. Soot and cinders spilled back on Tobias, more than necessary, he knew; Barney had control of the blower, and saved up pluming the smoke so it rushed back all the heavier. Covered in soot, coughing what he took in, Tobias knew but didn't care that he was all hat brim, wide eyes and grin; he was enjoying this privilege of riding to camp atop the tender. When the soot blew hardest, he looked back across the cars snaking behind, and he imagined rolling sixteen-footers across their decks where the brakemen now leaned on their jillpoke poles, solemn and gray as old fenceposts.

The screeches and screams of flanged wheels, their click-clack against rail joints, were a lumber-town lullaby to Tobias. He was keen to the voices of different logging locomotives, could pick out the solid grind of masticating gears peculiar to the brawny Shays, *stemwinders* the hicks named the switchback specials, stubby engines with a temperament they called short man's complex. And he knew run-in locomotives—like the one coughing cinders on him—just by the chugs and pops of their rods.

Tobias much favored the Shays and their cousin Climaxes—Pennsylvania-made up in Corry. One or the other he'd see on the job tomorrow. Their design owed to the sheerness of those hollows, iron mules made to test how treacherously steep or sharp lumbermen could build grades, then dare to ease log convoys down them. Shays weren't too proud to wear their pistons on their flanks. Power to every wheel, shoed to turn hairpins, they were to pulling railcars what oxen were to skidding logs: slow power and grit.

This run-in, on the other hand, was all speed and refinement, a retiree from a rich mainline, an engine with rods that pumped at the drive-wheels like suckling rabbits. It wasn't until these relics were old and worn that they had character enough to run on a logging railroad. Tobias had been indignant when the old engineers at the boarding house talked of loosening side rods so the snooty old aristocrats could run on the misaligned rails and irregular grades between the mill and camps. A run-in's duty was a mundane matter of exchanging log trains brought down from the ridges. Valley Darlings is what the Shay engineers called them, some still stained with their mainline lettering—*Chicago Southern; Baltimore and Ohio.*

Five miles down-line, time turned back to night as the train sided into the hulking narrows of Teaberry Hollow. Daybreak regained the train just as it closed in on camp, dawn spilling down swaths that had been timbered to the valley bottom. At the locomotive's last huff, Tobias recognized Old

Snyder moving toward the train, so stiff there might have been a line reeling him. The familiar tea-stain face sprouting its odd metal-stemmed pipe was welcoming in that new world. Old Snyder made for supply crates chained to the lead car.

"Hey, Mr. Snyder," Tobias said.

Old Snyder tipped his head up, neck so taut this required shifting his shoulders. He pinched at his pipe, and as Tobias knew he would, paused. Then, lighting like a match of recollection, he looked about and answered as matter-of-fact as he would greeting a camp hound: "Yessir. Young-fellow Meier. Same face, but sooty now—and it's got bones." Tobias just grinned and shook his head. He had, though, lately seen what Old Snyder meant. His body was showing everywhere its frame of poking bones. Even his face was all bluffs and coves from the jutting of cheekbone and chin.

"It's him all the same," Old Snyder said, with a nod while he looked down hard at the wheels of the log car. "Seems the last time I saw you was in a similar stall of a different barn."

"It's almost three years since I helped at the old Piebald camp," Tobias said.

Old Snyder spoke as if he all-of-a-sudden remembered. "You fellas run them laurel like cats in cornstalks." He rocked his head slowly. "So what brings you to this camp?"

"I've been put on." Tobias stood, the question a sort of summons.

"Swampin'?" Old Snyder said.

"Knot-bumpin'."

"Swampin', knot-bumpin', all the same. You'll roustabout most any job, I imagine." He pulled his pipe from his lips and stared harder at the flanged wheel of the log car. Tobias wondered if there was something wrong with it. Then Old Snyder looked up at him. The all-of-a-sudden remembering look. "It's a small operation. Good place to break in as a hick."

Tobias shouldered his satchel. Elating words.

*   *   *

He helped Old Snyder unload the crates before the train moved to drop its empties at a siding across from camp, then pick up a string of loaded log and bark cars.

"Crew out already?" Tobias said, toting a crate on his shoulder while he followed Old Snyder.

"Yep. Been to breakfast and out with the dinky a half hour now. Foreman's still in his office, though." They stopped at a tool shanty. "Set that crate round the doorway and I'll take you there."

"Dinky?" Tobias said.

Old Snyder frowned into his pipe bowl. Then he brightened. "Forgot you was green. A dinky's another name for them little engines that pulls the light loads. They got one here for moving empties and spotting cars."

Although newer than the one in Piebald Hollow, Teaberry camp was rough; a mishmash of twelve squat structures that seemed more chopped than built. The buildings were arranged in two cozy rows, but jagged as saw teeth. Every log structure, save one, was a single story, and the exception took half its second floor from the space of high-arched rafters. Some were shed-sized, a couple the length of a barn, and no roofline level, no pitch the same. Between buildings, long slabs of cast-off lumber crisscrossed in a web of walkways that kept feet out of a muddy sty strewn with pine shakes, horseshoes and the rings and staves of casks.

Tobias followed Old Snyder to a longer building, its end facing the tall one. The logs of its walls were heaped haphazardly as chimney stones. Bits of moss dangled where the chinking had cracked away during winter. Old Snyder pointed into the open doorway and spoke as if it was a new discovery. "There's the foreman's office."

Tobias tugged on his satchel and pulled down on his hat brim. Then he tapped the doorframe, not too loud, not too timid. "Mr. Fritz?"

Light stretched from a window and another opened door on the opposite side. Tobias could make out three rows of tables. By what lay scattered across them, he knew the office doubled as camp store. Overalls, cans and pouches of tobacco, socks, gloves, razors, underdrawers, suspenders, even a brimming box of sharp-pointed logger's corks.

A desk faced the wall below the window. Austin Fritz turned, squinting against the morning sunlight that framed Tobias. He was a broad man of forty in spectacles, dark hair tight-cropped to the sides of his head, which was long and widened toward the crown like a bucket. On top, his hair sprouted straight. A perfect carrot head, Tobias couldn't help thinking.

"Yes?" Fritz's voice was too flimsy for the broad body.

"Tobias Meier, sir. Mr. Blesh sent me out."

"Come here, then."

Tobias approached; Austin Fritz gave no formal greeting.

"Have you worked in the woods?"

"No, sir. But I've been about the camps and the mill. I catch on quick." He hadn't expected this second interview.

"Well, I didn't ask Blesh for experience. That sure as hell didn't save the one you're replacing." He looked Tobias up and down while Tobias considered the misfit voice—it nearly squeaked. "But I did ask for competence. And hardiness."

"I can work the day long," Tobias said. "I read well and been to school."

Fritz's eyes swam behind his spectacles, and Tobias chastened himself for so much as mentioning the word school in a logging camp. Fritz turned and opened a ledger on his desk. "Schoolmistress or not, we need to move every foot of timber before someone decides to shut me down. I'll put you on tomorrow."

While Fritz inked a pen and made a notation, Tobias stole a glance at the wares. He eyed a pile of red handkerchiefs. He coveted one in his pocket, saw himself unfolding it, smelled the new, dyed cotton as he wiped saw-dusty sweat from his neck.

"Sign to meal and board, plus a dollar a day. Take your pay here after work on Saturdays or against your account on anything in the store. Any day but Sunday." With that, Fritz shook Tobias's hand and told him to check in with the cook, then to find the lobby hog for a bunk.

Tobias stepped into the high-roofed building next door. He'd known this was the dining and sleeping hall by its tall upper loft and a shed tacked to the side, crooked stovepipe growing out of it. Smaller than the hall at the Piebald camp, it was still wide enough for two rows of black oilclothed tables with benches for thirty or so hicks. The joists were of un-hewn logs, and only one window in each long wall shed light into the room. Tobias walked to a doorway. The cook and his cookee were filling pecan pies that stretched end to end across a far counter, even onto the eight-griddle stove.

"Pardon me," Tobias said. "Mr. Fritz told me to check in. My name's Tobias Meier, and I've been put on."

"Well, ain't I a proud papa," the cook said, turning to Tobias. "Another mouth to feed." He cracked a dry smile while he spooned eggy pecan goo into a piecrust. Tobias could smell the sweet maple syrup.

"Just you?" the cook said.

"Yessir."

"Well, that'll be fine, Tobias Meier. I'm Jack Haney, and this is Elwood Davis."

"Woody," the cookee said, turning and nodding while he churned a tub of pie filling with a sort of short oar. "Oh," he said. "Just a kid. Or a sooty miner. What—did you ride up in the firebox?"

He laughed, and Jack Haney tossed Tobias a towel to wipe his face.

"The tender," Tobias said, and he wondered if every apprentice in the logging world had a chip on his shoulder. Like the fireman, the cookee was near twenty, but wiry as an egg whisk. The struggle of projecting what he would be over what he was showed on his pimply face.

A cookee was destined to be a cook, and Tobias knew as well as Woody that the occupation was revered in a logging camp, for the cook had charge of the hicks' chief benefit—food. He feared neither fight nor mischief; no hick bit that hand that fed him.

"Maybe you'll last longer than Hudson," Woody the cookee said.

"Who's that?" Tobias said.

"The one you're here to replace—a local knot bumper not liked by a pair of Canuck tree fellers." He shook his head in mock amazement. "Strange how their tree fell on him."

"That's enough," said Woody's boss. He lifted his chin toward the ceiling. "Geet will give you bunk orders," he said.

Tobias mounted stairs at the far end of the dining hall. Instead of a stall of tightly-aligned bunks like the one he knew from his stint at the Piebald camp, this was a squat room of wooden-framed beds, two pillows each, backed to the walls. True bunks would not have fit in these quarters, for the walls rose only thigh-high to where the roofline thrust upward. Crudely hewn, open joists spanned overhead, joining the middles of the rafters. Over them were draped stiff wool socks, underdrawers and suspenders. The hemlock roof boards, rough-faced and yellowed by tobacco smoke, were riddled with square nails from which hung the slings of lanterns, guns and satchels.

Blankets of wool covered the sixteen beds, melancholy gray but cheered by stripes—indigo from the dye of ragweed gulls, butternut-brown from walnut pulp. The blankets were so large they were folded over, still overhanging the bed tickings. An aisle-way split the room, clear except for the woodstove midway and a desk at the far end. Straddling the desk, a pair of windows let in the white light of the new day.

He stayed at the top step and smiled, breathing damp wool and the remnant of tobacco smoke. Feet, too. He'd waited his lifetime to be where woodhicks slept between days of exhausting work, played symphonies of growling snores and thunderous farts. He'd learned at the Whitehouse this was a place for practical jokes, for tall tales that blew in with hicks from the "down east" that was really up north, hicks from the Austrian Alps and the Adirondacks, Nova Scotia and Norway. Lots of local boys, too.

Finer details of the room came as he adjusted to the creamy light. A bamboo fishing pole spanning the rafters, corked boots powwowing around the woodstove, a razor strop tacked to a bedpost.

Then he saw him. As still and watchful as a pointed setter, the lobby hog sat across the room beside the desk, looking upon smiling Tobias. He was in an armed chair, his right hand wrapped around the hook of a cane he'd propped between his legs. He moved it slowly, as though to warn Tobias he was indeed alive. What a scowl, Tobias thought; looks mean as hell.

"Mr. Geet?" he said.

"Igidius Rakestraw," the old-timer snapped.

"I'm Tobias Meier, Mr. Rakestraw. I've been put on."

"I didn't say 'Mr. Rakestraw.'"

"Should I call you Geet, sir?"

"Geet alone—you're too damned close to geezer with that."

Geet's jutting brows and stretched eyes reminded Tobias of the salamanders he found under rocks for fishing bait. The cheekbones bulged like walnuts, and the lips were the clamped prongs of a clothespin. Thanks to the walnuts, his cheeks couldn't help dishing in, they and the lips and brows accounting for a fixed scowl. His beard hung over his collar in the way of old-timers to protect, as they said, their throats from consumption.

"Got pants rabbits?" Geet said.

"No, sir," Tobias said, assuring Geet he was no bearer of lice. He edged to the stove and tipped his hat back. Geet studied the big western.

Geet's hat was a common one among hicks—a saucepan crown with a wide, perfectly round brim. But unlike most hicks who curved, bent or pinned their brim to personalize, Geet left his level as a river pool.

Without moving his eyes from Tobias, Geet pointed his cane to his right. "You take that bed—share it with Cowboy. Hang your satchel overhead. I want nothing left on the floor except the thunder mug you'll find under the bed."

Tobias saw the edge of the chamber crock. And as Geet parked his cane with a thud of finality, Tobias wondered what kind of woodhick wore a name like Cowboy.

Tobias determined Igidius Rakestraw overdressed for the season—vest, coat, collar—age-worn, like the old-timer himself. And old he was. Tobias guessed eighty, though the sable beard was gray-tinged no more than a cottontail's summer coat. He wondered if his smiling moment at the top of the stairs accounted for Geet's hard stare. If so, Tobias desired to make him forget it, so he said, "I've got no assignment for today. I wonder if I can do anything around the bunkhouse."

Geet neither spoke nor moved. Tobias feared he'd insulted him. "Maybe I'll just go down and check with Old Snyder," he said.

"You know Old Snyder?"

"Yep. He was a hand at the Piebald camp when I shagged deer there for Mr. Ryder a few years ago."

"I worked that camp," Geet said. "That was eight years, easy." His eyes nearly creased shut. "What was Ryder doing there so recent?"

"He and Mr. Erhart and another fellow—a Mr. Hoehn—stayed there while they hunted thereabouts, mostly on Fiddlers Flats."

The old-timer's eyelids loosened, and he looked over Tobias's head. "Fiddlers Flats," he said. "A stand of grandfather chestnut that must have sprouted when the hills rose—they graced that place." He looked at Tobias. "Still there?"

"Yessir. Matter of fact, I heard Mr. Erhart say they weren't worth going after."

Geet smiled, mostly in the eyes, but a smile just the same.

"Well, maybe they will stay standing," Geet said. "The woods ain't the busy hive of hicks they used to be. Operations closing everywhere. I suppose this'll be next." The smile vanished. "They take everything from track to grindstones, ship it to New York or down to West-by-God-Virginia. That empty camp you seen in Piebald was the beginning of the end, boy."

Tobias knew that these overseers of sleeping quarters—combination chambermaids, lamp cleaners and fire tenders—had long histories in woods-work. Lumber camps were their homes, the crews their families. Lobby hogs moved from operation to operation—never drifted to permanent jobs, never sowed their blood.

Tobias wanted to know if Geet floated rafts in the days of the big pines. But Geet spoke before he could ask.

"You go ahead and check with Old Snyder," Geet said. "He probably won't know what to do with help, but check anyways."

"Geet, I was wondering about the hick I'm replacing. What happened to him?"

"Never mind that." Geet rose and swayed, but it was a motion as uniform as a flush of doves. He shooed Tobias by lifting his cane, then moved toward the stove.

Outside, Tobias realized there'd been something common across the sixty-odd years separating him and Geet—the chestnut trees. He lost the unease of knowing the old-timer had watched him wallow at the top of the stairs.

* * *

Old Snyder thought hard, then snapped to with "I think maybe so," when Tobias asked if Geet had been on the Susquehanna in times of the big log drives or maybe even worked on the rafts that were built from pine spars and then floated down the river like barges.

And Geet had been right: Old Snyder didn't need help, so Tobias whiled the morning seeing what sort of camp he'd been assigned to. Except for a teat-dragging hog, the only other creature about the place was the smitty. Tobias peeked through the doorway of his shack as the smitty poked the hook of a log grab into his forge with a gloved hand and turned his fan with the other. The smitty doubled as saw filer, for he'd vice-clamped a saw blade to a bench, and a silver galaxy of filings littered the dirt floor under it.

The sleeves of the smitty's union suit were rolled garter-tight above his forearms, which were tanned orange as his forge's embers. His apron was full-grain leather, and at his thighs, sooty black as his coal pile. Two trunks of muscle swelled along his spine. As he hammered the tip of the grab against his anvil, sweat-drops sizzled on the iron.

The smitty turned. "Who're you?"

"I'm taking Hudson's place," Tobias said. His position was seeming more replacement than assignment.

"Ah," the smitty said. Tobias noted regret.

"Did Hudson—" Tobias looked around. In the loose dirt away from the paths tamped by the smitty's boot lay cast tips of shoe corks, chain links and rail spikes, broken axe bits and cant hooks. There, a pile of horseshoes to be sharpened. "Did he get killed?"

"Killed, yeah," the smitty said. "Details I ain't got. They don't make their way to this shanty." He turned back to his forge.

*   *   *

Tobias sat on a stump near the smitty's shack, lulled by the dead ring of his hammer and the hiss of hot iron in his water can, until he spotted Old Snyder leading a pair of salt-and-pepper Percherons to the kitchen door. Tobias helped hang lunch baskets over the flanks of the horses. But Old Snyder did not ask Tobias to join him delivering lunch to the woods crew.

The cook handed Tobias a loaf of bread and a bowl of stew. Then he spent the afternoon counting rings in stumps by the tracks, awaiting the squeaks and thumps of the locomotive leading its cars of timbers down Teaberry Hollow.

It was full dark when the train came. Tobias made his way to the dining hall, hung his hat on a nail, and stood in a far corner. It was a custom for each hick to have his own seat, and a violation of squatting rights would draw more than fangs. Tobias guessed his place was near the corner he occupied, for the table setting had a plate turned right-side-up instead of on its fork, knife and spoon. Plates were washed only after supper. Otherwise, they were cleaned by crust, then turned over.

When the cookee rang the dinner bell with hammer blows on a holey bucket, the hicks filed into the dining hall, some from upstairs, some from the yard, all in Richie shirts.

The familiar face in the bunch was Old Snyder. But he sat across the room next to the kitchen door. The rest were mostly young, wiry men, and the only regard anyone gave Tobias came in glances as a few stepped past him. Tobias had guessed correctly—the upturned plate was his. He took his place.

Igidius Rakestraw descended the stairs. He stopped two steps from the bottom and lulled the din by scanning the rows of hatless loggers, his lids squinted.

His words cracked like splitting lumber. "New fella's been put on." He pointed at Tobias. "Name's Tobias Meier. Local boy."

Geet and the rest of the room eyed Tobias. "Tobias Meier," Geet said, "this crew's one of the finest I seen, and I seen many. You'll meet them one by one." Tobias returned stares, wondering if two Canadians were mulling that he was a local boy.

Someone yelled from a far table, "If they don't shut us down first like everywheres else."

Geet glared at the hick. Then, as other men chirped similar comments, he said, "It's got a couple years left." Tobias heard the strain of trying to convince even himself.

"Tobias has no woods experience," Geet said. "But he'll fill Hudson's shoes quick enough." Spotty laughs cackled about the room. A red-bearded man at Tobias's table turned and said, "Hudson is no longer with us, so those would be strange shoes to fill."

As each face in the room turned into a local-hating Canadian, Tobias told himself he'd waited too long for this day to doubt his aim, and he mustered all his will to grin.

Then someone at another table addressed Tobias's bedmate. "Hope you didn't get used to stretchin' in your stall, Cowboy." Tobias saw the speaker looking toward a lanky man of thirty. His hair and face were fair like those of the blue-eyed Scandinavians Tobias knew to board in Pigeondale. His hands rested beside his plate, veiny trunks that branched thin white digits. His features drooped in long and narrow rivulets. The man called Cowboy just grinned and shook his head.

The teamsters came into the dining hall, the rush of outside air delivering the offal tang of hard-worked horses. Six seats had been reserved for them closest to the kitchen. Something in their cool manner eased Tobias.

While the men passed great platters of pork loins, boiled potatoes and sauerkraut, only a few thrust out hands for Tobias to shake, their skin as course as the smitty's sharpening files. Then they ate, and ate, and ate, certifying every tale Tobias had heard about the swinish appetite of woodhicks who muscled trees and saws and horses twelve hours minimum.

During the eating, the only talk was food-related. "Slide the axle grease my way." *"That's butter, greenhorn,"* came a whisper slanted toward Tobias. "I'll take a splash of cow for my bean juice." *"That'd be milk and coffee, babe."* "Heap me some of that Dutch spaghetti." *"Sauerkraut, boy."* Few other words were spoken, as the price of talking was food.

The meal ended as abruptly as it began. The hicks rose, smokers reaching into breast pockets, each man moving either to the door or the sleeping quarters. When the room was empty, Tobias retrieved his hat and started up the stairs.

Geet occupied his chair by the desk. The others were lounging, talking or dealing cards. A bottle-spectacled hick hummed a tune on his mouth organ, the melody meshing into the men's slow, weary movements.

Lanky Cowboy lay on his half of the bed. He watched Tobias cross the room and hang his hat above his pillow.

"Nice hat," was all he said.

Chapter 9

He didn't like being called Johnny. But John Blesh learned quickly that to rise to the top of Erhart Carbon, he'd have to endure the name. That and the damned black dust.

In the carbon business, it was known as powder. All his life John had associated powder with good things. Soap powder; powdered sugar; the scented talc of Cashmere Bouquet when Celia Erhart stepped into the factory to find her husband. But this black dust was as indelible and stinging as gunpowder. And its smell bitterly reminded him of wet days in Pigeondale when his father had him shovel ashy cinders from locomotive fireboxes into the soot pile by the engine shed. It blackened the walls of the factory and every inch of the workers—floating eyeballs they were, blinking across the screen of a smoky picture show.

Not yet summer and already the vapor had thickened. More heat seemed impossible, and coming on suddenly, it seemed something separate, crammed into the factory, ready to burst the roof off with the chugs and slams of the machinery. That brick building was an oven containing ovens, and the cupola that spined its roof did little to vent the heat of those brick kilns. Nor did it admit sunlight through the shroud of black powder.

But this was John's first step into this carbon business, and he assured himself it would be a quick jump to the next one. At sixteen, he'd landed in the carbon-green department, the critical starting point of the process, the place that received top attention from Erhart, Ryder and that outsider, Hoehn. But it also put him in a room next to the kilns.

Most of the day he was sick, swallowing hard the coating in his throat, and lunch became nothing more than a better way of swabbing the powder into his stomach. He itched so badly at his brow and up to the rolls of his canvas shirtsleeves, even beneath the thin wool legs of the ready-made pants he'd bought from the Ryder Company Store, that he wished his hands were bristles to scrape flesh right to the bone where those miserable twitching nerves must be rooted. He scratched until he bled, and at night the stained gashes seared as if they'd been limed, burning him awake between short fits of sleep that were haunted by the stomps of machines pounding through the walls of the carbon-green department. Through that first month, he'd coaxed himself to the factory every day: *You can handle the heat, John, for as long as it takes to step up and out.*

Over the buzz and whir of the mixer John filled from a ladder, the word Erhart caught his ear. He looked to a silhouette in the doorway.

"Erhart wants to see you."

The shadow moved off, and John tossed away the tin bucket he used to fill the mixer's hopper with petroleum coke. Moving down the ladder, he glanced at his co-worker, who nodded that he'd heard the summons. John was in charge of the mixer, and though he was younger, he considered himself superior to his counterpart, for the man's job was merely to stock bins of coke, sop ladles of pitch into barrels, and wheelbarrow off to the pressmen the batches John mixed.

John stepped into the narrow cavern of the main bay—the factory was still a small operation of twenty men. The oven heat and mist of carbon powder conspired with the overhead arc lights in a whiskey glow that made shadow ghosts of the moving presses. But that was no doomful sight to John Blesh so long as he knew that at the far end of the building, all that black business was being bundled for a brighter, far-off world of flashlight batteries and arc lights—a world he'd someday be part of.

The office of Erhart Carbon was a separate, small building of the plant's same beige brick, so similar in shape that it appeared severed and nudged aside. To John, it looked like a schoolhouse.

Inside the doorway, John wiped shining black carbon streaks onto a rug. Erhart called from his office, "Johnny. Come on in." John made straight for him, not returning the smile of a sailor-suited girl behind her desk at the entrance.

Erhart leaned back from his desk, grinned, and lifted his big brows. "Still getting on well?"

"Yessir."

Erhart pointed to a chair against a wall, inhospitably far across the room, a carbon-soiled sheet draped over it and a narrow, stained rug leading from the door to the chair, the only mars to the neat, dark-paneled office.

"I see your father time to time," Erhart said.

John nodded and sat.

"I wish for his sake," Erhart said, "that woods work looked as promising as the carbon business."

"Will you have to close the Pigeondale operations?"

"We're feeding her all we can," Erhart said. "But soon enough we'll be making hard decisions."

Erhart grinned again. "Do you like boarding?"

"Don't mind it." In fact, John did not like taking rooms. He wanted an apartment of his own. But Erhart Carbon was growing, and John was sure that before long the company would move him well beyond Marstadt.

"Miss home?"

"Naw."

Erhart watched him a moment. "Johnny, do you know Ernie Groeger?"

He nodded.

"Ernie's know-how, you understand, is very valuable to this place."

John turned an ear. He would pick words cautiously, knowing now this had to do with Groeger.

"You know by now that carbon products are only as good as their materials, and how those materials are handled—the formulas."

"Sure," John said. "I mix green carbon."

"And you realize each formula you mix, whether for battery carbons or arc lights, is designed to result in a grade of product the customer chooses—by price?"

John nodded with an *of course I do* look.

"Here's the thing," Erhart leaned forward in his chair. "Any one of our grades is better than our competitor's, apples to apples. That, Johnny, will set us apart. We're banking on it."

Erhart stood and turned to one of his high, arched windows, which faced the factory. "This is a very competitive business. Worse than I expected. But with the new century, big changes are coming. Fast. The carbon company with the best ideas for new applications will do quite well." He turned back, rested his hands on the desk and raised his brows in a fraternal look; it piqued John's optimism about this conversation. "If we are very careful and very smart," Erhart said, "we'll be number one in this business." He pointed to his temple. "Think electric, Johnny, electric. Anything electric involves carbon."

John smiled and raised his chin in an "aha," sure that for whatever reason Erhart shared all this, it meant big things for him.

Erhart sat again. "Do you recall how this company started—with Andy Hoehn's proposal?"

"Sure. Three years ago at the Piebald camp."

The corners of Erhart's eyes creped with a smile. "Yes. And there was a golden nugget in that proposal—Ernie Groeger. It's true in this business— at the same costs, with basically the same processes, one company's carbons can last longer than another's. One company can call a higher price. And all the difference is some knack with carbon-green formulas."

John nodded enthusiastic understanding, sure this was leading to a promotion out of the grime of the plant, and into an office. Erhart laced his fingers, rested his hands on his desk, and became very serious. "Do you see, Johnny, that our greatest advantage is also our weakest link?"

"Well, yes."

"That happens a lot in business," Erhart said. "That's not to say we can't be reasonably sure of Ernie Groeger's allegiance—he favors Marstadt."

John cocked his head. He couldn't care less about Groeger, but he was curious about this. "Why would Marstadt matter to him?"

Erhart chuckled. "There are certain things about it he finds enticing. You may understand that better someday. But that's doubtful since you aren't from here. Let me just say that in Marstadt, Ernie feels as close to home as he ever will again. He's as happy here as he can be in this world. He's told me so." Erhart looked to the ceiling a moment. "Marstadt matches his constitution. He can be himself here."

John translated this into more proof that Groeger was plain weird. His apprehension about where Groeger fit into this must have showed.

"Johnny, it's important you understand something before I tell you why you're here. Even though the intuition of a formula man can't be passed on, what it makes can." He held up a hand. "Again, it's unlikely Ernie would betray us—money does not make him tick. But you can't be too cautious. And others concern me."

"Who?"

Erhart laughed quietly. "We may have been in business only a few months, but we're already making trouble for some big boys. There's no telling what they might do. We can't risk mixes of green carbon slipping out of here, landing up probed in another laboratory. If more than two eyes are going to know that lab, they'll be of our choosing."

Babysitter, John thought.

Erhart read him. "Johnny, you need to understand—what I'm offering goes far beyond watchdog. I'm looking at our future. And yours. You could be our formula maker someday, even if you merely learn to copy Ernie." He shrugged. "In any case, you'd have an important job."

"Why me? All of a sudden?"

Erhart gave a politician's parade smile. "I've been keeping my eyes opened for the right man. You're young and bright." Erhart rose from his chair and moved around his desk, holding out a hand. "I'd like to make you Ernie Groeger's apprentice."

Apprentice to that freak of nature? John stared at Erhart's ruddy hand. This wasn't a step toward getting out of Marstadt; it was a barring in. He calculated. If he said no, he'd never be taken seriously. If he said yes, then later approached Erhart about moving on in sales, he'd have betrayed Erhart's good turn. The lesser of two evils. He gave Erhart his hand.

"Don't be intimidated, Johnny. Things always seem bigger when you don't know them."

"Yessir," John said, looking down at the carbon-stained rug.

"We'll meet tomorrow morning in Ernie's lab. Seven o'clock."

*   *   *

John Blesh saw himself thrust into a world of oddballs. Ten hours a day now he'd be bound to Ernie Groeger, only to leave and live among the Bavarians of Marstadt, people he thought better suited to an asylum. Which is how he figured reformationists in eastern cities saw those German Catholics two generations before. Everyone on the tier knew that some such sentiment accounted for their setting off and establishing the town. To John, it rendered a strain too cold and quiet. He hated the sternness, thought of it as righteousness, thought they carried their past as entitlement to smirks they hid beneath their stiff features.

John Blesh counted against them their singular ways, that they didn't melt into the new century like people in *Life* magazine. To him, culture didn't come of knitting a shunned lifestyle into a wilderness. It was something determined by people in ballrooms and department stores. Marstadt's distinctive garden vegetables and grocery goods, architecture and rigid religion, its people's accent and attire, were the very absence of culture. Families were large, as were their sooty white clapboard homes with spanning front porches. They drank beer as water, any time of day.

Their cabbage was wincingly sour, and they ate sausages named for unpronounceable Bavarian cities. Making use of all the organs of cows and hogs, they pickled or cured anything. Every home had a backyard smokehouse one wouldn't know from the privy but for a tin chimney. On damp days, the smoke of hardwood overcame even the reek of the tannery, and it was said that a tree of green apples in Marstadt would be sacrificed if a hickory couldn't be found to keep the sausages smoking.

John took it all in walking home that evening, finding in everything he saw more reason to aim his energies at getting out of that parochial prison. Crossing Station Street, moving into the neighborhood where he boarded, he stared right back at the aged settlers on their porches. He knew by the sons and grandsons at the factory the odd ways of these ashen-faced and rheumatoid ancients; nothing about the bloodline ever changed.

Maybe the reason they wore those dry, unfeeling faces, spoke with no passion their throaty consonants, was that they held their gripe even a lifetime after escaping the self-proclaimed cities of liberty where they'd fended curses and sticks: Baltimore, Boston, Philadelphia. John fancied it had to do, too, with a raw deal they'd gotten.

From their ghettos they'd formed a league, pooled their money and bought the only eastern land they could afford. But when the first band arrived, underdressed on horseback in snowy December, they learned that even in the 1840s, their plot in the belly of Penn's Woods was a black cavern of ancient forest, panthers and snakes, beyond even Indian paths—a three-mile, dimpled mushroom-cap of plateauland splitting the headwaters of the Allegheny and Susquehanna.

John didn't credit that in less than a decade, using pit saw and axe, the refugees had transformed the place into pine-bark shanties and farm lots encircling a gristmill and brewery, church and monastery, even the blueprint of a mercantile square. All the while, the Bavarians had thanked God for delivering them to a place so like the forests of home they'd been compelled to escape, a place their ways would root into. It was as if a native seed had lifted with a trade wind and through all the mischance of an epic, landed an ocean away on the only other piece of earth it could sprout upon, where now with imagination and will, it could draw from the soil what it needed to thrive.

*　*　*

John, like everyone in the tier, knew how entangled the rest of the story was with the fixation of one man. Warren P. Ryder had been John's age in 1854 when he took an apprenticeship with a Baltimore surveyor, a time when such were in huge demand—vast chunks of eastern lands were still being sliced by grants and payment for military service. Baltimore-Eastern, the land management firm Ryder apprenticed with, had been hired by the brothers and nuns of the order that missioned to the Bavarian settlers, and been charged with developing that outpost into a town.

Young Ryder watched the process closely.

The mission had realized that vision and will alone would not guarantee its community prosperity. Pennsylvania had already seen its share of failed Utopian experiments; violin virtuoso Ole Bull's New Norway Colony had blossomed but died in its own deep corner of the tier. So Baltimore-Eastern recruited more settlers to cultivate the community, Bavarian Catholics, people with the same bent, the same scars; the company knew better than to mix the pot. It prospected land and managed investments shrewdly. And Warren P. Ryder followed it all. The apprentice had arrived early with a crew by horseback, and mapped and parceled land for homes, more farms, and timbering, while his company lobbied in Philadelphia for a stop on the great Pennsylvania Railroad.

At sixteen, Ryder recognized a seedling held dormant only by the wealth of timber that overshadowed it. Comparing the settlement to a wheel of progress, he persuaded the senior surveyor to lay out Marstadt with a town square as the hub of a wagon wheel, spokes of streets extending through home lots and space for industry, and a ring of farmland buffering the great forest. It unfolded as a quilt, all according to his design.

Ryder had seen that the Bavarians had heart. For ages, they'd conjured crops from slices of cleared forestland. Here, stalwart wives had gone right to work in shops. And craftsmen of wood and machinery arrived by the day, hauling their chests of tools. Modest and self-disciplined, they were just the people to fuel an enterprise.

So when he was twenty, Ryder gave up his apprenticeship with Baltimore-Eastern. He started with a mill to take in timber, and an iron works to put out tools to reap it. He leased small timberlands at a song, set his own crews to logging them. Then with every cent he earned, he bought plateauland.

By the time John Blesh became an apprentice, Marstadt had long been a stop on the mainline railroad, its square a place of beige brick hotels and banks, and the clapboard shops of bakers, tailors and cobblers, a milliner, and seamstress. There were butchers and a confectionary, second-floor offices of dentists and lawyers. And of course, the place to buy wares— the Ryder Company Store. Neighborhood streets named for Old World saints or Bavarian villages spread from the square. Out along the spokes of avenues, industry edged the neighborhoods: the shops for the Ryder rail line; the Ryder tannery next-door to Erhart Carbon; a chair factory and wagon works; a wood chemical plant; the brick, pipe and tile works. There were others, and the only ones of consequence that Warren P. Ryder didn't have a hand in were the breweries.

Beyond the smokestacks, farms speckled the edge of Marstadt's hump of tableland. And farther out, in remnants of the old lumber country, sawmills still reigned.

Warren P. Ryder had perpetuated the pioneer spirit of Marstadt. And everyone saw that of all his enterprises, none better suited those Bavarian temperaments and skills than Erhart Carbon. It couldn't have arrived at a better time, taking up the slack of a declining lumber supply, providing product to so voracious an appetite as the electrification of a nation. Nothing seemed so likely to ensure Ryder would leave a lasting legacy.

* * *

J. Hadley Erhart was waiting at the front entrance to the factory when John got there at a minute to seven. Erhart smiled and rubbed his hands together, elbows out, as if about to rally a team. "This is a big move for you and the company, Johnny. A big move."

He led John to the doorway of Ernie Groeger's laboratory. It was the one place on plant property not completely awash in the wet cinder smell of carbon. But only because of the smack of kerosene and chemicals. And Groeger's stink—sweat, cigar smoke, exhaled alcohol—as much a part of the room as his beakers and scales.

Erhart peered and called for Groeger. John wanted to laugh—a company owner begging entrance. Erhart even stepped back and waited.

The response was so indirect and conversational it might have been part of another exchange. "Who is that?"

"It's Hadley. And Johnny Blesh."

A head appeared from behind a marble-topped table of tools, instruments and a Bunsen burner, its flame jittering before Groeger's slouch hat like a tongue of fire. He did not stand. "What is it about?"

"May we come in?"

John rolled his eyes.

Ernie Groeger nodded, and his head disappeared. Erhart approached and leaned over the table. "Ernie, can we help you back there?"

"No. You talk, I work. I dropped something I cannot stop testing." Groeger popped up with forceps pincering a cinder-like chunk of calcified coke. He wagged it over the flame, the burner fluting a nasal whistle.

Erhart gave a grand smile. "Ernie, we've decided to put Johnny to work in the lab with you." The forceps stopped. Groeger looked at John. Erhart continued. "He'll become your assistant. Your apprentice."

Groeger dropped the forceps on the table. "Why?"

Erhart put a hand on John's shoulder, and John fought an urge to shrug it off. He couldn't help tipping his head away, resented being made to look like a kid, especially in front of crazy Groeger.

"To help you, Ernie," Erhart said. "We expect too much for one man here."

Groeger had only one good eye. Black-beaded and bloodshot, it canvassed John's face so thoroughly his skin felt kneaded. John couldn't look him in that eye, which forced him to the soggy, flour-paste orb left of the other. He saw the gray speck that pimpled it, rumored to be a shot-shell BB, then he looked away, knowing the rest would draw his stomach to his throat. The thought of enduring ten-hour days, six days a week with that face... Erhart must have felt him shudder, for he took his hand from John's shoulder.

"I don't need help," Groeger said. "No one can help. The formulas come from here." He pointed to his forehead.

"And someday, Ernie, this is where they'll go." Erhart pointed to John's scalp. "They have to go somewhere. Think of the future, think of posterity."

John glanced at Groeger. His good eye probed him again, interrogated him, peered for something inside.

"Just as you did," Erhart said, "we all have to start somewhere."

John held Groeger's stare the best he could, not hiding his disappointment. But he couldn't remain eye to eye, so he looked first at Groeger's soggy cigar stub, then at the blind side of his face, pocked and creviced as he'd seen on hicks who—fallen in a fight—had been kicked and clawed with a corked sole—logger's pox. That side of his face, dead as the eye, lacked a brow. The socket was ashier than the good eye's, which itself was gray as a rat's ass, John thought, sickly gray. And the rest of his hide was just a shade lighter. John made eye contact, then looked to the scars again, followed their lines to the ear—a fleshy lump with a hole in the middle.

"Johnny's already familiar with formulas," Erhart said, smiling from one to the other. "He mixes batches in the carbon-green department."

"Ach," Groeger said. With the forceps, he held up the cindery lump. "Here is the purest form of carbon we have." He pointed it at John, then at Erhart. "How do I know this? I know this because of many things I read in books. These things are very exact." He looked at John and shook the carbon. "Does he know things like coefficient of friction?"

"Ernie—"

Groeger cut him off. "Does he know specific resistance? Transverse strength? Many things go into grading carbon."

John turned to Erhart with a look to say, *see what I mean, he's cracked.* But Groeger leaned closer to John, pointing the forceps like a finger. John creased his eyes, thinking that if J. Hadley Erhart weren't standing there, he'd shove the carbon and all down the sonofabitch's throat. Groeger worked his eye all over John, chewing the cigar nub that was more a loose bunch of sodden tobacco leaves, his dirty slouch hat of herringbone tweed twitching up and down with his temples. He chewed as well the remains of mustache on the dead side, just a couple spider leg hairs.

"These things you would must need to know." Groeger threw down the forceps.

Erhart kept his smiling composure. "We realize that, Ernie. And we've chosen a young fellow with lots of time to learn, and then put it to use."

"I am not old," Groeger said, his words slow with wariness. "Only forty-nine."

"It's not just that, Ernie. We expect the company to grow to where we'll need more than one formula maker."

Groeger hacked out a sarcastic laugh, the wet stub of cigar adhered to his lower lip. "The only, only way for the company to grow is one formula man. It's the things that are not in the books that make the carbon even more best. There are things between the books. Two would foul what one does best." He reached and turned the lever of the Bunsen burner, the clatter and slams of factory machines falling in place of its fluting. "It is easy to think that things I read or see in experiments make the great carbon. Or makes it always the same. There is more."

"And another will learn to at least imitate what you make through all that." Erhart hadn't lost an ounce of his smiling optimism, but he'd wedged a slice of command into his voice.

Groeger held up his hands and grunted disgust. But he had one more thing to say. "Ach. The thing is to find if the person is right to make the carbon—if he has the way." He jawed his cigar and one-eyed John. "You don't just give a job to a man, you pick the man for the job. Or it will not be right. Something will go wrong."

"I believe," Erhart said, "that in my own way, I have chosen the right man for the job. If I didn't, the consequences are for me to bear."

"Well," Groeger said, then repeated it.

At that, it occurred to John that in his resistance he was allied with Groeger. While that made Groeger none the dearer, it quelled, slightly, his panic at being sentenced here.

Erhart patted John's shoulder, winked, and wagged his brows. He stepped toward the door, saying over his shoulder, "Teach him all you can, Ernie."

*   *   *

The rest of that day, Groeger measured and weighed carbon, graphite and charcoal flours, mixing them with pitch and lampblack in jars he held between his good eye and a lab window. To the tune of a glass swizzle stick, he'd monotonously recite ratios for John. Then he'd step to a journal on his marble-topped lab table and scratch with a pencil as he mumbled in German. Sometimes he stopped and stared, and when he looked where John sat on a wooden stepstool in front of a window—as far from Groeger as John could get—John saw that in whatever place his mind went, Groeger's good eye appeared as inward-turned as the doughy ball of the other.

Groeger worked at his lab table until early afternoon, leaving once near noon and returning with fresh exhales of beer. John stayed in his place, occasionally stepping to a window, resigned to being lulled and lazy on his stool the years it might take to figure a way out of there. He'd put in his time, watch out the window for the office girls taking breaks or fellows from the plant knocking off for a cigarette. Groeger wouldn't notice him missing, if he'd see him there at all. That would get him through. He'd manage until he found a way out of that lab, out of Marstadt, up with Erhart Carbon.

When the window light yellowed with the slanting afternoon sunshine, Groeger worked from his ovens. At three iron doors in a brick wall, he loaded and unloaded chunks and plates of carbon, using blacksmith tongs with lengthened handles. John's stool was three windows away, but each time Groeger opened a door, the hissing gas fires stung the side of his face.

"We measure temperature and time very carefully," Groeger said once, passing John as a timer buzzed. "Some carbon has been pressed, some not."

On a workbench, Groeger snapped, chiseled or sawed each glazed piece, at times tapping with a hammer as at a xylophone, turning an ear, and always probing at them with instruments John had never seen.

Groeger recited whatever his tests yielded. Sometimes he would suddenly stop and run to his journal to scribble, muttering German.

Near six o'clock, Groeger reached under his black-soiled apron and tugged a watch from his vest pocket. For the first time, he addressed John directly. "Well, we will stop making this formula here. I am tirsty." And at that, it came to John that all of Groeger's activities had been parts of one task, that he was trying to gain some preconceived outcome. He'd never considered that Groeger had aims, except maybe his jaunts to the brewery, never thought of his work in a recognizable form, beginning and end. A hunch told John this was all he needed to understand from the day.

Groeger etched the last of his notes in his journal, hurrying now without pauses or German mumbling. Then he carried the book to a counter by the doorway, beside which sat an unpainted trunk of deeply grained, splintered planks; in faded white stencil, "Henry Orch Schiff" was still legible across its front. After Groeger untied his apron and hung it on a nail over the trunk, he withdrew a key from his vest pocket, stooped, unlocked the chuck wagon lid, and opened it. John guessed this acquitted him for the day, so got up to leave as Groeger deposited his journal and pocketsful of test instruments, then shut and locked the lid.

Without a word, John walked out, eager as ever to get home, past the gummy-mouthed, porch-sitting pioneers who troubled his way.

Chapter 10

When Geet turned up his lantern flame and roused the crew on Tobias's first day of work in the woods, the windows by the sleeping quarters desk remained as black as when Geet had called for lamps out and traps shut.

Tobias took his place in line for the basin where the men doused their faces with wash water they ladled from a barrel. In the dining hall, he tried to match them in devouring bacon, eggs and prunes, which he heard a hick call sow bosom, cackle berries and belly birds. These men—most skinny as pole timber—ate like bears. Tobias gauged by their appetites the strain of the work ahead, but he felt ready as ever.

"Cooled down overnight, Dutch," one hick said to another as Tobias followed the gummy plod of loggers' corks across the planks to the tracks. The men didn't seem so eager to get to the woods as they had for their meals. Tobias had expected chatter and urgency. But the faces he could make out looked glum, businesslike, and the hicks trudged with the sarcastic, defeated mood their snickers cast over the dining hall last night with talk of the operation closing. Up ahead, the lamps of the engineer and fireman hovered and jabbed like burning moths about the gears and sprockets of the mini engine. Old Crawdaddy, they called the dinky.

Tobias's orders had been brief, handed down from Austin Fritz through Old Snyder before breakfast: Obtain a two-bit axe from the smitty. Go with the camp crew to the cutting. Swamp for Cowboy and his sawing partner, Billy Gaines—a gone-gray thirty-year-old, short with jutting, sturdy haunches and shoulders. Tobias squeezed in close to them as he picked a place to sit on a log car.

The little locomotive lurched, then began pulling them up Teaberry Hollow, its lantern beaming sharp in the mistless dawn. Cold now, the woods had withdrawn their sodden springtime scent.

"Worked much with an axe?" Billy Gaines asked Tobias. His voice had the oh-golly local dialect that Tobias had learned to single out in this mixed pot of immigrants, transients and natives—a sound that pleased his ear.

"No, but I've swung a sledge to split a good many cords," Tobias said.

"An axe ain't a sledge," Cowboy said. "You're comparing the sickle to the scissors. One's for the rough work, one's precise." His words dawdled out of his mouth in drawls as long as his face. "But there is something common," Cowboy said. "You let either do the work. You don't fight the tool, you guide it. It's the way of its stroke that makes for the bite of the axe, not the force behind it."

Billy Gaines cut in: "And you tuck that into your back pocket for when you know women."

At a narrows where the tracks arced up the flank of the hollow, the train stopped, and pairs of sawyers gathered their swampers, spudders and buckers. Then each group moved off in a different direction. Tobias—following Cowboy, Billy Gaines and their band—ladder-stepped up the slope while they fairly bound, focused and drawn as if on puppet strings. In the faint light and against the grade, Tobias soon had nothing to follow except the flim-flam of the flopping, sow-bellied crosscut Cowboy shouldered. Tobias compared this peculiar hick to the saw: long and skinny with a mournful twang in his way of talking.

Their climb ended at a narrow shelf. Woodsmen called these places benches, ancient shifted strips of ridge high above where the waters invisibly carved deeper and deeper. Upon the bench and upward, great heaps of hemlock boughs dimmed the milky light of dawn spilling down the ridge. The masses reared twice the height of Cowboy. Scattered among them, the trunks lay in various states, the freshest felled still bearing limbs. But most were bare, bucked into saw logs and denuded of their bark, which lay stacked about. The putrid tang of tree flesh lingered, even in the colder air. Tobias could not believe that only a small crew had done all this.

Cowboy walked to the broad trunk of a standing hemlock. Against the dark, furrowed background he no longer looked so tall, but all the more lanky.

"We work along the ridge from here," he said to Tobias while the spudders and buckers broke away. "You work behind us. Never alongside, always behind us. We fell thatta way." He pointed downhill. "So now you've been warned of which way the trees come down." Then Cowboy nodded at a felled and fully branched hemlock. "You chop limbs and bump any knots from the boles. Chop 'em tight and get 'em in the round. The peelers come behind you, and they want them even as a hoe handle. And blunt the butt ends so they'll skid easy."

Tobias nodded and pulled the big brim of his hat over his forehead, on the ready.

"Then you swamp. Swampin's to move branches and brush to make way for the spudders and buckers, and to open skid ways for the teamsters. The spudders peel, the buckers saw the boles to length, and the teamsters' hosses move any logs we can't roll to the bottom. Walk yonder later—" he pointed back the bench, "and note how Hudson cleared skid ways. Keep them straight and pointing at the slide." He threw a thumb over his shoulder.

Tobias shook his head to show he understood, though he was lost, swimming in the compliment of all this trust. Somehow now he added pull to the chain of the operation. And the teams, just how did they get teams up here?

Then thoughts of his predecessor took hold, and he pleaded with himself not to let Hudson's fate—whatever the circumstances—take this moment.

Cowboy concluded with a warning. "And mind your axe, Tobias Meier. The smitty don't stand for a lost axe. And the company don't stand for a dull one. It's your job to keep it sharp—I'd say sharp enough to shave your whiskers, if you had any. Whet it with your soapstone regular. And put it to the grindstone when you get back at night. To Ryder Lumber, a dull axe is slow work. Ryder don't like slow work, and mind you that the team of hosses straggles when just one leg's lame."

Tobias couldn't keep out of mind the broad-caped silhouette of a man aiming a gun, and the morning chill broke through the flush of his uphill hike. But he firmed against that picture—fear would not be what drove him to do good work today. He concentrated on J. Hadley Erhart talking to him as to a man. And he'd mind something else. It had begun trickling to him when he'd hopped off the railcar and breathed the peaty smell of earth drifting from this high ridge where men and horses scoured the ground by moving trees. Work in the woods, like stalking laurels for a bear, made him keen to a cycle, a code other than Ryder Lumber's. He had to match that to weigh into the pulse of the land, the command that gave it order.

Taking up their axes, Cowboy and Billy Gaines faced the big hemlock and started their notch, Cowboy swinging lefty, Gaines righty, woodchips the size of buckwheat cakes firing away. Tobias turned toward fallen trees that still bore limbs, and started off. The thump of the axes gave to the singsong of a saw, and Tobias figured the perfect rhythm of their sawing a sign of decent men, the right sort for crosscutting; he'd heard at the Whitehouse that good sawyers only pulled their turns, never pushed.

It was full light now, but moving among the great wilting boughs of felled trees was like stepping into a boxcar—dark and engulfing. The mint of hemlock needles fended the tang of fresh-cut wood. Overhead, emerald bud tips caught the morning light like so many lamp mantles. He made his way in, along a branch, his steps mute on the undersides of the boughs that had crashed beneath it. In spite of the murk, the pale bottoms of the needles drew the whitening sky; he could have been walking on clouds.

At the bole of the fallen hemlock, he sized a standing branch, a tree itself. The swing of his four-pound axe fell awkward, biting shallow and sidelong into the branch, and inches away from where it knuckled into the tree. He tried again and missed by more. He looked along the length of the trunk. How would he get every branch off this one tree in the span of a summer, much less all the others he was supposed to de-limb just today? He doubted the strength in his back to pull that axe until lunchtime, much less all day, all week. Tobias lifted it and started swinging, mostly to quell his panic. His strokes still sloppy, he concentrated on where the axe should fall. And it fell there, sometimes. Yet it was falling too square, and he knew that wouldn't notch out chunks. He concentrated on also turning the axe head, looking for that rhythm he'd so long imagined he'd have in his swing. But the distraction of two things to think about wobbled his stroke, and tucking his elbows to strike closer, he missed the limb altogether. The tip was at an angle, so when it hit his shin, it glanced off. But he might as well have severed his leg for the pain that shot clear to his crotch and watered his eyes. He squatted and squirmed until the ice started melting out of his skin. He'd bruise to a mound there, and stiffen with a limp by dinnertime.

Tobias leaned the axe handle against his waist as the piercing settled into an ache. He studied the tree limb. "How am I going to swing and think at the same time?" Cowboy had told him to let the axe do the work. He took it up, swung, concentrating on a clean stroke, but not acting on it.

The axe flew smoother, but off the mark. Next time he thought of nothing, just pictured the wedge he wanted to slice out of the crotch of that branch. And the axe swung twice, the bit tilting this way then that, a little chunk of tree flesh popping out. He felt no more effort in the two than he had in his first swing.

There came a rhythm, but it was staccato. He noticed himself driving the head at the end of each swing, and that, strangely, seemed to stop it short of how far it wanted to bite; he wasn't working full on Cowboy's advice. So he let the fall of the axe carry out all the momentum, Tobias nearly letting go, and the bit dug deeper. With each swing, he felt his strength slide through the handle and pour out the head like hot oil, sap spitting, the impact cracking through the woods like rifle fire. The axe was free of Tobias, just a midwife for where he pointed his will. Then he was not an axeman but a tree limber, a knot bumper, moving up the trunk, limb to limb, knot to knot. He was a hand now in the order of the operation.

By the time Tobias finished chopping clean his first hemlock, he'd numbed to the pungency of fresh evergreen sap, and had settled into the chamber-hold of the fallen timbers. When he paused to stretch the muscles around his swollen shin or to move to another knot or limb, his ears perked to the swish and sigh of saws bantering ridge-to-ridge—they sounded as determined in their purpose as gathering wolves. He caught the clinking of teamsters sledging grab hooks into timbers, the rattling of chains, the jingling of mane bells, and logs bumping along the flat sections of slides. And sometimes, in soft rumbles like distant thunder, and other times in slams as jarring as lucky misses, the felling of hemlocks came upon yells of "timber" and crackles of limbs as the trees roared heavy against the earth. Then he'd pick up his axe and get back to work, feeling himself move to the concert of the crew, the thump and rip of his axe adding his beat to the sculpting of Teaberry Hollow, the wail of the woods.

* * *

As the urgency of spring wilted with the last blossoms of dogwood, weariness left Tobias's back. Swinging an axe every moment of daylight, both sides of the noon hour had made his limbs sinewy and his mind spry, a team bred to the moods of the landscape. And his early concerns about malicious hicks had eased—many of the men lived up to his boyhood awe.

Through what was happening to the land, Tobias saw that getting used to something made it smaller. Sure he'd been jolted the first time he worked his way to a cleared ridge and looked across the desolation that had been his woods. But accustomed to the work, Tobias was less shocked than he'd have been otherwise. Anyway, he knew that the advantage of those beaten ridges lay under the sprouting brush. And yet, he began wondering if the plateau deserved more of an upper hand.

Tobias never looked long at the feats of the crews. He was a hick now, and the kind cursed with loving the woods, the might and heavy presence of the shrouding hemlocks, but woods work, too. Such hicks always looked beyond the wake of the saw, strained for some surviving treeline.

At the end of spring, Tobias's responsibilities changed. He'd held his own with the other knot bumpers and swampers, kept up with the fellers and ahead of the peelers, until the cuttings reached the slide, and the cycle of the piece was nearly complete. The trees felled and de-barked, Tobias worked the head of the slide. Time to himself, which he'd come to like, came less often.

"Git, git," snapped a teamster, urging his horses to yank ahead the train of two logs they'd just skidded to Tobias. The pair made one step, and at the teamster's "oh," waited.

"All yours," he said, releasing his skidding tongs from the first of the sixteen-footers. Sharp-pointed, j-shaped grabs were driven into the facing ends of the bare logs and coupled by chains. Tobias pried them out with his crook-ended grab skipper. He leaned it against a stump with his other tools, picked up his cant hook, and with upward thrusts of his body, worked each log across a scaffold of timbers and onto the slide.

"Bout, bout," the teamster said. And his horses swept around, readily as they'd turn for a rattlesnake. The chesty tan Percherons wore chains of ivory rings about their bridles and harness fittings. Tobias liked this show of pride by men who shared their better wages lavishing spoils on the partners that gave them their trade, who spent evenings in the barn bleaching the tarnish of sweat off those trappings, who groomed coats and salved sores, who undressed riggings in the months that horses scratched fly bites against the walls of their stalls.

Tobias had learned the language of each team that came to his slide. There were "hees" and "hoes" or "yips" and "yaws" for left and right; "ohs" or "whoans" for stop; even commands to put them in reverse. And by gruffness or sweetness, the teamster could tell the horses how much to brace up for a particular pull, or to slow down on a descent.

"We nearly cleaned off the top," the teamster said, hooking the log grabs to his horses' drag chains. He was a Scotsman with long whiskers bunched in tendrils like corn tassels, and as quiet-tempered as his Percherons—as were most teamsters. Tobias admired these men, and he guessed they sensed that through their teams, since teamsters cared only to understand horses, not men. He regarded teamsters beyond their privilege of easy walking behind horses. Skill earned their extra dollar a day. And Tobias counted it for a man, not against him, that he smelled like his passion.

Tobias leaned the cant hook against the stump and rested his hip beside it. "What do we do when the top's done?"

"From here to the landing, we keep skidding to the slide. You'll work downward with us." He pointed along the snaking chute of the slide, a trail of side-by-side log halves leaned into a v-shape. It followed the fold of a small side-hollow to logs jumbled at the head of the rails, the cables of a Barnhart loader plucking them to a train. After Tobias made up a string of five logs, horses dedicated to working the slide pulled the rear one, pushing the others ahead. Bump, bump, bump, like the hull of a moored rowboat against a dock. At the final, steep stretch, the logs were sent plummeting.

"Seems the trains keep bullying their ways farther up these hollows," the teamster said. "Times past, we'd have to skid quite a piece to get logs out."

"Ever work the rafts?"

"Never been on a floating operation—log drives, rafts. I worked mostly these parts, and there wasn't much rafting." He shrugged. "And they don't drive logs from up this far anymore."

"Do you think Geet worked the rafts?"

"Don't know," the teamster said, "but I guess he did. He's old as Adam, you know."

Igidius Rakestraw and the history of this logging business crowded Tobias's mind lately. There was something larger here than moving trees.

The Scotsman led his team along the furrow his logs had plowed through the brush and deadfalls. The morning sunlight still fell aslant enough to tinge every layer of thicket. So instead of vanishing into a wall of leafage, the team submersed slowly, diluting by steps from the heart of a lumbering venture into the recovering ridge. The last of the horses to sink into the thicket—their hams—were scalloped and manila-colored like hemp rope, each muscle distinguishable and flexing with its purpose.

Until he'd hear the approaching jingle of mane bells, Tobias could break. So he walked to the base of a spreading and gnarled white oak on a knob that marked the height of the ridge's brim. Anything bold enough to root on that crest fronted prevailing westerlies that whisked on fair days and battered on unsettled ones. In the rawness of that chafed piece of ridge, weather was seeable.

Atop the plateau, the leached soil was sour to plants that took to the valleys—especially sour on edges facing west. Tobias had come to notice the likings of tree types, and compared the handsome straight ones in the bottoms, sheltered from wind and ice, to fair-weather, snow-escaping birds, to people who complained about chill rooms and windy days, whose moods soured at a falling snowflake.

Majestic tulip-poplar and sycamore—trees already green with their big showy leaves—grew in the valleys, never on these windy ridges where spring reached last. This was sandy ground strewn with shards of gritty gray stone, a long-ago broken crust that Tobias had heard was ocean sediment. Moss-splotched pieces lay jaggedly against the trunks and roots of the white oak and of the few other trees, dwarfed and misshapen, that had somehow found footing here. Among these, wiry snags of laurel twisted up like Medusa's hair.

Stout as it was, the oak had been spared of the saw by its ugliness. It resembled in form the scrubby sassafras, pitch pine and bear oak that writhed around it, *waste wood* to lumbermen. Each distorted figure appeared to show the struggle of being sentenced to a stark ridgeline. But Tobias liked to think he knew better—they sought out that place; their figures were their nature: built to cope.

Something about the character of the knoll told him that the energy he felt move through him at times like the bear chase welled from such places. Celts, Tobias once read in a farmer's Almanac, called certain parts *thin places*, where through the earth they connected to a greater power. He'd eyed these twisted and knotty trees during his breaks, and it had occurred to him they were hardier than towering valley sycamores, which rooted into rich loam *because* of their weak nature. The trees up here reminded him of how he felt most alive when he was far from safety. He decided these were handsome trees that sprouted closest to what fed life. They gained their purer beauty not by the depth they rooted to, rather what they reached for, and how there was less to distance them from it in thin places. Some things thrived, he saw, not because of the rain, but the cloud, not because of the sunshine, but the sun.

Hicks had a way of honoring relic trees for standing against time and elements: they named them. This oak they called Old Fatbottom. For certain she was hundreds of years old, and her bottom bustled the way marbles fill a sack. Five loggers could put their toes to the base of Old Fatbottom and barely reach each other's hands.

From her broad haunches up, Old Fatbottom was simply confused on which way to grow—up, out, over, twist this way, send a branch there. The shrewder hicks knew by her outward-stretched arms that Old Fatbottom had always reigned on the knoll, with no other tall trees to compete against.

It seemed hospitable how Old Fatbottom's buttress swelled seat-like, and there sat Tobias. He took in the scrub oaks—digits kinked and knotted, rheumatoid—then the stunted, writhing laurels. All around them, the woods had been worked bare, right down to the bark off the stumps. All but this swath of saddleback. Now what's so barren?

The old-survivor oak put Tobias in mind of Igidius Rakestraw, who too had eluded his axe, and now was not thought much for function.

Tobias looked out where once stood tall and straight hardwoods and hemlocks, look-alike timbers compared to Old Fatbottom. Here she remained to stand over what they'd held. He rested his back against her trunk and believed Old Fatbottom sensed him there. Maybe this timeworn knoll would stay unchanged, a kind of reference point, indifferent to what lumbermen, any men, needed.

*   *   *

"Geet, how is it there were trees cut on this piece before we worked it? I see old stumps. Big ones."

Igidius Rakestraw sat porcelain-still in his chair beside the writing desk, one arm resting on the wooden arm, the other a guide wire to his cane. "White pine. Magnificent trees like you never seen." He creased his eyes and pointed his cane at Tobias. "A pine stump will outlast you. Unlike that sissy hemlock you boys cut—those stumps rot before the bole hits the ground." He replanted the cane.

Tobias well knew what the stumps were, conspicuous from others by their height and gray, worn wood. He'd resolved to ask Geet about his lumbering days; this was his lead-in. The time was right: Saturday night, the camp empty. The transient hicks were off to Marstadt, the locals at home. Tobias lay propped on his pillow, a copy of *Grit* in his hands.

"You don't see white pines big anymore," Tobias said.

"That's because we took them for spars. I'm talking trees shoulders above the rest. Giants. The finest white pines in the world." He stomped his cane. "Those trees stretched a hundred feet beyond your shade-loving hemlocks. Rubbed the sun's crotch at noon. And when it comes to the worth of lumber—" Geet paused, gave the slightest nod— "those pines were straighter-grained than a new nun." He waved his hand at the hemlock roof planks. "Nothing like this devil's wood, riddled with hellfire knots. Top-grade lumber, but for the bottom. Which is why we made our fell cuts high." He lifted his hand over his hat. "And why there's such big stumps for you to wonder at." He dropped his hand and watched Tobias, looking pleased he didn't understand. "See," Geet said, "the ankles of those tall pines cracked and splintered from shifting every which way, what with the winds tossing their tops."

Tobias sat up on his bed. "What's a spar?"

Geet echoed the question, scowling. "Spars were the great timbers for masts and yardarms on clipper ships, the fastest floating vessels in the world." He pointed his cane at Tobias. "You ever seen that kind of ship?"

"Pictures," Tobias said. "Frigates and such in books at school."

"We cut mast spars a hundred and twenty feet long. The might of those ships started in these hollows—the backbones of sails that stood tons of wind at a time." Geet shifted left and right, took a deep breath. "School," he said, shaking his head, then continued.

"Our one log would take six teams of your hosses to skid." A corner of Geet's mouth inched toward a grin. "But we used oxen, propped the spars and logs on skidding sledges."

"But oxen are slow," Tobias said.

Geet recoiled. "Maybe so. But those cloven-foot mounds of muscle were steadier than the pretty dancers your hostlers dress up in ivory rings for their beauty pageants. Not even counting all that finery, it costs half as much to rig an ox—like a man versus a woman. And an ox can wade snow and mud up to his belly."

"But their bellies are lower," Tobias said.

Geet narrowed his eyes, and stared hard on Tobias. "Not ours. They were skinny from working so hard. And long-legged on account of yanking their double shoes out of the mire those big spars made of the skid trails." Geet huffed, and lifting his cane and knocking the floorboards twice, capped the matter. "Consider this. An ox can go two days without water. In summer, you can turn him out to pick a living in the woods. And best of all, if one goes lame or you run low on vittles at camp—" Geet paused, then spoke with quiet triumph— "well, I'd rather eat ox steaks."

"Then, why do you suppose we don't use oxen nowadays?"

Geet looked over Tobias's head, figuring. "I suppose with the timbers getting smaller and times changing, faster's what mattered, sloppy as hosses pull, as many as it might take."

Geet was silent a moment, then said something that made Tobias shift to the edge of his bed. "It's always more and faster in this world. No sooner were the oxen gone, the lumbermen wanted the timber to market quicker than we could float it. So come along your year-round locomotives, took all the work and respect out of logging."

"Respect?" Tobias said.

"In slower days a hick was an all-around woodsman. He didn't need a tree selector to tell a sound bole from a hollow one. And he was as capable felling as he was hewing. He was a calculating man." Geet stared a moment over Tobias's head where underdrawers and socks hung from the timber joists.

"Of course in those days," Geet said, "felling a tree was like aiming a slingshot. These hollows were thick beyond imagination. Pine boughs eclipsed the sun. The only difference between night and day was whether the birds were singing."

Tobias had heard about that primeval forest—a dank tomb of mold and rattlesnakes, daylight no more than a shifting, shadowy murk that oozed through the vaults of swaying needle tops. The Bavarian settlers of Marstadt, arriving back in the forties, found it darker than their forests of home, and wild with wolves. They called the gloom *the shades of death,* and commenced on the spot in a desperate fury of axes to hack an opening to the heavens.

Tobias reached under his bed for one of his corked boots, and checked if its graying folds were dry enough for a Saturday beeswaxing.

Geet eyed the boot. "Shoes were different, too. A river runner's footgear wasn't so fancy, just shoes with nails pushed through the soles. The heads drove into your feet like thorns. Shoes, I say, not boots. That way you could take them off regular and get the sand out, else you'd have bones for feet."

"So you ran rafts?"

"Of course I did," Geet said. "So far we only talked woods work. That was just part of the job. We saw the timbers clear to market." Geet leaned forward and went on in almost a whisper. "It was for the Easter rise that we cut and chopped and skidded. Always there in the back of your mind. In your sleep, you felt the thaw and the rising creeks. All your eating was to get strong enough to stand the cold water. The Easter rise was like a wind, and you were a sail waiting in the fore-calm. Then we drove the logs and built the rafts and ran the rivers in the foulest weather. Not in spite of it—" he slapped his cane against the floor— "but because of it.

"Into the night by the light of torches, we moved the spars and logs into the splash dams of the little waters. The timbers pushed against the dams like penned pigs at feeding time. We called the dams *the gates of hell,* and hell broke loose when we opened them. We prodded the timbers through the chutes with pike poles. Out on the big creek, we'd ride the logs to the groundings to build the rafts, snubbing and prying and rolling and breaking jams, jumping in where needed, freezing our gizzards."

Geet pushed back the lapel of his rabbit-gray coat. His vest pocket squirmed like a sack of mice as his fingers probed. He pulled out an enormous case watch and put it in his other hand. He reached again into the vest pocket and took out a key. The watch turned with tired clicks as he wound it, his jutted-brow scowl not leaving Tobias. Never had Tobias seen a watch that wasn't a stem-winder.

"Hicks lived in shanties on those rafts, even quartered hosses to pull us along the low spots. Barn on one, bunkhouse and dining hall on another, stove and all. Always wet. See, the rafts run below surface, to the knees through the rapids." Geet pulled the key from his watch. "Then after the days of the rafts, we hopscotched down the river working log drives, mill to mill, far as the bay. Smell of sawdust the whole way."

He looked away a moment. "It was when I looked out over the logs that made it clear to the Chesapeake that I realized it all starts here. We feed the world her wood, sure as these hollows give that bay her water." Geet

127

nodded. "After we run to market, we walked back, Tobias Meier. That's hundreds of miles, and there's stories aplenty of what hell we raised in dry trousers with money in the pockets."

Geet put his watch and key back. "You're looking at me like I'm a stick of lit dynamite."

"I never saw a watch like that."

"Goes back to the war."

A Bucktail—Geet could easily have been one—that regiment that floated out on rafts, whitetails pinned to their hats. The First Pennsylvania Rifles. Famed marksmen, feared fighters. Tough backwoodsmen like Geet.

"All that woods work," Geet said, "and the only money we made was in the war."

Tobias knew enough that money and soldiering didn't go together. But Geet went silent, his gaze passing through Tobias, out of the room, the hollow, the new century. Then he raised a brow. "To clarify that matter for you, Tobias Meier, I'll just say that late in the war, some rich folks, including a young lumberman up in McKean County, bought their ways outta the bloodbath. I would'a stayed anyway, so I took his offer. But that money had as much worth to me as Johnny Reb's scrip." Geet's lips pursed as tight as an envelope flap, and Tobias knew that was all he'd hear of the war.

"Geet, do you think a hick can still count on a living of woods work?" The downheartedness about the state of timbering had become chronic in camp.

The old-timer appeared tired, the fire for his glory days fading. But eventually he spoke, and as Geet went on, it occurred to Tobias he was answering his question. "Just as soon as we blew the sin and money outta our trousers, we were back to the wilds. Men scattered off over the years, but it was always the woods for some of us." Geet traced the ceiling to its ridge. "Everything we did moved off with the water, just as these hollows take its shape. But the headwaters were where we liked to be, and our urge was to push back against the current. See, a man's a taker for a thing he can feel but can't see, and there's a pulse in the patter of these creeks. The farther downstream you go into the heavy and slow waters, the fainter it is." Geet nodded. "That made me all the surer of the heart of the beat. It called me back, gave me a way. It all starts here, Tobias Meier—you're closer to something in these parts."

He eyed Tobias. "Things still flow out with the waters, follow their course. We're just a step removed from the rush now."

"So we'll keep timbering, maybe in a different way?"

Geet's head bobbed with a silent laugh. "The water, boy, that's the A of the ABCs. We just don't have our feet in it anymore. But no matter, it's in the hollows here at the start where we still take timbers, however we do it, and coal, and who-knows-what next. Always something, always hauled away with the waters, even if on the railroads that follow them." Geet looked away a second, catching his breath.

"So," he said, "it's always richest here. Richest just as I say the folks are come to work, the ones hardy enough to take on the mean shape and make of a land so raw to the bones of the world. They'll keep on some way or another. And frailer folks on down the waters, on down your rail lines, they'll always be the other kind of rich, thanks to us." Geet leaned forward in his chair. "Look to that when you think of your woods work, Tobias Meier."

Tobias reclined on his elbows. The framework of his world unspooled: springs that fed the little brook outside camp added to the flow of Manooka Creek, feeder to the West Branch of the Susquehanna, heart-river of Pennsylvania and source of the Chesapeake. Port to the world. And the tendrils of uphollow staging track that terminated the Teaberry rail line were linked to the Manooka branch of Ryder's railroad. That was but one artery feeding the great common carriers, which mimicked the waters of the broader valleys to their junctions with the world.

Geet made him see cycles. Timbering meant change to the woods. The things that needed to last were trees, not pines; woods work, not rafting. Tobias felt lucky for crossing paths with Igidius Rakestraw, for seeing and hearing about his pioneer days—now he knew for sure that the pulse of this middle land was as real and old as the flow of its waters.

Tobias would find how he best added to it all. Sure, every job in the woods was important, right down to swamping. But swampers and sawyers smoldered away like wet tinder, off to town jobs, with rheumatoid shoulders and knotted shins. He was sure as April rain he had a temperament for leading draft horses. Maybe he'd start learning from the teamsters, help in the barn mornings and nights.

Then a thought seeped into his mind. Sycamores in the bottoms and black birch on the ridges could not hold against axes just because they grew in their right places. Maybe only odd waste wood was safe from the world downstream finally making of it what it wanted.

Geet dozed in his chair, still rigid, still holding his cane upright. Outside in the last light, a barred owl hooted, gruff and self-assured, as if his woodsy home was yet vast and unbroken.

Chapter 11

The engineer who was too big for ready-made overalls still piloted log trains between the mill and the waning woods work of Manooka Valley. Since the day Tobias had been put on, he'd worked off and on with the man he called Special Orders, whose large and willowy body had taken that sharp turn from life's prime to its early autumn—a gray-edge wilt muting the luster of hair and skin. But Tobias saw an accepting grace in his way of stiffening and slowing, as if it were a new lean in the track to slow-maneuver across. And he found something stable and devout in stalwarts like Special Orders who hadn't moved on.

At twenty-one, Tobias was back home. He hadn't worked from camp for two years, since the day Austin Fritz told his Teaberry crew they had another week to clear landings and draw pay, a day Tobias thought of more the farther he moved from it.

The likes of Cowboy and Billy Gaines had fluttered away, as gone as the hoots of owls that had no trees to perch in. The men's sad, humming songs, their work-earned laughter, their bunkhouse wisdom, all exiled to new timberlands—what there were—Teaberry Hollow bare as a wildfire's wake, quiet as a memory. The pair rode out one day on a flat car for Marstadt where they'd change trains to begin the next search for sawyer work. Tobias hoped the best for them, especially that this wasn't the inevitable step to a town job. Maybe they could hold on for one more turn. He liked to believe they'd found a corner of forest still whirring with saw-song, settled in for a stint, snug as goose eggs. Maybe down among what Cowboy called—with some enthusiasm—the knuckle-topped mountains of West Virginia. That's where Tobias put them in his mind.

But Igidius Rakestraw was different; Tobias knew he was out in some crevice in the plateau, probably at one of the camps still up North. Geet had to hang on here, where he could feel the ground drawing him in—like a lump of mossy humus that had been a mighty tree bole spared the axe, spared that ride downstream.

Four years Tobias put in on the Teaberry job, the last camp-based cutting to feed the Pigeondale mill. Now a few crews took log trains out to work the scattered pockets of smaller hemlock passed up in better times. Or skinny timber for mine props and lath. Even teams rode log cars out. Axe grinding and saw sharpening were handled by the engine shed smitty, the only man of his trade left in Manooka Valley.

That made brakemen of the youngest members of the small crews riding the trains back in, the riskiest of woods work, even more than felling, for unlike a falling tree, shifting logs gave no warning.

"We'll still have daylight when we go down over," Amos Newton said to Tobias's leg; the rest of his body lay under a log car where he sopped grease onto an axle using a wooden paddle he dipped into a tar pot. The business had the sucking sound of bare feet oozing through mud.

Amos was younger than Tobias, in his late teens, squinty-eyed—eyeglasses could cost five dollars a pair. You didn't need good eyesight to be a brakeman, just nerve. The best were agile men with squirrel-sure footing, and Tobias and Amos alone could adjust the stagger of brakes across a sixteen-car train as its weight changed with the grades, the pair holding speed to a horse trot. At least when the tracks were dry.

"And to boot," Amos said, "the load's light. Hell, we oughta just wildcat her in. I could dry my wet ass before we get to the mill. My feet are webbing."

"We needed the rain," Tobias said.

Special Orders made his way toward them, inspecting under every car and checking the tautness of the chains lashed over the pyramids of logs. The crew had been working an island of leftover timber six miles north of Pigeondale on a ridge above Manooka valley. Their return took an hour.

"Don't let the soft load and daylight get you off-guard," the engineer said. "This time of day, that track won't dry. Lock 'em up when we drop."

Tobias swung out from under the car. Before he stood, it took a second to collect all his motions, for he'd grown to six feet tall. His body, he'd noticed lately, had spread in all directions; he was on the solid side of lanky, with big hands and a bread-pan jaw, which—he'd seen in mirrors—stood out like his round, ready eyes—they hadn't changed.

On his feet, he took his hat from where he'd perched it atop a log on the car. He still wore the brim tight over his eyes, but he'd come to fit into the big western.

"I'm going to whistle the crew," Special Orders said. "You boys check the rest of the chains."

*　　*　　*

The load on the string of cars, hulking up out of the trackside brush, appeared as a long row of evenly peaked log piles. But with a huff from the Shay and kerchiefs of smoke shooting from its stack, the pyramids jolted onward. Tobias stood atop the pinnacle log of the foremost car, Amos Newton at the rear. One crewman fired for Special Orders, and four others, not young and nimble enough to brake, rode the tender.

Soon the procession approached the edge of the green matted tableland. Special Orders wanted no braking until the moment the running board at the nose of his locomotive peered where the rails dropped sharply across the slope into the deep valley. He blew the whistle, and it was business hours.

The engine spilled over the drop, and Tobias reached his jillpoke down to the coupling and jabbed hard against the flat pan of the brake lever. As if they'd just crossed a puddle, hisses and steam splashed from the wheels as they locked. He jumped to the second car, feeling fancy in the easy, daylight hop, for once able to see the height of the next top log and not have to fear a drop into that deadly gap. Log to log he cork-clawed as he poked his pole to trip each brake. Amos Newton added drag by setting brakes from the rear. Meeting in the middle, each turned and climbed down to work a brake on one of the sixteen cars—they'd release and add just enough for Special Orders to amble the cavalcade with a half load of steam.

Tobias always gave a soft hoot at the train's urge for speed as its formation got sloppy in the descent, the logs swaying and heaving as they might on river rapids. But working between cars during this part was unsettling. At least it wasn't dark, he thought, crouched on the coupling between the butts of logs. It wasn't the peril of riding the link and pin that storied the woods with gruesome deaths, rather loads shifting forward.

Special Orders was right: light load or not, they had to keep their guard; as they worked the brakes, the fickle wheels sometimes grabbed the damp track quicker than expected, making the descent all jolts and heaves. But they eased the load into the valley intact, and after Tobias climbed up, released all his brakes, and stood again atop the first car, Special Orders gave full steam, the quickening clapping and snapping of the train's wheels especially loud with the attendant squeals and whines dampened by the muggy dusk.

When they slow-chugged past the coal crib and engine shed, sunshine still fringed the clouds behind Tobias. Glancing back, he saw how their splotchy shapes and gaseous bulk looked like the tree fungus locals called sheep's head. The edges, electric orange and lacey, tattled the sun back there, blocked by the heavy clouds, or maybe by now the horizon of the high plateau. The truth of things—always eclipsed by what you saw.

And there was John Blesh. Over the clatter of the train, he called out "Tobias Meier," waving his arms where he stood on the plank in front of his father's office building. He was grinning and shaking his head, and the scene for Tobias turned from arriving home against a sunset to an awkward stance atop logs. The first thing John Blesh always seemed to do was make a person aware of appearances.

Tobias hurled his jillpoke into the tender and hopped down the descending logs onto the plank. He waved goodbye to Amos Newton.

"Still wearing that big-top like some would-be Texas marshal," John said as he shook Tobias's hand and tugged the hat brim over his eyes.

Tobias leaned his head back. John looked where Tobias felt his neck flexing tight against the rim of his undershirt. John's neck squeezed pale and fleshy from a tall collar.

Tobias pushed his hat back. "Home for anything special?"

John snorted. "If Pigeondale ever was home. Tomorrow I see the old man off. I helped him load his drawers of papers onto a boxcar an hour ago. Been waiting for you since."

"I didn't know today was the day." Tobias looked over John's shoulder. The front office window was boarded. His mind went to the day Emory Sundae looked out that window and reported the coming of Celia and J. Hadley Erhart. He realized he and John stood in the exact spot of the picture. Above the building, the clouds had lost their colored outlines— just cotton billows now.

"It's the day, all right, Mr. Woodhick. The mill's down to a shift, and the land's a desert. Not much use for a superintendent here." John tilted his head with a look of mock sympathy. "Won't be much need for hicks, either."

"There's still work," Tobias said. "Ryder left track where there's pulpwood to sell. And there's hemlock still around. You saw what I rode in on."

"Those little sticks mean nothing." John waved it off. "Do you think they'd be shipping my dad up North if there was any future in this operation?"

Tobias had quit listening to speculation on how much time Pigeondale had. From boarding house to barber shop, the remaining hicks and mill workers rumored the town's condition as if it were a sick centenarian: *Can't believe she's still holding on.*

He scraped his corks along a plank and looked at John. "So how's factory work?"

John's eyes, which became more fish-like the older he got, bulged all the farther. "You know I don't do factory work. I'm in the lab. And there's bigger things coming." He adjusted his compact bowler and brushed his square-cut suit coat. "My old man and mother leave in the morning," he said. "How long do you play lumberjack on a Saturday?"

"We cut out early," Tobias said. "Back by four."

John stepped past him, and leapt from the plank to the tracks. Tobias followed, knowing they were off to Pigeondale's one remaining saloon.

"I'm here full of boredom and ideas," John said when they got to the main street's plank. He moved quickly, stepping up the dull drumming of his hardwood heels. Tobias sensed he was trying to make that sound louder.

"The last time I saw you in Marstadt," Tobias said, "you told me there was too much doing there to come out to Pigeondale anymore."

"There is more doing—compared to this place." John lifted his chin at a boarded storefront across the muddy street. A woman leading a child by the hand mistook him and gave a flapping wave. "But I'm thinking well beyond Marstadt. I'm twenty-two years old and got plans. Plans that require a place a lot bigger and work more important than what I'm doing in the lab."

Tobias compared his own plans. They ended at finding work he fit, not finding work that fit his plans. "And that's where being full of ideas comes in."

"Yep." John moved along even faster. Tobias considered how ridiculous the pair must look—a lanky hick trying to keep up with a well-dressed, wall-eyed town fellow leaning his contracted brow toward some urgent matter.

"Ryder and Erhart are out of their league in that business," John said, "and altogether out of their era." He nodded up at the brushy ridge. "It's one thing to be king of the jungle." John stopped. "I keep atop of the trade magazines and papers. Competing today takes shrewd deal making. Not caution." He snorted. "There's more business savvy at my Elk's Club luncheons than in the front office of Erhart Carbon."

Tobias didn't get the argument, but he nodded anyway. John's brow and nose, habitually pinched, softened. "I've been in a situation in that factory that I've been waiting a long time to get out of. I've set my mind on coming up with the way out before I'm back in town Sunday night."

Then John was back to himself, stepping headlong down the plank. "Between now and then," he said, "I need a place with peace and quiet to plan things out."

The Manooka Hotel and Restaurant was the one square structure left among the pitch-roofed, false-fronted buildings clustered along the street. The pair stepped past the ladies' door and into the alcove entrance of the tap room. Cheap pipe tobacco and the tang of sour spittoons leaked through the double doors. Phlegmy cackles and tinkling glasses, too.

Tobias halted John. "So your planning has to do with the factory, right?"

John stepped back from the doors, letting go of a handle. "It has everything to do with it."

"What else do you need on-hand while you plan?"

"Nothing." John thought a second. "Your ears. Booze."

"Then why don't we go where it all started?"

John took a deep breath and looked around impatiently. "The Piebald camp? The place must be a ruin by now."

"It's not. I go out there and stay nights between fishing. Even the big table's still in the dining hall."

John lifted a corner of his lip. "I've come too far in the world to be sleeping on a camp floor."

"Don't have to. There's still bunk frames upstairs. We'd just throw blankets on them."

"We'll see about this," John said. But Tobias could tell the idea interested him, and after John stared at the door handle a second, he shrugged. "With my old man still in town tomorrow morning, I might have him call up a couple horses from some stinky teamster." Then annoyed, as if Tobias had pleaded for it, he said, "All right, knock off in time to get back by noon. By then I'll have horses packed with liquor and every kind of pickled food to be had in Pigeondale. We'll bring in the spirits to help me sift through this mess."

"That's fine," Tobias said. "But I can't get back by noon. We're working six miles out."

"Horseshit," John said. "My old man will make sure that train's in here by noon, half load or not." He laughed. "I'll tell him you have serious drinking to do. He'd believe that about a hick."

*   *   *

In the nine years since the hunting excursion, the Piebald camp had taken on that hollow stare of abandoned buildings. Some of its sheds and stables had been dismantled and railed away by the company; others offered themselves bite by bite to time, a few crumbs of rotting wall jutting among the briar tangles and saplings growing in what had been the camp's muddy yard. Amidst the tall pines and poplars spared for shade stood the barnlike living quarters, shifted now into shrubby skirts of chokecherry, the loin of its tired roof sagging.

They approached from a narrow trail on the rail bed, goldenrod and thorny blackberry switches parting against the breasts of the horses. "Damn," John said, "the place is as close to falling as this nag." He slapped his horse's withers.

"It's a fine camp for our purposes," Tobias said. "And that's a fine hoss."

They hitched their horses to aspen saplings by the kitchen door; it still held to its leather hinges.

Tobias untied two gunny sacks from his horse and set them beside the kitchen step. "Drinking fare," John said as Tobias sifted through the sacks. He found beef jerky and cured sausages bundled in butcher wrap, boxes of hardtack crackers, jars of beets and eggs, horseradish, oysters. The heavier bag held more jars—pickled turkey gizzards, rinds of watermelon, green tomatoes with garlic, turnips with carrots. John unstrapped a large leather case from his horse. As he shouldered it, they grinned at the sloshes and plunges of liquor, the dings of tall bottles.

Inside, the upturned log that had been the butcher block remained in the center of the kitchen. They carried the sacks to the dining hall, then

Tobias went and plucked a handful of ragweed stalks to sweep from the table and benches the droppings and seed hulls left by mice.

The whiskey and gin John pulled from his pack had labels. Tobias took from his own satchel two corked bottles. One contained clear spirits, tinged buttercup yellow. He held it up for John to see. "Honey-sweetened sunshine," Tobias said.

John winced, shivered. "I don't care what you call it. I ain't wasting a good drunk on some backwoods mash that never saw the insides of a barrel."

Tobias shrugged. "You label drinkers don't even know what your whiskey's made of. I sure do." He held the bottle toward the window and grinned through its golden hue. "Honey's the trick. You'd never know this redeye was brewed on a kitchen stove."

John waved him off and tossed onto the table a brick of cheese, so sharp it broke in two. Tobias held up his other bottle, its liquor the purple-black of caked blood, so syrupy it hung to the sides of the neck. "My own batch," he said. "Blackberry brandy."

"Holy shits," was all John said, his buggy eyes locked on the bottle.

By five o'clock they'd slid open what windows remained in the frames, airing the place of the skulking August heft. John poured whiskey into a tin cup, nicked and tarnished as an old nickel, then walked to a window and looked down where he and Tobias had piled slabs nine years earlier. He took a dram and exhausted it with a raspy exhale.

"All this land," he said, "doing nothing." He nodded at Tobias, who sat at a bench he'd pulled tight to the table. "Remember Ryder talking right here about keeping it, as if that might make up for the taxes?" He looked out the window.

"Erhart gave better reasons," Tobias said. "I still think about him saying the land's a lesson for handling business."

John laughed and gestured up the ridge with a lift of his chin. "What kind of business talk is that?" He shook his head. "Pitiful."

"He's scared of getting too far from what made them," Tobias said. "They may be away from it, but they're still working from what they earned here."

"Tobias, times are changing. In a fashion you have no way of understanding. The way of the future has nothing to do with land and logs. The world's moving indoors."

"I see the changes," Tobias said. "But there are cycles. In between busy times, there'll still be woods work to do."

John lifted a corner of his lip. "Like what?"

"Jobbers are contracting pulp wood. And small hardwood for chemical plants."

"Those are dago crews working at slave wages. Tobias, it's time you start moving where the world's heading."

"I have an idea of what I can do." Tobias took a drink of his corn liquor. "I'm saving for a team. I'll buy an empty lot in Pigeondale to stable the hosses, and hire out to jobbers—they sledge their small wood."

John threw his head back and roared. "He wants to be a shit-boot teamster."

Tobias didn't take it as an insult. John could be coarse, but he had a perspective on things Tobias would hear out. John was in a position to see a lot farther in this world.

"You think you're going to make a career out there?" John said.

"It's what I do."

"What you do? Let me tell you something, pal—it's a little secret for success. You don't just take up what you do. All the things you want determine what you do to get them."

Tobias squeezed the rim of his cup, looked into it. "What I want and do are the same to me."

"Holy hell. You really take this shit seriously. You'll stay out here in what was woods and maybe get by. And that'll be good enough for you."

Tobias pinched the brim of his hat and rocked it up and down. "I'm at ease out here." He shrugged. "We have different problems. I know where I want to be but maybe can't stay there." He searched John's face for what was missing in that. But John just showed a smirk of superior insightfulness.

"No," John said, "this is your problem: you've never been far enough to know what's to be had in this world."

"I go in and kick around Marstadt with you enough."

"Marstadt's nothing. Just a stepping stone to real cities where a man doesn't look out of place in a forty-dollar suit that tells people he's in a position. There's a world out there you can't imagine. Places I've been. Buffalo. Pittsburgh. One of these days, New York." He huffed. "And you want to wear this place like a harness."

"From what I hear, there's not so much freedom in a town job."

"Bullshit. There's money, security and prospects, and that, Tobias Meier, is freedom. Beyond that, there's a world where people take automobile tours, a place of dinner parties and restaurants that serve fine foods you couldn't pronounce, where bottles of wine have their own histories." John set his cup on the wide plank of the windowsill. He stepped to the table and shook a jar until a pickled egg bobbed out of the beets. He popped the whole egg into his mouth, then took a piece of jerky back and leaned beside the window, moving the egg to his cheek where it bulged like a third walleye. He tore a bite of jerky and slaked it with his whiskey.

Tobias could feel the liquor working—not to the point of clouding his thinking, but enough for him put down the gates of reserve. He was where ideas started swimming like liquid music, and his tongue wanted to hum along. He grinned. *Bottle barding,* hicks called it. He just about had himself convinced John would understand if he told him of the belonging he felt when he had an axe in his hand and a checked shirt on his back. But through the haze of the alcohol, he checked himself—maybe this was an important warning, maybe there really was something to the kind of freedom John spoke of. And that held Tobias to saying only this: "Yeah, I have less here, but I feel like I have more—given where I am."

He watched John, eager for his take. But John's eyes were downcast. The room got bigger and quieter, and when Tobias saw how embarrassed John was at those words, he wished the place would keep on growing, until he was but a crumb on the floor. It was true, though, and staying on had been comfortable, a momentum as inevitable and necessary as the chattery flow of Piebald Run—for sure, no one would second-guess its purpose of carving a hollow into the plateau.

John turned away. He leaned his nose to where it almost touched the window, and his head swept upward with the drama of the steep hollow, until his neck craned for the ridgeline. "All that was woods. Wasteland now, what with the trees gone."

"That land holds something even better than timber," Tobias said. "It's got what makes timber. There's ridges too rocky for trees to grow, but they do because they reach under stone for what accounts for growing. That's still there. Just look at the new oaks poking out of that brush."

John shook his head at Tobias, snickered through his nose. "In a factory, you'd get steady pay, not be at the mercy of the earth." He raised his brows and grinned. "And in town, you'd have women to choose from."

Tobias uncorked his bottle and filled his glass. "People are like bears. They find each other no matter where they are."

"But the pickin's a hell of a lot better in town. And there are things to spend your money on—shows at the opera house, dances." John looked deliberately at Tobias's open undershirt and suspenders, yanked at his own starched sleeve, then stretched his neck and stroked the flap of his stiff collar. "You can buy decent clothes. Have meals out, with company to treat."

Tobias grinned.

John stepped to the table, poured whiskey, and took a heavy swallow. "Uhrrr," he said, rubbing his breast. "Just look at what I've already got." He paced the floor, hands linked behind his head, elbows out. "My own rooms. I dine out every night, call on two, three ladies a week. And their fathers are as eager to see me as the girls are." He put his hands on the table and leaned toward Tobias.

Tobias thought of girls he visited in Pigeondale, bashful teenage daughters of mill men, limbs clubby, hands laundry-rough, girls with jaunty face bones and teeth they hid with pinched lips when they smiled. The idea of having extra appeal to a young lady because of his job was foreign. John, in his white shirt and tailored pants, was looking less ridiculous. Tobias mulled the power of a man's situation.

"Erhart is grooming me for big things," John said. He put his hands on the windowsill, and gazed up the steep of the hollow. "But I haven't shown him half of what I'm capable of. I'm a crouched cat, and my time to lunge is at hand." Tobias heard John's words exciting him, his voice charged as if narrating someone else's drama. "I can feel it—the world's calling me to move with it, to get out from under—" He stopped.

"From under what?" Tobias said.

Rarely a moment passed that John did not fidget: a hand turning a pen knife in his pocket, an elbow slow-rocking like a wing, a leg shaking, a shoe tapping. But now he became still, looking at the slope of the hollow. Tobias followed his stare, the window frame animated with the waning day's burgeoning bird song and the last liquid sunshine spilling into the bottomland, gilded gnats floating in it like slow fizz.

Must be something out there, Tobias thought. Deer? Bear? He whispered to John. "What do you see? A hawk?"

John held still, then shook his head, a grin unfurling across his face. "I'll be goddamned," he said. "What I see is my way out." He stepped to the table and grabbed a bottle, his eyes scanning the walls, his head bobbing yes to some new vision. He topped his drink and circled the room. "Why the hell didn't I think of it before?"

"What?"

But John continued parading the room, stopping again and again at the open window and putting his head through it to look back and forth, as if sizing the floor of the hollow. The only thing that kept him in the moment was the tin cup he sipped from.

Tobias poured from his own bottle. At the sound, John turned on him as if he'd spotted a game bird in a hawthorn copse. His gape had the feel of a predator. Then a dawning settled into John's distended eyes. He smiled and closed them, and laughed as mischievously as ever. "You *are* my man, Tobias Meier." He slapped Tobias's back. "And I'll be goddamned if that ain't the bonus on top of this place. Which is a camp, after all."

Tobias looked around the room. "Yes," he said, frowning at John's inventory of the obvious.

But when John went to the window, the way he grinned told Tobias that the place had become something else in his mind. It was a look he'd seen when John got determined and extra sure of himself, when he spoke of a woman or watch he was after. Tobias smelled John's love of the new and widely wanted. Which sounded alarms for things vulnerable. A ruby-eyed pigeon looking back at a boy fishing came to Tobias. The tall, blight-fighting chestnuts of Fiddlers Flats. Old Fatbottom and her contorted companions. There was a thread knitted through certain things, an ancient gossamer spanning past the ends of the earth and reaching high as Olympus, and something in John's eyes was sharp and menacing enough to sever it.

It was dusk. A band of crickets rasped a perfect accompaniment to the cloudy lull the drinks cast. Occasionally, tree frogs cranked like trunk hinges from the few tall, crooked trees that remained in the hollow.

John was back to walking around the tables, and Tobias guessed he swayed as much from musing at the ceiling, arms folded, as from the liquor. He stopped every few laps for a swallow from his cup and a grinning glance out the window.

"There's an old coot," John said, "name of Groeger. Works in the lab."

Tobias took a bite of hardtack as he eyed John.

"He lives outside town in a camp at the edge of a field."

Tobias set the hardtack on the table.

"Invites people out for parties Saturday nights." John stopped and turned to Tobias. "Why don't you come out next week?"

Tobias looked where the white light of dusk tried to push through the window frame.

"There'll be town women," John said.

"You say it's a camp?" Tobias said.

"You couldn't call it much else. Just a clapboard shack out in the country—like some bandit's hideaway."

"I'll go."

Chapter 12

From down on the wagon road, the bustle around Ernie Groeger's camp at the edge of the high field looked like sheets snagged and windblown in the brush. Tobias started up a path through a plot of mown wheat, stepping between ruts from horseshoes and the wheels of wagons and motorcars, all parked where the field leveled in front of the camp. As he approached, there must have been a hundred people staring back.

Because he knew coal ash covered his coat, Tobias had been careful to keep it away from his shirtsleeves. He'd walked two miles out of Marstadt after jumping from the tender of the afternoon bark train. He wondered if his face was sooty as his coat, even though he had wiped it with his hanky. He wished he had a horse, and not just because of the coal ash—it would have saved him the sweaty walk from Marstadt, out into this wrinkled quilt of sixty-acre wheat and cornfields, potato and cabbage patches, bitter land bent on bearing forests, but tamed by the outcast Bavarians. Unforgiving, it forever produced the fieldstone he'd seen heaved into piles pimpling the fields, or dragged to the toppling rows that bounded pastures from plow furrows, that rubbled the woods borders.

Close to the party and all the more stark in the field, Tobias took in the crowd and found a little comfort; his tan trousers and straight tie fit in with other men's clothes; he'd tried to dress as he knew town fellows did for casual, sportive affairs. No one else wore a vest, but in the woods he'd gotten used to one, and it had helped save his shirt.

John Blesh rushed out of the crowd and called Tobias's name as a mass introduction. He pinched Tobias's sleeve and tugged him in among staring, grinning faces. "From the backwoods of Manooka Valley," John said, "we have the honor of a bona fide woodhick."

Tobias heard laughs. Still he squeezed his lips into a smile and started touching his broad hat brim. But he let his hand drop when he picked up comments. "Marshal," he heard behind him. Then, "Where's his lasso?" John still pulled at his shirt, leading him around the camp, and a few catcalls came from farther in the crowd.

Though John might as well have seared a brand onto Tobias's forehead, not everyone took enough interest to shade and squint eyes against the low, late sunshine. That kept Tobias in tow, stopped him from heading fast for the corn stalks out across the mown wheat.

Taking quick glances as they walked along, Tobias saw how his hat made him a pear in a bushel of apples. All the other men wore either dapper bowlers or straw boaters with wide velvet bands.

When they'd gotten alongside the camp, John stopped and turned. "In between the everyday Marstadt Krauts, a few of these people are worth knowing. Bankers, a couple lawyers, and a fellow on his way to the top at the Pennsy. That's without mentioning some sons and daughters of Marstadt's better bred." He winked. "And lots of daughters, otherwise." John looked up at Tobias's hat and shook his head.

Tobias looked around and focused on the daughters. He conjured resolve to meet just one tonight, trusting they weren't all chatting him up as the token woodhick from Pigeondale.

He wasn't used to young ladies acting so casually. Most gathered in their own groups, but a few pairs mixed with fellows, and here and there a single girl stood with a circle of men. They each held a glass of beer. And never had he seen women look back so boldly. When they did, he felt them grinning at this outsider.

These women were daunting by their clothes as well, wide skirts and v-cut bodices of cascading frills—mostly floating white moths, but tans and baby blues here and there. Most hats spanned big around as table platters, heaped with dried flowers and feathers. Tobias had only known fashion from the few ladies he'd seen across streets in Marstadt, strolling the walks. The deeper details had come to him through well-traveled woodhicks: doctor-detested corsets, the deceit of bosom-padded bodices. Women that he knew, the women of mill men and woodhicks in Pigeondale, were utilitarian in their dress—flannel petticoats and camisole underclothes the only garments he could account for rounding out body shape. Here, up close, something called out from these tightly packed figures. The more confined they were, the more they seemed to shake their cages.

Nevertheless, he'd seen enough in town to notice in these clothes new liberty. What used to be stiff and contrived by whale bone and wire formed truer to the body now, mere elastic supporting the corsets; busts protruded freer to form, the roundness of feminine stomachs hinted itself.

"I don't suppose you'd know a soul here," John said.

"Nope."

John smiled all around at the crowd, tipping his head upward at the men, raising his brows at the ladies. He made the party feel like it was happening thanks to him.

"What about the fellow living out here?" Tobias said.

"The old coot's in the shack." John started toward the back of the camp, past a large and loud group at the corner of the building, the men coatless and slouchy, their shirtsleeves rolled. John grinned at them, his eyes making it seem as if at each person individually. Tobias couldn't keep from his habit of pinching the tip of his hat brim as he nodded face to face. The fellows turned quick grins at the giggling ladies.

As for it being a camp, the place was not as rough as John made it out to be. Most woods shanties that Tobias knew—ones used by hunters or occupied by backwoods folks—were built with just slanted shed roofs and see-through slats for walls. But this was a sturdy cigar box with a gable roof. It sat up on chunky fieldstones just far enough off the field that this Groeger fellow could probably shoot foxes and groundhogs for the farmer. Which probably explained the narrow, banister-less porch out front that looked over the wheat field. Lots of squatters earned a plot and all the privacy they wanted in return for keeping varmints at bay, handling a few chores and keeping out of the way. Probably a still around somewhere, too.

The camp's outside walls were unpainted hemlock slabs, mill castoffs in odd sizes. They'd weathered to a thousand brownish hues, some so rich they were more orange, all richly grained. Up close to the back wall a couple lean-tos kept firewood dry, and under the building's shored floor, wooden casks lay on their bellies—all the Bavarians were apt to make home brew. Behind the camp, the lot sloped slightly uphill to woods, patches of crabapple and sumac taking hold in between. Near the treeline, a group of men with rifles were arranging themselves in a row. Tobias lifted his chin.

"They're getting ready to compete," John said. They started toward them. Groups had gathered across the two-acre yard, which was dotted with ash piles from old campfires, and stumps splashed with limey whitewash. The yard leveled toward the treeline where the men with rifles stood at a rope pulled between two stumps. Some of the shooters wore suits, but it eased Tobias to see a few in overalls and shirtsleeves. Likely farmers. He recognized one of the Butsch brothers from Manooka Valley. Men were throwing boasts about their marksmanship, nodding into the woods toward clusters of tobacco cans, cigar boxes, whiskey bottles and jars, one bunch to each of the ten.

"Everyone's allowed seven rounds," John said as they reached the line of shooters.

Tobias counted seven targets for each man and sized the distance. About fifty yards, no more. "Easy enough at still targets," he said.

John snorted. "Kind of cocky, Meier."

Tobias just looked at him. "What's the prize?"

"No prize necessary, old buddy. Every fellow here knows the ladies like steady hands and a slow trigger."

"Well, that's good shooting in a word."

"That's good something else," John said. He shook his head at Tobias, an extra bulge to his eyes. People were moving from the front of the camp to the back yard. John turned slightly to face approaching spectators, lifting his chin at men, smiling at ladies as he reached for the top of his straw boater. He put Tobias in mind of a man outside a polling place.

Tobias looked down across the yard, the throng entirely anonymous. But out of it a figure called his attention. Not someone looking at him, rather walking through the crowd; a girl who seemed to rise from the rest of the chattering white-frilled moths just in how she carried herself. She disappeared into the party as fast as she'd stood out from it, but that had been enough to be sure of this: what struck him had nothing to do with her person, instead some subtle thing in her stride. He could read that she wanted him, at least someone in particular, to catch sight of her. How did he understand an intention in just a glimpse?

John looked where he stared. "It's chickens."

"What?" Tobias said.

"The old coot has chickens cooking over there." John nodded where a smudge of smoke swayed above the side of the camp.

"I wondered what that was," Tobias said. "Does he spit them?"

John laughed. "No. Balls them in clay—feathers and all—and throws them in a pit of coals he covers with planks. They come out hardboiled as bowling balls. We crack them with a mallet and they open like chestnuts. The chickens fall out bare of feathers as my ass."

"Heard of it," Tobias said.

His mind went right back to the girl. Something in that walk he'd known before, steps not to the tune of their place. By a newly stirred power that surprised him as much as the girl had, he believed that it was to him she'd signaled, and she didn't even know it yet. That both allured and repelled Tobias. It was as if he deciphered regions beyond the range of his senses, like that ghost sound dogs answer to when a whistle blows silent.

Someone called "fire," and gunshots cackled like splitting pine boards. Up among the trees a few bottles fell to pieces, and tin cans and cigar boxes tipped. Hoots, laughter and yells followed the last shot.

"What accounts for this guy keeping house out here?" Tobias said.

"He's that kind of Kraut that wants to be alone. When he does want to talk, he can do it in his own tongue with the farmers out here. Plus he's ugly as hell."

"But he has parties."

"Free food and booze is the answer," John said. "Ugly as he is, the only time he's at ease is when he's good and corned up."

"So he's one of the Bavarians."

"Yeah. But not a direct import. He's the one Hoehn brought up from Pittsburgh—thinks he's some genius. But the old coot's got them duped." John nodded with a sideways grin that said *trust me*. "I heard there's a tale to him leaving Bavaria. But he's no different from those backward Krauts in town. They all act like they got something due, thinking they got a short deal on that Luther business." He shook his head. "And now here they are, flocked in the middle of nowhere because they won't be lickfingers to their own people in Baltimore and Boston. All because of religion."

"I know their story," Tobias said. "They just want left to their ways. And they say this is country a lot like where they come from."

"I say too much cabbage got to their heads," John said. "Look at that crew over there." He pointed to people crowding the shooters. They shouted questions up to the scorers who were counting aloud the casualties among the bottles and cans. "Serious as doctors," John said. "No feeling in their nasally talk. Automatons without smiles, they are, faces firm as the baked clay on those chickens." He stiffened his neck and mouth. "He's struck three bottles and one box, Alfred." Then he turned his head and pretended to banter back, his expression blank: "Nice shooting."

John snorted. "When they talk to you, you feel like you have to reach over and contort their faces with the words. And beer. Look at them suck it in. It's either in their blood or they're too damned stone-faced to look drunk. What the hell are they made of, yeast and hops?"

Tobias believed he knew what they were made of. But he didn't offer it up; he doubted John would see it.

"I have to get out of this place," John said.

One of the men near the rope called for shooters. "Last winner got four of seven," he said.

"You shooting?" Tobias said.

"Hell no. I'm not mixing with that bunch."

"But you said the women like it."

John rolled his eyes. "Yeah, some of these local girls think it's big."

The Butsch brother walked up to Tobias. "Go up and show them what the boys from Manooka Valley can do, Meier." He held out his rifle, muzzle to the sky. Tobias looked it over. A Winchester carbine, like his own, like anybody's in Pigeondale. Most folks would shoot mark with a .22—the bullets were so much cheaper. But a Butsch from Manooka Valley shot what he had, anybody from Manooka Valley, for that matter. Tobias shook his head, not wanting to put himself any closer to the center of attention.

"I'd owe you for the shells," Tobias said.

"Seven shells on me," Butsch said. "Just do with them what I know you woodhicks can do. What I heard *you* can do." He handed the gun to Tobias and reached into his pocket for bullets. Tobias pointed the gun to the sky and looked across the barrel. The comb of a stock against his cheek sparked that ancient exhilaration that tuned nerve with muscle; it surged all through him, steadied his hand, sharpened his eye. Something bold in him said he should do right by the big hat and woodhick saunter.

"Give me ten shells," Tobias said.

"You're only allowed seven shots," Butsch said.

"Doesn't matter. I need ten in there."

Butsch grinned. He fished out three more shells.

Tobias put the shells in his pocket. Starting toward the rope was like tripping onto a stage, all around him heads tipping, hands to mouths. But the rifle in his palms had the comforting fit of his old corked boots, and he tried to put his mind to calculating the Butsch boy's size for how the sights would fit his aim. He glanced around and saw girls' eyes following him, noticed something less scornful in those smiles. And he could hear John all of a sudden walking behind him, probably gathering what scraps he could under the excuse of getting a better view of his friend. The playful grins made Tobias think of the girl he'd glimpsed, then of hen grouse he'd watched in springtime woods, begging notice by feigning broken wings, how they were casual in slighting the very ones they wanted to see them, to stay away from their clutches. A ploy for something more than passing attention.

He stood at the rope and loaded the chamber and magazine, given over to that keenness that came when he hunted. His will focused, body tuned. He did not yet need to concentrate on the targets, did not want to.

"Fire."

The gun came home to his shoulder, his big and slender fingers canvassing the for-end and bracing the grip. His cheek nested on the sweet spot of the stock, and as the front bead suspended in the crotch of the iron sight, tin can number one came into the other end of a familiar tunnel where there was nothing but gun, target and will. And in that instant he passed the limitations of his body, to a place where he could focus on three objects at once. And he'd do it seven times over, oblivious that between his determination to hit his mark and it falling, a gun fired. The butt of the stock never left his shoulder; he aimed, shot, lever-ejected, fluid and lethal as quicksilver. In his periphery, the others were lowering their guns to eject, raising them to sight their targets, pausing to concentrate. Tobias shot on like a machine, the gun a seven-pack of firecrackers and he a man who could hold them steady in his hand. No one in the crowds that had formed at the ends of the rope watched the targets or the other shooters. And even they, before re-aiming their guns, turned to see him. Finally, when the last to take his seventh shot lowered his rifle, somebody down by the camp let out a cat screech, uncorking a crescendo of yells, whistles and hoots for the big-hatted hick.

Tobias did not immediately realize the cheers were for him. He just tugged on his hat brim to block the setting sun while he looked down the line, waiting for someone to go check the shooters' marks. Though he knew how many he'd hit.

"I seen him load ten shells," a suited shooter from the earlier volley yelled as the cheers tapered into the buzz of people asking about the hick from Pigeondale.

"I watched him shoot," someone along the line hollered back. "I counted seven shots. Seven's all he took."

Another yelled, "You can't count that fast," drawing laughter.

"Or that high."

"And seven's how many targets he hit." This came from one of the men checking the targets.

"Bullshit," said the man in the suit. He was starting toward Tobias, looking very sure of himself. "What in hell did he load ten for if he wasn't going to shoot them."

Tobias knelt on one knee, facing all the people bunched near the rope. He pointed the muzzle toward the ground and worked the lever slowly, ejecting three shells.

"Well, he was bound to cheat." The suited shooter turned back into the crowd. "You can see he was gonna try."

Tobias shook his head side to side, slowly, and stood.

When Farmer Butsch walked up, Tobias handed him his rifle and shells, the seven empty cartridges, too.

"You don't owe me any shells, Meier. I just made enough in bets off'a you to buy a crate of brass." When he stepped away, he turned his head. "You loaded them extra three so the gun had the heft you like, didn't you?"

Tobias just grinned.

He assumed everyone was looking at him because of the controversy over the shells. That, he just wanted over. He looked for John. Most of the people staring were fair-skinned Bavarians. And there she was, deep-set eyes, shaded, drawing him in, and that instant it awakened in him that he'd been waiting a long time to see that person. It was as if a moment he'd always sensed would arrive had just been announced, and at the announcing, an old notion took its shape in a person. Something he was absolutely positive of, yet surprised by, the way that first stirring in a womb must feel.

He took in the face. Dark too, especially among all the others. Exotic. The contrast of her against that crowd made him think of hunchback Quasimodo's tambourine girl. But tricks or not, this was no dancing gypsy girl.

As the familiarness of her came to him, stronger than before, he realized she was standing beside John Blesh. Tobias walked to them.

"Seems you're suddenly great shakes around here," John said. He watched Tobias and the girl eyeing one another. "Cassandra, this is Tobias Meier. I invited him out here."

No impulse came to Tobias to pinch his hat brim. He just tipped his head and smiled.

She nodded back. Up close, the eyes were deep and shadowed as at a distance.

"Tobias," John said, never so polite, "this is Cassandra Erhart."

"That was some shooting," she said.

"He can get a lot of practice," John said. "He lives in the hinterlands."

Polite or not, John was going to take his own kinds of shots.

"Where are you from?" Cassandra said.

"Pigeondale."

"When he's not in some logging camp," John said.

"You work in the woods, then." Cassandra canted her head, and in a glance so quick that Tobias wondered if he'd seen it, she took him in, up and down. He could tell her words echoed something she already knew, though, and she did not seem at all repulsed.

He nodded. "I'm a woodhick. I work on a Ryder crew."

"My grandfather."

"I gathered that," Tobias said.

"It must be dangerous work."

Tobias smiled. "We don't think about that much."

John touched Cassandra's elbow and looked toward the camp. Most of the crowd had fragmented that way. "Let's go see how the food's coming along."

But Cassandra ignored him. "My father says, 'The earth shakes and thunder rolls' when those trees fall." She laughed up at Tobias.

"Tobias aspires to be a teamster," John said, still speaking politely, but with a saw tooth edge. "You know, following lathered horses through the woods."

Tobias shook his head. "A teamster works alongside, not behind—that's where the log is."

Cassandra tilted her face the other way, into the brighter western sky, and it broke the shadows so Tobias could see clearly that her eyes were the same brown as her mother's. Into the moment flashed the picture of Celia Erhart taking on eternity through a camera lens on the plank in Pigeondale, those nine years ago.

"I've heard talk of woods work all my life," Cassandra said. "It's something I'd love to see."

It was not what Tobias would have expected from the daughter of the Erharts. And what was she doing out among this group?

He caught her looking at his woolen vest, the one he'd picked because it was the least frayed, at the folded cuffs of his pants, and then up at his crossed forearms. Before he'd shot, he'd rolled his sleeves past his elbows, and her manner of looking at his arms made him conscious of the long and muscle-braided shape of all his body. He put his hands in his pockets, looked away.

"Seeing serious woods work in a Ryder operation," John said, "would take a long train ride these days. How 'bout it, Tobias?" He chuckled and slapped Tobias's shoulder, and the big hat shifted sideways. It was easier to take John's pessimism when he was himself.

Cassandra just smiled while Tobias fixed his hat.

John pointed toward the camp. "Look at that—the crazy coot's crawled out of his lair."

The twin-plank door was opened to the back yard. On a stack of fieldstone that made for a step sat Ernie Groeger, rubbing his face with the palms of his hands.

"Tobias's quick shots probably woke him from a drunken dream," Cassandra said.

When Groeger dropped his hands, Tobias saw even at a distance that beneath his slouch hat he was as gray as his sandstone seat, that the sockets of his eyes were ashy pits.

"Let's go see how sober he isn't," John said.

"We'd hardly get any sense out of him sober, let alone drunk," Cassandra said.

As they started away, Tobias thought of how she'd forced casual familiarity into those words, of how she tilted them and her eyes his way, as if to vouch she was indeed part of this scene.

Groeger looked out from his perch with no special interest in any group, not even the one approaching.

"Ernie," John said, "what woke you, the gunshots or the bed vermin?"

Groeger just kept looking on. "I woke because I was thirsty."

"I've got a hick here from Pigeondale. Tobias Meier."

Groeger stared up at Tobias with his one black eyeball, expressionless, the whole face dead as its scarred half. Tobias looked from the good eye to the other—yellow, doughy, brow-less. He searched for the lead speck John said was a shot-shell BB.

Groeger put out a hand. They shook without speaking, and Tobias could feel every bone—a fistful of tinder.

"I hear there's lots'a eels in the crick that runs through Pigeondale," Groeger said.

"Not anymore," Tobias said. "Something about the water's changed."

John grinned at Cassandra. "Everything's a dying breed out there, woodhicks and all."

But she tilted her head at Tobias, her lip and brows inched up in a way that conveyed that's so sad. "Anyone who's done such hard and dangerous work," she said, "could find a situation wherever."

Tobias went to thank her—it was comfortable how she spoke of a solution, not a problem—but he caught Groeger studying her. He looked on guard, a gaze as plain as his scars; something in her words or manner, he did not trust.

Cassandra had been clearly snubbing Groeger; it was obvious he repulsed her. But for a silent moment, she glared at him; she did not like that he looked at her, or at least that he looked at her like that. Then she drew back into the dark places of her eyes.

Tobias tried to resurrect her goodwill with a smile. Maybe he misread all this language of looks, maybe it was Groeger's odor that offended the lady, that cider scent he'd come to know among backwoodsmen.

John caught the smile. "Tobias thinks of the wilds of Pigeondale as home," he said, still polite. "Fancies he can spend his life there."

"It's the place I know, John." Tobias usually gave John's bullying the benefit of more experience in the world, but he'd never felt freer to shoot back. "Some things I just like about out there." He looked away, up the slope of the yard to the treeline. A few people in small groups watched him—still talking about the quick-shooting hick. "There's a different face to the land there." He looked back. "You just don't see that like I do."

"Face," Cassandra said. She deliberated. "That makes me think of people—what they're all about shows in looking at them. I know an Italian from a Swede in a glance."

"It's kind of like that," he said.

"Careful," John said, and looked around. "You could be saying you look like your place." John's laugh begged Cassandra to join him; they'd already been in cahoots, smirking sarcastically when Groeger had spoken. But Cassandra turned to Tobias for his say.

He shrugged. "Could be that a certain person searches out a kind of place. At least hears something in it."

John held down his straw boater as he lifted his chin and roared.

But Cassandra did not laugh. Nor did Groeger. The stare of his probing eye lay now on Tobias. "I know about that," he said. And Tobias feared Groeger was talking about his own marred shape. Really though, he had not struck Tobias as hideous. Groeger held his head with dignity. There was grace—despite the crusty appearance—in how he sat and watched quietly. That somehow veiled the deformity of his face; with Groeger there showed more person than appearance.

Tobias took in the scars, the scant hair of half the mustache. Definitely not logger's pox; he'd seen enough mutilated men working the woods to recognize where boot corks had torn flesh. These ridges and dimples, the mangled flesh left of an ear—he'd never seen anything like them.

"The sun moves over some places just so," Groeger said, "and the color and smell there fit me better. That's what you speak of, Tobias Meier. I know the thing you say."

John laughed. Cassandra looked around, unsure, then laughed with him.

"The face of a place ain't going to feed you," John said, then pointed across the mown wheat and canes of corn that had faded gray-green in the dusk. "Unless it's got potatoes or a factory on it."

Torches of kerosened cressets glowed against the new, bluish twilight closing on the party, and a bonfire of tree limbs was drawing a crowd in the yard. Its blaze already made shadows against the camp. Despite the firelight, the nooks of Cassandra's eyes were still idle black gaps where Tobias could read nothing. So he reasoned by her willingness to listen that she understood him.

A man walked up to Groeger and handed him a quart-sized mug of beer. "Thanks," Groeger said. As the man stepped away, he slapped Tobias on the shoulder. "You're the talk of the party, sharpie."

Groeger looked hard on Tobias, his one eye probing like a blind man's finger. "You'll make a home of a place so long as it's right." He looked at John. "No matter what the rest say. Think about this, Tobias Meier."

John's hand shot into the air. "But how can he be sure another place isn't more right if he's never been there?"

Tobias rolled his eyes. What was John up to, why was he even in the presence of a man he hated? The polite tone Tobias could explain; the daughter of J. Hadley Erhart stood there. The rest didn't match John's impatience.

"How does Tobias know," John said, "a place like a carbon factory isn't right if he's never been there?" He looked face to face. "As just an example."

Groeger stopped gnawing his cigar and squinted his good eye at John.

"Maybe he'd like it," John said.

"Would you want to work at Erhart Carbon?" Cassandra said.

Groeger clapped his hands together. "Carbon work's not for everyone. It's in the blood of some men only."

"But if the woods work in Pigeondale is moving out," Cassandra said, "maybe you should consider it."

What bothered Tobias wasn't that the same old harping came now from Cassandra Erhart, rather how she just muddied what he'd made of her. Or maybe she was just being polite to John. Tobias smiled in appreciation of her concern.

John moved closer to Cassandra and touched her arm. "That's something I'd like to handle," he said.

"What should you handle?" Tobias said.

"Yes, John," Cassandra said, "what are you saying?"

John looked toward the bonfire. "Well," he said, long and drawn. "It's time I gave Tobias some advice. Do him a little favor."

Groeger had been back to working his cigar, following the exchange. He clinched the wad of tobacco under the straggly half of his mustache, and sucked from his mug with the good side of his lips. Tobias saw in Groeger his same suspicion.

"What's on your mind?" Tobias said.

John took a cigarette and a box of matches from his shirt pocket. "I think factory work is the way to go." He struck a match and drew it to the cigarette, the flame magnifying the bulge of his eyes. "Don't wait until you have to find something," he said. "I can get you in at Erhart Carbon."

A surprising warmth rolled into Tobias at the prospect. He looked to Cassandra. "I suppose I could be missing something." In Tobias's periphery, Groeger's cigar froze between his lips. Tobias glanced at him, lifted his shoulders.

"Thatta boy, Tobias." John smiled all around.

"If my father knew your situation," Cassandra said, "he'd give you the next opening at the factory. All it would take is me passing the word."

John held up his hand. "Why don't you let me do the talking to your father. I have an idea for Tobias. It's going to take me just a little more time."

"Not necessary," Tobias said. "No matter how I decide, I'll do fine myself."

"Nonsense," John said. "Just wait and see what I cook up."

Groeger shook his head at John, then said to Tobias, "Careful of who pulls your bridle."

"Well, since you and Tobias share all those special feelings," John said, "maybe he bleeds black carbon, too. Maybe it's you that ought to bring him on board." John took a step toward Groeger, who stared past him at the bonfire. "C'mon Ernie, you're the big carbon man, keeper of the secrets you lock in your trunk. You should be recruiting young help. You and Tobias would make a good pair. Never know, Tobias may one day be your apprentice."

The cigar in the folds of Groeger's rag face became still, and his good eye went straight to Tobias. Tobias felt for the backwards Bavarian.

But maybe John, in his ruthless way, was right, maybe Tobias and this Ernie Groeger were a common pair, and despite what Groeger had said, that's what Tobias should above all take from this. There could be something to this carbon business, to the world moving indoors. After all, this singular Ernie Groeger fit the work, and they both seemed to pull the same saw. Damn, he'd never had to reconcile such confusing messages.

Groeger got on his feet and rocked to find balance, putting John to sharing grins and eye-rolls with Cassandra. Groeger stepped up to Tobias.

"I go get the chickens," Groeger said. They shook hands. "You come by here any time, Tobias Meier."

They watched Groeger shamble away. "So, Tobias," John said, "what do you think of the old coot?"

PJ Piccirillo

"I liked him. Good enough sort."

John nodded agreement, opposite of what Tobias expected.

"He knows the business," John said. "There's a lot to learn from that guy."

Tobias watched him.

"It gets in your blood. You need to give it a try."

"I'll consider it."

Cassandra smiled up at Tobias. "I hope you do, Tobias. And I'm offering whatever help I can."

"No need," John said. "It'll all be taken care of."

Tobias went to protest John's meddling, but Cassandra spoke up. "I'm off to see Ernie crack open the chickens. I can hear him hammering now." With the tip of a finger, she touched Tobias's forearm. "I want you to come and tell me stories of timbering later."

"I'll catch up," John said.

Cassandra moved away, and as she rounded the camp, she turned her head. Though the eyes were obscure as ever, Tobias was sure she looked particularly at him, and that she wanted him to know it. His understanding of this was as indefinable as what accounted for shooting seven of seven targets, or whatever made him sense more in her mother's photograph than a woman posing for a camera.

"Shouldn't we walk her over there?" Tobias said.

"She's an independent one," John said. "Used to moving from one crowd to another."

* * *

Near two in the morning, Tobias walked off in the darkness, across the mown wheat and into the still, pea-sweet canes of corn that bristled the soft sweep of the hill. He desired to walk alone, away from the wagons and motorcars carrying away the partyers, away from offers to ride with people who'd found the sharp-shooting hick their latest novelty. He planned to go to the rail yard and board a loaded boxcar coupled to a train pointed toward Pigeondale. He'd sleep there against a flour sack and awaken at dawn to tick-tocking wheel flanges and thumping casks of beer.

There shone enough moon to wade the rows of corn—well into tassel, yet still just shoulder-high. A woodsman always carried a compass. He knew that the road spoked northeast, and he lit a match from time to time to check his bearing against it. Field to field, woodlot to woodlot, pasture to pasture.

His compass. Its needle sought north, but not the north people called true. He veered his steps a little, minding that. For to keep safely on course, a compass reader had to heed declination, that space between the made-up north and the elusive magnetic pole, a thing invisible and ever moving, though it was the pulling force, was alive. He found it odd—and an eerie echo of some problem in his own life—that only by calculations contrived by humans could a man find a straight and safe path out of a dark and dangerous forest, lest he be—God forbid—at the mercy of a force that moved by its own laws.

He'd come to see that only things that could be held down, to which lines could be drawn and at which they could end, were trusted, not a thing that moved with laws without regard to people.

As he lifted a foot over a stone fence, his eyes adjusted to where moonlight ahead pooled in a pocket of heavy mist, and there he leaned into a stride, his vest whisking leathery blades of corn stalks, his mind full of the night.

He liked the surefootedness of the factory idea, how the thought of it took away that feeling of walking an edge. It quelled the constant gnawing that made him question, question. Which nobody else he knew did. There must be something to read in that. As there must be in that peculiar carbon man who lived at a camp and seemed to home right in on the heart of things. As there must be in Celia Erhart's very daughter offering to put in a good word for him. And as there must be in John, coarse manner or not, trying to get him to look at matters in a practical way.

Close to Marstadt, where Tobias could taste the acid of the tannery and see the hazy orange glow of the gas lamps on the square, he made his last compass bearing, by which he'd turn down to the road.

As the shimmering light of his match showed the needle yielding to its pull, Tobias thought he'd start looking out for more signs.

Chapter 13

Section crews on logging railroads always worked in reference to the end of the line, that point to which track was laid, then pulled fro. Around Pigeondale, the only work was pulling fro. Everything a man touched was sent off for use elsewhere, or as the hicks said, on down the line.

And so woods work for Tobias went from timbering to salvaging what went into timbering; he'd been assigned to a section crew.

Track was coming out of side-hollows all around Pigeondale, mile after mile of it piled onto stake cars. Tobias would have rather worked any section than that one, Teaberry Hollow, where six years earlier—still a boy—he'd been put on as a hick. Leaving every day from home for Teaberry Hollow, instead of starting from right there in a dining hall, stung him with the reality that camp life was gone from those hollows.

Worse yet, while berry briars reclaimed the rail beds, Pigeondale itself was being dismantled, goldenrod and purple aster covering empty lots. Crews tethered to the spines of former log cars the timbers and wallboards of houses and company buildings, shipping them away for operations elsewhere. Still, not all. There just wasn't enough woods work in the Ryder empire, even beyond, to take every nail and machine, board and person. Much of it followed the course of the new century to little plateau towns of tanneries and brickyards, chemical plants and coalmines, paper mills and refineries. The whole damned world was moving indoors, so it seemed to the woodhick in Tobias.

Parts of Pigeondale remained. A few families bought their company houses, men shipping off daily to work section gangs or to peddle wares or blacksmithing among the backwoods farms. But most left, Tobias's family on their way. With a declining barrel market, the stave mill couldn't operate independent of the saw-log mill. His parents and sister—who'd yet to marry and had lost her job when the post office closed—would move elsewhere on the plateau, Herbert Meier looking to finish his workdays around acrid-smelling vats, whether filling them with pulp in a paper mill, or sloshing hides in the liquor of hemlock bark at a tannery.

And that left Tobias to decide if he wanted to buy their house from Ryder Lumber.

*   *   *

Every morning he rode with a train of empty stake cars to the mouth of Teaberry Hollow where the section gang lived in a weathered wooden boxcar, sided there on a length of track. Ryder Lumber policy called for a seasoned woodhick among the sectioners it contracted to pull its rail, a man to ensure the loads were correct.

The crew were mostly dark and spare boys, tentative as choke-collared circus bears. Pulling track was as close as most Italians got to logging—being latecomer immigrants had relegated them mainly to the boom business of mining in the valleys south of Marstadt.

Tobias wondered what happened in the evenings around that boxcar. Little Italy in the woods. Raisin wine and bocce ball. Or maybe not—two of the twelve were neither Italian nor friendly—probably planted by the contractor who hired out the gang, put there to give the Italians enemies. Without enemies, the Italians were apt to fight among themselves, and that would lead to factions, then defectors, which cost contractors.

And they were an intimidating pair. Two wandering flunkies who made it clear they disliked dagos, as they said, and Tobias, reveling in knowing he was no more their boss than these foreigners whose English amounted mainly to: yes; no; push; pull; lunchtime. All except Matteo.

Matteo-the-tomato the pair called him, the one who translated for the crew. The only one the two needed to mind with their references. Tobias wondered just how selective Matteo was in what he interpreted to the others. Day one of his assignment, Tobias saw in Matteo's squat coffee-and-cream face the man who would determine the success of getting the Teaberry spur sent on down the line.

The brink of fall, and all but two of the seven miles of rail had been stripped to a corduroy of beech-wood crossties. Teaberry Run trickled invisible through its bed of cobblestone, and even where the men worked now in a broad, lush flat of the lower hollow, the leaves of the willow shocks were parched dry as sandpaper. There was no escaping the season's last hurrah of heat in a clear-cut hollow, and that had soured tempers across the gang. And the closer to the mouth of the hollow they moved, the more anxious the Italians became about new work beyond. Tobias's job increasingly entailed easing their concerns. His, too.

Matteo pointed to one of the iron squares that held the rails true. Daylong, he pried spikes from them. "Tobias," he said, inclined to break from his work every time a thought struck. "Why do they call them fishplates?"

Questions or pining were what Tobias always got from Matteo. "A hick from French Canada told me fish is their word for peg," he said. "So instead of calling it a peg plate, they call it a fishplate." Tobias glanced up the steep, timbered slope. "New words like that spread through the camps quicker than lice."

Matteo looked worried. He always looked worried when he thought. "Then I call it *pesce* plate."

Of the intimidating pair, Grant always spoke out first. Doing, as usual, the easier job of gathering fishplates and spikes to fill barrels, he said, "The only things pesky around here are the mosquitoes and the whining wops." He stopped at the foot of the grade to look straight at Tobias with a smart smile and a cock of his chin. Tobias held his stare, not as a challenge, rather to keep him from moving it to Matteo, which would start trouble.

Grant's friend, Moon—a name he must have earned with his round, shiny face—hacked out a laugh.

Just two more miles, Tobias thought.

"If I didn't have a promise to myself," Matteo whispered to Tobias, "I'd tear the cheeks of his ass wider than these tracks." He swung the heel of his pry bar between the rails.

"What's your promise," Tobias said, glad Grant and Moon were making their way to the train cars.

Matteo patted his breast. "I promise to Matteo that I will own a house, property."

Tobias nodded.

"And a gun."

Tobias raised his brows enough to move his big western. Matteo chuckled, and Tobias followed his glance down the rail line to where his countrymen were lifting loosened rails.

"At home," Matteo said, "we are not allowed to own guns. If we could, we not could afford. Here, I become a citizen, then I own a gun."

"And then, after the gun?" Tobias said.

Matteo squinted at him, his squat face bunched like a raisin. Tobias saw he hadn't thought beyond the gun. Come all this way, and hadn't thought beyond the gun. "Tell me something of Italy," he said. "About home."

Matteo dropped his pry bar and stepped from the rails, crossed his arms. "It's not like here." He looked up at the ridge of Teaberry Hollow. "Here all the towns are in the valleys. In Italia, all the towns are on a hill. Or on the side of a mountain."

"What's the matter with the bottomlands?" They seemed logical—drinking water, shelter from wind, the rivers and streams for trails and roads to follow. If nothing else, you always hauled your firewood downhill.

Down-line, the crew dropped an iron rail onto the cross members of a car, and it trilled up the valley. But Matteo continued staring at the ridge. "In Italia, the streets are skinny and the houses tight and pressed up to the church like kittens feeding. Old. And many years of one family in every house. Around the towns are walls of stone—always walls. From a town in Italia, you always look down."

Tobias picked up Matteo's pry bar and fitted its notch around the head of a spike. "That doesn't tell me why." He pried and nodded for Matteo to pick up the spike.

But Matteo was grinning, looking from side to side across Teaberry Hollow. "We always watch out. We are born with that." He looked at Tobias. "It was what I saw first different in America. In Italia, a man will walk to those stone walls, or sit on his step, and turn his head into the end of the daylight and just stare. Like a turtle. The women say it is from old ways—just looking out."

"For what?" All the spikes out, Tobias pried the fishplate loose and tapped it toward Matteo.

"For those that wanted to keep us in the walls. Or for those that wanted to break in." He shrugged. "Even those that might take you away to do service. One of these things has torn at us since always. Italia has seen many flags." He paused and looked at Tobias. "Here, all you think about is where to go cut more trees."

"So there aren't any woods at home," Tobias ventured.

"Ah, forest. Yes. But only some, and not near my home. In my part of Italia, there is wheat, wheat and more wheat. Then some olives for the *olio,* and *uva* for the *vino.* But my people only know wheat. They work the fields. That is all the work they can do."

"There must be other work."

"Ah, Tobias. Don't you hear that sonnabitch Grant call us peasants?" He lifted his chin down the tracks. "Speak of sonnabitch."

Grant and Moon approached. The rest of the crew were ready to start their lunch break, leaning against the rear log car, looking past Tobias and Matteo, silent. There wasn't a dry shirt in the gang, except Grant and Moon.

At ease, the Italians wore that look that made Tobias think they weren't quite happy, a pang, a tentative sadness. But something in it he liked. Pointed stares, stares that made Tobias turn quick to glimpse too, out and away.

Their quietness came, too, from bashfulness about broken English. Matteo drilled them, insistent they learn. So Tobias picked up on some of their words. To be affected by that language though, there was no need to decipher it, just submit to the lapping waters of the murmur, and the occasional accents of passionate swells.

And as Matteo drilled, Tobias had come to recognize manners that bespoke each individual; men began to emerge from the band.

"No *treno!* Train!" Matteo would demand of Narciso. But the carefree joker, who grinned and goosed, would just give a backhand wave and a laugh.

Then there was Anastasio, who always took off his hat when spoken to. He shed his apt nickname *Pinocchio* for an English depiction of his Roman nose. By the waters of Teaberry Run, he'd been re-christened Hookie.

Matteo even had little Sabatino, the youngest—maybe twelve— squeaking out "water bucket!" instead of *"secchio d' acqua!"* as he stumbled up the grading, shrugging against his big wooden pail and ladle.

Tobias gleaned that their talk was mostly of family and home. "Sister! Not *Sorella,*" Matteo would insist. "Father! No *Padre.*" "Dante, you say my Angeline, not *Angeline mio.*" And lately, midday talk surged with words that said as much in tone, Matteo complaining when Armondo, the pensive pipe smoker, carried on in his bluesy and distant cadence. "No more talk of the olive groves," Matteo said, "and sweet *siestas,* and mama's *pane.*"

After Grant and Moon passed, Grant said: "Your rail monkey flunkies are waiting for you to bless lunchtime, tomato Matteo."

"Go on," Tobias said to Matteo, glancing at the sun. "It's close to noontime."

Matteo waved off the others. "I stay here with you today," he said to Tobias. "Too damned hot for me to climb."

The Italians took lunch buckets from the railcar and moved up the line past Tobias and Matteo while Grant and Moon ambled well ahead. By their nature and too-long lunch breaks, Tobias guessed the pair went for shade somewhere up-hollow where they'd found hemlocks still standing.

Since the first day on the job, the Italians had found their own places to lunch. Matteo always invited Tobias, but he declined. It was their time to speak freely, talk about home, drink their raisin wine. Plus he needed to maintain neutrality between the Italians and the other two, though they still all saw where his favor lay.

They typically lunched high on the south side of the hollow. To find a breeze, Tobias figured. A few weeks before, Matteo told him they found an outcropping of great rocks extending over a narrow bench. One massive stone jutted to make a grotto, and from under it they could see down the hollow and up it all the way to where it split with the headwaters of Teaberry Run. Now Tobias wondered if they were drawn there by some security learned over generations in places looking out.

Tobias walked with Matteo toward the railcar for their lunch buckets. "How do you know English so well?" he said.

"Since I was a small boy, I read to learn. And I spoke to the soldiers of my village. I did everything I could to become a citizen someday."

"You knew as a boy you wanted to come to America?"

"Ah, I tell you when it started," Matteo said, and he stopped. "I was playing in the *piazza* behind the cathedral. I heard shrieks and yells. I knew the voices—it was Mamma and her sisters. I ran and saw a great confusion of people in the street where our home huddles with those of my mamma's sisters."

Matteo drew a breath, and Tobias followed his gaze down the hollow.

"My mamma and her sisters were beating a man with kindling sticks. My aunt Eugenia—they called her *semplice*—the simple one—lay on the ground, wailing and beating her own face. And my cousins were all crying around her. They did not know what was the matter, but were scared of her face—bloody from her beating and scratching herself." Matteo shrugged and started along the rail bed. "I was scared, too. But I walked up to the man. I had never seen him, but I knew who he was—many times I heard my mother whisper about my uncle Riccardo. He had gone off to join the cavalry, while my aunt carried his third baby. But I had heard them hiss *America*, too, and this became a bad place in their words. And in my mind." Matteo pointed to his head.

"But when I looked down on my uncle, I did not see a terrible man that came from a bad place. I saw one with a happy way, even though they beat on him." He glanced at Tobias. "He had a finer look than any man I ever saw. And something more."

Tobias watched Matteo's round face redden as he searched for the word. "You could tell," Tobias said, "he'd seen the world, was sure of things."

Matteo nodded. "Even while my mamma's sisters cursed and beat on him, he laughed and laughed, making fun of us *stupida* little peasants." Matteo slowed and looked down at the loosened tracks, grinning and shaking his head. "What a suit. White stripes on the pants, black coat and cuffed sleeves. Even a vest of a yellow like straw." Matteo tugged at the sweaty neck of his shirt. "His collar was stiff and tall with a black tie. Silk. On the ground beside him was a hat tall as my waist, and it had hardly a brim. I thought, imagine a man needing a hat with so little a brim." He laughed. "He kept trying to pick up a little stick cane, and out of his pockets fell cigars as thin as my fingers. Tobias, my people all of a sudden were plain and simple, while there my uncle laughed and laughed like he played in a box of puppies."

Matteo slowed even more. "His face was the face of my people, but with the look they would have if there was no wall around our little town and we found these riches. To me, that face, his fine clothes, they all meant America. A place where there was not poorness and sicknesses waiting always."

The two had come to the rear railcar where they'd hung their lunch buckets from nails in its underside. Then they slid down the rail grade and leaned against its hogback where a high carload of iron rails shaded the sun.

"Tobias. Your hands are as big as your *panino*—your sand-a-wich."

Tobias grinned.

"What is it with your tomato?"

"Bacon."

"Ah, *pancetta.*"

Tobias tried it, drawling the syllables and splitting them with the leisurely pauses he heard the Italians use. "Pan-*chet*-ah." He reached deep like he thought they must to add passion. Or maybe that came naturally out of being so damned passionate. No wonder their bodies and hands lurched when they spoke.

"Eh, you might talk it all right," Matteo said, "but if you would go to my village, they would chase you out. '*Aristocratico.*' They would think a brown-haired man with those olive eyes and that lean face is a *ricco*, high-nosed northerner."

Tobias grinned. He liked the way Matteo's tongue strummed over the *r*'s in *aristocratico* and *ricco*.

"The people of my village are proud," Matteo said, squinting and staring as if they looked back from across Teaberry Run.

But it seemed Matteo was just saying his people had nothing to be proud of. "Matteo, wasn't it hard to leave, like roots would come up with your feet?" Tobias rested on an elbow. "Or were you sure it was the thing to do?"

Matteo did not answer right away. His lips were clenched, his face ripe-red. "Didn't you hear the story I just said?" He'd been eating an apple, and he snapped its core at a stump.

"Sure."

"Tell me anybody would not take after such a fine life. We had nutting. *Non.*"

"Not everyone leaves. I'm guessing some see as much to like, but no farther than their sight."

"Ah, like Nunzio, my *fra.*"

"See."

"He thinks he will be all right. Stay on that hill. But—" Matteo pointed a thumb at this chest— "I will show him."

"Show him what?"

"That he is wrong, that the same thing he likes over and over—like the smell of olive groves coming across a sea of wheat—is not so great. Pressing someone else's grapes for a bottle of wine is not so dear." With two fingers in front of Tobias's face, Matteo imitated legs. "I'll show him that walking through town every night, everyone he knows sitting on benches or chasing *bambini* around the *piazza,* that is not worth staying on a little hill to live in a beehive where the homes of aunts and cousins are so close, you hear them laugh at a fart, and the fart, too."

Matteo gestured as if pushing the whole business away. "He will end up like the rest. Toil in the wheat among the snakes, go home to everybody's business. One week hungry, one week filled. One baby die of the consumption, another of pox. He says 'for love of family—for our name—forget the riches, Matteo. You can be happy here.'" Matteo laughed.

Tobias clinked his bucket with his sole; he hadn't timbered in a month, but he still wore his corked boots. "Maybe over there," he said, "the land routes water and wind just so. The air carries what the breezes jostle. And that fits the shape of some people."

Matteo laughed and stood. He spoke into the hazy vault of humidity. "Tobias Meier, just like my brother—you better hope you can eat dreamy words. He in his land of wheat and you in your valleys of no trees. You both talk nun-sense." He turned and started up the embankment toward the railcar.

Tobias called after him. "Then tell me why you go to the ridgeside for lunch."

Matteo looked back and shrugged. Then he disappeared beyond the railcar.

*   *   *

Across the hollow, on the edge of the bottom, a maple rose above the brush, contorted like a crack in a frozen puddle. Another one, Tobias thought, spared by ugliness. His eye went to a lump on the trunk, just about where it gave itself to its disordered branches. Porcupine? he wondered. He squinted. Coon? He started away for a closer look.

He pushed willow shoots where hemlocks once shrouded Teaberry Run, then hopped the exposed stones of the summer-shallow waters.

It wasn't an ancient tree. A seasoned hick could tell in a glance it was no more than fifty years old, especially a hick who spent his lunchtimes reading in stump rings, thick and thin, the up and down life of a forest.

He looked along the maple's trunk. Just under its first fork, big as a bushel basket, erupted one of those odd knobs, a burl.

Tobias grinned at the deception, then thought of Ryder Lumber passing up this crooked tree and missing that burl. In that ugly fist of bark flowed the most elegant grains of hardwood, prized for their waves and hues.

Considered the most beautiful veneer in the world, burl wood commanded a lot of money. Steep prices paid by people on down the line who were unaware that such beauty came from a tumorous gnarl, people who wanted grand bookcases of maple, but wouldn't know this from an elm.

He took in the denuded hollow. A single tree now meant as much as a forest—there was a chance for a forest in that maple. If people appreciated trees for what they made, mere sprouts should hold for them all the beauty of their eventual great tall forms—one's in the other. But he knew on down the line, people were forgetting the trees. The decor of a grain, the flavor from a barrel stave, the strength of a wagon spoke, stood alone in minds anymore. That was dangerous.

"Matteo, Matteo..." Nine Italian voices poured down Teaberry Hollow, more animated than usual.

Tobias went to the rail bed. The Italians were swarming to Matteo while Grant and Moon approached along the grade, for once back early from lunch. Nicolo held something in cupped hands as the others spoke rapidly to Matteo, pointing high on the ridge.

"*Quanti, quanti?*" Matteo asked Nicolo as Tobias stepped up to them and looked over Matteo's shoulders, Grant and Moon pushing their way in.

"Speak goddammed English," Grant said. He looked down on the tiny pieces of flint Matteo stroked in Nicolo's hand. "I'll be damned. Arrowheads."

"Spear points," Tobias said.

"What the hell do you know, wop-lover."

He knew a lot about Indian relics, had even known Indians. Every gardener and farmer in Manooka Valley turned up the colorful points and set them out on windowsills. Springtime, boys scoured the ground for the flint and chert triangles among the plowings of rail beds or potato patches.

"Those are sacred," Matteo said. "Grandfathers left a mark on the land."

"Your grandfathers drank camel milk," Grant said. "Give me those. That's American property you're greasing up." Beside Grant, Moon snorted as if a gnat flew up his nose. The points Grant didn't snatch from Nicolo's hands fell to the ground. Ten tan faces went red, and Tobias knew their words were curses. We'll never pull these last two miles, he thought.

During the earliest autumns Tobias remembered, a band of Senecas still came through Manooka Valley, hunting on foot with old-time muskets, carrying elk-skin packs. A farmer in the valley had told the town boys they started from the reservation up near Warren. Keeping an annual ritual, the Indians camped for weeks in the great flats of McKean county, the long vanished kingdom of Chief Cornplanter. They hunted from that main camp and smaller outposts, foraying the dark forests of the Susquehanna and Allegheny headwaters for deer. These Senecas, Tobias knew, were of the clan who'd come for the pigeons before they were wiped away.

When word was out that the hunters were nearby, boys would mill around the company store where the Indians knew they were a novelty. There were men older than Tobias's father, women, too. He remembered the faces, not red as books avowed, but russet prunes that looked no more extraordinary than the immigrants who worked section gangs. They talked in tired tones as if they doubted their own words, which sounded more like announcements than conversation. He remembered even the names they spoke among themselves—Old Testament names: Jacob, Moses, Daniel, Ruth. Ruth, he remembered well. Outside the store, Tobias had shown her his polished flint pieces, a few long, thin and notched, others rounder, like little chicken hearts. "Not Seneca," Ruth said, bowing over his hand.

She wore pants. Tobias had never seen a woman in pants. Old-time buckskin—the only native attire she wore. The rest was white and male—soft collared shirt, braces and an overcoat of bracken-matted wool opened wide across her chest. "Not for arrows," she said. "Spear points. A grandfather nation. They lived in this valley long before any Iroquois people came. Before any whites. A giant people." She stood erect and reached with her hand as if she greeted someone at a window above the post office. "Gone. All gone." A gesture to show the height of that lost race. A wave.

But the saws had sung, and the woods disappeared, and the Senecas no longer made the old journey. Like the pigeons, there remained no remnant here. Except for the regal names they left on the flowing waters: Kinzua, Tionesta, Sinnamahoning, Tobyhanna. Except for the sounds they painted across the land: Dahoga, Tidioute and Oswayo, Towanda, Moshannon and Nittany. Thousands of places in every county of the state, words Tobias heard through the pipeline of hicks who brought into the camps the streams they'd forded, the hollows they'd cleared, the towns they were off to. But only a trace of that race who'd named the rivers and ridges remained, and remained only faraway. That was very confusing to Tobias, still.

Matteo bent and picked up the spear points.

"Where'd they find them?" Tobias said.

"You mean stole them," Grant said. He held one close to his face with the serious look of someone who could tell by the mineral that Adenas of Ohio mined the flint and came here to trade it for a Teaberry mink. But Tobias knew there was as much contemplation behind Grant's eyes as he'd have taking a bite of the point.

"Doh-vey," Matteo said to the Italians. They pointed to a ridge and responded in their words.

"At the stones," Matteo said. "In the *grotta* under the big rock that juts out of the ground."

"Give 'em up," Grant said. "You dagos got no business with those."

Tobias pleaded hard with his eyes for Matteo to hold his temper. Just two more miles of track.

Matteo threw the spear points at Moon and turned to the Italians. When he spoke, they all grinned. Then they walked by Moon and Grant, laughing. Moon looked as confused as ever, but Grant was livid.

Just two more miles.

Tobias took his time following the Italians back to work at the end of the line, his mind full of the ancient Indians. In an instant, in a timeframe as minuscule as the acorn to the oak, that race was gone. Then the traveling Senecas and the golden-throated, gentle birds. To what end? Or did it really add up to something big being diminished?

Matteo was already prying spikes out of fishplates. His feet left the ground as he dropped his weight onto the bar's handle—like a thirsty child working a water well.

"What did you tell them?" Tobias said.

Matteo's face flushed and crumpled with a smile. "Tomorrow we'll get more relics. There are many there." Matteo leapt onto the handle of his pry bar. "Relics are good luck to us," he said, riding back to earth. "Like grandfathers welcoming us to America."

"And what will you do with the spear points?"

"Every one of us will keep one. Our *talismano* for good luck. Ah, they are a better welcome sign than the statue in New York. They speak to just us. Not all. I will carry mine until the day I own property."

"Well, I hope they bring you luck," Tobias said, stepping around Matteo. "But leave some of those spear points. The grandfathers would want that."

Matteo stopped smiling. He became very serious. "Yes. They would."

Tobias started toward the other Italians who, in pairs, were returning his way heaving iron rails. Grant and Moon were nowhere to be seen. He was off to find them.

Matteo called out. "You are a good boss, Tobias, this place and you I like." He gave a shrug, but there was no doubt to his frankness.

"I'm not your boss, Matteo. But I'm glad you like this place." He looked high on the ridge, then walked toward the end of the line.

*   *   *

The most decrepit locomotives were assigned the menial work of picking up spur track. Their tired lungs could only give the wheels half-steam, the rest going out leaky seams in their jackets. The old Shay gasped along as if fording water, steam waving from its flanks while the smoke dome hacked onto the coal bin where Tobias rode hunched like a coach driver. Summerlike weather keeping hold, there remained in the hollows until late morning a leftover evening mist weighted eerily by some residue of the moon's creamy glow.

After letting off the crew and spotting the day's empty cars, the locomotive started back to Pigeondale to haul rail from there to Marstadt, from where she'd return to pick up the day's load.

Work was quieter than usual. Tobias knew the Italians had on their minds getting those good luck charms. But Grant and Moon didn't seem wary of the calm—they walked up and down the line picking up spikes, un-fazed by the indifference to their mocking today.

"Lunchtime yet?" Matteo kept asking, all picks, pries and shovels stopping while the others waited and Tobias pulled out his watch to declare that, no, it was not.

An hour before noon, the hollow's mist had not risen at all; instead, it turned to plain nagging humidity, drawing gnats and the sear of the sun.

"Now?" Matteo said.

"Go," Tobias said.

"You come?"

"No." Tobias shook his head. "Paperwork."

The others were already on their way up the grade. "Ah, paperwork," Matteo said. "I did mine this morning. Someday I will own everything Mr. Sears sells."

"Not that kind of paperwork," Tobias said.

Tobias walked to the first of the two log cars they'd loaded, rows of rail chained across its ribs—iron track where he'd known piles of great timbers. He pulled a leather satchel from between the car's front beam and axle, and made for Teaberry Run where he had set his lunch bucket in a riffle.

Sitting against the rail grade, he gnawed on cheese and waved off gnats. He leaned back on his elbows. It was nice being alone out here, better than any pay or prospects.

Tobias reached to his satchel and pulled out the next car's manifest so he knew how many rails to load. The manifests fascinated him, records of the tug of man and this land. Every car of track they sent on down the line followed lives and livelihoods. Sometimes the rails went to the yard of a paper mill, where a little switching locomotive would move pulp cars. Others went to the mines down in the coal country. Occasionally they sent carloads off to logging railroads—just tiny spurs up in Potter and McKean where a few tracts remained.

He propped the manifest against a fern, its fronds shadowing through like a watermark. He began reading. And there it was—the inevitable, which he'd nonetheless pushed out of mind. He shook his head and grinned a melancholy grin.

"Five hundred feet of straight, 60-pound rail to be shipped via Ryder Railroad to Erhart Carbon, Marstadt, Pennsylvania, for construction of an inside loading dock." Track from right there headed to Erhart Carbon. A manufacturing plant—where he'd been coaxed to work—now reaching all the way to Teaberry Hollow. The world really had moved indoors.

Tobias looked across to the crooked maple, its dark burl, then turned his head. Too damned many signals.

From well upstream, faint voices trailed down the hollow. He listened. "*Vipera, vipera.*" The words registered nothing, but their cry for help was unmistakable. He ran up the bank and started along the corduroy of crossties.

Vipera? Tobias mulled it. He'd sometimes made out the meaning of Italian words by snipping off an A or an O. Viper. Snake. His stride became leaps, five ties at a time; a hick accorded rattlesnakes the respect a mill sawyer gave the teeth of his blade.

The grade followed a bend in the bottomland, and rounding it, he saw trails of brush and saplings give way where the Italians bore down the steep wall of the hollow. Their voices and bodies slapped the thickets, and they tumbled out, every face crisscrossed in a horror of expression, blood, cuts, scrapes. Matteo was last, Dominico dragging him like a sack. But it was a screaming, soaking sack, its yells those of pain and fear and anger all at once, *Madre* and *Jesus* peppered among unintelligible words.

On the floor of the hollow, Dominico kept dragging him by the leg, propelled blind-wild by the hysteria of his friend. Tobias tackled Dominico and knelt beside Matteo, who writhed all the more.

"Tobias, the *vipera* strikes."

The others watched, and Tobias yelled for them to start down the line for help. "Run for Pigeondale." But they just moved back. Pigeondale meant nothing to them.

As calmly as he could, Tobias said to Matteo, "Where? Just tell me where the bite is." But Matteo only wailed. His shirt had gathered at his chest, and his midsection and hands and face were thatched with the soil and leaves of the valley, blood trickling through bright as foxfire.

Tobias held down each of Matteo's legs, ran a hand along them. As he was about to grab a wrist, he saw the hand was more a pillow. "Hold that still," he told Matteo while he dug for his jackknife. But Matteo pounded the ground with the swollen hand as furiously as he did with the other. When Tobias grabbed his arm to cut the shirtsleeve, the yowl from Matteo rang as hard against Tobias's chest as it did in his ears.

The arm looked inflated with fire, red and already thick as Matteo's leg. Tobias saw the fang marks midway up the forearm. Cutting, he knew, would likely do no good. But there were four hours of walking and trains between here and a doctor, and Matteo was so hysterical, the poison would course everywhere inside. Tobias had to try something. So he sliced.

How strange the sound—a tear, like peeling an unripe banana. He sucked and licked and squeezed at the incision, and along with the blood, out trickled a rank yellow fluid.

Between blows that thudded Tobias's head, Matteo tore out hair, but Tobias sucked, Matteo's punches and scratches and gushing arm bloodying his face. And Tobias cursed that land for gathering its vital tremor in serpents that coiled where relics lay, for a strike of evil from what he'd heretofore fancied pure.

Then he drew his head back and pressed his hands against Matteo's chest to still him, but his face only added to Matteo's terror—he must have looked to his friend like some beast paused to mock the prey it ate alive. "Listen to me Matteo, listen to me." But he wouldn't.

"Oh, *Dio,*" Matteo screamed, his bulging eyes white polyps against his soiled black face.

"You have to stay here." Tobias's mouth beaten and already swelling, his throat sour with Matteo's blood and sweat, he grunted his words. "Wait until I can get help, and don't move. That poison's got to settle."

But Matteo moaned and tried to writhe from the clutch of this beast feeding at his arm. So Tobias turned and yelled widely spaced words, telling the Italians they must wait until he returned, to make Matteo lie still if they wouldn't carry him to the mainline while Tobias ran for help, that when Grant and Moon showed, have *them* carry Matteo. But they glared at the bloody face that licked where the serpent had struck.

Tobias turned back to tell Matteo that if someone did not find help and a train for the long journey to a doctor, the infection from what he'd just done would set in to kill him as likely as the poison would. But now Matteo's body stiffened, and he drew back from this face soaked in the sap of his own life, and he ground the crown of his head into the forest's moldy black duff. In that otherworldly stare Tobias had seen come before the eye-glaze of a fallen deer, Matteo's terror gaped more distantly than ever had the Italian's sad, pointed gazes. Tobias saw into the hollow horror of a man realizing he was about to die far, far from home.

Chapter 14

For the longest month of his life, John Blesh had put in time at his stool in the lab while old rat face, as he thought of Ernie Groeger, moved constantly to and from his marble-topped table, littered always with chunks of charcoal and coke, scale weights, chisels, charts, paddles sopping with pine pitch, and bottles smudged with lampblack fingerprints and full of whitish, soupy fluids. Occasionally Groeger snapped from his work and took notice of his charge, who either stared through one of the tall windows or studied a business journal. Groeger would speak some token task, more to the stool than to John. "Write down the weight of the carbon on the scale, then put it in the oven." Or, "Go to the shed and get me a bucket of pitch." The orders fed John's contempt, not to mention his hurry to take the route up and out of here that he'd determined in August at the Piebald camp.

He ignored the temperatures, resistances and densities that Groeger recited by duty. John's only care for work involved the finished brushes that Andy Hoehn spoke of when he came to request formulas for new applications.

Away from that backwoods settlement, a carbon's composition would mean merely what he'd sold it for—arc lights, flashlight batteries, new things. John doubted that anything other than the luckier odds that come with extra trial and error accounted for old rat face making his carbons conduct electricity and resist heat so well. What he mumbled in German and scratched into that journal were just the trials that by happenstance didn't come out errors. Why else would he so abruptly drop whatever he worked on and run for his pencil?

John could learn nothing of use from Ernie Groeger. Everything he had to offer had already happened—a party at his camp where John had set his plan into motion, and a month of stool-sitting to refine the idea. He'd be free from Groeger before the leaves fell.

"I go for the walk," Ernie said on his way out the door.

John gave him a moment, then left the lab, off to see J. Hadley Erhart. John was expected to report lab activity once a week—a duty that required a convincing show of enthusiasm.

The front office had become crowded with occupied desks, filing cabinets crammed now even between the doorways of Erhart's and Andy Hoehn's offices.

"Hello, Johnny," Maura Schlim, the receptionist said. John knew she liked him, and that he set the girls buzzing as rapidly as their typewriters about her prospects.

"The place is tighter every time I come," John said.

"The addition will be up in spring," Maura said. She gave that frank and eager smile that said she was ready for conversation. He liked direct girls, not these others who blushed and looked away. As if they wouldn't be chit-chatting about him in a minute. Too bad he couldn't return Maura's frankness and let her know that some Bavarian settler's granddaughter, playing office girl in Marstadt, didn't have a chance in hell.

"Good," John said. "The place won't look so much like a schoolhouse."

He glanced toward the heavy carved doors of the offices of Erhart and Hoehn. Erhart's was ajar, which meant no appointment necessary. John grinned, tapped his knuckles against Maura's roll-top desk, and made his way to Erhart's office.

"A week already?" Erhart said, rolling his chair from his desk. Its rich stain matched the office's wall panels and arched-brow window frames.

"Not quite. But enough happened in just four days. I thought it best to get with you sooner than later." John sidled along the narrow rug and sat on the sheet-covered chair, keeping his boots off the waxed wood floor. "Will the new rail siding lead right into the factory?" John said.

"Not exactly," Erhart said. "It will lead to a new loading dock. Then we'll build on to the factory—over top of it."

John nodded just enough to say this is what he expected. He glanced at photographs of Celia and Cassandra on a credenza behind Erhart.

"How's Mrs. Erhart?"

"Well, fine," Erhart said.

"I have to admit, I forget to ask about Mrs. Erhart the few times I see Cassandra."

Erhart gave a polite grin, but cocked his head, on the ready for news.

"Cassandra and I have been such good friends. I wish we could get together more often." He shrugged. "Then again, laboratory work isn't the most interesting occupation to a young lady."

Erhart considered this for a second. "Johnny, what are you getting at?"

"Nothing really, just a thought."

"You said you have news."

John leaned ahead. "Ideas, sir. I have some ideas. All from what I've been learning."

Erhart arched his great brows.

"Building on to the factory," John said, "must mean our formulas are winning over more customers."

Erhart nodded.

"And we're testing carbons for a lot more than batteries." He put a finger in the air and recited a phrase he'd picked up from Andy Hoehn. "In any terminal of electricity or in any machine is an application for our products."

Erhart grinned. "You're learning your craft."

"Maybe learning craft's not enough."

Erhart turned an ear. "Pardon?"

"Take motor brushes. You've said they're the keystone of the electrical era. But how could we ever know all the customers for them in this day and age?"

"We have salesmen finding them," Erhart said.

"But what are they missing?" John pulled his chair ahead, his boots creeping over the edge of the rug. "Maybe there's a better role for me. With what I've learned, I can ferret out applications the salesmen couldn't imagine."

"What kinds of applications?"

"There are electric trains and flying machines today. New wonders invented every minute. We need to have someone watching the hotbed of ingenuity."

"Which is?" Erhart said.

"New York."

"We have a man in New York."

"But unless some new customer calls *him,* he's concentrating on what carbon can do today. And that's fine." As John said this, he tipped his head while turning up the palm of his hand, a concessionary gesture recommended for negotiations by one of the magazines he pored over in the lab. "We need someone bidding on bread-and-butter jobs. But we should have an exploratory man out there that understands the science of formulas, one to root around for new places carbon will work—before even customers see them. That'll keep us ahead of the competition." He paused for effect. "And it will prevent price wars."

Erhart leaned back, crossed his legs, and touched together the tips of his fingers. John was drawn to the broad face of his Hermitage Club ring, then to his shoe, a blucher, which he knew from studying the clothing pages of the Sears, Roebuck and Company catalogue: *The swellest thing in Fine Shoes is the BLUCHER STYLE, and by actual observation we have found that four-fifths of all the swellest dressers in New York are wearing this style of shoe.*

John let out a line he'd rehearsed a hundred times pacing the lab. "Why not position us as the innovators of the electrical age."

Erhart seemed impressed. He stood, knitted his thick brows, and turned toward one of the windows. John regarded the suit—worsted charcoal with a light weave of gray plaid. Wouldn't see that cut in a catalogue. Not a mail-order, made-to-measure stitch on Erhart.

"I like that spirit, Johnny." Erhart looked out at the factory. "I'm not sure about the concept, but we need that kind of thinking." His head tilted as he traced the beige-brick smokestack, Erhart Carbon spelled out in blocks of chocolate brown bricks. "Your idea of creating markets may not be smart at this point."

"Maybe I'm not making myself clear," John said.

Erhart turned and raised a hand. "I understand perfectly. What *you* need to understand is that the opposite of reactive is not necessarily 'assertive.' It can be 'rash.' Do you realize the modifications we'd have to make to build those products?"

"But with the expansion—"

Erhart turned back to the window.

It's time, John thought—go for that charitable streak. He carefully measured pleading into his voice. "How will I ever put what I've learned to anything worthwhile?"

"We need an apprentice, Johnny. I explained the value of that position. And aside from Ernie's occasional claims that you lack interest—which by the way, we need to discuss again—you've given every indication you're thrilled with the work."

Shoot for the heart, John thought. "Even Cassandra thinks I have better prospects in sales."

Erhart remained still and quiet. Presently he nodded, slowly, then called out. "Maura, ask Andy to come in here, please." He took his chair. "You're obviously unhappy in the lab." Erhart clenched his lips, sighed. "I'm always willing to consider opportunities for our people. And I'll take your father's loyalty into account."

John looked at the soiled rug. Damn. He never thought of bringing his father into this.

"Since Andy handles sales," Erhart said, "I want his involvement."

Andy Hoehn coming into the picture at the verge of John playing his ace, might, John realized, work in his favor. It would appeal to Hoehn—he'd been a sucker for that wasteland around Pigeondale.

"You know," Erhart said. "I'd be at square one in the lab if you moved on."

"I have a solution for that, sir."

A brow raised.

Andy Hoehn walked in, his usual enthusiasm flushing his boy face. "Johnny," he said, jumping back in a feigned startle. "News from the lab?" He pulled a chair toward the desk and sat.

"Johnny has been working by moonlight as a market analyst," Erhart said. His voice was admonishing, impersonal. On cue, Hoehn straightened. John understood that Erhart had sent a signal—it was business time. The chain of command tautened. Erhart leaned back and crossed his arms, no lively flare to the big brows anymore. He went from generous patron of Marstadt to shrewd principal in the Ryder empire. The air of the office took on the chill of a courtroom. John would get to explain his case, but the hearing of it would be as much a trial.

"Well then," Hoehn said, "I gather he has some market intelligence—"

"Whether it is intelligent or not is for you to determine." It came across as an order. Erhart looked down at his desk—may the best man win.

"What have you come up with, Johnny?" Hoehn forced a corner of his mouth into a grin. The puffy boy face was near scarlet now.

John wiped a finger along sweat at his hairline. "I'm thinking I could put all I'm learning about formulas to good use in sales."

Hoehn looked to Erhart, likely to gauge his response. Nothing. "Working in the lab," Hoehn said, "doesn't necessarily make a salesman."

John cleared his throat. "I don't have in mind just any kind of salesman. Something new."

"What would we need new?" Hoehn said. "We're hardly six years along, and orders always beat forecast."

"Just look at American Carbon," John said. "Both of us fight for the same batteries at the flashlight and electric sign companies, carbons at all the arc light makers. And now brushes for electric generators." His voice rose and fell, and the sweat around his scalp came cold now. Hoehn let him have a pause, and John borrowed from a marketing journal. "That way of business is making a commodity of our products. It's all about price." The words felt heavy with authority, strengthened his voice.

Hoehn put a finger to his chin. "You're talking about new applications that aren't price sensitive."

John nodded. "And I'd be where the latest technology is—New York."

"New York?" Hoehn glanced at Erhart, who shook his head up and down slowly, still looking at his desk. "I understand your theory," Hoehn said to John. "But you'd need to learn to sell, and New York is *no* training ground, no place to unleash a greenhorn. You'd get eaten alive." He tugged at his dog-eared collar.

"Maybe a novice from the little town of Marstadt is just what we need." John reached for his ace. "There's a trend in sales the old bid-customers would be ripe for, and new-style customers even riper."

Erhart rose from his chair and lifted the window behind his desk. With the fresh air came the stomping of the factory presses, the humming of their motors.

Hoehn watched Erhart. "What's the trend?" he said, his voice flat.

John got to his feet. "It has to do with attractions. A kind no one in the business has except Erhart Carbon."

Erhart turned from the window, reached under his coat and took out his watch. He glanced at it, but not at the men.

"Or I should say," John said, "a kind Ryder Lumber has." Now Erhart gave his attention. "The landholdings," John said, pacing now.

Erhart's eyes followed John while Hoehn looked down at the black crescents of carbon John's shoes left on a Persian at the base of the desk. Hoehn held up a palm. "Let's slow down—"

"Let him go," Erhart said. "We have an apprentice formula man at stake."

"Mr. Hoehn," John said, stopping, "the wilds of the tier first drew you here, right?"

Hoehn shrugged. "Forbidding as they are, they have an allure. Sure."

John waited, hoping to tease one or the other's curiosity.

Hoehn let out a long breath. "What does this have to do with selling carbon?"

John smiled. "Picture a lodge." He paced again, looking at the ceiling. "A retreat in the woods that customers in forty-dollar suits daydream about." He shrugged. "Let American Carbon sell to them while they look out over Manhattan thinking about hunting or fishing away from the bride, courtesy of Erhart Carbon. Or maybe horseback riding—it's in vogue with the upper crust, you know." He'd read that standing boosted confidence. But this pacing made him feel like he owned the room. Maybe he'd write his own article.

Hoehn looked confused. "A hunting camp? Do you know the caliber of these men?"

"Get rid of that image," John said. "I'm talking first-rate accommodations—all the comforts of home, and then some." He held up a finger. "But in a rustic way—make them feel like real Davy Crocketts."

Hoehn shook his head. "With the lumbering and the locals, the deer are all but gone, and you can hardly move among the little timbers left of the woods, what with all the brush. Hell, the trout aren't even what they used to be.

"We have deer brought in," John said, "pheasants reared and released. We make the land off-limits to the locals. It becomes a preserve."

Erhart was giving his total attention, one brow lifted.

"As for the brush," John said, "we burn swaths and have trails cleared. Then we have patches of fast-growing spruce planted as refuge for game."

"You call that hunting?" Hoehn said.

John laughed. "What does hunting have to do with it? I call it sales. As for trout, we do the same. Rear them big and stock them in a stream. And we dam the water for a pond."

John let silence do some of the work. Let them think about it, he thought. Objections would keep the discussion going until they heard him out.

He'd drawn his idea from magazine illustrations of the entertainment estates of eastern bankers and industrial barons—villas and lodges on private lakes where board members and influential politicians escaped for daytime charades of hunting and sailing, and evenings of fine cigars and brandies.

"I know the perfect spot," John said finally. He stopped pacing and made eye contact with each man. "Imagine a fireplace of cobblestone, beams of open rafters. Antlers on the wall over a bar, card tables, a picture window looking at the pond—" he grinned— "and at deer and bear in the yard gorging from buckets of apples and lard. Every one of those city customers feeling like he's on an expedition with Teddy Roosevelt."

John walked with one hand in his pocket, eyes tracing the decorative ceiling plaster. "Hell, they'd ask to have the hollows named after them. And who's to say we wouldn't? One week Bill Smith Hollow, the next week Tom Jones Ridge. We'd hang a new map on the wall every trip, let them fill it in."

Andy Hoehn looked from John to the smudges of black carbon he'd tracked. Erhart creased his eyelids. "Just where is this 'perfect spot'?"

"A place all three of us are familiar with. A lumber camp." At this, Erhart and Andy Hoehn lit with recognition. "The Piebald camp," John said. "It was left intact after the logging, and that leaves us shade trees today. We'd raze what's left and build our lodge." He looked to Erhart, knowing his soft spots. "That's the very birthplace of this company."

Erhart faced a window. "What do you think of this, Andy?"

Hoehn's eyes flittered back and forth. "Well, I don't know—" He smiled. "Wait a second, didn't a crew pull the track out of Piebald way back after we hunted there?"

"That's right," Erhart said.

"Then a lodge is impractical. We'd never get material in."

Erhart turned and raised a brow at John.

Particulars John could overcome; he'd weighed them. "It's 1907," he said. "The day of the motor carriage. Just as we'd take our customers by automobile, we'd haul materials by motor truck."

"In that case, roads would have to be built," Hoehn said.

"And how convenient," John said, taking his seat, "that the old railroad gives us a road bed."

Erhart looked at Hoehn. "Our apprentice here has given us two things to consider—a transfer to sales, and a lodge." John smiled and nodded agreement. "And I suspect," Erhart said, "they are related." He put his hands on his desk and regarded John. "Tell us how, so Andy can make a decision." It was the closest to neutral John had ever heard business talk; no overtones or undercurrents to lead the listener to his own agenda. How dishonest, John thought.

He pointed to himself. "I bridge the two ideas. I have an eye for the possibilities of carbon in more profitable markets. And a man that grew up out there is ready-made to promote a wilderness lodge. I can make the most of the two lumped together."

"Andy?" Erhart said.

"Am I to decide on Johnny moving into sales *and* a lodge?"

"They're both in your department."

"I still say New York is no place for an experiment. But I have to admit that a place to entertain puts us right with the big players. He's got a point: the Ryder lands are something we could make use of."

"Make a decision," Erhart said.

Hoehn straightened in his chair and regarded John. "Then a compromise. We send you to Pittsburgh. That city is an industrial beehive, and every day Westinghouse is spawning industries with his inventions. I've got contacts there." He tapped a knuckle on his chair arm. "Pittsburgh suits an experiment better than New York. Maybe someday, Johnny. Not yet."

"So you're for the lodge?" Erhart said.

"Why not?" He studied the ceiling. "We'd need someone to oversee the lands, get things set up for the next visit. Stock the trout and birds, keep the horses. All the duck lodges and boating clubs I've known, they have that kind of man." He looked at John. "You're from out there. Any ideas?"

"No," John said definitively.

Hoehn thought a moment, then looked at Erhart. "What about that fellow who prepped the Piebald camp. They call him old-something or the other, but he really isn't old—just acts it. He still around?"

"Old Snyder," Erhart said. "Kind of a loner. I can round him up. He's got the background."

"And a cook," Hoehn said, more animated. "Those kinds of places always have lots of good food. Big hearty meals. Pies and pastries out all day."

Erhart grinned. "Put out platters of pork, and your lodge will be the reincarnation of a lumber camp." Everyone was grinning now.

"But the cook should be a woman," Hoehn said, "not one of those drill sergeants that feed loggers. Someone good spirited, able to take ribbings—that's another thing all those places have. This burg oughta be able to supply her—some chesty little Erika in a French roll, spooning out liver dumplings. Top quality booze will have to be on hand. Fresh beer sent out—Lord knows this town's the source for that."

But Erhart was done grinning, and back in his chair. "It seems you've made your first sale, Johnny. But—" he held up a finger— "I have to include a condition. We need an apprentice. What's this solution you have?"

"A friend of mine's eager to take my job. Someone reliable."

Erhart turned an ear.

"Tobias Meier. He helped on the hunting trip at Piebald."

Erhart mulled this. "He's been with us a while, just worked with a section gang pulling track out of Teaberry. Actually, track we're running into the factory."

"You know he's dependable. And he wants out of the woods."

Erhart narrowed his eyes. "I thought he liked working the woods—he's hung on to every job he can. Matter of fact, I was ready to accept an offer he made to team pulpwood."

"No, sir, he's ready to come to town."

Erhart watched him. "Does this have to do with what happened in Teaberry Hollow?"

"Not at all," John said. He wondered what had happened in Teaberry Hollow.

Erhart looked him up and down. "What are you now, Johnny, twenty-one?

"Twenty-two."

"Meier's your age?"

"A year younger."

"Do you think he'll mix well with Ernie Groeger?"

John smiled. "He's met him and thinks he's swell."

Erhart thought a second. "Have him here as soon as possible so I can make clear this is a long-term position." He tapped his desk. "Your plan depends on him."

Erhart swiveled to face Hoehn. "Put numbers together on this lodge. As soon as Tobias Meier is on board, start training John for this sales assignment."

Hoehn nodded and walked out, and John started away. But Erhart stopped him. "Johnny, that haste of yours concerns me."

John nodded.

"I wouldn't consider this without bearing in mind your father's dependability. Don't shame it." Erhart pointed at his Persian rug. "And think before you act."

John nodded again.

"Another thing," Erhart said. "Your plan, like everything else we do, capitalizes on the land. That makes you as much a steward as Old Snyder will be. You're accountable."

*   *   *

As he walked through the office, smiling and tapping the girls' desktops, John decided Warren P. Ryder was the only one around there with any business sense. Whatever Erhart had meant, it put John in mind of Tobias Meier's blather. Pickling the past didn't build empires. No wonder Erhart had to ride his father-in-law's shirttails.

By the time John reached the factory, some of his elation had seeped away. He'd won the battle, but not the prize. One way or another, he'd get to New York.

For the first time, though, he looked forward to getting back to the lab. He'd play lame duck, refuse even errands.

But Groeger was already at his trunk, depositing one of his journals of German scratch. He closed the chuck wagon lid and turned its key.

"Night," he said.

Chapter 15

Danger was typically honest in the woods; it could be touched or heard first, smelled in a gathering storm or a dead opossum in spring water. Even snakes gave fair warning, most of the time. Outdoor hazards confronted a man more straightforward, looked him in the eye, wherefore he could feel accountable for what befell him. But in the factory, caustic specters lurked everywhere, slow eroders that sneaked into the mouth, scorched the insides. Some burned outside, too, and of all times for Tobias to learn that, it was the day before Cassandra and Celia Erhart came by.

"You worked with pitch before?" Ernie Groeger asked a few weeks into the job.

"Sure," Tobias said. Every boy in Pigeondale sealed windows and patched roofs with the resin of pine pitch. It wasn't so black and thick as this coal tar, but what could be the difference?

"Then go and fill a bucket and distill some in that glass." Groeger pointed to a jar on his marble-topped table. He sifted through tools and vials and gave Tobias forceps as thick as a smitty's pincers. "Hold the jar over the heat until it bubbles. Then I mix it with carbon flour."

Tobias didn't feel where the fumes of coal tar had seared his face until that evening.

*   *   *

Inside Erhart Carbon were a few places where, between machine stampedes, Tobias could hear the wooden heals of his work shoes tapping hardwood floor planks, a sharp sound, opposite the tacky slaps of logger's corks against pine boards. He told himself he'd get used to that. And the odor, too, a fume distinct only outside the factory where just a smudge from the smokestack didn't smother the senses, the way campfires smell more like woodsmoke away from the flames. Far enough away, he could fancy the exhaust of baked carbon almost sweet, but only because it put him in mind of rainy-day cinder piles along the tracks of logging railroads.

"Learn how each operation fits the process," Ernie Groeger had told him. "You'll know both better." So Tobias had moved for a week from department to department, learning the machinery and procedures that transformed coke into conductors of electricity. Then with the self-possession he'd planned to put to steering horses, he weighed ratios of green carbon with oils and metals, and memorized baking times and densities.

Tobias saw that making carbon products came down to pressure and temperature, which meant plenty of noise and heat. Chaotically stomping presses. Hot mist that left a metal taste he took home to the rented rooms he'd inherited from John Blesh. Each night he coughed ashen phlegm into newspapers. Then in a place between sleep and delirium, the perpetual thump of machines echoed through his head.

It caused a weariness as much of mind as body, which he was not used to overcoming. Still, he worked hard, and still yet he was glad for breaks. Not from the heat of the factory. Hot work, he had known. Rather from those blackened walls packed tight with carbon fog, a drum roaring with the noise of the pressure part of making carbon.

But even more, there was that different danger. Not the danger you watched over your shoulder for in a falling tree. Not the danger you minded in toes and shins when your axe fell, in your flanks when you pulled a crosscutter. This was something far outside your senses. The dishonest danger.

* * *

The day he saw Cassandra came after a sleepless night suffering his encounter with the boiling jar of coal tar. He'd spurted and gurgled the water of his washbasin as he plunged his face over and over. His knuckles bled from driving them into the wall behind the washbasin as the aftershock of the fumes of coal tar branded his cheeks and forehead. Tobias believed Ernie Groeger had intentionally exposed him to rid old ways of wariness, to tell him old guard was no guard there, and make him weigh carefully whether he was suited to this.

John Blesh had assured Tobias, though, that he had the constitution of a carbon man, that he'd been handpicked by J. Hadley Erhart. He'd sharpen to a charge in the air here, as he had other places. And he already felt a companionship with this peculiar Ernie Groeger.

He was grinding copper powder in a spice mill when the door opened, and Celia Erhart took shape against the haze of carbon powder. Unchanged in the nine years since Tobias had last seen her, she commanded that doorframe as much as she did the picture in Josiah Blesh's office.

"That's Tobias Meier." It came from behind Celia, where Cassandra peered over her mother's shoulder. "The one who was a woodhick."

Groeger had stopped rummaging a cabinet shelf. His eye poked back and forth between Tobias and the two ladies. He'd never looked so confounded. Even the cigar was still, his temples fixed.

"We're looking for my father," Cassandra said. "The office girls said he might be out here."

"I haven't seen him," Tobias said. He looked for some hint that Celia recognized him. But she seemed oblivious of the room; the doorway could have been a mirror she stared at.

Cassandra squeezed past her and made for Tobias. He watched her mother. The curiosity that had taken root that day of the photograph had grown fingers over the years, and they squeezed him now to near breaking.

"Tobias," Cassandra said, an arm's length away. "What's happened to your face?"

He made himself smile and could feel every crease in his face.

"Maybe it's just that you're not wearing that big ranger hat," she said. She craned her neck. "But your cheeks and forehead. They're red."

She turned to her mother. "I'll catch up with you at Dad's office," Cassandra said. "I'm sure you want out of the dust."

Then Celia disappeared into the noise and darkness of the factory.

"So, Tobias," Cassandra said. "What do you think so far?"

He grinned. "I have to be careful of what I say around the boss."

Cassandra turned up a corner of her lip and glanced over her shoulder at Groeger. Her skin was even darker than he remembered, such a contrast against the fly-ash gray of Groeger's face.

"You call him your boss?"

Tobias shrugged.

"John never did."

He just looked at her. She stepped past him to one of the tall windows, and leaned against its sill. Tobias went up to her, and she put her hand to the false-front blouse of her suit. She stroked the collar.

"You look so different without the hat," she said. "And your face—did they have you loading those big ovens out in the plant?"

"Something like that." He made fists to hide his blood-crusted knuckles. "I must look like a regular bakehead."

"A what?"

"Firemen on locomotives get red faces. Feeding the firebox."

"Have you done that?"

"Once. But with trains, I've mostly braked and coupled."

"My father told me of brakemen falling when they jump between cars," she said.

Tobias nodded. "But it can be worse without even falling."

Cassandra's thumb stopped stroking her collar.

Tobias glanced back for Groeger. He hadn't moved—just stood watching them. "On the downhills," Tobias said, "you brake from the coupling. Brake too hard and the logs might shift."

"And the brakeman is crushed."

"Some part of him, at least," Tobias said.

Cassandra looked him up and down. "All parts of you escaped."

Tobias looked away.

"Never even had a close call?" Cassandra said.

She shifted away from the windowsill, closer to him. Against the fetid air of the factory, she smelled fresh; this put Tobias in mind of the lilacs women planted by their privies in Pigeondale.

"Once," he said. "Luckily I was stooped low on the coupler, kicking a pin that was binding such that it might snap." He grasped an index finger and pretended to try to twist it out of his grip. "I had a hunch the pinched pin might make the cars lurch. Sure enough, the top logs slid."

"Did you jump?"

"You can't hardly jump squatted like that. I just cat-crouched over the coupling."

She nodded and sighed. Again, in a glance, she took him in, shoes to pate. Her eyes rested where he crossed his arms over his chamois lab apron, hiding his knuckles. Close enough to reach him, she made Tobias tensely aware of himself, of his exposed forearms, lean and broad-topped and corded as hemp rope, still holding a Teaberry tan. Where her mother, in her indifference absorbed all his attention, Cassandra's tight presence and dark-window eyes shouted it back, a mirror that had to tell Tobias that she stirred him. He wanted to nudge Cassandra toward her mother's alluring way of private extravagance, the keyhole to that world he wanted a better look at.

"There must have been danger every day," Cassandra said.

Tobias shrugged and looked out the window at the slab-sided shack where the pitch was stored. "We always said it'd be more worthy dying of a thing you kept guard against than some slow, sneaky bed-death."

"Tobias, there's something I'd like to ask you."

But his mind went to the woods for the moment, *give take, give take, the pant of the saw.*

He heard her say, "Tobias, will you be at the company picnic?"

A hemlock bole parting from its stump crackled, every nib of the tree's boughs splaying like emerald wing-tips as they caught air. The understory of the forest quaking in the palms of oak and chestnut leaves shimmering away from the fell, the air flushing with the musky flesh of hemlock. Then in seeped the soot of carbon.

What sent him off like that? Must be that he felt comfortable around her.

The ground shook, and Tobias looked from the window. "That's what they call the 'big press.' Tons of pressure." He glanced back, hoping Groeger would hear him, but he was not in sight. "Every cycle churns out slabs of carbon made with a formula concocted right here."

"What are you talking about, Tobias?"

"The thumping you feel. I ran that press to learn how slabs are molded."

"Oh."

He lifted his chin at the window. "Cassandra, the days working in the woods, they're over. I hope you're still in favor of me coming here."

"Just because I'm interested in what you did doesn't mean you should still be working out there. It's just something that makes you different. I like that. Are you all right?"

"Sure." He nodded, glanced away.

She tilted her head to see behind Tobias. Her sour look told him Groeger was back there again. "We can talk more about those days," she said, "somewhere else. At the picnic?"

Tobias heard Groeger at the lab table. "I need to get to work," he said.

"Then go." Cassandra made no move to leave. She nodded over Tobias's shoulder. "I pity you having to put up with that."

"I didn't know about a picnic," Tobias said.

"Why, it's always in October when the leaves are brightest. That's next Saturday—at the Riverside Park, on the way to Buffalo." She tilted her head at the window. "My grandfather's railroad runs a special. There are ball games, boating on the river, even a ferris wheel and merry-go-round." She narrowed her eyes. "Have you ever seen a ferris wheel, Tobias?"

He shook his head no.

"An orchestra from Olean even comes for dancing in the pavilion. I thought that's all anyone here talked about this time of year."

"I'd have to work," he said.

"The factory is closed all day."

He nodded. "Then I guess I'd be going."

Tobias turned and saw Groeger gnawing his cigar, listening, the pink furrows of his scars bright in the window light. His good eye was aimed at Tobias, while the errant gray dot in the doughy one seemed pointed at Cassandra.

Tobias turned back to her. She shrugged and shivered in a show of repulsion. "I'll come by some day before the picnic," she said. Then she moved toward the door.

Tobias's eye, inured in watching draft horses strain and step with their purpose, accustomed to the cadence of deer and bobcats stealthing to the tune of the land, caught in her walk that feigned, stiff strut of one trying to be watched. It seemed at once crafty and enticing.

But where was whatever he saw in her mother? It must be hidden there somewhere.

When she was out the door, Groeger stopped gnawing and looked back and forth between the doorway and Tobias. "What do you think of all her talk?" Groeger said.

"About?"

"The picnic. You and her there."

"You heard what I heard. I don't make any more of it than that." Crotchety drunkard eyesore that he was, Groeger rarely annoyed Tobias, rather piqued his curiosity. But his manner of going bluntly where most people danced always made Tobias more self-aware than he liked.

Groeger sneered. "You don't know anything of women, do you?"

"I'm here to learn about carbon, Ernie."

"And that you are. Still, all the time you talk of work in the woods."

"I was a hick for six years."

"What did you like about the woods work?"

"Being out around trees, cutting them. Just doing what hicks do."

"What did you not like about it?"

Tobias thought a second. "The way I saw hicks get to thinking of trees just for what they're worth on down the line. That cheapens the work, shames the tree."

Groeger's eye kneaded Tobias. "But what did you move on for?"

Tobias shrugged. "Some things just told me it was time, right when I was wondering if it was. Like Mr. Erhart wanting me to take John's place, them believing I was the one for the job."

"I learnt John Blesh only believes what serves him best."

"John was good to me," Tobias said.

Groeger said nothing. Tobias took in the laboratory, the vials and scales, the table littered with forceps and jars, the iron doors of the brick ovens. Here circumstance and people had pointed him from the decay of the timbering business.

"It's never time to move on," Groeger said, "only right to move on."

"That's what I meant," Tobias said.

"No, I don't think you did." Groeger was gnawing hungrily on the wad of tobacco that remained of his cigar, the spider-leg hairs glistening.

"Well, what of you?" Tobias said. "You're here. And from a lot farther away. What was so right for you?" Tobias wanted the truth on Groeger's past. Word was he robbed a baron, that Groeger escaped with his shirt and scars. Yes, Tobias suspected trouble had chased him here—a German accent was common in Marstadt, but a scarred head and a foggy past made him a turnip in that cabbage patch. But in Groeger's secretiveness, in things he keyed on, Tobias suspected that he and his scars were misunderstood.

"I can't be made an example of you," Groeger said.

Tobias recalled John Blesh saying, *Business moves people, people don't move business.* "I came from the woods," Tobias said. "You came from Bavaria." He shrugged. "I see where you and John Blesh are, and a good direction to go."

"I ain't John Blesh," Groeger said. "And I don't think you are either." Groeger's temper came out now in sharp-ending words and flinches of his head. "The hand can't be made to fit the glove." Groeger looked at the door, scoffed at it.

They were silent, and Tobias thought of how at first Groeger seemed the same as the brittle and firm-mouthed Catholics. Where they hid in their hearts scars of their journey, he'd thought Groeger must bear some incident on his face. But the closer he'd watched, the thinner that ugly veneer became. Groeger was unappreciated by people who didn't see him for his face, and Tobias had a feeling that would cost Groeger.

People dismissed his skill as pure knack. But Tobias saw how hard he worked. Groeger read industry periodicals and books on ceramic sciences, tested carbon with chemicals, even experimented with compacting metals; he had a toddler's curiosity. He'd stare for long periods, his brain flexing as rapidly as his temples, and he ended every day in a trance as he scribbled his last notes, furiously, as though struck dumb and only that journal understood him. Tobias would give this carbon business a chance. Maybe his own knack would come of working at it.

Tobias studied Groeger's scars. They streaked in a pattern he'd seen before. Pulling and firing on a grouse once, Tobias had watched his shotgun's pellets graze the decaying flesh of a standing dead tree just that way.

Yes, scattershot could have lashed him, gouged pink creases across the ashen cheek, taken most of his ear. That gray dot in his doughball eye just might be a piece of shot.

Groeger let out a huff on his way to the counter beside his trunk, and began scribbling.

Tobias himself was annoyed; he'd moved his life along finally, caught a good current and put signals out of mind.

No matter. He had a picnic to look forward to.

Chapter 16

The first thing John Blesh saw when he stepped off the motor cab was Cassandra Erhart, leaning into the swayback of her crimson and pearl-striped bodice. She seemed to draw the very sap out of the sugar maples flaunting around the white-washed picnic pavilion of Riverside Park. The second thing was that Tobias Meier stood beside her, dressed up like gentry in a new cap and bow tie. Even from a distance, John could see Cassandra smile as Tobias handed her packages from a picnic basket.

John took his bag from the rear-facing seat of the red and black Oldsmobile, a mere tiller-steer, single-cylinder buggy called a Curved Dash. He paid the liveryman who serviced the town's lone cab, made a note in a pocket journal for his expense account, and started straight for Cassandra and Tobias.

Three rail coaches were staged on an excursion train siding, which ran beside the flagstone path John followed toward the wrought iron entrance gate. A trace of rooster sneaked into his strut; he'd looked forward to an audience of the plant people, guessed his pending arrival was a topic of discussion.

The first two cars were regular Ryder Railroad coaches. At the third one, Ryder's personal Pullman, J. Hadley Erhart knocked at a window, then dropped an upper pane. "Glad you made it, Johnny."

John grinned and nodded, but continued on his way.

"Wait a minute," Erhart said. "I'll be right out." Celia Erhart sat across from her husband, facing the park. She motioned for him to close the window.

John shook his head. Sixty degrees and calm, and it's too damned cold for her royal ass.

He had a better view of the picnic, Cassandra laughing now with Tobias, the two of them leaning across a table, setting out plates, utensils. Most of the men were out on a field beyond the pavilion, some playing tug-of-war, others practicing wheelbarrow racing. John rolled his eyes and refocused on the pair. He tried to catch Cassandra's notice with a wave, but the chatter and the dispersal of picnic items hemmed their attention.

"Johnny, good to see you." Erhart approached, rubbing his hands in his on-the-ready way, then offered one to shake. "Andy Hoehn must have just missed you."

John cocked his head, not understanding.

"He left for the station ten minutes ago," Erhart said. "Took the trolley."

"My train from Pittsburgh got here early." John snorted. "Imagine that. The livery next to the station offered cab service."

"I saw. A motorcar at that."

John shrugged. "It's what I've gotten used to. Never thought of a trolley." He nodded at the pavilion. "Looks like I made it for lunch. I'll catch up with you later." He went to start away.

But Erhart put up a hand. "There's been a change in plans, Johnny. It wasn't just to meet you that Andy went to the station. We tried to ring you in Pittsburgh all day yesterday. We never got an answer."

"I was on calls."

Erhart nodded. "We finally got an appointment with that new generator company we've been trying to get into. Andy wants to take you along. Great training on presenting our products for a new application."

"Sure," John said. "When he gets back, I'll find him."

Cassandra still had not looked his way. She and Tobias sat now on folding wooden chairs at their table, side-by-side, backs to John.

"That's the thing, Johnny. The meeting is first thing Monday. And one o'clock is the last train from here to Buffalo. Andy brought his things so you fellows could go from here—no sense going back to Marstadt tonight and coming back through tomorrow."

"One o'clock?" John reached under his coat and tugged out his watch. "That's just an hour away." He looked over the expanse of the park, caught the arc of the ferris wheel above the treetops. Erhart couldn't take him from this picnic. People in that pavilion wanted to hear about dinner meetings in the city, ball games and new tall buildings.

Erhart squeezed his lips and shook his head, and John knew Erhart saw his disappointment.

"Sorry, Johnny."

"Well, I have no way to the station now."

"Andy will come back for you when he learns your train was early." Erhart touched John's shoulder, but it was like an annoying pin prick. "Come on into the Pullman. I need to catch up on your progress in the smoky city. Your call reports haven't been making their way to me."

John laughed and lifted his shoulders. "Wooing customers all day has me a little behind." He watched Tobias turn toward Cassandra and put an elbow on the table. Why would she give him that much attention? John flicked his eyes at Erhart. Wasn't he seeing his daughter over there?

"Too many appointments is a good problem to have," Erhart said.

John still looked at the pair. "Maybe I should ride back to Marstadt with you anyway. We need time to talk about the lodge. I'll take a train to Buffalo on my own." He lifted his chin toward Tobias and Cassandra, trying to turn Erhart's attention. "It would be useful to spend some time with the factory people."

Men, hands in pockets, were moving in from the field, toward barrels of beer in the front of the pavilion where it had been left open for dancing. Groups of children holding hands skipped through a grove of shaggy scarlet maples. From behind them, the oom-pa-pa of the carousel's band organ rose and fell on a breeze. Against one of the maple trunks, Ernie Groeger sat sipping beer, looking sulky.

"No, Johnny, there's a lot for you two to discuss between now and Monday."

Now Tobias stood. He put his hands to the back of Cassandra's chair. She rose, and John had to keep himself from starting forward. "I'd like to go over and say hi to Cassandra at least." He nodded that way, but Erhart still did not look. "And have a bite to eat," John said.

"Of course," Erhart said. "We'll talk as I come along."

Just as John started ahead, Erhart pointed toward the road. The motor cab was grinding through mud, Andy Hoehn waving from the passenger seat. John looked over at the picnickers and debated the appropriateness of just walking away while Erhart awaited Hoehn. The pavilion was packed now, maybe seventy-five people standing, sitting at tables. Tobias in tow, Cassandra made her way to the front where most of the men still stood in circles, mugs in hand. John was sure that for an instant, as Cassandra squeezed between chairs, Tobias put a hand to the small of her back where the tail of her crimson bodice wedged downward. Then Tobias leaned to say something, and they stepped up to a pair John recognized as pressmen. He could tell by their gestures that Tobias made introductions. John looked to Erhart. Was he seeing his daughter among that common crowd?

But Erhart was waving Andy Hoehn along the walk. Hoehn picked up his pace, his puffed boy-face flush from the effort and the motorcar ride, pinched fingers holding down the brim of his felt boater. "Our crack salesman," Hoehn said, catching his breath, "fresh from the city."

John gave his best smile, eye on the pavilion.

"Has Hadley told you the news of the lodge?" Hoehn said.

John shook his head *no* while Erhart grinned and nodded Hoehn on.

"The old rail grade's been tilled into a road bed," Hoehn said. "And—" He looked to Erhart.

"I haven't said a thing to him, Andy."

"A design's been drawn up by a Buffalo firm. You and I meet with them to review it tomorrow night at dinner."

Erhart touched John's shoulder. "We wouldn't move on this without involving the man who conceived it."

John turned away from the picnic to face Hoehn. "When do we break ground?"

"Spring thaw," Hoehn said. "And we've already got a crew damming Piebald Run for the pond."

"We could be ready this time next year." John looked at Erhart. He paced his next words one at a time, as if he drew them from his mouth by hand. "There's no time too soon to put me in New York. Among the innovators."

Erhart gave his politician's parade smile. "Patience, Johnny. Patience. We need to get you seasoned."

John thought for how to counter this, but Hoehn spoke up. "So, how's life in the Burgh? Looked up any of my old friends?"

"No time, no time," John said. "It's all I can do to keep up with Mr. Westinghouse's enterprises."

"And your apartment?"

"Fine. I'm just on the edge of Shadyside—a fashionable section. And I'm out of the smog of the mills, close to all the new industry of the eastern suburbs."

"No place within twenty miles of Pittsburgh is out of the smog," Hoehn said. He drew through his nose a deep, dramatic breath and looked out at the countryside. "What's really fashionable in that city is to say your section is out of the smog."

He and Erhart laughed.

"But I say, gentlemen—" John cocked his chin up and looked from Hoehn to Erhart— "New York is where the greater potential lies."

Hoehn pinched the lapels of his overcoat. "You are determined. But what of the ladies down there?"

"Busy, busy, busy." At that, John turned back to the pavilion to see Tobias and Cassandra standing by their chairs. Tobias looked as if he'd been jigsawed out of a pine plank, all stiff and awkward in his suit coat and starched collar, his flaring gray bow tie. John could see the effort of his formal smile, the tense attention Tobias held to the chance she might beckon his aid or favor; she had him on a leash. John decided Tobias was her novelty of the day, and discounted it for its worth.

Hoehn tugged at a watch fob under his coat. "I have that town cab waiting on us."

"I've *got* to go say my hellos," John said.

Hoehn looked at Erhart and shrugged. "We have a few minutes."

"I'll be right back," Erhart said. He picked up John's valise bag and took it into the Pullman car where his wife still sat at the window. John followed her gaze to the picnic pavilion. Her daughter was sitting again, chin turned on her high tube collar toward Tobias Meier, as if her head had been detached and replaced and all that held it there was the black satin ribbon wrapped from the bun of her hair to where it was tied in a bow beneath her chin. What did Celia Erhart think of her daughter in a picnic pavilion with factory workers and barrels of beer, spending her day with Tobias Meier?

The moment Erhart returned, John started toward the entrance gate, his steps setting their tempo.

"Automobiles, Johnny," Erhart said. "Andy and I have been talking quite a bit about their potential."

"They're the rage in the city," John said.

"Exactly," Erhart said. "Even the wagon works in Marstadt is selling them. And just as they do with any machine these days, someone's going to come along and make them affordable. Next thing you know, everybody will have one. And that makes a hot market for carbon brushes—all those automobiles will soon have electric starters."

Closer to the maple grove, the bright moldering of the season was so heady it put John in mind of the wet sawdust he and Tobias sacked from the pile behind the mill in Pigeondale. It turned his stomach. "The trends in the cities will tell us what's to come," he said. "Automobiles are simply a convenience for the better off."

"Johnny," Erhart said, stepping aside to let them through the entranceway in the wrought iron fence. "The line between the better-offs and everyone else is fast fading. We need to heed that when we look to new markets."

John shrugged.

As the three closed in on the pavilion, heads turned. Erhart smiled and gave general nods.

"So what's Cassandra doing with herself these days?" John said.

Erhart shook his head back and forth. "On the go, who knows where. I used to hear of charity balls and bazaars. Her interests seem to change. Perhaps she'll go to school yet." He paused, looked skyward. "But she's a woman now, with her own private and brooding side." He mulled it as much as said it.

"Well look," John said, "there she is."

Erhart lowered his voice. "By the way, Johnny, that Tobias Meier is as reliable in the lab as he was in the woods. Good pick."

John did not respond.

They entered an opening in the pavilion's white clapboard banister where Tobias and Cassandra stood waiting. Cassandra, arching her chest out with the swayback of her dress, her neck impinged by her high collar and head ribbon, stepped toward John, leaning on her parasol as if it were a cane and she had a sore spot in the middle of her back. She put her free fingers to one of John's cheeks and kissed the other. Tobias stood away, hands in pockets, crooked grin.

"John," Cassandra said, "we looked so forward to seeing you." She tilted her head and pouted. "But now they're sending you off to Buffalo."

She cast her father a glance, and John stole a quick up and down. Contorted and overly stylish as she was, she looked good, somehow polished, refreshed.

"Have to keep things moving," he said.

Tobias stepped up and offered his hand. "I thought we'd have some time in Marstadt," he said. "We haven't gotten together since you moved."

"It's been a while," John said, shaking his hand and glancing at the new cap and bow tie. "How things change in your wake." Tobias just looked at him.

"I wanted to give my regards to Cassandra," John said, "and say hi to you, pal. I even talked my way out of a meeting with Mr. Erhart in that fancy Pullman." He grinned and turned to Erhart, but he'd stepped to a table where people sat before plates of fried chicken.

"It's quite a coach," Tobias said.

John noted a matter-of-fact tone. "How do you know?"

In the same matter-of-fact voice: "I rode up on it."

"You?" John looked from Tobias to Hoehn and then over at Erhart. "They let workers on?"

"Just Tobias," Cassandra said with a titter of laughter. "I invited him."

John studied Tobias, wondered if he had any sense of what he was doing. Tobias stood stiff in his Sears Roebuck suit, wide-eyed, looking as eager and nervous as a new waiter, first day on the job.

"You must come to the city sometime, Cassandra," John said. He caught her glance at Tobias. "We could take in a concert, or a show."

"Well, sure, I'd love to," she said.

"All the streets in my section are paved now," John said. "Perfect for a motorcar ride."

"John," Cassandra said, her voice lightening. "You're not getting an automobile?"

He shook his head. "Oh, no, not yet. An automobile would tie me down, restrict me to a flat with a garage. I need to be light and portable." He glanced at Hoehn, who'd joined Erhart with the fried-chicken eaters. "Any day now I'm off to New York." He held up a finger. "As in the city, as in Madison Avenue. So, Cassandra, we'd hire a cab."

"You always said you'd make it to New York," Tobias said.

John nodded. "You too, pal. You'll have to come down sometime."

"And you'll have to come up next month for deer hunting."

John raised a hand. "No time for that. The next hunting I do will be from the lodge. With customers."

"That will be something," Tobias said, "having city fellows out there." He grinned. "We might have to hold back a few secret spots though."

"Sorry, Tobias," John said, "but we'll just have management doing the entertaining. Besides, pal, you can't possibly think it'll be the same there."

Tobias looked out of the pavilion and shrugged. "I just thought I'd offer. Knowing the country and all."

"You know, John," Cassandra said, "everyone talks about this lodge as if it's yours—John's lodge this, John's lodge that. The whole thing sounds exciting." She drew her shoulders to her neck and spoke in a husky, soliloquizing voice: "Adventures in the wilds." Her smile enchanted it all the more, and John thought he heard a little lift on the word "wilds."

"Only my idea," he said, flashing the palm of his hand. "Something I came up with, learning the industry. But it'll be the finest getaway any New York businessman ever saw. I'll be wooing them to come, and escorting them there."

"A sporting affair, then," Cassandra said.

"Horseback riding. Trout fishing." He pretended to aim a gun. "Bird hunting and deer. Bear even."

The pavilion was full of chatter and children's laughter now. Picnic baskets lined the plank-topped banister, half-lids open. Homemade linens and napkins garnished the table settings, bright ones made of sun-bleached blouses, others of flannel or old dark dresses. Most every adult was at table, picnic foods of every kind spread before them: chicken pie, corn pudding, pickles and coleslaw. There were sweets of waffles and honey, walnut cake, apple turnovers with whipped cream. Women spooned from cans of Van Camp's Beans and Tomato Sauce, spread molasses on brown bread, poured cider into tin cups. Children carried away plates with treats of peanut brittle, honey popcorn balls, and chocolate fudge.

When John saw the orchestra players setting up chairs and music stands at the open end of the pavilion, slow fingers of regret grazed his gut. He looked away. A group of children in caps and bonnets ran across the playing field for the carousel. In the foreground, Ernie Groeger sat now on the banister, brooding under the visor of his old slouch hat, gnawing on his cigar and sipping from a tin of beer.

Winding his watch chain around his forefinger, Andy Hoehn stepped up to John and said they'd best be going. J. Hadley Erhart moved behind them and put a hand on each man's shoulder. "Time to send the soldiers to the line," he said, "while we tend business on the home front." He winked at Tobias, and John felt his jaw tighten.

"Off to Buffalo," John said finally, "to draw up the lodge."

Cassandra smiled and flinched her chin. "Exciting," she said. And John saw the dark pools of those eyes stir with a hint of the fancy he'd tossed there.

Tobias stood away, as if he awaited John or Erhart or someone to summon him. John put a hand out, keeping an eye on Cassandra. As they shook, Tobias touched John's shoulder and nodded, formal as his new brown suit. But his palm was still coarse as sandpaper, as John had always known it, strong and sure and steady, big as a mitten over his own, and John pulled away quickly.

John looked up at the cap. "It's a different kind of growing you'll have to do into that hat," he said.

Tobias slowly shook his head up and down. "I'll keep that in mind."

* * *

Think about the lodge, John told himself as he followed Erhart and Hoehn onto the slate walk. Take one step at a time. That back there's a novelty.

The three men walked abreast now, John in the middle. When he mentioned that he'd never known Tobias and Cassandra to be so friendly, Erhart raised the cinnamon tips of his brushy brows, slowed to nearly a stop and looked up at the entirely blue sky. He shrugged, then moved along.

Erhart ascended the Pullman to get John's bag. Celia Erhart still looked out the window, and John saw there the pinched brows of concern he'd expected from her husband. He told himself again to just think lodge. But John couldn't crowd out the nagging idea that he'd set more into motion than a replacement lab apprentice. An alarm was sounding, warning that something had taken root, would grow to menace his way.

But then he grinned, getting a shot of reassurance as the frown in the window deepened.

* * *

"Automobiles, Johnny," Erhart said, tapping the red mudguard of the motor cab as its engine chop-chopped and John and Andy took the rearward seat. "They'll be common as shoes soon, and the common fellow will be our money man."

John nodded and tugged at the thighs of his trousers. Let Erhart think the common man would determine where carbon brushes sell.

Erhart put a foot on the high spoked wheel, an elbow on his knee, and leaned in close. What he said turned John's attention. "When it happens, Johnny, you put our starter brushes in these cars, and we'll talk about where you go next." He reached over and spun the wooden knob of the side-mounted engine crank.

As the Oldsmobile tottered into the ruts of the road and started up a grade, John looked down at the pavilion to meet eyes with Cassandra. Among the dark suits and white day dresses, her cinnamon and pearl bodice drew him like a lodestone. But she was not looking his way. Instead, in front of where the orchestra players had set up their music stands, she had one hand on Tobias's shoulder, the other at her thigh, lifting the trumpet hem of her skirt as they practiced steps for a round dance, Tobias stilted, but grinning. On the banister, Ernie Groeger had turned to watch. The flashing of his temples showed even at a distance as he gnawed his five-cent cigar. Then, just before the pair stepped in front of Groeger, that ashen face canted, and he looked in John's direction.

John looked away, past Erhart to the Pullman car, and he forced himself to laugh.

Chapter 17

Even after three years, the figure that faced Cassandra when she woke still slapped the breath from her. It stood naked now before the glass-paneled French doors, had for weeks, though for much longer than that she'd been losing enthusiasm to arrange evening gowns over the mannequin. It was hard to get excited about balls and plays when there was no winning against Mother. For all her shame over Cassandra now shunning the society life of Marstadt—what there was of that—Celia had always made as much of a show ignoring gowns hanging on the mannequin. She'd wanted Cassandra to interpret a personal affront, she a woman who—despite the means—hadn't been allowed such privileges, growing up in Warren P. Ryder's household. So in all, Cassandra's indifference of late doubled Mother's indignity.

If she just had someone to get excited with. But it was hard to keep friends among her set, granddaughter of Warren P. Ryder or not. As soon as she tried the talk of whatever circle she moved to next, tried to take on their interests in books and styles and music, they did not take her seriously. Maybe she just wasn't made for a world of dance cards and parlor parties.

This morning she woke blind to her mannequin. Her sleep had been so shallow, her senses were already tuned to the birdsong and draft squeezing through the crack she'd left between the doors to her little balcony. Her head was full of the eager, green-bottle sheen of Tobias Meier's eyes, of his rough hands and corded forearms. He brought to mind the long tendrilled willows that stood graceful and indifferent, even to wind, where they reared out of the seepy black soils down the hill from her balcony, down in the marshes behind the tannery buildings. Tall and serene. Enveloping.

All was quiet, save the birds, the autumn air's sharp, leafy bite snapping away the brine of the tannery. She closed her eyes and thought of that big hand steady on her waist as they round danced yesterday in the pavilion. She wanted him to wield her, deft and sure as he had the smooth handles of the logging tools he talked vividly of using, and which she imagined him pulling and swinging and heaving precisely as piano notes. Even his breath was steady, distinct and telling as a voice in that man who spoke few words.

She'd never considered rawer, simpler beauty hiding beneath the varnish of that world at which she'd been clawing to catch hold. Finally, she thought, the key that fits. And she let the weight of those big hands and the current of his breath sink into the deepest pockets of her mind and heart and body, the aching places that were always searching but never fulfilled.

*   *   *

Downstairs, in the center of the parlor, stood a marble-top coffee table with brass, licorice-twist legs. Except that a sofa and chairs surrounded it, the table had every appearance of a short altar, for on it sat a morocco-bound Bible. It had drawn Cassandra since she'd learned to read. Many mornings she went there with the thrill of a girl returning to her Christmas doll, went there as if the voices of people named in the Bible promised to answer all she longed to know of herself.

But not voices in Scripture. Rather those of lives recorded on the inside covers, and the blank pages before and after the text.

By following the dates of relations' milestones written in hand-drawn boxes, Cassandra had determined that the Bible started through the generations from her great-great grandmother, grandmother of the French-American whom Warren P. Ryder had married. From the earliest notation, written in French—*Maman est morte aujourd'hui, le 28 septembre 1829*—to her own birth date, Cassandra could recite them all. Perhaps if she traced along the branches enough times, coursed up and down the trunk, she might color that inner haze she tried to give shape as she moved into her twenties, running from one interest to another. But her path along that tree always stumbled over an existence grayer than her own.

This morning, she did not dress, instead went straight to the parlor in her nightdress to open the Bible, a map to consult against new bearings. Sitting in the sofa, which looked across the coffee table to the cold hearth, she opened the cover onto her lap. She breathed the comforting must, scanned the years of births and deaths drizzled within the boxes, assured at once of both her own existence and the power of mortality. When she looked at those pages, death seemed less trifling, for her life, visibly rooted to something, did not seem so arbitrary.

Then she landed her eye as always on the blank space, empty as the core of her, which like the void on the page stunted the story of all the rest. She'd deducted long ago that the space was for an unrecorded wedding date, the threading of new genes into the family patchwork. Not the dead-end digit of an unmarried daughter or a stillborn son, not the incidental notation of an in-law uncle's death, rather sap of the trunk from which she'd sprung.

It had occurred to Cassandra one day, reading the 1839 birth date of her grandmother, Manon Dozier—the woman who'd become Mrs. Warren P. Ryder—that the wedding of Manon's parents was not mentioned. In fact, the only reference to Manon's mother was in Manon's own birth entry. But there had certainly been a wedding, for the birth notation referred to Manon as the daughter of Didier Dozier—as daughter of him and Cassandra Dozier.

So the wedding day void remained as a covered-mouth gasp amidst that solemn telling of family history, left there, she guessed, in case some sin be later forgiven. Nevertheless, Cassandra identified most with that deliberately neglected spot, a moment more personal, more alluring than all the antiquated milestones of her maternal bloodline.

Cassandra brushed a finger over the empty box and looked away. The varnish of the mantel beam lustered in the silver light feathering through the parlor window's sheer voiles. She closed her eyes. Since yesterday, she'd felt she'd uncluttered a path to her own empty space, let in air and light enough that she could sure-footedly make her way there. She'd found finally, certainly, the right shape and color to fit and fill it. Nothing had been so easy as sharing Tobias Meier's unpolished existence, his simple conversations about taking things of the earth, about how nature's pieces fit one with the other in that world that provided the material for the one she occupied. Nothing had moored her so securely as the tethers of arms made strong working that material. For once, she'd been someplace where she was free of the frustration of wanting approval a mother would never give. She even felt comfortable in his talk of crude things like coal oil and carbon, trees and trains, the work of teamsters, sawmillers and machinists. Maybe she was made for plainer conversation, maybe she had eyes for seeing through all the finery. After all, she hadn't felt anything but babysat by the affairs Mother arranged and then begrudged her, had felt an imposition to people who chattered and moved among one another with ease, who would return home to encouragement. She must have needed to scratch beneath the varnish of her world, to callous her sensibilities against the raw stuff that made worlds. She opened her eyes and flipped the page to random news of distant cousins.

"Circle left, circle right, into the middle and back." It came from the hallway, her mother's voice mocking in song, weary with the usual martyrdom. She paused at the parlor doorway, lifted her eyes as if her feigned surprise were a struggle. "Oh," she said, "you're downstairs already."

"I was up early," Cassandra said, playing the charade—her mother had well known she was in the room.

"Not early enough to dress first," Celia said.

Cassandra sighed, smoothed the knee of her nightdress.

"Can't seem to keep that noise out of my mind," Celia said. "Circle here, circle there." She leaned her forehead against the doorframe and traced a finger up the molding. "Of course, you think of it as music. You and your dancing woodhick."

"We were joining in on the fun of the picnic," Cassandra said. "Would you rather us sit and listen all day from a Pullman window?"

"What I'd rather is that you show as much interest in ballroom dances as picnic trots."

"You mean the dances you insist I go to?" Cassandra finally had the nerve to chuckle at her mother's contradictions. "The ones that if I bring up, you walk away?"

"You're ungrateful, Cassandra." Celia's weariness became more dramatic, her voice the exaggeration of a whisper. "I've given you opportunities I never had. And you discard them before me."

Cassandra studied her mother. Dressed already in a gold-trimmed, chestnut dress. The sash she'd pulled tight around her waist gave her a morbid stiffness. "It's not opportunities I need," Cassandra said.

"You mean want, which is obvious, considering you reject them for round dances with woodhick factory hands."

Cassandra shrugged and strummed the ruffled bib of her gown. "It doesn't matter—you're offended no matter where I dance. The only difference is you actually pay attention when I'm among people who might reflect badly on you."

"I would think," Celia said, even her nose now on the doorframe, "that a mother should take notice of a twenty-one-year-old daughter who suddenly shuns socializing with her set—" she drew a breath and her voice wavered— "yet continues to go to beer barrel parties at backwoods camps."

Cassandra shooed this off. "This is Marstadt, Mother. Such is acceptable, no matter what your name or address." Cassandra had had enough. She turned back the page to the vacant box.

"It's a shame you don't read beyond all that scribble," Celia said.

Cassandra blew out a breath and shook her head. "All this scribble is what we're made of."

Celia gave a feeble laugh. It trailed into a feigned sob of grief. "My dear. You have no idea what we're made of."

"Why is that such a mystery?" Cassandra traced the empty box. "Even as I hold the family tree in my hands?"

Celia went sighing to the mantel and took down a tintype of her mother. The image was framed in blackened pewter, the slits of Manon Ryder's eyes set in even darker skin, darker than an Egyptian. The complexion of a middle easterner maybe, or of a Bombayan. Shadowy as a secret. "There's more to that story than what's written there." She wiped her thumb over the glass covering. "There's the journey of that Bible itself."

Cassandra looked to the first French entries. "A journey that started in Bordeaux."

"Oh, but you can't learn the travels of that book by following the trunk of the tree. There is a detour, a story not written." Celia's eyes narrowed as she looked from the tintype to the Bible in Cassandra's lap. "That book was not handed down to my mother through her own."

Cassandra nodded. "It bypassed your grandmother—the woman whose marriage into the family is not recorded."

"Um-huh. My grandfather had to marry that woman, and therefore had to take his disgrace to America. And his mother would certainly not let his wife lay hands on that Bible." She tapped the tintype. "So, years later, when their oldest daughter—my mother—was grown, the Bible came to her from Bordeaux. From an unmarried aunt."

"Cécile," Cassandra said. "I've seen her birth date." She turned the page. "And I've seen, too, that the name of your grandmother, this woman whose marriage was never recorded, was Cassandra. Only her daughter mentions it—just once—where she wrote in first person of her own birth."

Celia's snicker was dry with the irony Cassandra expected, loathing and indulging at once, as though she gnawed at some hated prey. "The forbidden name. What took you so long to ask?"

"You gave me a forbidden name? The name a mother-in-law would not write in a Bible?"

Celia snapped back. "Why not loudly put a name to all the whispered explanations for dark-skinned Frenchies, Frenchies cut adrift here from their past? I would not have us bear shame and not utter it, too."

"So to spite the world, you've marked me with some family stain." Cassandra had known since childhood by Celia's constant ire that only spite motivated her. But in the choice of her daughter's name? Her eyes went to her lap. "Who was this Cassandra?" she said.

Celia let out a drawn and quivering, "Oh." Then she closed her eyes. "Not who, rather what. A gypsy, a vagabond. Forsaken even by her own caravan of lost vagabonds when she seduced my grandfather among the vines of Bordeaux."

Cassandra looked away to the window and leafed through this. She'd deciphered many of Mother's grudges, hearing about the things Celia had missed, hence resented. That's why Celia belittled her daughter's every interest, from the idea of a finishing school to meetings of the lyceum society. But this was the first her mother admitted one of her spites. And in Cassandra's pent disdain for them all, multiplied now by knowing her very name was another display of indignation, she could feel a shifting fault of fury quake clear to her fingertips, clear to her lips. She could not calm her mouth enough to shape the words that knocked to break free and call her mother's selfish ranting.

Celia must have seen how she yet again baffled Cassandra, made her hate her place while she left no place to run, no place Celia would ratify as right. She stood straighter, smugger than during a usual belittling. As always, Cassandra would utter her rage only alone in bed—sobbed whispers that echoed throughout her inner hiding space. But as she began closing the shutters behind her, retracting like a frightened turtle, a wedge of light showed beneath a door in that dark interior. A place to run. A sliver of hope dawning into her black sanctuary, and it stirred Cassandra to the point she could have rushed past her mother, away to what must at last be right for her.

She turned back the page and tapped the empty space. "What was the year of the forbidden marriage? Was it the same year the baby—your mother—was born, or in the year before?"

"Why would you be so interested in marriages?"

"The year?" Cassandra said.

Her mother shrugged. "One or the other, there's no difference."

Cassandra set the opened Bible on the coffee table and went to the seat of the piano, which faced a tall corner window. She used to practice there, long ago. But Cassandra had lost interest; she never had an audience, whether her busy father or her spiteful mother who never suggested she play even for dinner party guests. She lifted the hinged piano seat, sifted through sheet music and books of songs, and found a pencil. Her mother watched closely as Cassandra returned to the sofa and took up the Bible. She thought a second, and decided she liked using the year before the baby's birth. And in that box that had been blank for some seventy years, she wrote what she imagined: *Didier and Cassandra Dozier were married on a fine crisp day in October, 1838.*

Celia tilted her head and strained her eyes at her daughter. "What have you written?"

"It's time to fill in the blanks," Cassandra said. She held up the pencil. "And isn't this much better than ink? If I learn more about Cassandra—" she paused and tapped the Bible with the tip of the pencil— "I can easily change things."

Her mother's face tamed a moment as she fumbled in confusion. "You have no business writing in that Bible."

Cassandra gave her own smirk now. "Why? Have I committed some sin that the Bible should bypass me, too? Will it always bypass Cassandras?"

"What's the matter here?"

Mother and daughter turned to see J. Hadley Erhart in the doorway, dressed for church and holding his hat. Celia sighed, and Cassandra tossed the Bible onto the coffee table, loud enough to raise the brows of both parents.

"She's learned of my grandmother," Celia said.

"And so she should," Hadley said.

Cassandra watched her mother, who leaned now on the wall beside the mantel, turned away to the parlor windows. "The forbidden name of a stain," Cassandra said.

"Ridiculous," Hadley said. "It's your inheritance in name and flesh, no matter the buzz that surrounded it. Wear it proudly." He walked to the back of Cassandra's sofa and tapped her shoulder with his hat. "I've waited a long time for you to be in on that. Since the day your mother picked that name, I've liked how it recalls a neglected part of who you are."

Cassandra still watched her mother. "And just what is that part of me?"

As Hadley smoothed Cassandra's hair, Celia whimpered out, "A common dancing girl I suppose, whether in a town square or a picnic pavilion."

"Celia." Hadley stomped his foot, and his wife's whimpering became a quivering of her shoulders. "You can't mean that—you smear the very dignity of her name." He patted Cassandra's head, and she hardly contained a laugh, wondering if he'd say next, *There, all better now.* "And let's quit interfering at a big time in her life," he said. "What harm is dancing at a picnic?"

Celia's shoulders went still. She turned. "Of course there's no harm," she said, "dancing with a woodhick." Then, to the ceiling: "Or is it a factory hand?" She tilted her head at Hadley. "Just what is that boy, the long-limbed yokel she invited onto the Pullman? Tell me, was that forest or factory grit under his nails?"

Hadley laughed. "Who am I to knock a man for rolling up his sleeves? Give her a little rope, Celia. She's a grown woman who needs to find what's best. And please, let's not spoil Cassandra's idea of her name. Think of her self regard."

Whenever her father rose against the gloom, optimism bellowed in Cassandra's chest. But it had become optimism jaded, as that of a moth finally wearying against a lighted window. Her father was always somewhere between ready, set and go, a busy man who thought it important in his frantic quest for causes to constantly cheer someone anew in the Ryder empire.

But competing causes or not, he only ever left off at his wife's final word.

"Affording a daughter *correct* opportunities," Celia said, "is not so simple as pep talks at the shop. It is a thankless battle against indifference and ingratitude."

Cassandra looked back at her father. She knew he was already thinking of the day's next task.

"Well," he said, pulling at the chain of his watch, "we can talk through all that later." He turned and started for the doorway. "I'm off to church." He stopped, looked over at Celia, and raised one brushy brow. "After that I'm sneaking into the office. So if anyone calls, they're not to know. It's Sunday, after all." He stepped through the doorway, putting on his hat, then called from the hallway, "I'll be at the Hermitage Club afterward."

While Celia stared again at the tintype of her mother, Cassandra rose, silent in the soft cotton of her nightdress, and returned the pencil to the piano seat. She let the seat-top swing on its hinges. But her mother, absorbed in her sadness, made no show of noticing the thump.

Chapter 18

It was difficult writing to John Blesh. Tobias seldom wrote letters, only to his sister to read for his family who lived now at a tannery town on the upper Clarion River where Tobias took a train to visit some Sundays. In an unpainted plank house—same as the one he'd grown up in—he passed those afternoons on the sofa, listening to his father wonder aloud about Tobias working not in a factory, but in the laboratory of a factory.

Tobias wished Herbert Meier still spent his Sundays on his feet, out for berries or fishing. Now he just sat in his chair, fifty-three and arthritic in limbs and back, his arms covered in salve for the scorchings of the lime and hemlock liquor he sloshed hides in six days a week. Edna Meier knitted on those Sundays. She'd occasionally hold troubled eyes on her son and daughter until the heavy fear that neither would marry tipped her lollipop head again to her needlework. Frieda worked mornings for a widowed baker in an oven-hot shack, spent her afternoons planting or weeding the garden or reading dime novels. There were a lot of men in a tannery town, but fewer came calling Saturday nights on a woman of twenty-five who'd lost her interest in dance halls. As for his own situation, Tobias wished he could reassure his mother, but he couldn't speak of Cassandra Erhart in front of his father.

Asking John to be his best man directly would be easier than writing a letter; he could even involve Cassandra since John would be honoring his friendship with her as much as his with Tobias—what was left of that. Tobias rarely saw him, John always busy, always traveling from Pittsburgh, mostly to Detroit these days. Word was that he'd be at this year's company picnic that Saturday. But Tobias would have to get a message to him after that, couldn't risk letting it out before he and Cassandra announced the engagement. Which had to wait until he had a private moment with

J. Hadley Erhart—Cassandra had insisted Tobias speak to him away from her mother. He had an appointment in Erhart's office next Tuesday.

He was jotting ideas on how to start the letter when Cassandra came, unannounced, to the third floor where a year ago he'd taken John's rooms. She'd only come to the house a few times, and never beyond the boot foyer.

The landlord, Frank Nussbaum, a spare-built dentist with hoarfrost hair, knocked and opened the door. He was frowning at the impropriety, but he couldn't maintain the frown as his eyes widened in middle-aged envy. She stood behind Nussbaum on the unlit landing, the black puddles of her eyes washing into her dark skin and bare head, so depthless in the dim light, she could have been a hanging portrait.

Tobias remained a moment on his bed, back propped against the wall, held there by the presence of Nussbaum in this unusual arrangement. Finally he tossed his pad and pencil to the bureau. The pencil landed on end and arched into his four-legged wash basin. Then he was up and over to Nussbaum. When Nussbaum stepped aside, he nearly fell off the landing. He stood looking from Tobias to Cassandra, who stared now at the hem of her dress.

"I need to talk to Tobias a few moments," she said.

Nussbaum turned the palms of his hands to Tobias.

"Privately," Cassandra said.

Tobias lifted his brows at Nussbaum. "I'll walk her back out."

Then Tobias stepped into the room and pulled a chair from beside the chest of drawers. He took the thong of his sassafras-handled shoe horn from the chair post and moved newspapers from the seat. He waved her in from the landing and saw by the light of his nightstand lamp that her face and steps were rigid with worry.

"Your coat?" Tobias said.

"They took it—downstairs." She seated herself. "Sit down, Tobias."

He sat at the edge of the flannel bedspread his mother had quilted of his old Richie woods shirts. He'd rather her not see the quilt, his room.

Cassandra removed one of her black leather gloves and crumpled it as if wastepaper, then took in the room. "There's just the one window," she said. "And the slanted ceiling—it feels as if it's pressing down."

He shrugged. Tobias liked the feel of sleeping among rafters, a womb of comfort it was recalling nights aloft at the Teaberry camp. "Snug in a way," he said, "and I have another room."

"Oh. A sort of parlor?" She leaned forward, perhaps to get up.

He smiled. "An unfinished one. I guess it's just a big closet."

As if she just remembered a puppy had followed her in, she probed the floor. "It smells of that lab in here."

He lifted his shoulders. "It can't be helped."

"You'll be out of there someday. And away from that foul Ernie Groeger."

"It's a good job, Cassandra. Your father picked me for it with the trust that I stay there."

She let out a deep and weary breath.

"What's the matter?"

Cassandra unfurled the glove onto the thigh of her dress and looked everywhere but at him. "Oh, Tobias," she said. "They know."

He'd expected this. "I haven't told anyone," he said.

She shook her head. "Nor have I."

Tobias looked to the bureau where he'd thrown his tablet. The first page lay open, a corner of it clinging to the mirror, pointing at the nape of her neck. "You and John share letters," he said. "Have you written something to him?"

"How could you suggest that?"

He thought she said it too quickly, on the ready. He lifted a shoulder and rubbed his knees. "Cassandra, what would it matter if you did? We're announcing it anyway."

"But only after you speak with my father."

"And I can't do that until I'm alone with him, away from your mother."

"Well now," she said, "Mother's gone to him and demanded we be stopped."

"We never thought she'd accept it anyway. Not at first."

"It's worse," Cassandra said.

He followed her gaze to the window beside the bureau. "Am I to lose my job?" he said.

She didn't answer right away. "My mother's anger, I expected," she said. "But not this."

Tobias turned an ear.

"My grandfather. It's scary, Tobias. He's furious. That's how I learned it's gotten out. He's probably still ranting in my father's study."

"What's he saying?"

"Tobias, I don't understand. He hardly knows you."

"Cassandra, look at me." And she did, but stiff and slow, as a headstrong child. "You have to tell me now," he said, "what your mother holds against me."

Cassandra watched her bare hand stroke the glove she still wore. "I can only tell you what I know of my mother's problems." She drew a breath. "It's me she resents."

"Cassandra, you'll do us no favors hiding things from me."

"I didn't expect you'd understand this." She closed her eyes. "It goes back to my grandfather, and my grandmother whom I hardly remember. It's about my mother spending her life as I have—in the shadows of smokestacks with the name Ryder painted in blue, getting on and off trains with it gilded on engines, painted on boxcars."

"Cassandra," Tobias said, and she opened her eyes. "So did we."

"Oh, but Tobias, neither of us grew up in Warren P. Ryder's house on the hill with its spiral turrets and leaded glass, under that man's rules of piety and duty—a man who thinks he's entitled to control people, to pen his daughter like a chicken. Neither of us feeds a sorrow like she does for the things she missed, a sorrow that's turned to self-pity. It's not about you and me, it's about calling attention to herself. This is just another way to look scorned."

Tobias shook his head back and forth. "There's a problem on my part you don't know about, Cassandra. Your grandfather—" But she cut him off.

"After a life where everything I go after is made little, I know things about a person." She leaned ahead in the chair. "That self-pity turned to jealousy for her daughter. She dismisses anything I'm interested in. I was made to feel guilty for even going to a good boarding school. And a finishing school was out of the question—it would have been an insult to her because her father never gave *her* that chance. It's a wonder I'm content in that house at all, where sighs and rolled eyes tell me anything I do is wrong."

"She'd be against us because you'd be happy?" Tobias said.

"She'd say she's bitter because she wants the best for me. But Tobias, her interest in my happiness can't be real, because to her there is no happiness." Cassandra leaned forward. "Don't you see, Tobias, it's not you. My mother would not approve of anyone."

"There must be more. Worse things happen to people than growing up in mansions where the rules are strict."

She was shaking her head, eyes narrowed. "The things we've missed are more crushing than all the horrors the world can throw on us. People with everything lie over train rails, Tobias."

"But she married a great man."

"She married a laundry man, one my grandfather reminds her he made into a hero of the tier."

"That, I know, is not true. Your father is what he is because of something in him. If he lost it all tomorrow, he'd get it back on his own."

"What's in my father," Cassandra said, "is a sharp pang of remembering how quickly life can end. So he races to accomplish all he can." Her voice sharpened. "I've told you his past."

Tobias shrugged.

"It sentenced him to work so intensely that he's numb to what's happened between his wife and daughter. Too busy championing anyone who might have half his ambition. Almost anyone." She slapped her glove against her breast.

"I thought your father was the one person who'd back us."

"He already has," Cassandra said. "Over and over he challenged my grandfather for a solid reason against us. The question remains if he'll try that hard with my mother." She pulled off her other glove. "I never expected it to go this way."

Tobias plucked at a square of red flannel in his bedspread, the pocket still on it. "Did your grandfather give any hints to his problem?"

"He just booms, 'That woodhick will be no heir to Ryder land.'"

"For such small potatoes, I'm a big threat."

They each found a spot on the floor to stare at.

"What are we to do?" he said.

"What we planned."

"They'll prevent it," Tobias said.

"We're twenty-two years old."

He shrugged. "So."

"We'll elope," she said.

Now they met eyes.

"Cassandra, I'll not make you the butt of a scandal."

"I don't care what my mother thinks."

Tobias held up a hand. "Let's slow down."

"They'd never fire you if you were married to me," she said.

"I'm not doing this to keep a job."

"You'll keep me."

He did not answer this; it was not where he'd hoped things would go. "We haven't even thought of where to live."

Cassandra looked around the room, then at her lap. "We'll take a train Friday and get married up in McKean County. Then we'll be off to Niagara Falls. You talk to Nussbaum about us staying here a few days afterward—until we find something."

"I need time to think this through. Our reasons have to be right." He smoothed his bedspread.

She tilted her head, and he saw the hurt.

"I'll be of a better mind Friday," he said.

"We'll meet at the station, then. First train north."

"Cassandra."

She turned an ear.

"Saturday's the company picnic—there'll be a train waiting that morning. It would be even more of a disgrace if they all found out by us not showing up."

"My parents will know by then—I'm already writing the note in my head."

Both their eyes shifted to the opened door. Cassandra reached and touched a sweep of her hair held aloft with a nacred comb. A petite crown, a diadem, it looked to Tobias.

He stood, because he did not know what else to do, and Cassandra did the same. Then she stepped to him and smiled and tugged at his braces, and he inched toward her, stiffly. She rested her face against his shirt buttons. When he put his cheek to her hair, he saw the pair in the mirror, framed against the darkness of the landing. He watched his hands trace around her waist, Tobias wanting to act in the tenderness he knew the moment called for. But his taut elbows trapped her arms and she could not return the embrace, and Cassandra pulled back and kissed him.

*　　*　　*

On the third day at Niagara Falls, as they bicycled upriver on a gravel path in Queen Victoria Park, Cassandra pulled aside and told Tobias she had a surprise.

"I suppose I haven't had enough surprises," he said.

Grinning, she opened the single button at the neck of her shawl, which she wore over a straw-yellow knickerbocker suit. She reached behind her collar, and out came a key on a loop of green yarn.

"It's to John's lodge," she said.

"It's not John's lodge." Tobias immediately wished he hadn't said it.

"In any case, it's there to use," Cassandra said. "It sits new and grand and empty, back in your country, Tobias. And I thought it would be an adventure, finishing our week in the wilds where you used to chop trees and sport about the woods. We'll camp away from the world before we go back to whatever it's preparing for us."

Tobias turned his bicycle handlebars, looking down where the tire grinded the drab autumn lawn-stubble bordering the gravel; he breathed deep the taste of river-foam misting out of the great Niagara cataract. The hydraulic stomp of the falls beyond the park trees charged the ground even where they stood. "We'd never make it there unseen," he said. "Somebody'd spot us waiting at the station in Marstadt. And from Pigeondale it's a hike to Piebald Hollow and up to the lodge."

"That's another surprise." Cassandra reached beneath her collar again. This time she held out a metal trinket on a blue piece of yarn.

"I'm afraid to ask."

"It's the coil key for our Ford motorcar. The newest model—a T."

"Cassandra, how could we afford a car?"

She laughed and leaned toward him, her bicycle canting, then percussing against the ground between her splayed legs as she passed the necklaces of yarn over his cap. She tipped back her straw hat, stretched her neck, and kissed him. "I have it all arranged. We drive from the wagon works once we arrive on the evening train in Marstadt. We'll steal away in the dark. Like a couple of bandits."

*   *   *

From a slight knoll on the valley floor, the lodge looked down on the site of the Piebald camp, little trace of that structure left but the square it occupied among the poplars and pines the hicks had spared for shade.

Like the chimneys, the haunches of the place were all cobblestone, as if a cairn had shoaled itself up out of river rubble in the shape of walls and porch pillars, then snagged around its crown a flotsam of pine shakes and pitch that made for a roof, gables, dormers. Tobias guessed the masons had dredged a mile of Piebald Run for all the shoe-sized stone that mottled gray, beige and sorrel those walls, stout chimneys and porch piers.

Inside, by the beam of the Model T's acetylene lights shining over the stone banister and through the broad glass of a picture window, Tobias found an oil lantern hanging by the door. Back on the porch, he checked the firewood—enough for a couple days.

On blankets they took from beds in the south loft, they spent the first night at the foot of a riverstone fireplace, one of two that bounded the long lounge of the lodge. Tobias had already learned that Cassandra was hungry of the flesh. And something of the sharp autumn air in Piebald Hollow, or that honing of awareness that came in the woods, increased her appetite. Or maybe it was the part of a bandit she imagined. Whatever, it stood out as one of several things he could have learned only living with her. Her love, once spent, cooled quickly, though briefly, then revived, and she kept away. She was an untidy woman who strewed clothes and left hairpins and petticoats in any of the rooms. And from the time they'd departed, she'd started four dime novels, finished no more than twenty pages each, and dropped them in trash cans at stations, one at the hotel in Niagara Falls.

At daylight, they laughed at the ridiculousness and irony of the sign hanging from an exposed beam that spanned the lounge's cathedral ceiling, the words seared into an oak slab: *Welcome to Erhart Carbon's Piebald Lodge, the businessman's haven for respite and jollification.*

They stayed indoors the first day, tending the two fireplaces, eating biscuits and canned fruit they'd brought, drinking spring water and brandy, and moving their talk and lovemaking from the lounge to the balconies and bedrooms, even the empty quarters of the groundskeeper and cook out back of the lodge. And in her brief periods of detachment, Cassandra read from her fifth dime novel of the honeymoon.

The second day they strolled down the new road, which had been that overgrown trail on a rail grade where ten years earlier Tobias walked with John, talking of passenger pigeons and beech saplings that held their leaves, thinking of the clearer cycles of old times. It had been then the forbidden path from his home in Pigeondale, and other times, a way to go fishing, all when the hollow—logged-over though it was—had been a place of only wild trout and hunters and woodhicks.

The place seemed different now, less personal; for some reason he couldn't help seeing it through Cassandra's eyes. The hollow that used to feel as aware of him as he was of it appeared now just a lifeless, cut-over wake, felt empty as a grounds of flattened grass the day after a circus.

In the afternoon they went beyond the lodge, above the new pond, walking along the receding rail bed that he'd always known, where the hollow was left to reclaim on its own terms the old-time work of locomotives, saws, men. The swellings of Piebald Run had begun scraping at the mound of the old grade wherever the winding waterway made a bank of it. Up here, he took more notice of the twenty-year saplings crowning with bright, crisping foliage. And something of the old feel of the land weighed in on him. No, it tried to well up from inside; he no longer believed in such a power possessing these places.

Nor did he have the old desire to be out there counting tree rings or looking for deer sign or just watching and wondering how the pieces of a place all moldered together. Or wondering where passenger pigeons went.

Cassandra pressed for stories he no longer cared to tell. She urged, and finally he ceded with depictions of runaway logs on slopes over in Teaberry Hollow. And she'd stop and hold his waist to hear about men who couldn't outrun them.

It seemed pleasantly innocent how she had no interest in what was most memorable about those days: how hard work erased anxiety of time to come; the way deep hollows compressed the perfume of nectar and sap; the middle peace of working alone, of rare quiet.

*   *   *

He never heard the automobile approach. Near dusk, carrying firewood around the porch after handsawing cleared trees behind the staff quarters, Tobias saw it parked beside their Ford. J. Hadley Erhart leaned against his Buick, one foot on the running board. He peered up at the lodge, drumming his fingers against the car door as if awaiting someone late for a meeting.

Tobias's first thought was of Celia Erhart. He looked to the passenger seat. Not there. Inside the lodge?

Erhart glanced his way and lifted his chin toward the porch. "I thought it would be strange to knock."

The usual benevolence was gone from his eyes and tone. But there seemed no animosity. He just appeared a man holding against something he'd rather not have to say.

Tobias wanted to meet his stare, but the ground kept sucking at his eyes. All he could think of was the Ford motorcar; oddly, it seemed more between them than Cassandra, a four-wheeled monument to audacity, to taking things unearned. Owned on credit, nonetheless, credit Cassandra got by just her name. No matter the circumstances, that car rose suddenly as the thing really taken from this man. Tobias's urge was to run to it, release the brake, and let it roll to the pond.

Rust-colored ants from a punky piece of the firewood were scurrying into his shirtsleeve, carrying their little eggs before their heads. "I've got to put these on the porch," Tobias said, nodding at the logs cradled in his arm.

Erhart turned up his hands and looked away to the pond.

From the porch, Tobias saw Cassandra peering from the edge of the picture window. He dropped the firewood and held up a hand for her to stay put. She simply closed her eyes.

Brushing off ants, he approached Erhart and stood at the bumper of the new Ford. "It's not how I wanted it to be, sir."

Erhart snorted. "So what does that mean? That my daughter abducted you?"

"No, sir."

"You've put me in a hell of a position, Tobias Meier. I'm squeezed from all ends. If it's not the company, it's Mrs. Erhart. If it's not her, it's the man who prospected this land." His eyes swept the hollow. "Why didn't you come to me?"

"We believed Mr. Ryder wouldn't favor it. Neither would Mrs. Erhart."

Erhart shook his head back and forth, glancing at the ring on Tobias's finger, then the lodge. "And she'd favor all this?"

"She can't prevent it this way."

Erhart jerked his head back. "There's a whole town back there saying you did this to get a piece of the company."

"That's not my way, sir, not my interest."

"If that's so, I want to know something from you, Tobias Meier." Erhart pinched the lapels of his overcoat, lifted his shoulders, and took his foot from the running board.

Tobias looked at the hood of the Ford. The name of how he felt came to him. Cheap. Even with all his father's harping, he'd never given his station a thought, never even considered himself in a station. For the first time, he was aware of commonness, that being whatever common meant was cheaper than something else. And he'd gotten someplace where that would rate his say.

He looked over his shoulder at the picture window. He'd thought there'd be other obstacles in the beginning: a place to live; his tendency to take things seriously versus her fickleness; sharing a home with a woman—he a man who'd lived four years among ripe and hard woodhicks.

He nodded for Erhart to ask his question, and looked at the ridge shouldering Piebald Hollow. The old feel of the place was entirely gone, and he thought he had no world anymore, not here, not wherever *there* meant.

"Did you do this," Erhart said, "for fear you'd lose your job if you came to us? Just tell me that."

Tobias gasped out a chuckle. He shook his head no, stared at the ground.

"Tobias, look at me."

The old J. Hadley Erhart was back, congenial grin, raised, brushy brow. Erhart whisked his shoe over the straw on the seeded ground. "I expected that. But I needed to be sure. Tobias, I understand your situation more than you know." The grin faded. "There are things I wish I could tell you. I'll just say there is a fear in my heart of a difference of intentions." He looked back for a moment at the tall pines and poplars where the Piebald camp had stood. "When you were just a boy, I saw an eagerness in you I liked—the very day this company was conceived. I don't want you to lose that. But—" Erhart tapped his car— "more than that, I have to protect my daughter's interests. I'll do all I can to defend you, so long as those interests are safe."

They stood a moment in silence.

"From Cassandra's note," Erhart said, "I understand you plan to live awhile where you take rooms."

Tobias nodded.

"You realize you won't be able to stay at the house, even after me coming here."

"I wouldn't expect it."

"Mrs. Erhart will come around," Erhart said, "just not right away." He tipped back his fedora and looked uphollow.

With the last-hurrah light of the set sun glancing off the paling sky, patches of sassafras and blackgum glowed yellow and maroon on the far ridgetop, like the skin of a peach. The musky scent of autumn dusk flooded the bottomland, a few weak-kneed crickets still scraping out *treeb treebs* where grass had taken hold around the pond.

"It's my father-in-law I'm not sure about," Erhart said. "I don't believe he'll talk to you. Perhaps he'll change his mind." He lifted his chin at the lodge and raised the big brows. "Mind if I go up?" He grinned, and Tobias guessed it was at the strangeness of asking.

Tobias stepped aside.

"It's quite a place, isn't it?" Erhart said. He took in the expanse of the cobblestone porch, then traced one of the jutting chimneys. "All native material."

Tobias turned and studied it with him.

"A fitting monument to these wilds," Erhart said, glancing back and eying the sharp fold of the hollow, already entirely an even olive drab. "He did a good job."

"Who?"

"Johnny Blesh."

Chapter 19

Married more than a year, and Tobias had never been to the home of his wife's grandfather. But it was always there, always looming from the hill, no matter whether business on Marstadt's east side took a person to the station, Erhart Carbon, Ryder's tannery, or his brick works.

Tobias turned the Ford onto the drive and looked up at the twin turrets and piercing gable of buff brick, rising naked as the bare hill they crowned. With neither trees nor shrubs hedging the house, the mighty louring of it seemed to huff in breaths.

There hadn't been much snowfall, but now the tips of the turrets tickled the bellies of gray, pregnant clouds. Five o'clock, nearly dark on Christmas eve—the first holiday he and Cassandra had been invited to spend with her family.

Like everything for Warren P. Ryder, the affair was more a company event, the top men and their wives from his operations joining to toast the success of his empire. The extra guests were a relief. In the time Tobias had been married, Ryder had no more than lifted his brows in passing at the factory.

Tobias parked the car by a lighted side entrance, helped Cassandra out, and started for the steps.

"No, Tobias," she said, pinching his coat sleeve. "That's the children's entranceway. Put there for my mother." Cassandra nodded to the second floor. "She even had her own stairway—my grandparents did not favor a child dirtying the house." Cassandra started for the covered carriageway at the front.

The door opened, and Celia Erhart stepped back to accept them. She flicked Cassandra a smile and kissed her cheek, then gave Tobias her customary glance, which she always concluded with a quick closing of her eyes. But then J. Hadley Erhart was there, arm around Cassandra and hand out to Tobias. "Merry Christmas," he said.

"Same to you, sir."

"All the company men are in the parlor," Erhart said. "Andy Hoehn's here. And Josiah Blesh, and the Midwest salesman. You already know a few people."

Cassandra handed Tobias her coat, plucked at the hips of her strawberry gown, and patted the matching velvet bow atop her head. Sprays of ostrich plumes jiggled from a bundle of curls. "Is John coming?"

"Due any minute," her father said.

"It's been so long."

Cassandra followed her mother into an adjoining reception room. The far end was rounded with one of the turrets, its leaded, stained art windows illuminated by the carriageway lights. Women in evening gowns sat at the edges of parlor chairs and couches.

Tobias considered the incongruity of a mother and daughter, so similar in height, dark complexion and black hair, hardly speaking to one another.

J. Hadley Erhart took from Tobias the coats and his hat and passed them to a woman who'd come down the hallway from the kitchen. Tobias recognized her as Gerda Zissl, Ryder's chief housekeeper, whom Tobias had seen at the factory delivering meeting luncheons—a short, stout woman who pointed aloft her bowsprit of a nose.

Erhart nodded across the reception room to a brightly lit archway. "I'll take you to the parlor."

Along the way, Erhart put a hand on Tobias's shoulder. "I know this is hard for you. But be patient. Not everyone is quick to accept the hand they're dealt."

Expansive and furnished only along the perimeter, the parlor could have been a small ballroom. Two dozen or so men stood about. Tobias's eye went immediately to Josiah Blesh, his bald pate aglow in the yellow light of the crystal chandelier. Tobias hadn't seen him since Blesh left Pigeondale two years ago. Even in a long-tailed dress coat, he carried his broad waist as a staff of authority.

Then Tobias spotted Ernie Groeger sitting near a white-pine Christmas tree and staring into his glass of beer, the only man at a seat. Erhart saw Tobias looking. "I persuaded Warren to invite Ernie this year. With no family, living way out at that camp, it must be lonely on the holiday."

Andy Hoehn stood with Warren P. Ryder near the fireplace. Erhart led Tobias that way, and the nerves in his gut jittered as furiously as the hearth flames. Ryder regarded Tobias, head tilted, lips puckered.

Hoehn grinned. "Our formula man."

Tobias smiled best he could. "Apprentice formula man," he said, glancing at Ernie Groeger who—within earshot—was looking his way.

"A drink?" Erhart said.

"Beer would be good," Tobias said, still watching Groeger, wishing he could take the chair beside him.

Erhart took his own empty glass from the mantel and made for Gerda where she stood in a doorway to the hall. Tobias concentrated on the two logs burning on the andirons, the flames yellow-tipped. He drew in through his nose. Birch, he guessed, black birch.

Andy Hoehn watched Tobias. "Quite a fireplace," he said, nodding at the hearth, then smiling at Ryder. The host said nothing, face fixed, head still tilted.

Tobias took in the mantel. Chestnut. The elaborately carved columns suspended a mantelpiece of marble, below which spanned a diamond mosaic of inlaid tile. The tile mirrored the design of the hearth, which arced out level with the floor, its tile inlaid with diamonds of five differently shaded hardwoods. Alongside the fireplace, a gold-plated fire poker, ash shovel and broom hung from decorative ironwork, knobby and brass like the andirons.

The preponderance of the thick pillars made the fireplace the focal point of the room, and Tobias could see in the way everyone was positioned that they reflexively gave it attention. Of course Ryder probably drew them, too. Still, Tobias sensed something else pulling everyone's eyes.

Like the parlor, the mouth of the fireplace gaped in impractical enormity; the little two-log fire did not heat the room. Must be another source. He saw no floor registers, so looked for what might be hiding a radiator—just reasons not to look at Warren P. Ryder. That's when Tobias caught in his periphery a veiled frame reaching from above the mantel to the twenty-foot ceiling. He'd been so nervous, he'd missed the biggest thing in the room.

Andy Hoehn followed Tobias's gaze, then turned to Ryder. "When will they unveil it?"

Ryder did not look up, just sipped his brandy, the snifter lost behind his big hand. "Before dinner, we'll have a look."

Erhart returned with Tobias's glass of beer. "Andy," he said, "let's go speak with the brick and tile men about how they're building those new kilns."

They stepped away, and Tobias had to hold back from pinching Erhart's coat. But he knew Erhart wanted him to break whatever ice Ryder kept between them, and if Tobias did not speak, Ryder would be gone in a second. "I take it," Tobias said, "we're in for a surprise." He lifted his chin toward the veiled frame.

Ryder let out a loud exhale.

Tobias raised his glass a few inches. "Thank you for having us."

Ryder, as though not to be outdone on propriety, took his brandy from the mantelpiece and matched the toast, but without quite looking Tobias in the eye.

"I'm learning quite a bit in the lab," Tobias said. "Ernie's a great teacher."

Ryder drew a breath and looked around the room, then half-dropped, half-set down his brandy where it clinked against a walnut-cased clock. "Let's get beyond the pleasantries."

Tobias waited.

"Don't expect anything to be easy for you, Tobias Meier."

"Sir?"

"Don't act naïve. You pilfered my granddaughter from this family."

Tobias shook his head. "It's not like that."

Ryder reached and stroked the beveled edge of the marble mantelpiece, still not looking at Tobias. "What beyond your disdain for me made you do it?"

Tobias was taken aback by the admission of guilt in this, but only for a second. After all, there was no denying he'd made him face his own poor judgment, was probably one of few with reason to doubt his integrity. Tobias would always be the boy who'd seen too much.

"Mr. Ryder, I have much respect for you."

"If I can ensure it without affecting my granddaughter," Ryder said, "you will be heir to nothing. I will always be on the lookout for a way."

Tobias sensed a very dangerous threat tucked in this. He already had reason not to trust this man, knew his rashness.

Cheers erupted through the archway. Tobias was glad for the distraction of John Blesh in the reception room. He walked among the ladies, hands out, all smiles, playing the late arrival as if he jumped from a box after being sawed in half. John kissed his mother's cheek, then moved along, feigning modesty to women doting on this young man fresh from the city. He went to Cassandra where she stood with her mother. John embraced and kissed Cassandra, took her mother's hand a moment. Cassandra beamed.

Tobias glanced at Ryder, who watched with interest. He seemed finally pleased, whether at John being there, or at Cassandra's delight. "Now there's a star," he said.

"Mr. Ryder, I'm not after anything I don't earn."

Ryder turned on him, sharp. "How did you, a common woodhick, ever earn that?" He flinched his chin at Cassandra.

John pulled bunches of cigars from his pockets and waved them at the men through the archway. Ryder started away.

Tobias gulped his beer. He wished he could wash away the conversation with it. He took in the room. Clearly the parlor of a lumberman, a stained and polished forest. Bird's eyes peeked from maple paneling as rich-grained as the butt of a log. Novel heartwood, all right.

Two windows, nearly tall as the ceiling, reflected the shine of the chandelier. Feeling awkward, alone against the murmur of the room, Tobias stepped over and reached behind a velvet, tight-girdled curtain. He ran an index finger along the cherry molding, slow and speculative, as if the egg and dart carving sang back in braille. Turning to see if the doorframes were of the same design, he caught Ernie Groeger rising from his chair. They met at the mantel.

"Glad you came, Ernie." Tobias raised his glass. "You don't know how glad."

Ernie sipped his beer, his good eye watching Tobias so intently it drove him to the doughy dead one, then to Groeger's crooked tie and dandruff-dusted coat.

"You don't belong here," Groeger said.

"You're the second person to tell me that tonight, and I've only been here ten minutes."

Groeger lifted a shoulder. "No more than me." He glanced where John Blesh and Cassandra moved through the room. Cassandra pointed John's attention to the veiled frame on the wall, neither of them taking notice of Tobias and Groeger.

It was time to greet John Blesh, something Tobias did not relish. Ever since the marriage, John had kept a cool distance when in town, never stopping by the house to go for drinks and billiards, no calls to go hunting.

Tobias started away. But Groeger stopped him. "Maybe you belong here *even less* than me."

"Pardon?" Tobias said.

Groeger shrugged and waited while an outbreak of laughter from the Josiah and John Blesh circle ebbed. "You tell yourself you're everyone's idea of you."

Groeger tipped his head back and emptied his glass of beer, his gullet twitching with fast swallows, the corduroy scars of his face raw and welted against the glare of the chandelier. He finished and breathed out. "You're a different man from when we met at my camp. Now you think being like me means being me. That ain't for you any more than this." He waved his empty glass around the room of black coats and varnished hardwood.

Cassandra and John were headed for Tobias. Cassandra's face was blank as the veil that covered the wall hanging, soberness Tobias knew came of his company. John was all smiles, though, in his jaunty gait, not cold and indifferent as he'd been the few times Tobias had seen him at the factory lately.

Tobias shook the hand John had put out five paces away.

"Merry Christmas," they said together.

John pulled a cigar from his coat pocket.

"No thanks," Tobias said, smiling at Cassandra.

Groeger grabbed the cigar.

"So, Cassandra," John said, raising his chin at the covered frame. "You say it's a gift from your mother and father."

She nodded. "But don't ask me for details. I've been told nothing."

"Who are you fooling?" John said. "The girls always talk."

The comment hung in silence while Cassandra and Tobias both glanced away. John watched them. "Sorry," he said. "I guess she still hasn't warmed to things." Tobias would have preferred John had not brought up this subject he and Cassandra avoided anymore, for it made her distant and tearful, days on end.

The ladies from the reception room were filtering in among the men, voices gradually quieting with anticipation for the unveiling. Celia Erhart stepped in from the hallway, head cocked, eyes severe, and the decrescendo of voices seemed to follow a new movement—the subtle slant of men's glances. In the chandelier light, the lavender of her tight-waisted evening dress radiated as if its own lamp globe. Her usual indifference was regal now. She wore tendrils of diamond earrings and a French roll bunched high with red and green ribbon. In what looked offhand, but Tobias guessed was an intentional part of her entrance, she reached to the square breast-cut of her dress and stroked a silver broach at her throat.

Tobias looked to Cassandra and remembered something the justice of the peace up in McKean County had said when they married, part of a quasi-sermon he gave after their vows. *Look through each other's eyes, the windows of your souls.* A cold, constricting needle stitched through Tobias's heart at the idea that he'd only wanted the window for a view to that world that had tantalized a mill-town boy all those years ago. But the stitch unwove when he looked back at Celia Erhart. For sure, though eclipsed by the darkness of eyes, the bright shine of a soul made windows that ornate, and so must have drawn him to her daughter with her own dark eyes. For sure, experienced men of the world pursued such women for something deeper than the sockets of enticing eyes. The warning instincts of a Pigeondale woodhick were not reliable.

Then J. Hadley Erhart stepped behind his wife, and Tobias affirmed his judgment through him.

Cassandra waved her mother to her. Celia's gaze, tight as her French roll, swept the faces around her daughter, and as if she'd taken in nothing more than the fireplace, she looked away. J. Hadley Erhart touched her elbow and steered her into the room.

"Guess it's time to let the curtain drop on this show," John said as he nodded up at the wall hanging.

Cassandra, defeated in eyes and voice now, said, "The curtain drops when the show's over, John."

He shrugged. "My guess is it's a likeness of your late grandmother, Cassandra." He flicked his eyes at Tobias. "What do you say?"

Tobias looked to J. Hadley Erhart and considered. "I say it's not that, and that's as far as I'll guess."

John rolled his eyes and waved Gerda to him. Before she arrived, he said, "Scotch"—a little too loud and forceful for the lull that had come over the party.

In the center of the room, J. Hadley Erhart put a hand in the air. "Excuse me," he said, and the crowd widened around him and his wife, who stood so still and stern, she could have been the subject posing for whatever hung on the wall.

"Many of you know the history of Warren P. Ryder." Erhart made a show of checking himself. "Well, maybe the time's come to say the *legend* of Warren P. Ryder." A few chuckles came from the perimeter, and Erhart cupped a hand to his ear. "Did someone say *myth?*" This drew polite laughter, and heads turned to find Ryder. He stood in the archway of the reception room, head perched aslant on the tall Edwardian collar of his black coat, eyes, pug nose and pointed lips aimed at the chandelier.

"In 1854," Erhart said, "he came here by horseback. Sixteen years old, and he already had visions for a place towering in timber and boiling with gases and oil and black coal."

A few heads turned Ryder's way in acknowledgement.

"He also saw the pioneering pluck of the Bavarians. Through their good hands, and the leadership of many of the men in this room, Marstadt took the shape of his plan."

Erhart raised his glass, and up came a chant of "Hear, hear." Celia Erhart remained unmoved.

Erhart lowered his glass. "A railroad and engine shops. Landholdings, sawmills and lumbering operations, the brick and tile works. An interest in practically every business in the region, from the furniture factory to merchandise establishments and banks, even the new opera house."

Erhart pointed to his eyes. "Warren continually looked ahead, and now, through Erhart Carbon, he's invested in the electrification of the nation and the coming of personal transportation."

He raised his finger in the air. "But it all sprang forth from a looming presence that greeted my father-in-law that day he arrived on horseback. The canvas on which all his early visions were drawn, and the backdrop of all our future enterprises."

Erhart paused on this, and John glanced at the veiled frame. He leaned toward Cassandra and whispered, "I think I know what's coming. And I sure hope your grandfather's more flattered than I think he'll be."

Erhart turned to Ryder, who remained smug and still, eyes narrowed now in wariness. "Business is booming," Erhart said, "but in new places. Lumber is down. Tanning is down. So instead of flatbeds of logs and lumber, the Ryder Railroad is moving coal from the mines to the South." He held up his glass. "In only eight years, we've become number one in carbons for dry cell batteries and arc lights. And now, motor brushes."

Huffing *hear hears* came from the quarter held by Andy Hoehn and the factory floor supervisors, and Erhart moved his glass their way. Then he nodded toward the hallway.

Nose extended, Gerda Zissl made her way to the mantel, and held her hand out to the cord hanging from the top of the muslin veil. Erhart pointed to it. "It all proceeds from the trees, from the land that issues them, that endows lumber with the strength and beauty and grain of its native place." He nodded to Gerda. "To Celia's father, on this Christmas eve. And for his seventy-first birthday."

Gerda pulled the cord, and Tobias knew the scene immediately. The chestnuts of Fiddlers Flats. Titans that demanded such a large canvas. But this rendering was certainly in the imagination of the oil painter, for the crowns stretched green and lush into faint blue heavens. The chestnuts of Fiddlers Flats—spared centuries by inaccessibility—were in fact withering in their reaches, death spreading from their foliage down to where the cancer of the imported fungus blight had traveled and girdled away their flow of sap.

Tobias had seen the leafless, barkless bones of branches at their crowns the one time he'd gotten away to hunt the Flats that fall. He'd looked up from exactly the artist's perspective—at the end of a long alley between two rows of the great trunks, lines that Tobias suspected weren't accidents in old woods, rather somehow fit nature's chain.

Sunlit mist beamed through the passageway, but the thrust of the scene was all upward with the hope and power big trees drew from the sun. Tobias liked the painting, even if—or maybe because—all it contained were a leaf-mottled ground and the illusion of infinite furrowed trunks trailing into deeper wilderness, reaching with their leaves into that glowing haze. The strength and movement of the scene told that the painter sensed in Fiddlers Flats what thin places were closest to.

The initial reaction from the crowd struck Tobias by its indifference, just a couple sighs. Then a few men half-uttered, half-grunted *hmms*.

J. Hadley Erhart looked around, gauging the reaction. When he saw Tobias's smile, he looked relieved. He winked.

Erhart spoke up as if they hadn't quite gotten it. "The scene is a tract beyond Pigeondale where Warren used to hunt. One of the last native stands of hardwood, just as it might have greeted him all those years ago. Almost pure chestnut." He stretched his arms as if measuring. "Folks, these are enormous trees spared of the axe. A living symbol of our legacy."

John had given the painting a glance, and now, with a bored and superior frown, was concentrated on his glass of scotch. Cassandra had studied the scene, but Tobias could tell in the slight shrug she gave John that she'd counted on the likeness of her grandmother. She showed no intention of stepping in line with the people shaking her grandfather's hand; she'd joined John in his superior embarrassment. Cassandra, Tobias decided, was not an imaginative person. Just one with a strong imagination.

Ernie Groeger was smitten by the painting, though. Gnawing his cigar, neck bent, he traced every tree trunk, up and up, again and again, just as the painting seemed to call for. The Bavarian eccentric who appalled people with his yellowed collar and crooked tie was the one admiring the painting, while the uncomfortable ones were Tobias's better-born wife and a man in a tailored suit. The scene, the absurdity of the whole night, had Tobias wondering if Groeger was right about him.

"So what do you see in it?" Tobias said to John. He couldn't keep a challenge out of his voice.

John shifted his look of boredom to Tobias. "In what?"

Tobias nodded up at the painting.

"Furniture."

"I guessed so much."

John snorted a laugh, and turned his boredom to the room.

"What about you, Cassandra?" Tobias said.

Groeger studied her closely, too. She looked at John. "I like what John said. Maybe that's the point of it after all. Furniture. I mean, just look at what my father said."

Eye still on Cassandra, Ernie Groeger said, "Tobias Meier, what do you think of the picture?"

"To me, it's about something in the angle."

John rolled his eyes, and Cassandra bunched her face, annoyed. Ernie looked from her to Tobias, good eye probing.

Cassandra missing his take would not have bothered Tobias except for an insight gained after a year of marriage, of watching this girl reincarnate ideas as often as she tired by page twenty of the characters in those dime novels she sampled like chocolates in a confectionery. He knew that had she not already taken John's view, she'd have been as likely to agree with Tobias.

But darker than this loomed the real picture of Fiddlers Flats, the last native hardwoods, defenseless against that venom from afar.

Even after J. Hadley and Celia Erhart went to offer Ryder their congratulations, the circle they'd occupied remained open, a vacuum of uneasiness, a collective breath everyone held as they awaited Ryder's acknowledgement. He'd shown no reaction, face sour as always, even as he took people's hands.

Then Ryder stepped into the opening, turning his thick shoulders as he looked face to face, and finally to his painting.

Ryder nodded, then spoke as if a stray thought struck. "Hadley is right. When I arrived at these headwaters fifty-five years ago, this land was simply coarse material for something greater."

Then Ryder's eyes fell on Tobias. His look said that he'd moved merely from a common woods scene to a woodhick. Raw material.

After having promised against it, Tobias cowered. He let Ryder shame away the satisfaction he tried to feel at being rated with the grade and grain of heartwood that made this polished room so grand.

Ryder turned his attention a moment to his granddaughter. He smiled, then raised his brandy. All the glasses in the room went up—but to Warren P. Ryder, not his painting.

Still smiling, Ryder went on. "Thanks to a few select men, we've moved from axes to prosperity in an era of machines and electrification. The real tribute today should not be to trees, but the persistence of men like Andy Hoehn, who believed his idea would serve us well when I knew it was time to diversify."

Heads turned to Andy Hoehn.

"Companies like Westinghouse," Ryder said, "laughed us off at first. Now they take our shipments every day. That kind of conquest will continue our success. As will the kind of man who represents us to Westinghouse." Ryder nodded to John. "The future of any enterprise that carries the name Ryder or Erhart is ambitious young men like Johnny Blesh."

As *hear hears* started from Josiah Blesh's corner of the room, Tobias raised his glass higher and wedged his lips into the same proud smile his wife beamed for her friend John.

"So perhaps this vision my son-in-law speaks of was always for the modern world, which men like Johnny Blesh will continue forging into, far from forsaken wilderness. A vision not for the coarse raw material of trees—" he lifted his chin at the painting— "rather in spite of them."

Tobias looked for Erhart. He could see only the top of his head, back in the cherry-framed doorway. He was sure the crimson brows were raised with a polite grin.

Beyond him, Gerda and another server waved the crowd into the dining room.

*   *   *

After the meal, Tobias and Cassandra visited with John again under the painting in the parlor. Then they went to the reception room to thank Warren P. Ryder for the evening.

"I appreciate the kind words," John said, shaking Ryder's hand.

"No kindness at all," Ryder said, watching Tobias. "Just the truth."

When Ryder took the hand Tobias offered, he still spoke to John. "You have the vision spoken of tonight, Johnny. Nothing will get in the way of what you want." Ryder let go of Tobias's hand. "Just picture what you're after." He leaned forward for Cassandra to kiss his cheek. "And take it."

Chapter 20

Other than seeing Cassandra at company Christmas parties, and twice for lunch during ladies' shopping excursions to Pittsburgh, letters had been as close as John Blesh had let himself get for three years—until finally the sting of things had faded. So he was surprised by the part of Marstadt he found himself walking through to find her address. Nice enough, but not where he pictured the daughter of J. Hadley and Celia Erhart. A neighborhood of clapboard two-stories on a knoll, not far off the square, probably homes of shopkeepers and clerks. Paved streets at least.

John had seen little of Marstadt in that time, little of Erhart Carbon, and as little of Tobias Meier as he could.

Marstadt was just a place he passed through as he took customers to the lodge, the factory just a stop on the return to give customer tours, pick up product samples. He avoided Ernie Groeger and his lab when he could, spoke a pleasantry to Tobias when he couldn't. Said, "Hey Meier," and moved on to look over the latest expansion of the plant.

But he'd never lost touch with Cassandra, exchanging letters, keeping track of the path she'd taken, that one he'd never expected.

So where had three years gone? A stretch so busy it didn't seem divisible by thirds, so quickly it unraveled while he chased things he'd set out to catch. And ignored ones that got away. It was a ledger's-worth of dinners on the expense account, too many drinks on top of them, and a rasp in his voice from all-night cigarettes and fawning fibs to prospects—customers or women.

Now was time to account for those years, redeem all he'd promised himself. He was spending the week in Marstadt. A last hurrah of sorts, the place he'd begin his reckoning.

He had put millions of carbons into flashlight batteries, arc lights, moving picture projectors. So what if he hadn't gotten around to finding those new niches he'd promised, or to selling any of Erhart's beloved automobile starter brushes. If he'd been in New York among the real innovators, it would have happened. But there was no convincing the fool ownership. Give them a lodge, and they stretch his territory to upstate New York, out to Michigan, down to Cincinnati. The "northeast man," they called him. But it was interior northeast, Boston and New York still handled by the most senior rep. Philadelphia was his, though, and look what he'd done—beaten the American Carbon man on the contract for generator brushes in all those electrified locomotives built there. A new factory wing to manufacture just those, a warehouse to keep them on hand. Four hundred people in that plant now—three bays, the warehouse, a two-story office building. He accounted for a good share of it. And more locomotive business was to be had.

So it was logical to be in town for this stint, logical to go yesterday to the lab to request samples for new proposals, there where he'd gotten Tobias Meier's starch-stiff reception—where he'd had to tear down the fence of awkwardness that separated old friends who'd lost touch, who had little in common anymore. Except a wife with whom one shared friendly letters.

Tobias—son-in-law of an owner, still doing Ernie Groeger's bidding. He'd refused John's invitation to dine out, as John knew he would. And that had left Tobias obliged to invite his wife's correspondent to dinner.

*   *   *

Knowing the factory shift finished at five, John reached the house number a half hour early. The Model T was parked on the gravel drive. Meier walked to work—he should have guessed. John stood a moment on the walk, ridding his vision of the home he'd pictured for Cassandra. He glanced at the low gray sky and drew in the must of November, curdling now with sharp hints of winter. Throwing his cigarette, he looked the place over, the color wrung out of even the lawn. Other houses had dabs of life about their limed siding and black shutters: evergreen shrubs, painted porch chairs, a sign in a window for ice delivery. There, a red bicycle leaning against cement steps.

He stepped to the door, which was cracked open, an indefinite whiff of cooking shimming through. He tapped with a knuckle, pulled in his sales-luncheon paunch, and stepped into the foyer. It opened to a large sitting room as wide as the house. He called.

All smiles as she came into the room, her hair pinned tight, Cassandra looked like the wrong woman cast on a domestic stage set, a self-conscious star who knew she called for too much imagination to play housewife. She kissed his cheek and took his bowler and a bottle of wine, then his overcoat. She offered him a seat on the sofa.

"It's French," John said as he sat.

"Delightful."

She reached to hang his overcoat on a high hook behind the door. He thought less flesh shaped the skirt of her lilac dress, though he couldn't be sure—skirts themselves were less full these days, nothing but loose kimonos tapered to the shins, the Boticelli figure. A little too urbane for this place.

She joined him on the sofa, and even by her face he might have thought her frailer, except that Cassandra Erhart—er, Meier—always seemed to wane into those dark features.

"I didn't know," John said, "if I'd be allowed in this town with a bottle of wine."

Cassandra looked around a moment. "Oh, the Germans." And she laughed, then watched him, and he saw her try to read his face, wondering if she should be critical, or if it was just a good-natured poke. "Well," she said, "you get used to it being a beer town. The brewery is just over the hill." She pointed across the back of the sofa. "It's convenient. We just go with a bucket and fill it from a barrel there."

When he didn't respond, she looked down at the bottle cradled in her lap. "Well, for our dinner, Tobias won't have to go down for a pail full."

They looked away from each other, and John tried to reconcile a sentence like that out of the Cassandra he knew. He started shaking his leg. He needed a cigarette. Something. Probably not a drop of bourbon in the neighborhood.

His eyes traced the wall running up the stairs. "Those look like the pictures from the stave mill."

"Tobias wanted those so badly when they tore that place down. I think he pestered your father to help him get them. He insisted they hang in this room, so I compromised that they go along the stairs. Just old woodhick pictures."

John had an urge to write that last line in his pocket journal. Then the note: *The novelty has worn away.*

"In your last letter," he said, "you mentioned taking on something part-time."

"It's a thought. Maybe help somewhere at the factory. In an office."

He leaned her way with a show of concern. "Not something you *have* to do?"

"Of course not."

Which he didn't believe. But neither could he believe that J. Hadley Erhart would let his daughter get into that financial strait. Her mother, maybe. He knew she still hadn't warmed to the couple—*endures us for visits*, Cassandra had written. John reasoned Erhart had submitted to the queen's spite, cut them off to make Tobias earn whatever piece of the company might come his way, like John's dad had made him hump as a kid to learn whatever lesson was wedged up his ass. But that plan made Celia look more like a tyrant than the martyr she liked to be. He was missing part of this.

John went to say that Cassandra was too fair to breathe that carbon powder and be around coarse factory labor, when another angle struck. Grandfather Warren P. Ryder, who still held reign over even Cassandra's mother, had all but disowned Cassandra for marrying Meier. He'd heard all about it in telephone conversations with the office girls. But never a word from Cassandra.

"How's your grandfather? I don't hear much from him these days."

She bit her bottom lip. "Fine. Seventy-four now. Spends most of his time between the railroad offices and the plant. Still visits the little timber contracts your father runs up North."

"See him much?"

"No, not often." She stood the wine bottle on her thigh. "I have to put the biscuits in the oven. Would you like a drink? We have Coca-Cola. Chilled in the icebox."

"No, just an ashtray." As she set the bottle on the coffee table and crossed the room, he reached under his coat for a cigarette and breathed the lavender water she'd bathed in. He struck a match and narrowed his eyes as he held the flame to his cigarette. He drew heavily and writhed into the sofa with that excited energy that swept him whenever he lit up, or poured bourbon. He seemed to need the boost more and more. His body felt sopped all over his bones lately, wet and heavy, his every step a wading against tide. Until he telephoned for a date, or situated himself at table before a nice steak.

Cassandra returned with a terra-cotta ashtray, put it on the coffee table, and sat next to him again.

"Tobias should have let me treat us to dinner at the Stauffer Hotel," John said.

"That would have been nice." She stared across the room.

He smiled and shrugged and tapped his cigarette against the ashtray. "So what are you cooking? I'm sure we'll be glad we stayed in."

"Corn chowder, roast and potatoes. Plain fare." She nodded toward the foyer. "The house smells of the grease I started the roast in. That's why the door's cracked."

Cassandra picked up the wine bottle, looked at the label a moment, and gave a little laugh. "I had to think about whether this was the right color for a roast." She rose. "After the biscuits, John, I want to hear about all the places you've traveled to."

He watched her go through the pair of doors that opened to a dinette. The way she moved hadn't changed: forced composure, shifting eyes peripherally alert to being watched, as if she walked in a boutique with a stolen scarf in her purse. He'd always liked that self-consciousness.

Now he had a moment to look around for what had been tugging at his sleeve as odd in this room. First, it was dark. Two windows, curtains drawn. Just one electric lamp burned on a bookstand near the door.

He took note of the furniture. The sofa, part of a matching suite, was framed in black walnut and upholstered in sorrel horsehair. All the pieces had foliage-incised, cabriole legs and claw feet. Expensive. Very expensive. And the lady wanted a job?

The coffee table was marble-topped. Over on the mantel, beneath some nickel-worn gun of Tobias's, a mahogany clock tick-tocked, brass candelabra, six sockets each, flanking its sides. He walked to a corner by the side window where stood a Chippendale lowboy with scrolled drawers and brass handles. He picked up a decorative water jug nestled in a basin of gilt-stenciled china. A mirror of beveled glass hung above it, flowers leaded into the corners, interlaced fruit and flora carved into the mahogany frame. All the finest.

He stared back at himself. His face seemed bloated lately, his eyes swelling out all the more. He tugged his coat over his paunch and sucked in. Then he patted each side of his parted hair, turned his head to see if the traces of gray showed in the room's pall. Not bad.

He scanned the room in the mirror. The place had a defeated air of enduring the wrong occupants. It was all the finery that made the house feel off-key, furnishings that appeared temporarily quartered, a grand estate held for auction. Everything mobile—not even carpet or wallpaper.

He could only figure that this was a home of belated wedding gifts and gestures passed on as Celia Erhart accepted that her daughter had eloped with a man such as Tobias. But her pride stood in the way of liberating all this to a better home, for that required patronizing Tobias with a better job. Or maybe that's where Grandfather got in the way.

The absurd wealth of the room slapped John with what he usually made himself ignore: just how poised Tobias Meier was to step up in Erhart Carbon. At that, he wanted another cigarette. The taste of bourbon caught in his throat, twitched his nose.

He heard Cassandra setting places at a table. So Tobias came home every day to reminders of what could be, yet lacked the means to properly house the goods, probably barely afforded that five-year-old Model T.

What if this was a life sentence? Maybe Tobias, the dreamy woodhick, would be dumb enough to do something drastic, thinking he'd help Cassandra break from her well-appointed cage. Whether so hardly mattered. Just that it was conceivable could help John. If everybody in Marstadt thought Tobias was frustrated in not getting a piece of the company, John had a second insurance policy if things backfired. He'd get a better sense for that at dinner.

He pressed down his hair once more and went to move away when he caught the other thing the house fairly heaved to expel. He'd had to bend some to look in the mirror, and straightening, he could see the floor beneath sofas and chairs, the bottom shelves of bookcases. The place was not just opulent, but a mess. He turned and stooped and strained his eyes into the dim light. Stuffed under furniture were papers and magazines, lidless shoeboxes of pencils and tablets and coasters and every miscellany that a person would keep in drawers—at least a person who cared at all for her situation.

John stepped to a corner chair, its back the shape of a lyre. He brushed a finger across the top—thick with dust. Behind the chair stood boxes, three high. Books. He pulled one out. Dime novels. There had to have been a hundred. He flipped through others—spines hardly stretched. She wasn't finishing these any more than she even pretended to play house with Tobias.

The jittering in his chest that had him reaching for cigarettes and tasting his whiskey calmed; finally a clear take of the whole picture: fickle Cassandra, the unheeded daughter. Tired of all those tries to get bitter Mother to approve some or the other joy, she went for simple attention, married a woodhick, then told a Cassandra she didn't even know that that was the thing for her. And lost interest in the second chapter.

The doors to the dining room swung open.

"Oh, don't mind that mess, John. I haven't had time to pitch it."

He returned the book, put on the smile he wore to sales calls, and sat with her at the marble-topped coffee table.

"Let me ask you a personal question," John said, holding the smile.

"Only if I can ask you one." She smiled, too.

"In all our letters, there's one thing you never mention."

She waited.

"Children."

Cassandra looked at her hands on her lap. "Everything is always different on the other side," she said.

"Of what?"

"Of what you want." She waved her hand around the room, her voice suddenly weary. "Oh, John, nothing ever feels right once I get it." She was quiet a moment. "Now, does that answer your personal question?" she said.

"I haven't completely asked it."

"It answers it, though. Now my turn."

But John held up a hand. "Is it that you don't want children because marriage with Tobias didn't turn out as well as you thought? Or that children would make commitment too real? Realer than you'd anticipated."

She smiled and looked away and said it was maybe a little of both. And he could see she was going to leave it at that.

"Here's my personal question," she said. "All your letters are of new cities and shows. Restaurants and big deals. Not a mention of a lady." She spoke slow and teasingly.

He chuckled, then sighed and fibbed that the job kept him too busy for more than occasional dinners with friends, that he feared his chance for the right woman would pass him by while he gave his life to Erhart Carbon.

*   *   *

The moment Tobias came, John could smell the factory. Then he was up and over to the door, hand extended, smile turned on.

"Thanks for inviting me," he said, taking that big sandpaper hand, so different from the cold manicured fingers he usually shook.

Tobias nodded. The last few years had wiped the eager boy from his face. The eyes were still wide, but now with a trace of that general wariness John saw in most men. When Tobias said "Glad you came," it was in his voice, too.

Cassandra stood beside him now. Tobias touched her shoulder, a tender slowing in his movements. "Tell me what I can do to help," he said.

"Why don't you change out of those clothes. I'm sure the last thing John wants is the odor of Ernie Groeger's experiments."

John laughed. "You can take the boy out of the lab…"

* * *

The furnishings of the dinette were as elaborate as those in the living room. Cherry-everything, right down to the china cabinet, which held all the crystal of a wealthy couple who'd had a real wedding.

John pulled up a chair, and Cassandra came in, carrying the bottle of wine. "John, I have no corkscrew."

"I'll get the cork out," Tobias said. He rose from his place and went through the kitchen to where Cassandra said he'd built a shed in the backyard.

While she brought their dinner to the table—a royal blue apron splayed with the contours of her body—John marveled at what Cassandra Erhart had come to by the age of twenty-seven: existing in a house of unused crystal where she dippered beer from a bucket without knowing a red from a white wine.

* * *

They'd started dinner with the conversation cordial, but stilted and bare, Tobias distanced by the estrangement of the staled friendship.

"So how's the old coot," John said.

"Groeger's a headful of wisdom," Tobias said.

John shrugged, moving a mouthful of biscuit to his cheek and soaking it with a slurp of wine. "Wise in a way, maybe. I guess that old trunk of his could be a regular Smithsonian exhibit." He swallowed the bread. Another slurp of wine. His glass was near empty, theirs still filled, which put him next for a refill—only one left. "But that would be just one trunk in a universe of exhibits." He turned to Cassandra. "The Smithsonian's endless—I've seen it." Then back to Tobias. "There's a whole world of real knowledge out there, away from that old coot's witchcraft." He nudged his glass toward the bottle by Cassandra's plate.

Tobias tapped his fork on the table. "Groeger draws on other knowledge, and sorts it with his knack. You've seen him study."

"Study?" John shooed it off.

Tobias lanced back, sharp as he ever had. "You don't like him because he isn't something he dresses up to be." He pointed his fork at John. "Seems you profit by his work."

John looked at the fork. Ought to make him swallow the goddamned thing. Tines first.

Cassandra sipped from her wine, face blank, not even trying to look interested in talk of Ernie Groeger.

John nodded to the bottle. "Cassandra, would you please pass that?"

He filled his glass, glad she didn't top off her own.

"Explain his oddness however you want," John said. "But you can't trust some old coot keeping our best advantage locked in his head." He lifted his brows. "And in that old trunk." He looked askance as if he just thought of something. "I guess that puts you in a dangerous position, too, Tobias." John looked down and bit his bottom lip, glanced at Cassandra.

Cassandra was about to take a bite of potato. "Tobias would never…." She looked at her husband. John caught the nudge of a squint, a fleck of doubt. "He'd never steal those formulas."

Tobias just rolled his eyes. "Seems it's our New York man holds our future. Groeger and I spent two months just cooking up samples for that AutoStart order we're trying to win against American Carbon." He put his elbows at each side of his plate. "That business could double production. We'd need another bay, another warehouse, twice the size of the one we have."

John took a drink and shrugged. "I know about that order."

"Well, tell me about it," Cassandra said, looking from Tobias to John, who poked with his fork at his last bites of roast. "Tobias never mentioned it was that big."

"All anyone at the plant talks about," Tobias said. He glanced at John, then back to Cassandra. "Your father and grandfather call it the future of the company. If our carbons get approved, it'll add enough workers to put us over a thousand."

Cassandra turned to John, and he forced a smile to acknowledge this.

"You'll get to New York," she said. "Whatever this order is, we all know it would be won if you were the New York man." She nudged her hand from where it lay beside her napkin, toward him. "You *will* get to New York."

"Oh, I'll get there," John said, reaching for his wine. He held up the glass as if for a toast, which no one met.

"So," Cassandra said, "what does AutoStart make to account for this big order?"

"Automobile generators and starters," Tobias said. "Thousands every day. Every generator takes three carbon brushes. And every starting motor, four."

"You seem awful interested in this order, Tobias," John said. He pushed his plate away, pulled his wine glass toward him, and leaned back. "This, Cassandra, was not plain fare. It was a dish that would be recommended in the finest restaurants. You," he said with a grin, "have your own knack."

"Of course I'm interested in that order," Tobias said. "We're trying to concoct the best carbon-graphite formula yet. Working with the engineers to make it the most affordable."

"Have you done it?"

"We'll find out a week from Tuesday. That's when the order gets awarded."

"You'll be a hero if we get the job." John winked at Tobias.

Tobias shrugged.

"What if we don't?" John said.

Tobias shrugged again.

John finished his glass, took out his matches, and lit a cigarette. "As far as your personal situation, Tobias, you're in a pretty good position no matter what."

"How's that?" Tobias did not turn, just looked at John sideways with a shift of his eyes.

"If things go right, you'll be keeper of formulas someday."

John drew from his cigarette, tapped a few crumbs of ash onto his plate. "But AutoStart order or not, you could write your own ticket to any carbon company you pick, considering the reputation of those mixes you two devise." He glanced at Cassandra. "'Course that would be treason to your own father-in-law."

"John," Cassandra said. She gave a little laugh, a weak attempt to turn it into a jest.

Tobias kept his eyes turned on John. Blinked.

"Just an observation," John said.

Cassandra rolled a corner of her napkin between her thumb and forefinger, staring distantly ahead. His words were doing their duty. Just look how he got even her imagining Tobias turning on the company. How easily would anyone else?

His two glasses of wine were doing their work, too. As boldly as he'd scrutinize a diamond in a jewelry shop, he studied her face, still smooth as pumpkin butter, hardly changed but for the tautness of skin that stretched the corners of her mouth. The face—taking so much identity from those deep-set eyes—it seemed there just to hide them.

John turned in his chair, put an elbow on the backrest and crossed his legs. With his other hand, he tugged his pants waist where it chafed the spill of his paunch. He caught something moving on the table—Tobias inching his hand toward Cassandra's.

He watched her face. He knew the short life of Cassandra Meier's enthusiasms, knew jaded eyes. He was seeing resignation for this husbandly gesture. John had made a lot of money understanding that a resigned person was ripe, vulnerable as an October apple fallen on the pasture side of a fence.

He waited. No response, not a move.

Tobias laid his big gawky palm atop Cassandra's fingers. John supposed he did this hand routine every night, part of his big role as husband, a miniature of how Tobias fumbled over her upstairs. A grin broke out of the laugh John held back.

Tobias looked back with the confidence he used to wear in his corked boots and big western hat. But somehow his pluck now was the wrong size, fit him like a little girl's dress.

John arched his back luxuriously and started counting prizes he could win.

"I do believe," Tobias started to say. But John stopped him.

"I don't—" he chuckled— "I don't believe it's time for me to go. And I wonder if you, pal, have the best intentions for the company." He looked back as boldly as he could.

Tobias drew his hand from Cassandra's and stood.

But John sat. Tobias wouldn't try anything in front of her. She remained still, except for her eyes blinking at John, her hand remaining where Tobias had held it.

"Seems the waterboy's at it again," Tobias said. "You've been spitting into buckets since the day I saw you in Piebald Hollow."

John's cigarette had burned to a nub. He snuffed it on his plate, kept grinding it with his thumb. "I don't know what you're talking about, pal." He stood.

"John, don't," Cassandra said.

"Don't what? Leave? After being insulted like that?"

Tobias tipped his head to the side. "Why are you so bitter about that day, John? Because of what they did? Or because I happened to see it? I'd like to know—there's a big difference."

John snorted, rolled his eyes.

"Such a little thing," Tobias said, "but you've been doing it over and over all your life."

"Here he is," John said to Cassandra, "calling me a waterboy. Insulting me because I warned him from biting the hand that feeds him." Then to Tobias: "And here I am, the one that accounts for everything you have. You'd be nothing if it weren't for me, never would've moved out of some hinterlands hollow. Still be out there looking for a tree to cut while you whine they're all gone."

"Just what is it about me, John, that bothers you so much. So much that you always make my life your business?"

John laughed. The first glint of rage he'd ever seen in Tobias Meier's eyes was already collapsing into deliberation, as though he were fishing for an agreeable answer to his own question—typical, annoying Tobias Meier, the ready believer, the eager contemplator of even this. Rage was something John knew; he'd rather be leaving on a note of that. "Cassandra," he said, standing, dropping his napkin on his chair, "great dinner."

John went to the foyer, and before Cassandra got there, he took his overcoat and hat from the hook. Tobias stopped by the sofa, hands in his pockets, head lowered.

Cassandra, who'd already had a droop to her shoulders and a shuffle to her walk, was entirely wilted now. John reached for the door, nodded to her, and stepped through the doorway. But he stopped midway and craned his neck around to see Cassandra. John narrowed one eye and nudged his cheek into the whisper of a grin. "Would you like me to leave it cracked open?" he said.

Chapter 21

Only a couple inches had fallen overnight, turning already to flurries, so Ernie Groeger's absence was the first sign that told Tobias something was wrong that morning three weeks later. Unless snow piled too deeply for Groeger to wade his way to work or catch a car ride, he was always in the lab before Tobias arrived at ten of six. Groeger hadn't been himself the day before—had hardly talked to Tobias, testing pieces of finished product, spending most of the day looking out a window until he left for a long jaunt to the brewery. He'd come back so drunk he only made it as far as his trunk by the door, stumbling, limbs lurching as if pulled by strings, until he collapsed onto the trunk. He hadn't moved from a slouched stupor when Tobias left at five thirty.

The second sign of something wrong came when the door of the laboratory slammed behind Warren P. Ryder, melted snow glistering on the heavy wingspan of his shoulders. Ryder typically avoided the lab, and always shunned Tobias Meier.

"You're done," he said, pointing at Tobias, thumb up like the hammer of a gun.

Tobias stood near a window. He'd been pulling strings to turn on overhead lights. What he saw beside Ryder, against the wall, sent a warning as clear and indisputable as a rifle crack.

Ryder glared as though he'd just gnawed flesh from Tobias's neck. He took a step toward the lab table and lifted a cane—really a swagger stick, for age had not seeped to his bones, only to his frosted hair and sag of face.

Tobias keyed on the glint of the metal tip. And when Ryder swung, Tobias's muscles tensed like the coils of a spring. The glass jars and beakers that did not break against the stick smashed on the floorboards. Ryder back-swung and swung again, batting books, chisels, stoppers and lumps of coke.

"You're fired, you bastard. Fired."

A hatch holding some feral part of Tobias unlatched, and he did not try to hold it back. This time he let no baron of timber and industry cloud danger. He saw clearly the bristle of menace in the eyes.

Still, in the periphery of his mind was the open lid of the trunk behind Ryder. He tried to ignore it. The nerve and fiber, bone and gut of Tobias were equipped, he sensed, so long as he kept beyond the cause of this. To try to explain would be to let down that feral wariness, to open himself to the confusion that almost cost his life in a bear hunt. "Where is Ernie Groeger?" was all he said.

Ryder threw his hat onto the lab table's litter of glass shards. He came around closer to Tobias. "How can you say that name after betraying it?"

Tobias's impulses sized the distance to the iron pincers he used for loading carbons into the brick ovens. With hardly a step, he could reach where they leaned against the wall. Something about the proximity Ryder had advanced put him on the edge of moving that way.

"Five hundred jobs," Ryder said. "Twelve years' reputation." He counted off by raising fingers. Tobias locked on the hand, gauged how much its quake of rage would delay Ryder from reacting.

Ryder stepped to within two paces, and Tobias slid a foot toward those ten-pound pincers. He saw Ryder interpret it as fear, heard him draw more authority into the slowing of his voice. "Who paid for the formulas?"

Tobias was tempted to reason, say how this could look like one thing but be another. He couldn't help looking to the gaping trunk, the opened journals on the countertop beside it, stubs where pages of German handwriting had been. There was no reasoning here. Groeger was the only person Tobias would talk to, had to talk to, knowing what he believed of this, and what it would do to him. So all Tobias said was that he did not trust the world of Warren P. Ryder.

At the instant Ryder reached under the drapes of his mackintosh overcoat, Tobias had hold of the pincers, both handles squeezed within the expanse of his right hand grip—there would be no sorting of intentions, no guessing what was under the coat.

As Ryder's forearms braced his head against the impact, carbon brushes pattered on the floor from the hand he'd reached into his pocket. A child's "no" squeaked from his chest, and he cowered away as the iron tongs came round in the dead aim of an axeman. With the crack of a final kerf cut, the handle snapped Ryder's wrist, and the lip of a pincer tine thudded his skull—dull, as if away in the distance, another axe bit sunk into pine bark. Ryder collapsed and gathered himself into a fetal cringe, arms around his head, the fingers of his limp hand smeared with the blood in his hair, his eyes squeezed tight against pain, or fear. Tobias held the tongs high over his head, put his left shoe on Ryder's hip.

Reasoning seemed as unnatural as thinking through saw pulls. But he couldn't help his mind tightening reins on what he was about to do. He leaned into Ryder's hip, jerked him. Ryder opened the nearest eye, but immediately squeezed it shut and curled tighter into the ball of himself, clamped his elbows before his face.

It was a quickening current Tobias held against to stay the tongs above his head. "Just tell me where Ernie Groeger is."

The stomps of presses increasing with the first shift stirred wider awareness. Tobias lifted his foot. Ryder raised his eyelids, and Tobias saw he was barely conscious, eyes rolling. Then Tobias knew that someone was about to come into the lab. One blow to the skull, he told himself, and this threat is gone forever.

A knock shook the door's frosted glass in its frame. Tobias turned to see a man's shadow. His chance to explain it to Ernie. Tobias let go of the tongs and started toward the door.

But Ernie Groeger would not knock at his own lab. Only J. Hadley Erhart, in his courtesy, knocked. Hisses and clicks from the factory spilled in as the door opened and Erhart stepped through. "Has my father-in-law found you?"

"Where's Ernie?" Tobias said. Even in the din, he was close enough to hear Ryder sighing heavy exhales where he lay beyond the lab table.

"Tobias, you can't be in here." Erhart nodded at the countertop where Ernie Groeger's journals lay opened. "What more do you need to see?"

"You mean what more do *you* need to see."

"The only thing I haven't figured out," Erhart said, "is why."

Tobias watched the open doorway while Erhart held out a handful of carbon brushes. "Samples sent by our man in New York. The American

Carbon brushes that won the AutoStart order." He pocketed them. "Ernie ran tests and reported back that they match our amperes, our specific resistance, contact drop, everything. They behave as though made in this plant." He frowned at the broken glass on the floor. "It struck me last night that maybe Ernie's notes got out. So we came in, and there he sits." Erhart pointed at the trunk. "Then out he runs. And what do we find?" He picked up a journal. "Missing pages."

Erhart took a step toward the lab table.

"I've got to find Ernie," Tobias said, "but hear me out on this."

"Tobias, you're the only one who could have taken those pages. Ernie wouldn't sell his own formulas—he doesn't even show up to collect his pay half the time."

Tobias was opening and closing his hands into tight fists, watching that opened door. "And Warren P. Ryder thinks I wanted to spite back the family."

Erhart threw the pillaged journal onto the lab table and pointed to the littering of broken glass. "Now what have you done?" Then he locked on his father-in-law's hat.

"Listen to me," Tobias said, voice cracking. "All that matters is Ernie Groeger. You don't understand what he might do." He waved around the room. "This is all there was for that man."

But then Erhart went blank as he looked over the table. Tobias turned to see Warren P. Ryder pushing himself toward the wall, alert now as his son-in-law moved around Tobias. When Erhart was within view of the iron pincers and the blood in Ryder's hair, Tobias was on the run.

"Stay here," Erhart yelled.

Outside the factory, tailing dregs of the evening snowfall sifted through the glow of streetlights, still luminous against the ashen sky of an overcast dawn. Workers carrying lunch pails and quart bottles of beer moved away and watched him run past.

There existed one necessity in Tobias's mind: to get the Ford and find Ernie Groeger.

* * *

He reached for the smoky cold steel of his double-barrel shotgun with its cracked stock and secret tale. He'd drunk himself to vomiting on his shirt, then drunk more to do it over until four in the morning.

At the windowsill, he slid open the hatch of a small wooden box and took out two paper-jacket shot-shells. As he stepped to the door, he dropped them into the gaping double bore. He snapped tight the breech.

He'd sat in a wooden chair through the night, watching the black window, waiting for dawn to tarnish it gray. When it had come, he'd known it more by something shifting inside him than by the seeing of it.

And he'd heard something, too.

"Ernst."

It came from outside, by the woods. But nobody had called that name for forty-three years, and not ever in this country.

He lifted the latch and dragged the bottom of the door planks across the floor, then stepped onto the fieldstone step. He kicked away the lantern he'd set there when he'd returned in the night.

He turned to the field, toward Marstadt, and the cold air sifting across from the distant woods-line wicked moisture in his nostrils, and he keened to the acid stink of vomit and to the musky urine that drenched his pants—long before in the night, he'd stopped bothering to rise and piss on the floorboards.

Soaked and without a coat, he shivered, but not so much from the air as something else out there.

Dawn's nickel grayness cast enough light to show the depressions of last night's footprints, softened now by intervening snow. He grunted, wrenching out another of the heaves that had come all night while he'd thought about what was to come, and he moved along his tracks. Ahead, half a white orb still arced over the woods from the distant streetlights of Marstadt.

*   *   *

The car was gone, her footprints in the snow showing she'd moved in and out of the house many times. But had the car never moved, he'd have known she was gone by the feel, as if the place had just steadied itself from coughing something out of its throat. He sensed it even before he saw the boxes she'd pulled from under furniture, contents spilled in search of...what? A hatpin? A glove? Maybe a letter.

Still that single necessity drove him. So only by the sharp pang in knowing what this scene meant did he force himself to stay a moment to think out whether the events of the day were of a piece, or if this new thing was its own ugly truth. Not coming to an answer, he made himself

PJ Piccirillo

feel guilt for believing that what he saw here mattered less than finding Ernie Groeger to explain what he could. And he took that guilt upstairs to see what else he would find.

* * *

He used the gun as a cane now, his cold, numb palm squeezed fast to the barrels. A dog barked in the distance, probably at deer out to feed.

He didn't fall until he crossed the field and the big woodlot along the road darkened his way. Trying to decipher his snow-softened tracks under the blackness of pine boughs, he slipped on a root, and the forward knee concussed against one of those unceasing fieldstones farmers threw from the ends of their rows, then his mouth slammed another and a top-front tooth snapped and caught in his throat without him even feeling the break. He gagged on the tooth and groped for the gun, and the familiar handhold of the poplar grip drew a picture from beyond the fog of his mind and the sickness of his body.

He lay still, and through the stink of him and the smell of these pines came *spruce and the wet leaves of birch.* And the lullaby Hilde sang to the son he hoped had survived the croup and worms after that day of leaving, so many years ago, another time when he carried this gun, which all but pulsed memory into the veins of his hand.

Back on his feet, he trudged along. He hardly felt the snow drop from his collar down his wet shirt, insensitive as he was to the moment.

The picture in his mind was *heady with the preened stalks of barley* that sifted into the spruce forest from the field he'd crossed that dawn, entering the forbidden woods. The sure and sober stealth of a young man took him under the fence of barbed wire that was strung through the woods on pickets, then up the hill, between pillars of blue-green trees, to where he knew the roe deer fed at daybreak in a small meadow in the baron's forest. Not so far onto the property that he could not escape Odo the overseer.

He huddled into the dark backdrop of a spruce trunk and looked out at that half acre of meadow where deer came to nip at forbs and paw for grasses. Before the chill of dawn broke the heat of his uphill hike, a tentative doe stepped to the far edge of the opening. He drew up the barrels of buckshot, pulled back one of the hammers, and waited, hoping for the deer to stop swiveling the white palms of her ears. He prayed she would hurry and move ahead—he'd have to shoot quickly, before Odo and his dog started walking the grounds.

* * *

256

Seeing the dresser drawers she'd left opened in taking a few last underthings, Tobias realized she'd been leaving for two weeks. In that time she'd kept laundry out, piled in the room where she ironed, her suitcases and hat boxes stacked there. Then it had signified nothing more than a rare binge of housecleaning. Now his mind, tense in its focus on finding Groeger, was at the brink of clairvoyance. In a flash, he saw two weeks of smug remoteness, feigned smiles and an indifferent, dreary voice. And her body, begrudging as it had become over the years, was lately as cold and uncomforting as a stone slab. Especially the last time, and that had been at least two weeks ago.

She'd been gone all that time, right in front of his eyes. This morning's event had not given rise to this.

He did not linger or look for a coat. He ran downstairs and out of the house, before someone came after him.

*   *   *

The deer held tight to the edge of the meadow, a few steps beyond lethal range. He knew to keep still while it watched for danger. The gun barrels had become excruciatingly heavy, as if someone pushed down on the muzzles; his arms ached and swayed. Needles of pain pricked where muscle fibers in his shoulders seemed to be tearing from their lashings. The deer moved its head to the left and the right, pointed its nose in the air, flicked its ears.

It was full light now. Odo would have started his rounds, walking across the baron's vast lawns to the fence line.

But he needed the meat. The boy coughed always now and did not sleep. Lately his eyes stared limp from what looked like old purple wounds. Hilde's milk was thinning.

The deer bobbed its head.

The weight on the muzzles inched the barrels down, the pain spreading as though a dull knife ripped through his back to his buttocks. And the gun quaked as much as it swayed now. But he had to make a good shot so the deer would not run and die far from the barbed fence. A swelling of air, hardly a breeze, puffed uphill from behind him, across the meadow. The deer stomped a foot.

He squeezed shut his eyes.

Following his tracks in the snow had lulled him into reverie, for there was no such wind at the moment. He looked through the tree limbs and saw it was full light. He dragged the gun now, swaying and crisscrossing last night's tracks like a serpent. Down the hillside, he could see the road to Marstadt, along which he moved.

* * *

Tobias saw the Ford as he ran by the station. But he did not have a key, and anyway, the car seemed something he'd only borrowed until now. It had never felt earned or deserved or lived up to.

People he saw on Station Street turned and looked ahead of him for where the fire or some other catastrophe might be. Then he was panting down a spoke-road in Warren P. Ryder's wagon wheel design, toward Ernie Groeger's camp in the farmland.

* * *

His stomach retched more and more, rank, cottony fluid squeezing out his throat and gnawing at his teeth with every thought of what he had to do. He'd lost control of his bowels, warm, fluidy feces gushing down his legs with each wrenching of his stomach, tottering his bearing.

He veered headlong into an oak and reeled to the ground. Under his hip, the bottom of the gunstock broke off where it had cracked that day, forty-three years ago.

He lay still and closed his eyes and *saw the deer turn* its head back, as if to take flight, and he lowered the gun from his shoulder, the shearing pain pouring out his arms while his hands tingled back to life. He trembled, though, from new weakness.

Odo would surely be along the fence by now, close enough to hear the shot. But if after he killed the deer he ran, pulling it downhill…

It turned its head back to the meadow when the fawn stepped out, still dappled in white spots, tiny, nearly as short as Odo's shepherd dog. But there was all the meat he needed to make rich Hilde's milk, so pale—like her—now that the shared crops went for the war the Prussians were making with the French. A broth, too, would help the baby.

The doe stomped the ground, but the fawn continued into the meadow of green forbs, pausing and staring in a new direction with each step.

The fawn lowered its head to feed, lifted it quickly and turned its neck to its mother. The base of its skull was in profile to him. He raised the gun. The mother locked on the movement and stomped again. His arms shook as he sighted down the barrels to the rear of the fawn's jaw, and he squeezed the trigger just as the fawn stepped toward its mother.

It wheeled and fell on its side, legs cycling air. At the gun's report, Odo's dog had barked, still far enough that he could get the deer beyond the fence, and maybe home, the fawn so small he could run with it over his shoulders.

But before he got to it, a front foot caught ground. The fawn rolled upright and plowed with its rear legs into the woods, trailing blood from where the buckshot had torn the nape—not the center—of its neck.

He dared not shoot again, thus leading Odo directly to him. So he followed the deer, back on its feet now, but falling every few steps.

So much blood, he thought at the sheen of its trail in the leaves. He'd have to stanch it with his shirt when he carried the fawn, lest Odo trail him. Maybe the dog, rapt with the blood here, would not track his scent.

He got hold of the deer where it fell in brambles, and clubbing it to death, he cracked the stock of his gun. The fawn had run far—too far, he feared. He caped it over his shoulders and stumbled downhill, across the meadow toward the fence, Odo's nearing shepherd barking in a gruff frenzy, the way of even an obedient, trained dog at the smell of new blood.

* * *

Half a mile from Groeger's, Tobias slowed to a walk. Each breath had become a wheezing cough from the cold air grating his throat, and the pain at his kidneys pierced with his exhales so much he'd come to hop with each one, as if landing on a pebble in his shoe. His shirt was soaked, and hammers knocked at his temples.

What if Groeger was not at his camp? Where would he have gone? Back to Pittsburgh? Germany? Tobias just needed to find him. For he knew that Ernie Groeger drew his very breath from his gift now stolen.

* * *

His whereabouts came and went, the black trunks of oak and pine appearing as pillars in the snow, propping above the ground the mirror of itself that was a toneless sky. Back in the moment and on his feet, he saw that the snow-softened track he zigzagged and stumbled over flanked the Marstadt Road closer than he'd thought. Then he went adrift in the scourge of his body and visions of the business at hand, and he lost his way. So he turned back on the stain of stink and piss and watery feces he'd left like the trail of a slug.

The deer had left its own course, glistening on the leaves, despite his trying to stanch the wound. Above the meadow the dog picked up the trail, its barks feral with the taste of blood. He'd shoot the dog when it reached him, and maybe he'd still outrun Odo to the fence—maybe beyond.

Back on course, he looked down the bank at the road to Marstadt and then to the woods before him where they flattened in a basin of heavy, widely-spaced hardwoods. It came back to him, the lay of this place last night in the glow of his lantern, and he began sobbing with every inhale. Tears dislodged pus which smeared his vision, and he fell, his head striking the face of the spade he'd left last night. And he was looking at the mound, the snow having melted against the warmer earth and stone of it. He crawled back along his tracks to a black cherry tree where he writhed himself to sitting, and he pulled the gun across his lap, looking toward the road to Marstadt.

As he reached to rub away the smears in his vision, his fingers strummed the pocks and crevices of his scars. And that moment came back to him so clearly, the road could have been *the picket and barbed fence* he was just that close to when he turned and pulled with one arm the gun to his shoulder and fired into the face of the German shepherd, which pranced and growled at the bloody carcass over his shoulders.

He should never have pulled the deer as he crawled under the fence. The fawn was so small, he could have thrown it to the other side, as he had his gun. Ah, hindsight. But his mind at the time was clouded with worry for Hilde and the baby, and he tugged the deer while he bored like a mole under the wire.

Otherwise he could have wriggled like a worm, as he would through trenches in the war. His coat caught between the shoulders, and as he reached around with his knife, he saw Odo peering over the barbed wire. In Odo's eyes burned the rage of a man who'd lost his prized shepherd and who believed he should shoot a poacher the way his dog had been shot—in the face.

Even his coat sleeve caught now, and he could not turn away his head when Odo aimed the black holes of his barrels.

* * *

Soaked from his sprint, Tobias couldn't stave off the cold that had him rubbing his arms. But he would not run again until his breath quit coming in wheezes. It wasn't far, for the up-slope of the road had leveled where the woodlot opened to big timber. Just one stretch down a slow grade and he'd break to the field by Groeger's camp.

He looked into the woods. He thought he'd heard a cough, words, but saw nothing.

* * *

The heaves were drier and more frequent, and between them he kept seeing Hilde and the baby. He may have called their names, too.

Then the movement between the trees stilled his gut. At first, it didn't register as a man walking the road, and when it did, his mind went back to Odo and the black holes of the gun barrels, and that he'd never have vengeance for what Odo had done.

But he would not be ill-used again.

Fully in the present now, he braced his shotgun with both hands. Something in the way the long legs flapped over the snow-whitened road, like a raven in mist, told him it was Tobias Meier, and he felt himself swooning into the current of what was to come. He stretched his legs before him, cocked the hammers and lifted the gun, and it swayed in his arms. He'd thought right, Tobias had come for him.

Why had he done it? Why had Tobias Meier taken the only worth left of him? Taken his *Bedeutung,* all he was? Tobias had turned another's part to his own advantage, heartlessly as he might sneak off with someone's woman, coldly as he might with a poacher's fawn. And for something unworthy as ill-gotten dollars.

There are only two things in the world men want, the nurse he'd found in Kosbrunn lectured him that night as he begged her not to send for his wife: *Sicherheit und Bedeutung.* Safety and worth. Did he think he could have worth away from his family? Did he think he could give himself safety? Only a fool thought so. But he'd given up his family for any chance of *their* safety. And then, in work, he'd gained worth again. Or so he'd thought, until that man on the road took it. The man he'd thought of as his one friend.

Though rooted firmly on the ground, tight against the tree trunk, he had the sensation his body spiraled downward, a one-eyed man off balance in a flushing eddy, no one to take his hand. He kicked at his shoes and looked for the figure moving along the road.

Despite the feebleness of his body, his mind was sobering, and out of flurrying thoughts came the reason Tobias Meier had taken what worth he'd found. He had no *Bedeutung* of his own. Tobias looked so hard for what that meant, he gave himself up to every fool's mistake of it. He couldn't trust that it was in the journey of his soul rather than the business of men. All a man had to do was make himself worth his own liking. Look what it caused if he didn't.

He thought about that a moment—making himself worth his own liking. But he let it go, exhausted of his courage, tired of the toll.

He looked into the black holes of the waving gun barrels. Odo had kicked the deer away, and through the fear of death rushed the reality that Odo had moved that fawn because he did not want a trespasser's blood on it, for Odo had planned to take the meat that would save a baby's life.

He steadied the gun, and the roar and flash of it across his face was as if the sun had exploded within him.

* * *

A gunshot—so close it slapped a beat from Tobias's heart, a punctuation, his gut warned, to being late. Or had he sensed the shot was at him? He moved with new urgency, looking where the gun had fired. He saw only a sentinel crow landing in the top branch of a cherry tree. Just a hunter, he thought, sprinting now.

* * *

All the world was darkness, and in one ear a gurgling seep of blood muffled the after-ring of gunshot. Then her voice came to him through the fire that scorched the side of his face.

"Ernst. Ernst."

Again and again she called from the edge of the field, and once he thought he heard the child's croaking cry.

He reached for his eyes, and when he brushed his cheek, realized what seared—the torn flesh of that half of his face.

Still she called. But he could not answer. He knew not if Odo remained nearby, the shell in the un-fired black chamber for her should she find him.

Through a red, clotted veil, the light of day trickled to him, and he knew the eye was merely blinded by blood. He reached for leaves and willed himself to keep the eye open as he wiped until he could make out shapes.

The calls faded.

He could never go to her because now he was dead to the baron's man, Odo, or he would have to be made so if Odo knew he lived. Odo had shot him for killing a prized dog. What would become of his wife and the boy if they knew, if he made a trail of blood to their door? Yes, he was dead, whether in body or not.

So he would cut free his coat and staunch the blood with his shirt. By night he'd drag his gun to the nurse, and she'd dig out all the buckshot—except that one in his eye. And he'd make the decision that he'd spend his life enduring: to not send Hilde word for fear she'd live—if she might—with the hope of him. He would run, and fight the French for the Prussians, be taken prisoner and stay in France to work in a factory. And there he'd learn Mr. Carre's charcoal inventions, then understand he had another worth—with carbon. Then to America, never to return.

But this time she still called. There was no unbearable fading of her voice to stab through the pain of a gun-shot face, to redouble the agony of holding silent and letting her move away across that field. She drew closer, into the woods toward the fence, and the boy, he could hear him too, not croaking, but cooing.

His eye was clear of the blood. He could see her and the baby coming through the woods. He could call out.

Hilde's smile, the boy's health.

Das Paradies.

*   *   *

The wide-open door and fresh tracks were good signs to Tobias. He'd wait inside for Groeger to return. Maybe it had been him hunting.

But when he stepped onto the fieldstone, he saw the chair pulled to the east window, the yellow, phlegmy vomit glazed over the spilled beer and piss. And the menace in the stink of it put him hard on Groeger's tracks.

As he ran across the white field, the land seemed flopped over: whatever illumination sifted through the low, slate ceiling, pooled brighter in the snow cover, as if that should have been the side with the sun behind it.

He took no comfort despite telling himself that maybe Groeger really was hunting, albeit drunk. He'd find no warmth from the steely cold, breaking now to the pith of his bones, no peace of mind, until he found him. But what if that shot along the way had been Groeger attempting vengeance?

In the woods he couldn't make sense of the tracks. They zigzagged as if Groeger were trying to flush rabbits from brush tangles—but there were no brush tangles. Tobias could see that Groeger was trailing someone's older tracks, and that he'd fallen. He dragged a stick, or his gun. Then Tobias came upon a trickling, a grainy tea that looked and stunk like the bowel juices of a gut-shot deer, but no deer tracks broke the snow. And an increasing acid tang of vomit drifted in the air.

*　　*　　*

Tobias moved carefully; if he was coming upon a man hunting and apparently drunk, he'd best not spook him.

The woods canopy so far had been blotted by young pine. Just past a place where the tracks had branched to and from a dead end, Tobias broke into a stand of open hardwoods. Tracing the footprints with his eyes, he caught an odd sight: a thigh-high mound of earth and stone, black against the snowscape of the open woods. Then, closer to him, a pair of legs extended from the opposite side of a big cherry. The smell of him came to Tobias like an un-limed privy in July.

He drew to within a few steps, then thought he'd better make himself known.

"Ernie."

No response.

Passed out, Tobias guessed. Careful. Who could say what Groeger might do if Tobias came dropping from the clouds.

A pace away, he found a fallen, snow-topped limb. He stretched it toward the tree, the hook of its branches turned Groeger's way. But Tobias stopped before he poked at him.

What would he say? Give his regrets that Groeger's gift had been ill-used, for no one took seriously an ugly man who spoke only the hated truth? Or was Tobias going to explain how his doubt in proceeding his own way had led to all this? He'd just shrug? Say, "Sorry, Ernie, in pawning myself, I let all you lived for be destroyed."

He dropped the stick. What would happen, would happen. Let Groeger do the saying, however he chose.

Then he stepped around the tree and took Ernie Groeger's vengeance.

And immediately Tobias turned up and away, the web of black branches seeming to fall as a shattering of clouded sky, and one screaming word pounded out of him like a universe of echoes: "No-o-o-o-o..."

Forcing his feet to stay, his eyes to look down, was the effort and agony of tearing himself out of his skin. Ernie's head leaned back on the tree. A stump of red teeth and jaw bone showed where the gunshot had blown his cheek away. Flesh and ear and chunks of bone matted the tree trunk, blood glazed his neck. Like a loose button on a rag doll, the doughy dead eye bloated over the sheared bone that remained of its socket.

Tobias's eyes catapulted to the tree limbs again. Snowflakes penciled jagged tendrils as they materialized out of the gray sheet overhead, so it seemed to shatter and fall all over again. Looking down, his gut knotting, Tobias made himself see the most piteous part. Ernie's mouth remained intact, the lips opened and distended by exploded bone and tooth and tongue, but complete, owing to a thread of flesh remaining between laceration and lip. And despite the disfigurement of the blast, the lips and the cheek that survived were undeniably tugged into a smile. The expression—that there was an expression—was all the more hideous. Tobias was so sure of the smile that he reached under Ernie's chin and felt beyond hope for sign of life. But in touching him, the aspect released, any ember gone.

Tobias turned and saw a shovel and pick. He looked to a dark pock in the earth, the mound of stony soil. Good God, he dug his own grave.

He fell to his knees, then slumped onto his side, his head resting on the gun barrels where they'd recoiled from the bare toe Groeger had put to the trigger. Tobias held the gun, squeezing the barrels with one hand, the stock with the other, in such desperation that his mind engaged in nothing but begging God to undo what he'd caused, or at least erase what Ernie Groeger had died thinking.

His head close to the ground, Tobias could hear the snow's whispered patter drawing the great velvet pall over all the world's doings.

Except the chickadees alighting overhead where they huh-huhhed as they husked tatters of bark to get to their food stores. And then a squirrel descended, then another, and they commenced pawing leaves from their own caches. A dog barked from a farm. It seemed too quick—an insult to Ernie Groeger's departure.

And maybe that's why he did it. Or from hearing—out of his senses—a plea of urgency in the new snow. Or maybe seeing the papery black glide of a raven where it jittered against the cloud cover.

He rose and grabbed Ernie Groeger's wrist. When he pulled him onto his side, blood in the cavity of Groeger's chest sloshed—faint and deep, bringing on the notion of Ernie Groeger having helplessly drowned in that blood, making the ache in Tobias's gut ball into his throat, gag him and come out in a moan. But he moved toward the grave, embracing Groeger against his side, half-carrying, half-dragging him, warmth from the body breaking the iciness of Tobias's skin where he wore only a shirt. Though he'd begun cloying to the stink, he retched now, the stomach acid on Groeger's bloody chest so close to his face.

Each time Tobias heaved Groeger, clots of blood, brown and purple and livery, spewed out with bits of bone from the hole in his face, and the mush of it steamed in the snow. It was beyond real, this dragging the corpse of a man you'd loved, doing it according to the plan he wished for his own death. Groeger, he realized, knew he would come.

He thought this as he rolled him into the hole Groeger had dug, the body thudding face-down like a punky log. And only then did the gravity of it all settle in. The world already believed he'd violated this man. Tobias turned up his bloody palms. He sat and pulled his shirt away from his skin; it was soiled in a mix of his own sweat and Groeger's body fluids. He looked back at the shovel, then up at the sky, dropping its whiteness over his world, starting to erase proof of what he hadn't done.

Now he looked back at the gun.

He squeezed his eyes and chided himself to come up with the last time he acted in his own behalf. If only he hadn't wanted to know the world a woman struck a pose for, had given himself over to the self-regard he'd had in his own world. So just what was his own behalf now? He opened his eyes. They remained on the gun.

His thoughts, sundered to pieces, fell paralyzed where he tried to resuscitate them before they faded out of reason. He began to persuade himself to start away, then lost track of what that meant, unable to process the idea of *away* into any actual place; the walls of his world had contracted to contain only the dark facts before him.

He crawled toward the cherry tree, his eyes and mind moving between the gun and shovel, some thought telling him there remained a thing to be done with one of them. The cold cut into what he willed his limbs, his movements weak and intractable—but at least the ache in the bones of them had numbed. He came first to the shovel. He looked at his fingers, stiff and waxy as candles. He begged them to take up the shovel. Then he'd concentrate on what remained to be done with it.

Not knowing he had the shovel except that it moved, something Cassandra said slipped into the moment, then overspread the whole scene, as thoroughly and snug as the snowfall. *The things we've missed are more crushing than all the horrors the world can throw on us. People with everything lie over train rails.* He vaguely recalled stepping to someone's bidding, missing a destination, and so landing in this bizarre white death-world.

He went for the gun, fumbling as much with the shovel as with why he might want the gun.

His wayward fingers would hardly grip as he dragged the gun and shovel between his legs, crawling toward the grave with his elbows now, his feet repeatedly catching the face of the spade and yanking it from his hold.

His whole body quaked in a palsy, his mind picking and choosing from scraps of clipped thoughts, and sometimes he would arrange them in a way that repelled him at the idea of using the shovel. But then they'd scatter in a gust of black and white certainty that no other necessity existed. And he'd be left to grope for why he had this gun.

By the time he pulled the gun and shovel onto the mound, he no longer trembled, and that seemed all that had kept him awake. Free from the pain in his bones, his body felt light as the thoughts wafting through his mind. He looked down at the twisted body in its too-small grave, pictured himself stretched peacefully over this heap of earth beside it.

His blood at last coursed tepid, the warmth lulling him, and he drifted away.

Chapter 22

"This is highly unusual, Mrs.... Your surname again, Madam?"

"Blesh. Mrs. John Blesh."

The long-mustached clerk behind the marble counter thumbed through a box of index cards. "Mrs. Blesh," he said, "I'm sure you understand that the Plaza is very respectful of our guests' privacy. I have no note here about Mr. Blesh expecting anyone."

"But I'm his wife." Cassandra drew a breath to calm the pleading in her voice, and squeezed her left hand into a fist when the clerk glanced there. "This is a surprise visit. You can give his own wife his room number."

Another man appeared beside the mustached clerk, this one taller and clean-shaven, his hair combed back tight to his head. He looked over the clerk's shoulder, watching him scribble on paper Cassandra could not see. The taller man's smile was both honest and somehow presupposing; it seemed to measure off a perimeter, which, crossed, would switch the smile off. Altogether, it was a look Cassandra had heard described as *New York*. "Mrs. Blesh," he said, "perhaps we could ring and ask him to come down to meet a guest. I'm sure he'd be just as surprised and delighted to find you here."

Cassandra closed her eyes. "I've been changing trains for a day and a half. Sir. It will not do for you to spoil this. If I must, I will sit in this lobby until he comes through. But I do not think Mr. Blesh will be pleased."

"If you must, madam," the tall man said. He vanished as quickly as he'd come.

"Perhaps," Cassandra said to the mustached clerk, "I could wait at a table by the bar and you could stop him when he comes through, send him my way."

His eyes snapped wide open. "That would not do. Ladies cannot wait in the bar."

268

Cassandra jerked her head up as haughtily as she could. "We'll see where I can and can't go."

The clerk shrugged and tugged up his long mustaches, then stepped aside to wave forward a man behind her.

So Cassandra checked her bags and saw that indeed she could not wait by the bar, for a peep into the room revealed not a single woman. So she went back to the lobby and took a seat on a spherical, velour couch, the back of which was a great urn. She faced away from the marble counter, she and her hot indignity hidden by the palm fronds that sprouted from the urn.

Then she watched the most confident and beautiful people she'd ever seen as they moved through all the gold gilt and marble and scrolled plaster, more of it than she thought could be assembled in one building, let alone a mere lobby. Each person, each group, walked to and from the elevators with the urgency of important business, even if it was five o'clock on a Friday evening.

She couldn't decide whether to watch the entrance doors or the elevators; John could have been in his room or out to dinner, maybe away yet for hours. So she stared back and forth, and intermittently into the pastel depths of the floral-patterned Persian rug that stretched end to end across the lobby.

Half an hour later, upon a ring of the elevator bell, she turned to catch him stepping off. She straightened, smiled, waiting for him to look her way. When he did, nothing registered; he simply gave her a sweeping glance as he moved along at everyone's business pace. Just as he reached a door, Cassandra said his name, and he stopped and turned on her.

The spunk she'd taken to the registration desk wilted when all he said was, "You're a day early," neither pleased nor surprised. He started toward her, slowly now.

"I couldn't wait any longer, John. Since the moment I decided, I haven't been able to keep it out of my head. It's so hard to hold something like this off." She waved her hand, indicating this lobby, this place, this city. Through the palm fronds, she saw the clerk watching this stilted meeting.

"There wasn't any other reason you left?" He stepped very close. "No kind of trouble?"

She tilted her head. "What do you mean, John? If you're talking about Tobias, he knows nothing."

"Not about Tobias," he said. "Trouble with the company."

"I don't know what you mean."

He studied her, then loosened, his irritation fading. Cassandra let out a breath she hadn't known she held. "I realize this must be jarring," she said.

He reached for her, and when she stood, he drew her to him and kissed her cheek. "I'm sorry, Cassandra. I'm not good with surprises. Don't let that make you think I'm not ecstatic over this."

Cassandra wrapped an arm around his shoulder in a half-embrace, looking at the mustached clerk. She convinced herself the hug did not look as awkward as it felt.

*   *   *

"Top-class," Cassandra said as John held the door opened for her.

"New York's finest rooms," he said. "Practically brand new." He shut the door. "The first name in the register of this place was Vanderbilt."

John walked past her and pulled back curtains. "Our window looks over Central Park." He turned and watched her take in the room. "It's called a parlor room," he said. "Twenty dollars a day."

Cassandra shook her head. Walking into this room was like stepping out of prison stripes, out of a dark pen called Marstadt. "Perfect."

At the window she looked with him over the dusky park and the possibilities that stretched away across upper Manhattan. People walked the lighted paths in pairs. Evening strollers. She thought New Yorkers must be the happiest people in the world. "The company puts you up in places like this?"

"Not exactly," he said. "This is a treat for us. To celebrate my debut in New York."

"How could you ever afford this on your own?"

John stepped from the window and lit a cigarette. "Let's just say that from now on, I'm in control of John Blesh's destiny. Erhart Carbon has no choice but to heed what I've been telling it." He pulled a chair from a desk and sat.

"So it's for certain—we'll be staying in New York?"

"Westinghouse has manufacturing in Newark now." He pointed across the room. "Just over the river. The New York man doesn't touch Westinghouse. So I've told Hoehn and your father that after I call there, I'm working New York and New Jersey. And they had little argument now that their man here lost the AutoStart order." He drew on his cigarette and leaned the chair back on two legs, tapping ashes onto the desk top. "You and I are going to look for an apartment next week. And the way things look, we can do it on Madison Avenue if we want." He grinned. "I believe I'd like to have a Madison-ave address on my card."

He set his cigarette on the desk, the burning side over the edge, and stepped behind Cassandra where she faced the window again. He put his hands on her hips. "Now how would you like to have that on your calling cards?"

She smiled, let out a purring sigh.

"Things are falling into place, Cassandra. The way they were supposed to be." He leaned his chest against her and spoke into the soft collar that covered the nape of her neck. "There's New York. And here you are."

But she was thinking how John did not look like a man who'd gotten all he wanted, how he looked much different from the one who visited the house just three weeks ago. Wearied. She'd noticed right away a jaundice wanness around the eyes, and a sagging of his lids. It left his stare vacant. Or distant perhaps. No wonder he hadn't recognized her; his attention seemed beyond this place.

The telephone rang. He tensed.

"Who the hell's that?" he said.

He went to the desk and took the earpiece, picking up the stub of his cigarette and tapping ashes onto the floor.

He leaned toward the microphone. "Yeah?" He drew the last of the cigarette, flicked off the hot ash and dropped the butt on the desk. "I won't be making it tonight. We'll do it tomorrow."

Cassandra mouthed the word "go," waving him off. She hadn't thought to ask if he'd been headed for an appointment when she saw him in the lobby. But he rolled his eyes and shook his head.

"Let's just say I've got business." He picked up the microphone and turned away from her. "We'll meet tomorrow for drinks. After lunch. Say two o'clock, in the bar." He set the microphone down and went to hang the earpiece in its cradle, but put it back to his ear. "Don't worry about it. I'll pay for the extra night's room." Again he went to hang up. "You mean *if* I'll need you again." Now he pushed down the cradle and threw the earpiece on the desk.

"John, I'm sorry if I ruined your plans. Was it a customer?"

He waved it off. "You could say that." He picked up the earpiece. "I'll have them bring up your bags so you can get ready. We'll get a table at a window facing Fifty-eighth. Looking right at the Cornelius Vanderbilt Mansion."

* * *

What John called a window was actually a pair of great glass doors, each wider than the table, with their velvet curtains tied back with gold tasseled ropes. Cassandra was lost in the scroll-work and curly-leaf gilt of the arches surmounting the doors, the elaborately carved trim of the ceiling cross members, the rows of chandeliers, their dangling crystal pipes glinting and spilling like fountain water. As much as she dared, she looked at other diners, men wearing white bow ties and long jackets, women with trailing gowns and lace. The angel-motif seatbacks were so bright and lively that the diners with their backs to her looked to be wearing shawls of kimono.

"Scotch and a drop of water," John said to the waiter, a balding man of sixty in a waistcoat and black tie.

"Perhaps a glass of wine, madam?" the waiter said. Cassandra could not distinguish his accent, but she guessed French, for she had heard Frenchmen could be bold or haughty in their own way of civility, and this man held his chin as if ready to be either.

"Tea, please."

"Live a little," John said. "Bring her a bottle of Bordeaux. I'm sure you know what that is, eh Pierre?" The waiter rolled his eyes and spun around fast as a weather vane.

"It's so international here," Cassandra said, stealing peeks. "In one glance I could be in New Delhi, in another, the Orient. And with the mahogany chair frames, we could be in South America." She glanced at the ceiling. "No, I must be in an Italian cathedral."

John laughed and held up a cigarette for a light. "Except those chairs are likely stained English oak—the place is loaded with it. And I doubt cathedrals have such chandeliers." He made a circular motion with the cigarette he held between two fingers. "Keep looking around like that, and you'll start drawing glances."

"I don't mind being watched. At least not here."

At that instant their waiter arrived and poured Cassandra's wine. John took his scotch from the tray, and toasted. "I'll second that Cassandra, I'll second that."

*   *   *

John ordered them gougeonnette of flounder, and before it came, Cassandra was high as the lights from the endless glass of wine the waiter kept filled to the rim.

She looked around the dining room more openly. Bold as a Frenchman, she thought, and giggled.

"What is it?" John said, the big walleyes, glossed from three glasses of scotch, looking wherever the joke may be.

"Oh, nothing," she said. "Just that child with the wooden soldier."

Three tables away, a boy sat with his parents. He pulled the string of a red and black cutout, its wooden legs and arms waving in a hopping dance. Every time Cassandra glanced that way, her eyes were drawn to the child.

John leaned and looked. "I wouldn't think you could have a kid in a place like this." He shrugged. "Then again, if you've got money in New York, you can do whatever you want." His attention went back to his asparagus and the piece of flounder she'd given him.

So Cassandra let her mind wander through the marble lobby and down the dark hallway to the bar she'd looked into this afternoon. It had been dim and smoky, its coffee-dark paneling set with high wooden arches, their apexes capping lighted Bavarian castle scenes and carved coats of arms. In a glance, she'd seen it was a place where even distinguished men roared with barroom laughter—still just a smoky corral of tinkling glasses and stale alcohol, no matter how refined.

"The bar," she said, "and the café we passed down the hall, they're so different from this. All that wood. You wouldn't expect places like home in New York."

John just looked at her, took a sip of his scotch. "Too damned much water in this." He held the glass up to one of the chandeliers.

"Tobias could spend an entire evening," she said, rolling her eyes, "talking about how tools and barrels and clocks and what-nots are made best from one kind of wood or another." She sipped her wine. So petty, she thought. He'd probably sit here and try to figure out what wood the little soldier was made of.

John puckered his brows. "You don't have to worry about that anymore." As he chewed his last bite of flounder, he took out a cigarette. "So you didn't tell him anything?"

"I thought I'd write him a letter. But me leaving was no surprise. An idiot would have seen it."

"Even a woodhick idiot?" John put the cigarette to his mouth as a passing waiter stopped and lit a match.

Cassandra closed her eyes a moment. She wanted to laugh, but could not. "It was silly, marrying him," she said.

"Why in hell did you jump in?"

She shrugged. "Maybe revenge at my mother for always making me feel like a fool." She thought about that, her mind lucid with the wine. "Or maybe I really believed in it at the time."

John turned his head to exhale smoke. "What will your mother make of this?"

"I don't think she'll be disappointed. It always pleases her to say I was wrong." She did not notice the waiter at her side until he began reciting the dessert menu.

"I bet you recommend the crème brûlé, eh Pierre?" John said. The waiter said nothing. "Well, that's what I'll have. And a hot toddy of brandy."

"Nothing," Cassandra said. The waiter about-faced and walked away.

John watched with Cassandra the child and his toy soldier. "You didn't quite answer something when we were together at your house," he said. "Never exactly told me why you didn't have children."

She looked at John. "It never seemed like a real marriage, especially after I quit trying to feel what marriage should feel like."

"Then you were careful—about not getting pregnant."

She nodded, looked back at the boy, a churning in her stomach that was not entirely from the wine.

"But you agreed with me when I guessed you got scared thinking children would make the marriage real."

She shook her head back and forth. "It was more that children would have made whatever I was in real."

"So what should a marriage feel like?"

"I don't know, it must feel like something." She shook her head back and forth. "I never *feel,* John. I can't even *make* myself feel things."

"I'll make you feel things, Cassandra." He exhaled smoke across the table.

*   *   *

She was glad for the wine now. At the moment John locked the room door, the weight of what she'd done settled at the bottom of her stomach; the wine at least made it buoyant.

"That suit's smart as any I've seen on a native lady of this city," John said. She'd had the pearl-white outfit with a stole and cuffs of emerald velvet made two weeks ago just for this night. "But you should relax. You're tense as the hobbles of that skirt. I'll call for champagne; we'll take our ease."

So with a boldness she took from her dinner drinks and the promise of champagne, Cassandra went into the bathroom and changed into a dressing gown. She undid the wrap of her hair, which she'd pinned under a new velvet hat, bought to match the stole. She waited to go out, though, until she heard room service.

John sat at the desk chair, undressed down to his shirtsleeves, tie-less, shoeless. He handed her a glass as she stepped to the window. She looked across the lighted lace of the park's paths.

"Tomorrow," John said, "we'll rent a hansom cab and ride through that park, snug under a blanket."

"You have an appointment at two."

"Sure," he said. "And after I'm done, we'll do a show."

"How far I've come," she said, "with just a decision—one made through our letters, at that."

"It was more than a decision," John said, a trace of question in his voice.

"Well of course," she said. "I've always been moving this way. Here and to you."

"By the time that park turns green, you'll think you never called any place else home."

"I look forward to the day this all blows over—with my family and Tobias. The company."

"It will," John said. "Soon. And everyone will be better for it—you and I, J. Hadley Erhart, Celia Erhart, the company."

"And Tobias, too. I'm sure."

John did not say anything.

Spangles of snow sprinkled through the lamplight along the paths. "Is it the first snow?" she said.

"The what?"

"Has it snowed yet in New York?"

"Hell, I only checked in this morning. But I don't think it has. New York doesn't get near the damned stuff we did."

"It snowed overnight in Marstadt. Just an inch or so before I left. And then again on my way here." She leaned her forehead against the glass and took in the park grounds as best she could in the general glow of the city lights. She would have thought the land was flat—from pictures she'd seen and from knowing that Manhattan was a river island. But bare hillocks, pimpled with boulders, swelled among the trees.

"Tobias told me once," she said, "about his first encounter with you." John was silent. "It's colored your picture, like I know you so deeply. I see how all you've done un-spools from that moment."

"What did he say?" John said it almost indifferently.

"He told me," Cassandra said, "how your father made you work in the woods when you were a little boy. He said hicks treated you rough, and he believed those days weighted you too early with the worries of men. I just want you to know I understand you, John."

"Why is Tobias Meier all we talk about? You wrote in your letter that you'd be coming here free of him and that past."

She turned from the window. "Truly I am. I'm sorry."

He snuffed his cigarette—in an ashtray now. "I think we've agreed," he said, "to stay to this side of the past." He came to her, put a finger under her chin, rested his hand on her hip.

His kiss was sharp with scotch, and dry as his cigarettes. He nuzzled to her neck, his hand caressing her breast. She closed her eyes when he pressed her against the window, then his mouth was back on her lips, wet and opened, and his hand squeezed her breast. But against any exhilaration, she said, "I can't." Still, he put his hand to her thigh, lifted her leg and pressed more heavily, until she was sure she would burst into the snowfall. She opened her eyes, only to see he was looking out the window. "John, we can't."

He used her body instead of the window as he pushed himself back, wiped his mouth. "And what use is waiting?" He stayed within a breath of her face.

"I'm sorry. It's not good now."

He laughed and stepped toward a bureau. "Not to worry."

"Please," she said, and he stopped opening the drawer. She made herself smile. "It's really not a good time."

He watched her a moment. "Oh, that. Well, that doesn't bother me. At least we know we're safe. And we don't have to use anything." He closed the drawer and grinned.

Cassandra turned to the window and pinched at the satin of her dressing gown. "John, that fear of being pregnant is real, suddenly in a new way." She rested her forehead on the cold glass. "It's early, but not too early that I may have reason to be worried. Wouldn't it just figure?"

"But you came here," he said.

"We had this planned, John. It's unlikely anyway. I just need you to understand why I stopped you." She lifted her head and watched a circle of breath fade from the window. In the reflection, he stepped to the desk and lit a match.

*   *   *

They'd go shopping for an evening dress when he returned—he said by three. But it was fifteen minutes past, and she was bored of the novel she'd bought in the gift shop, bored of waiting. Sitting seemed to aggravate the ache in her skull from last night's wine. She'd take their coats and find him downstairs to give them a head start.

The entranceway to the barroom spewed smoke and murmur into the glare beaming through the hallway from the far door to the park. When she stepped in and searched that cavern of dark paneling, every eye turned her way. In the ensuing hush, a man she could not see said something, and laughter lit a course table to table. Heads leaned for a better look.

"Madam," said a maitre d'hotel in a tuxedo, approaching in a hurry from the bar. "*Can* I help you?" Like the tall man at the front desk yesterday, he wore that New York smile that threatened to be switched off any second.

"I'm looking for—" she strained her eyes at the bar— "my husband."

His smile relaxed into a look that seemed at once sympathetic but coolly unsurprised. "Your husband is Mr.—?"

But then she saw John coming from a corner table. He brushed past the waiter and took her elbow—not gently—and pulled her to the hallway.

"What in hell are you doing here," he said.

"You said three o'clock. I thought I'd come and find you. It's half past."

Glancing back through the doorway, held half-open by an inquisitive patron at a near table, she saw a man approach and peer through intently. He was in shirtsleeves and suspenders, carrying his coat over his forearm— a short, graying man whose round middle furrowed the top of his pants.

All the effort of his face seemed toward arching his lips up and hooking the tip of his nose down. Cassandra immediately did not like that man's eyes: swimming black beads, untrusting and untrustworthy.

"Don't you know that women aren't allowed in there," John said.

"Who is this?" the man said, squeezing through the doorway. His German accent was throatier even than that of the old settlers of Marstadt. He canted his head and looked her up and down while he thumbed the brim of a gray fedora.

"Never mind," John said.

"John?" The rudeness, Cassandra thought.

John exhaled, put his hands on his hips and shook his head. "Friedrick, this is Cassandra."

"Friedrick Taub," he said, stepping forward, his head still canted, close enough that she could smell the sweat-damp wool of his suit. Again he looked her up and down, then grinned at John and turned back. He closed his eyes as he nodded very quickly. "Cassandra who?" he said, and shrugged. John held up a hand as if to tell her to stop, and she fumbled for what name he'd want her to use. Well, what could be more suitable than her maiden name? Time to begin using it anyway.

"Erhart," she said. "Cassandra Erhart."

Friedrick stepped back, almost into the wall, as if the name had grown arms and shoved him. "A joke?" he said to John. Then he moved sidelong, toward the door facing Central Park.

"Wait, Friedrick," John yelled after him. "I'll explain."

Before John started away, he turned to Cassandra, teeth clenched. "Goddammit," he said, "Do you have any idea what you just caused?"

Then he grabbed his overcoat from her arm and was out the door after the German.

* * *

She moved toward the elevators, her cheeks afire, alarms sounding in her mind.

At first she didn't decipher that the mustached clerk called her as she walked by the front desk.

"Excuse me, *Mrs. Blesh.*"

She was about to step into the elevator. She turned and saw him waving an envelope, and for a moment, she just stared. She was thinking it was too late to have doubts about John. Or, really, too soon, much too soon. She started toward the clerk, not curious at what this man wanted, benumbed to his smirk over the delayed response.

"A telegram for your husband," he said.

Cassandra removed the manila page from its unsealed envelope and went to read, but noticed the clerk watching, his grin a sort of gloat now. …*the Plaza is very respectful of our guests' privacy,* she recalled.

She walked to the flower-urn sofa, sat facing away from the counter and began reading.

MARSTADT, Pa.   DECEMBER 5, 1913

Mr. John Blesh,
    Guest. Plaza Hotel, 5th Avenue at 59th Street, New York, N.Y.

Itinerary said pass on important news. The Plaza—my my. Old pal Tobias Meier in hospital. Held for murdering Groeger. Hadley found Tobias half-dead of cold where he tried to bury body. Think he attempted scapegoat for stealing formulas. There's more. Cassandra missing. Scandal scandal scandal.
Best
Office girls

She concentrated, staring ahead into the gray swirls of a marble wall, but she could not make the events of the past two moments sensible.

Then in her periphery, an elevator dial reached its apex, a bell rang, a door parted, and all the thoughts she turned in her mind suddenly nestled into a chain of events, something recognizable because it had a design— no, a scheme, one she'd have never guessed imaginable.

She rose and started for the elevator, stuffing the paper into her coat pocket. As clearly as she saw the trail that led to the telegram, Cassandra knew she was the only person in the world who could save Tobias Meier.

Chapter 23

He had the room to himself, looking over the snow-swept fields where the nuns rotated buckwheat and corn and potatoes. Nobody would be assigned to a ward with an accused murderer.

No need for surveillance other than a policeman checking in a few times a day; he sure wasn't running out of here. Funny how the loss of just one toe could put a man off balance to where he'd have to learn a new way of walking. Stranger yet how fingers that weren't there could burn as if skinned and limed.

The only other people he saw were a long-bearded priest who came by daily, and the nuns who floated in and out in their black robes and habits, keeping hospital. Nothing left for the doctor to do but let him heal to the point he could be led to jail. Though it wasn't the wounds that seemed to hold him down, rather how damned tired he was, still, from the effects of exposure.

He liked that the sisters treated him no differently than had he gotten his frostbite saving a child fallen through ice. Especially Sister Wulberga, a bespectacled, round-faced nun who squinted out from her habit like an old hooded Eskimo, and sang hymns while she looked at his stitches with a magnifying glass she wore on a lanyard. She was the one who came and put a hand on his shoulder and told him his wife had come, her words chanted and soothing, as if to console for some sad fate in this.

Though it took the wind out of him to even picture Cassandra, he'd hoped she would come; he hadn't known a soul could feel so forsaken. And yet he hadn't brought himself to contact his mother and father, even his sister.

The nun left Cassandra at the doorway. Tobias watched her unwrap her scarf and unbutton her coat. Blood throbbed so hard at the seams of his amputations, he feared the stitches would burst.

She stood and looked at him, and he thought she might turn and leave. He pulled the cover away, tugged at his gown, and waved her in. Then he mustered his muscles to sit, carefully moving the leg of his wrapped foot over the edge of the bed. She came and took the wrist of the hand that was a club of bandages. Her smell was of musty coach seats and cigarettes. He saw she was deliberating a kiss—a kiss with her husband. What more did he need to see?

"Ever since yesterday," she said, letting go of his wrist, her eyes on the hand, "I've been thinking of what I'd say. And I've come up with this: There's a greater plan in what we do, just as in what befalls us." She did not raise her head. Tobias saw she waited for him to respond to this.

"So you're saying you found something good in a thing you did," he said.

She nodded. "And I have news."

What more could he take?

"You've been cleared," she said.

So that was it. She'd come to be his savior in amends, and was turning the saving into the reason for what she'd done.

"Cassandra, I don't want any kind of pity or a name or money to rescue me. That road got me here."

But by her confident smile, he saw he might take heart that she held more than the hollow shell of a favor. "They know you didn't kill Ernie Groeger," she said. "Tobias, my father never believed it from the moment he tracked you down. But I was able to give proof you didn't steal that formula, and that's all the police needed to confirm it was the suicide it looked to be. We know you're innocent."

He hadn't let himself lose a tear—either for self-pity or for Ernie Groeger. But now that he saw her certainty, he craned his neck for the window, looked over the pearly play of snow-shadows in the plaits of the fields.

"All will be fine, Tobias. We've both learned from this."

"What have you learned?"

"Where I belong."

He still looked out the window. "That's what I've been thinking on, how it shouldn't take something bad to learn that."

She did not respond to this. "My father wants to see you."

"You know, I can't remember him finding me."

"You were nearly dead of hypothermia, Tobias. They told me your temperature was eighty degrees. With the snow covering your tracks, my father would have never found you except for the—" she paused— "the crows in the trees."

He looked back at her. "Why does your father want to see me?"

"He understands what you did—in the lab."

"He wants to work something out to keep your grandfather from pressing charges."

She nodded.

"I'd say it's more important that your grandfather understand things over your father."

"My father will do whatever it takes so we're all satisfied, including defend you to my grandfather. I'd say that's quite an effort, considering you could have killed him."

"It always comes down to your grandfather."

She twisted her scarf. "And what does that matter if he's willing to forget what you did so long as it doesn't get out? That's all that's important to him."

Cassandra stepped away and pulled a chair to the bed. She let out a long breath and sat. "I've been up for two days."

"What about your mother?" Tobias said.

"Same as always. Sighs as though she's the one suffering it all." She leaned toward him. "Tobias, let's go home."

He closed his eyes a moment. "I don't know where you went, Cassandra. But I know who you went to."

She watched the window. "Don't you understand when I say there's a greater plan? Going where I did, I found out you didn't steal that formula— I could not have saved you otherwise."

He went to say that had the car been home, he might have saved Ernie Groeger. But he would not fall into her error of whitewashing. "I hoped you wouldn't say something like that," he said.

Cassandra was looking at the bandaged hand again. Tobias worked the fingers of the other one, the left one. They still hesitated, but the doctor said that in time they'd serve him as well as ever. When he thought of his three missing fingers, his mind went always to how he might wield an axe or pull a saw. Even though that didn't matter, he felt lucky they were from the middle of his right hand; a woodhick relied on the grip of the other, the right more a guide. Useless thoughts he couldn't contain. Funny, the things that came to a person.

"It won't slow you down, Tobias. There's plenty of work you can do with a hurt hand. We'll find you something right."

He watched her. "I hobble like a three-legged horse."

"And we'll work together to get you walking tightropes. My mission in life will be to make you healthy. And happy."

How ready she was to say these things, how quickly they came on the heels of all else.

"We'll start," she said, "with a baby."

He laughed. "How can you say all this when you left just three days ago?"

"I know things I didn't then."

He credited her sincere tone. "About me or you or someone else?" he said.

She hesitated a moment. "About both of us." Then she smiled. "And maybe, just maybe, somebody else." She touched her stomach.

He lifted his bandaged foot onto the bed; the wound throbbed all the more when it hung over the side. "If things appeared differently, if whatever it was that proved my innocence hadn't happened, you wouldn't be here."

She sighed and looked everywhere but at him. "That's the way life happens, Tobias, falling dominoes. But no matter what, I'd have come around." She smiled. "I understand it's not easy. But after you're home a while and we straighten out this last bit of trouble with my grandfather, we'll all be better for this." She looked at his hands the second she said it, then away.

"I have to stay here another two days," he said. "Until I can at least put weight on this." He lifted his bandaged foot. "I really may have an awkward walk."

She shrugged and flicked a hand as if to say it didn't matter. Then she stood and leaned over him and said she'd be back later. "I have to start getting the house ready." She kissed his lips and turned, buttoning her coat as she walked away.

* * *

A moment later, Sister Wulberga came and looked through her magnifying glass at the bandages on his foot.

"Sister," Tobias said, "do you know I'm innocent?"

She did not look up from tugging the dressing. "Your guilt or innocence has no bearing on our care."

He went to apologize, thinking he'd insulted her. But he stopped, overtaken by the clearer view of things that came upon her words.

"Sister," he said, "I need to reach my parents."

* * *

For a moment every morning when he awakened, Tobias believed he was back in his boyhood home in Pigeondale. Same size room, same musk of pine floorboards. But newspapers weren't pasted with buckwheat to stop drafts. The room was wallpapered. Blue cornflowers. And the air seeping around the windowpane had not the smell of sawdust, but tannin and sour cowhide.

He would let it sink in that he was in his parents' house in a tannery town, then stare for a time at the strip of bandage hiding the three knuckle stubs that looked like the stitched ends of burlap sacks.

He had a lot of thinking to do, and a lot of time to do it. He walked daily through the hillside streets of the company neighborhood, trying to work out the lopsidedness of his gait and the chill he couldn't leach from his bones. As the days passed, it occurred to him that his thinking ought to be on what he already knew. It was around the time his scars started to itch, and January's snap of windy frigidness set in, that he came to see this in a conversation with his sister, and then in the way of his father.

Because she worked at a bakery, Frieda was always home early in the afternoon bearing yesterday's rolls or muffins, flour in her hair and the smell of doughnut grease about her.

Tobias appreciated her company; she did not pester him as his mother did about his intentions with Cassandra or why he wouldn't take her calls. Nor did she question his work plans as did his father.

"I'm leaving, come summer," Frieda told him one afternoon as she sat in the kitchen over a bushel basket, sorting out soft potatoes while he fanned a new fire in the woodstove.

Tobias never expected those words from her at thirty years old. She's got a man on the sly, he thought. "Where to?"

"Pittsburgh. I've been saving all these years for nursing school."

He took a seat at the table. He realized he'd assumed his sister was content staying where she was—or else had surrendered to it. He spoke before he thought. "You sure that's right for you?"

This brought a smile to her eyes. "Of course. I've planned since before you went to the woods. You'd think a wish made that young is a real one, wouldn't you?"

A chick pecking out of its egg, he thought.

"It's the Mercy school," she said. "Run by nuns. Afterwards I'll likely stay in the city. So now you'll understand that I'm dying to get a look at that foot." She pointed at his shoe propped on a chair. "And under that bandage on your hand." Tobias started unwrapping it without another thought.

"I haven't told Pop yet," she said, pulling her chair up to him. "You know how he can be."

*　*　*

That night in the front room, dim lights and little conversation, Herbert Meier made it clear as he did every night that the situation with Ernie Groeger would never have happened, nor would Tobias be separated from a wife, had he taken work as a laborer instead of an apprentice in a laboratory. "I warned you," he said. "You had no business marrying the daughter of an industry man, let alone the granddaughter of Warren P. Ryder."

Tobias looked at his mother, who said nothing. She believed he'd simply misplaced his spirit, which he had every right to have.

When Tobias had first come home, he'd seen his stiff and angry father as a window to his future. But they were not the same; he knew now he had something his father did not.

When Tobias hobbled to his room that night, he thought this meant he would thus make a better life no matter if he decided on a job at the tannery. But something about places, places where he was and wasn't vulnerable to all this questioning, kept washing into his reasoning, and then into his dreams. So when he woke the next morning, long before daylight and ahead of even his sister the baker—but soon-to-be nurse—he did not dwell on his maimed hand. Instead, he removed the bandage. Then he dressed and packed his clothes and put on his blue-checked mackinaw. He pulled on a hat with rabbit fur flaps, put a glove on his left hand and a mitten on the other.

He tapped on his sister's door and woke her, said goodbye and started for the station.

He sat at the edge of the platform, feeling the same calm resolve he saw in dawn whitewashing the valley. First it brushed the denuded ridges and the smokestack of the tannery's boiler building, then the gables of the bark mill and leach house. When he heard his south-bound chugging down the Clarion River valley, full sunlight made a jagged salt and pepper of snowy roofs and seasoned wall-planks all through the tannery complex and up the rows of company houses.

He boarded the single coach that trailed the train of box freighters, and took his seat bound for Marstadt. Only a handful of other passengers rode the car, Buffalo businessmen heading to points south.

At a small stream a few miles down the valley, the engine turned off the trunk line, taking an alternate loop for the Marstadt stop. As the train ascended the divide—up the Allegheny watershed, closing on the headwaters of the Susquehanna—the land showed a different signature. Back along the Clarion, the earth and trees and slower waters were softer, a place of aspen glens and soil-banked riverbends. Now, nearing Marstadt, there was a sharpness to the snowscape—beneath it lay strewn sandstone, upheaved and rent and whittled by movement of earth and elements. A jaggedness even to the treeline—oak-dominant with scattered scrub pines and laurel copses.

It was as if he moved from a region as pliable as river clay to terrain like himself; he sensed a coarseness under his skin, ridged and brittle as this land. He felt a comforting pull toward the horizon, where just beyond Marstadt the earth roughened more, and had a tilt to it few were keen to, channeling and hastening gravity into the reaches of the Susquehanna's headwaters—brooks gushing from the hollows to power the river's current. Source-land of the world's fuel, of the energy that pulsed up out of those ancient mountain roots, which time had chafed clear to their innards. Where it all starts. *A man's a taker for a thing he can feel but can't see.*

The pulsing had weakened in the loam of these six years. But the ebbing of it, he realized, had sharpened him to the heart of the beat. It called him, laid a course. He like an old-time raftsman done with his run, his back turned to the slower waters.

At the depot in Marstadt, Tobias inquired at the grilled ticket window about a train to Pigeondale.

The station agent turned and leaned to the trackside bay window, took a sweeping glance up and down the line, and looked back at Tobias with an apologetic frown. "Only one coach passes out there," he said. "Won't come through till two o'clock."

"Freight?" Tobias said.

Again the agent turned his face end to end at the bay window. Tobias saw this was his habit. The agent shrugged. "Probably empties leaving the tannery in that direction sometime next hour. They've been getting bark from a tannery just closed out East. Been running through Manooka Valley between the common carriers." He eyed Tobias's satchel at his hip, caught the bare, two-fingered hand, then went to the other, which held his mitten and glove. "Not much to be found in Pigeondale," he said. "Anymore."

"So I hear," Tobias said.

The agent again glanced at Tobias's hand.

"Can I have a scrap of paper?" Tobias said.

The agent pushed a tablet of Ryder Railroad stationery and a pencil to the edge of the ticket counter. Tobias scrawled a note, best he could with his left hand. He took the note next door to the livery stable and paid the boy who tended horses fifty cents to deliver his message, then started for the tannery.

Tobias stopped along Station Street and looked over at a narrow, false-fronted, box-of-a-building nuzzling the boardwalk. He rested his sore foot on a mound of shoveled snow, and considered this steam laundry his father-in-law ran after all these years, leasing it to a family who'd worked the trade in Munich. J. Hadley Erhart believed in holding on to what accounted for where he was—not for the material of it, but for its lesson. Erhart's generosity, his appreciation for his place and good fortune, were rooted in not forgetting where he came from, a quality Tobias would call to his attention.

Between rows of hemlock bark on the knoll above the Ryder tannery, Tobias found a worker pushing a wheelbarrow. He assured Tobias that the train on the siding was going his way, but to note that it lacked boxcars.

"I've ridden lots of flat cars in the cold," Tobias said, glad he'd be headed out on his own kind of train.

He found a car to the rear and sat on his satchel. He knew he could ride in the tender but did not feel like answering questions. And when the engineer and fireman finally came and stoked the locomotive and put the train in motion, they gave him no more than a glance.

On out the line, the train picking up momentum as it slanted into Manooka Valley, Tobias turned up his collar and tugged at his earflaps. He faced away from the rush of air and engine soot, took in the trees crowding the track. Pole timber.

Just before Pigeondale, Tobias hopped cars to the lead empty and signaled to the fireman. The engineer slowed the train as they rounded to where the engine shed once bordered the tracks. Tobias shouldered his satchel and jumped onto the snowy strip of ground where the plank had been. Grimacing at the pain of his wounded foot, he turned to the engine and waved a thank you, then looked to the void in the distance—open sky where once loomed the knotty plank walls, long cupola and smokestack of the sawmill.

He squinted across the snow-covered valley; no mill saws screeching, no musk of fresh-sawed hemlock.

In the thoroughfare that was the main street, a few tire tracks indicated that at least one person here had a car. The hotel still stood—visible from the railroad now that the intervening businesses were gone—the dentist's office, the barbershop, the post office. A strip of plank fronted the building—had even been shoveled. But it was merely a barroom and residence now.

Across the way, the hulking uprights of the old company store held firm where they'd been planted. Skeletons robbed of their clapboards and trusses.

Beyond this town-stubble, at the base of the valley, a smattering of faded gray structures persisted where had been the rows of the company neighborhood he grew up in. Some places had become hunting camps—as had the Whitehouse—but a few were still homes, occupied now by the families of section crew bosses and pulp contractors.

The emptiness of it was like the leavings of a cocoon on a chunk of tree bark—refuse, faded reminder that the life nurtured there had fluttered off. Life shaped and colored in its womb, the womb just a moldering husk now left to fertilize that earth. There was a hint of deliverance in a thing forlorn.

He looked along the tracks. On down, one old shanty remained—probably a tool shed for a section gang. But nearer him still stood Josiah Blesh's retired office: boarded windows, padlocked door, sturdy as a cigar box. It looked maimed now with the plank gone, the door inaccessible.

In front of the little building, Tobias probed the snow with his better foot until he came upon the ladder used to reach the door, and he leaned it there. He looked around the side to confirm that the tin stovepipe still poked out of the roof, saw that the outhouse and well pump remained out back. In the stead of railroad sheds, he kicked enough pine shakes and broken wall slabs to make an afternoon's-worth of firewood, which he piled at the base of the ladder. Then he sat on his satchel alongside a pier of the office.

With an unfettering of warm hope that so conflicted with the chilly ruin, he looked across the shadowless snow blanketing the slag of his hometown, and he waited, not knowing whether to listen for an automobile or a train.

*   *   *

Tobias was recalling mornings he'd come to this office asking to be put on, when down along the tracks, on the road from Marstadt, a covered Buick came into view, tire chains jingling. J. Hadley Erhart stopped across from the office, and peered out at Tobias. He got out of the car and came across the tracks.

"Why here?" Erhart said, looking from Tobias to the office.

"Did you bring a key?" Tobias said, standing.

Erhart took off a leather glove, reached into the pocket of his greatcoat and held out a skeleton key.

"Stove still in there?" Tobias said, taking the key.

"I believe so. The company used the place while we dismantled the town and moved out the equipment." Erhart turned to look over the remains of Pigeondale. His eyes stopped on the opening where once stood the sawmill.

Tobias slung his satchel over his shoulder and gathered an armful of wood, then moved up the ladder. With the key between his teeth, he said, "I'm going to start a fire."

Inside, after his second trip for wood, Tobias pulled away a board nailed over the window by the stove. Then he took a newspaper from a pile on the floor and crumpled it into the stove's belly. He made a teepee of wood, and lit the paper while Erhart climbed into the office and leaned against the door frame, arms crossed.

The room was little changed. Josiah Blesh had removed only his framed maps and file drawers from behind the desk. He'd left the two spare chairs along the wall, even the apple crates by the stove where Tobias and John had listened in on Josiah's business.

Tobias laid his satchel on the desk where sixteen years ago Emory Sundae spread his map and explained how a logging crew would forge into Teaberry Hollow. Tobias pulled out the chair and sat, indicating for his father-in-law to pull up one of the others.

But Erhart remained leaning in the doorway. "What's this all about?"

"You sent word you wanted to talk."

Erhart nodded. "Been trying for a month. Cassandra, too."

"I got your word. And now I'm ready."

"Why here?"

"For one, Warren P. Ryder. It's best I'm not around him." Tobias lifted his head to indicate the opened door. "It's not getting any warmer in here."

Erhart shut the door, then pulled a chair to the desk. "Tobias," he said, "I've told my father-in-law that I'd be offering you work with the company, no matter what he thinks. You have that coming." He put his gloves into a pocket of his greatcoat. "We all know you thought you had to defend yourself. You felt trapped."

Tobias just watched as Erhart unbuttoned his coat, crossed his legs and put his hat on his lap.

"You have no idea," Erhart said, "how far out I'm going for you. I'm standing up to a man you could have killed, and telling him you come back or I sell my share."

"Why?" Tobias said. "Because of Cassandra?"

Erhart shook his head back and forth. "Many reasons. One is selfish. It has to do with the consequence of a terrible mistake I made. I let myself be deceived thinking the best of someone. Hell, I built a lodge as a monument to my gullibility." He paused and blew between pursed lips. "I began piecing together my mistake after you ran out of the lab. Since then, I've had Ernie Groeger's death on my shoulders."

"And I haven't?" Tobias took off his hat and tossed it onto the desk. "He died believing my guilt. From the second I saw those opened journals, I knew he'd do something—those formulas were everything to him. But I was too late."

Tobias pulled off his glove and mitten and stuffed them into a pocket of his mackinaw. He saw Erhart lock on the maimed hand. "Don't you understand? If I'd have acted on my own, John wouldn't have used me to move on. He wouldn't have had someone to take the fall. I was the key to John's design."

"No, Tobias," Erhart said, pointing back and forth between them. "We both were."

"Either way, no one's swaying my course anymore."

"No one but a ghost," Erhart said. He leaned forward. "The only place my misjudgment will live on is your gloom."

"So I'm another one of your good deeds?"

"Tobias, I'll always have causes. Before I was your age, I lost a father and four brothers—that made me acutely aware of the frailty of life. So I've rushed to achieve all I can, and to help others do the same." He glanced away. "Unfortunately all that rushing caused me to neglect Cassandra."

"As did Mrs. Erhart," Tobias said.

Erhart nodded slowly. "Tobias, I know where Cassandra went."

Tobias shrugged.

"But I didn't need her to tell me you were innocent. In fact, I went after you once I understood why you were so adamant about finding Groeger. When I got there and saw his bare foot, then his shoe by the tree, I knew what he'd done. But everyone needed proof. That came where Cassandra went. In the meantime, I could not defend you until my missing daughter turned up and I knew everything."

Tobias limped to the stove. "What was the proof?" He used a piece of shingle to poke at the embers before he threw on more wood.

"A two-bit translator—some normal school German teacher Blesh met in a bar in Philadelphia. They found an American Carbon apprentice who wanted to be a hero matching the performance of our carbon. So Blesh fed him mixes he'd stolen picking the lock of Ernie's trunk. When American realized they had a grade of formula as good as ours, they resubmitted samples and kept their price low so they'd be sure to win that big order and get a jump on us. Hell, the apprentice knew all our costs—Ernie kept everything in those journals. And Johnny got a pittance for it—the apprentice's life savings. Sold the company for a week-long spree in some gaudy hotel. He thought we'd fire the New York man and give him the job. Then he'd make himself a darling rebuilding what he destroyed. Who knows what would have been next." He watched Tobias a moment. "Tobias, the cocky son-of-a-bitch didn't think we'd find anything. You were not set up."

Tobias dismissed it and went back to his chair, tempted to tell Erhart he was wrong, that though John hadn't expected anyone to find out, he'd certainly figured in fall-backs—Groeger first, Tobias if that went bad. But he simply said, "What kind of trouble is John in?"

"Naturally, he's been fired. But he's not worth anything, so we can't recoup any loss. And with Ernie gone, we lost our best offense in a case against American. Besides, they were probably as surprised as we were. So we run the risk of making a case and getting nothing but a charge on the apprentice." He looked to the window. "And since I don't bring it up with my father-in-law in the little we speak, I doubt it will go anywhere."

Erhart looked back at Tobias. "But you can be assured that Johnny Blesh will one day come to a bad end."

"I don't desire that John Blesh come to a bad end."

"Why can't you be as forgiving of Cassandra?"

"It has nothing to do with forgiveness, Mr. Erhart." He looked away. How would he explain this?

"All this time I've been looking for what's right for me. That destination you spoke of. I let John Blesh make me think it was in trying his way. And Cassandra was part of how I saw that path. But Ernie Groeger was telling me all the while it wasn't in taking paths, theirs or his own, but letting a path be a destination. That's different from most people, especially John Blesh—his destination is whatever he wants to have, and so goes his path."

Erhart looked around the office. "So what are we doing here, Tobias?"

"This is part of my destination," Tobias said.

Erhart gasped out a chuckle. "Pigeondale?"

"You said you'd give me any work I wanted," Tobias said.

"I meant it."

"I want woods work."

Erhart turned up his palms. "We're not timbering anymore. Even up North, we're contracting that work now."

Tobias went to the window and looked out. "I remember like yesterday you giving your reasons for keeping the land." He turned and leaned against the wall. "My fit with all you said is coming clearer and clearer."

"If I don't say so," Erhart said, "it's providing a surer inheritance than any factory ever will." He lifted his chin toward the window. "Most of that pole timber is oak. There's veneer and furniture cropping up in these hollows. And all the competition that logged around us and moved on, they've already squandered their ventures."

Tobias nodded to this.

"Tobias, you were on your way to something. And that opportunity is still there."

"Of anyone," Tobias said, "at least anyone living, I thought you'd understand."

Erhart regarded him, the great crimson brows pinched. Then they loosened. "I've not been listening to you." He shook his head up and down, thought aloud. "When you give a man an opportunity, consider what he's fit for, as Ernie tried to tell me."

"That's part of it," Tobias said. "Just the beginning, though."

Erhart pondered his hat, then glanced at Tobias's hand. "I know just the job for you."

Tobias gave his attention, but he doubted they had the same idea.

"The lodge. You could oversee the place. Old Snyder's finally getting old. He needs someone to take over."

Tobias stepped to the stove. He crouched and opened the door and checked the fire, then tossed in pieces of pine shake. He went back to the desk, and remained standing. He could see that Erhart realized the folly in making him lord of John Blesh's invention, the place of Tobias's own honeymoon.

"You do know the land, Tobias. Directly." Erhart stood and went to the window. He leaned his forehead to almost touching the frame. "And so it belongs to people like you in a way it never will to us."

He looked over his shoulder. "You do know this land." He turned back to the window. "Today's surveyors and geologists don't know places in the ways I saw Emory Sundae know them. You would be helpful to those men."

"You might be near to my thinking," Tobias said.

Erhart shrugged. "The farther we get away from timbering on our own, the more we become a landholding company. At any time we've got pulp contracts going or bark jobbers bidding or gas lessees calling. With hundreds of thousands of acres, it'll just get busier." He was shaking his head up and down now. "We'll need someone in the woods, someone who knows timber and access roads to mark boundaries and make maps, check on gates and contractors." He nodded up at the snowy south ridge of Manooka Valley. "Someone who can cruise that timber coming back."

"To answer your question from before, Mr. Erhart, *that's* what this is about. And now I'll think about it and decide if I'm interested."

Erhart turned from the window and raised his brows while Tobias took his seat. "This is something you'd do from Pigeondale?"

Tobias nodded.

"Where would you even stay?"

Tobias gave the room a sweeping glance. "This would be a start." He pointed at the stove. "I read once that heat is the first necessity."

"I like to give a man an opportunity, Tobias, but not if it means him leaving my daughter."

"It was your daughter that left me, sir."

Erhart considered a moment. "Do you remember me saying when I found you and Cassandra at the lodge that I feared a difference of intentions?"

"I figured that out," Tobias said. "You saw in me something that happened to you. At one time, there was what you might be. Then there came what Mrs. Erhart intended."

"But you see," Erhart said, "even so, I've been able to do all a person could dream of."

Tobias was shaking his head. "No," he said.

Erhart drew a deep breath, looked around the room. "Well then," he said. He tipped his head, groaned and said it again. Finally he looked at Tobias. "I guess I don't have to lecture you as I did Johnny Blesh when he came to me with the lodge idea—to always remember you're accountable." He nodded out at Manooka Valley.

Erhart put on his hat. "When I look back," he said, "it always amazes me how prophetic we can be."

He turned and started out. "And all the while I've had a man working for me—a son-in-law—who saw it, too."

Erhart opened the door, and the white glare of winter sunlight washed the room. He turned and stepped down the ladder.

*   *   *

As soon as the jangle of tire chains shushed into the snow cover of Manooka Valley, Tobias went to the door. As he pushed it closed and the brightness swept from the room in a retracting wedge, a small square stood out in the dimness above him, a reflection of window light. He looked at the photograph where it had hung these twelve years, there where he'd ignored it today.

Now he saw the whole picture: a big-eyed boy who wanted to be a woodhick; the eager heir, J. Hadley Erhart; Josiah Blesh with his cynical scowl; the corrosive discontent fermenting in his son's eyes.

And of course her, the woman who'd come to this hicktown and—before the backdrop of a sawmill smokestack—struck a pose that had given him that teasing taste of the big world.

He reached with his left hand and lifted the frame from its nail, turned the picture away, and walked to the stove.

Using the tip of his shoe, he lifted the stove door, swung it open. With his two-fingered hand, he tossed the picture into the flames. He shut the door, stepped to the window and leaned his forehead against the glass, taking in what remained of Pigeondale. Then he turned to the pale square where the wall planks hadn't darkened, as if time paused for that story, as if he could pick up from there now—now that he'd acted on his own account. The first time in a long, long while.

Epilogue

Before he got too far, Tobias did turn to watch his grandson walk downstream to fish for stocked trout where the road traced the water.

Tobias started upstream.

He always liked that a place's lure took from what it was called, from something that spoke of it. Piebald. Patch-coat deer. This hollow could have no other name. It was in the stream patter, the wind on the cheek, the salty smack of wet, mossy sandstone. Just as beyond the ridge, the musty sweetness of teaberry was on those waters.

Tobias baited his hook, drew the pole from behind him, and dropped his worm into the gurgling froth at the head of a pool no wider than a washbasin. An invisible eddy twitched the drifting line, then the bait surfaced where the water tapered into a riffle.

After Tobias's many tries, a little brook trout took the worm. In a motion, Tobias yanked it from the water, and staying all its wild vigor with a squeeze behind the gills, he unhooked the fish and admired its red speckles, its blaze belly, its shape and wiliness so beautifully suited to this gossamer of spring water. He still wondered at how these delicate fish made their way to this nook, took to it, thriving natives severed from their kindred.

He could taste that trout as he dropped it into his wicker creel, feel it fueling him with whatever fueled it in the depths. And he thought of how a man could love a trout and kill it—maybe love it more than men who did not kill trout—just as he'd loved trees and felled them. He saw no contradiction in that.

He continued upstream; all morning he'd felt an urge to forge up this hollow, alone. He watched the tracks of a coon in a pebbly sandbar, his mind full of this woods that had come of the old, quietly, imperceptibly—

to most. Full of the rings he'd counted in the stumps left of pines that long-forgotten men like Geet Rakestraw felled for ship masts. Full of his axing and sawing broad-waisted hemlocks, his gazing at the spanning arms of chestnuts before the blight. Full of the hardwoods he'd known as saplings, palisading now the ridges. Full of the crowns of the old pines' offspring poking there above the treeline, of second-generation hemlocks shading again Piebald Run. So he was mindful today that he was the link; he beheld the succession of timbers, from the work of Geet Rakestraw, to this new forest. Which carried something of the old.

But the strength of timber was as delicate as respect, as delicate as passenger pigeons. The chestnuts of Fiddlers Flats were long gone, no more than a memory, no more than oil paints on a canvas that hung now in the home of the woman he still—after fifty-three years apart—abidingly thought of as his wife.

Walking wide of the stream, he turned to the drumming of a woodpecker and saw that the clouds remained a low sheet of rumpled grays, like an oyster shell. He crouched and fished the next pool through. After six drifts of the bait, he tried a salted minnow. Nothing. He moved on.

He walked a stretch of mounded embankment, the flanks of its hogback eroding, its ends washed away where Piebald Run had shifted its course. No trees grew in the center of the strip, and he staggered his steps between corduroy depressions where beech crossties had rotted from the old rail bed. The earth was reclaiming what horse and plow and shovel had long ago arranged according to the design of mapmaker Emory Sundae. The effect of this place on humans was greater than anything they did to it, the old rail grade hanging on as precariously as dew to the new dogwood petals.

If Tobias feared anything today, it was that he was the memory of this place, and that with him would die that pang of confounded instinct in the ruby eye of a passenger pigeon.

With that thought nagging him, he put a rubber knee-boot in the water, and crossed Piebald Run. He'd pass from the other side the rise of earth and creek-stone left of the rail siding where a bark car was parked seventy-two years ago, the place he'd seen the boy John Blesh and the incident wherein rooted John's spite. Whatever came of him, Tobias did not know.

The stream bank was steep where he ascended. He paused to catch his breath, but did not rest, given to that sense of needing to move uphollow.

He fished another hour, caught trout at hole after hole, even in the rippled water, which still surged from the Easter rise. It was coming on lunchtime, but he did not want the sandwiches in his creel. Exercise had flushed the stiffness from his hips and knees. And the grogginess that anymore settled on him through the day was instead lifting out of his mind.

There was something freeing in this walking—an outbreaking, as if the gate of a bygone splash dam had lifted and he spilled through the valley. He thought no longer of fishing.

Near the head of the hollow, the walls drew tight, canyon-like, the remains of the old rail bed snug to the water. Much of the grade had washed away, but he followed where a faint path still traced its course. He stopped and leaned his fishing pole against a yellow birch, un-slung his creel, and left them.

The ground steepened, the stream dropping between sandstone boulders in a ziz-zagging staircase of falls and pools. A remainder of grade he mounted dissolved into a pile of rocks—an abutment where the rails had crossed the water on stringers of broad pine logs. He half-crawled down the strewn stone, stepped in and out of the water and up the opposite abutment.

The next stretch of rail bed arced up the side of the hollow. Away from the stream it was smoother, letting him regain the gait he'd settled into over the years, only a faint sway to the side of the maimed foot. But his breath was not so even. Every few steps he'd pant in fits—no way of controlling them. Still, where the sweep of the trail reached its peak, he turned up, a vane in him aligned toward the ridge, sure as a compass needle.

He could climb only a few steps at a time, resting to look up through the picket of tree trunks reaching stoic against the downward thrust of this cut in the earth. But he rose, too, needing to get to the top, squinting against the beat that peened at his temples fast and hard in a warning he ignored.

He thought of his grandson. He hoped the young man had not followed him.

*   *   *

Pauses lasted much longer than steps; his feet became heavier and heavier. He'd been inching upward for two hours and could still hear Piebald Run. It sounded up here like the muffled gurgle of the underground springs that fed it. The headwaters—rain of the sky percolating through this place. Blood of the plateauland, urgent and cold and rushing with energy that he knew welled from the thin place ahead.

The temple-peening—more a sledge now—had moved to his ribcage, dizzying. Still he moved upward.

Then the wall of the hollow reared so steeply, the sandstone scales of it lay ready to loose under the leaves, and he slipped often, coming down on a knee or shoulder. But they weren't hard falls—the face of the ridge, in its abruptness, was not far from his body. He kept on.

Finally, laurels barbed the brim, and though they made a maze of his path, he could hold on as he pulled himself to the top. Daylight ebbed toward dusk already and the trough of the hollow behind him was muting from canvas brown to gray. But up ahead, the light of sun still saturated the cloud cover.

Tobias leaned against an oak and looked across the open understory, waiting for his breath to slow and deepen. But the pounding in his chest seemed to have seized on an outward stroke, cramming his lungs, tightening even his throat.

Squinting for the pain, he scanned the terrain, weighing against memory its faint folds, the slant of the place cresting into tableland and sky. He studied the treetops.

There. Flanking him. He could tell by the crowns, trailing in two rows, that the trees had grown along the disturbed earth of a skid road. Against his bloated chest and chasing breaths, he started away.

No trace remained on the ground, but by the two columns of tree trunks and the strip of white sky between the tops, Tobias could follow the course where the succession of trees had not regained footing. It would lead to the head of the slide he'd loaded with logs, back when the century was new and these woods lay freshly timbered.

It was easier walking on level ground, but not much. The fullness in his breast staggered his steps, pushing now to his shoulders. And the harder he tried to deepen his breathing, the less air he seemed to take in.

But it was only another quarter-mile to Teaberry Hollow. Damn, if he just didn't have to step over fallen limbs and timbers. He rested and looked through the alleyway of trees. There, a stretch of trough the teams had gouged dragging logs, still visible under sixty-five years of leaf mold.

He spooked deer, and not from beds—out already for their twilight feeding. Finally, the brighter abruptness over Teaberry Hollow showed through the trees. At the rim, he eased his back against a hollowed and gray, chest-high stump.

Looking down the side-hollow before him, he saw it in his mind, the log slide snaking to the jumble at the landing. He heard the bump-bump of butting timbers as teams moved along the oiled groove. The smooth handle of his cant hook came to him, the tang of fresh-cut hemlock. But that wasn't what he'd come for.

He reached back to steady himself as he leaned away, and it occurred to him this stump was not from any new timbering—these parts hadn't been logged since his day. Besides, those stumps were long gone, and never so tall. He turned, and with a chill, he recalled Geet Rakestraw saying, *A pine stump will outlast you.* He could still run his fingers along the brim of the flat crown, course of a saw that sang a hundred and twenty years ago through a woods forgotten. Who'd know such a stump now?

He started along Teaberry's ridgeline. Despite the disorienting pain, he stepped to the pull of the knoll with the homing a bird hears in lengthening days, a salmon in its death call. When he trudged onto the rise, last light sifted from the pearly cloud cover over the far shoulder of Teaberry Hollow. It lay across the valley's abyss like a pool, something he could step through, a ford, a shortcut home.

The spreading limbs of Old Fatbottom wreathed dense, a shrouding embrace. Even sitting, he panted. He pressed the sides of his neck to stifle the ache that welled out of his chest, and took in the writhing pitch pine, bear oak, sassafras, the kinked snags of stunted laurels, unseen but by the snow and rain, the insistent wind.

Tobias tried to draw strength from these haunches gained in rearing beautiful, infinite limbs against the elements. But the same muck of gravity that had weighted his steps in climbing here countered the effort, the field of some lodestone he'd never known—until today's weakness. So it had tugged at his cuffs all the years he worked, and he hadn't felt it for his strength, becoming more than the logger he always wanted to be—cruising timber and property lines, charting tracts to lease, even drawing road grades for the CCC. He'd tuned to an inner rhythm, become a woodsman, a man of the place.

Out of the milky light of dusk came a raven croak from Teaberry Hollow, the call of day's end, of things finished. Behind him, chipmunks rushed their last in the moldering of yesteryears' leaves, searching out the new shoots of another spring. He did not turn, couldn't with the pain that swelled his neck. Besides, he wanted right now only this knoll's indifference.

A breeze streamed across the plateau from beyond Teaberry Hollow, curled under the brim of his hat and whispered into his ears. It was the new wind, the soft one that always came before dusk this time of year. It told of darkness nigh, that the evening creatures—the coons and opossums and owls and bears—would start their shifts. He knew every cycle of this place. He'd owned it, in his way. Who now?

By this time, his grandson would be well upstream, looking for him, calling against the babble of water and descent of darkness. That's what it was for—for that boy—the understanding of the land that had cost the oblivion of birds and chestnut trees.

The weight roared all through him, wringing even the bones of his fingers, pushing at his skull. He squeezed his eyes, leaned hard into Old Fatbottom, bearing against the rending of every fiber, the fear. When he looked again, the last pale band of sundown edged the treeline across Teaberry. He tensed his legs to fend the gaining pull of the earth. But it slipped under his flesh like a skinning knife, and he startled at the tremor of it, as if he'd touched a snake beneath a rock.

Tobias strained for that faint strip in the west. But he could no longer see. There was something good in that, for now he knew for sure that what he'd sought wasn't a passing light, but the fire at its source—somehow he could feel warmth on his face.

He pushed his eighty-year frame into Old Fatbottom, holding against the undertow. He felt the tremor coursing the tree's sapwood, too, and it embraced him as completely as it did the dead heartwood within.

His panting was not even an effort for breath anymore, rather frantic spasms of his lungs trying to bear him up for the answer he realized he'd come for. He would not go down until he knew, the problem that had burned since childhood, that had so often confounded his life.

Tobias turned his face upward, into the fire of the light. It seared now, tongues burning through flesh.

"Why?" he said in a wheeze as rough as sandstone, the heart of him tearing, gushing, though his mind held clearly the ruby eye of that passenger pigeon. "Why?"

He drew what breath he could and listened, listened to the wind fifing through the kinks of Old Fatbottom's limbs, to the rasp of night creatures on the go, felt the sway of treetops, of the living earth, felt himself moving with it, seeping into the completeness, like the last moldering of a windfallen pine, resistant as an old stone fence.

THE END

Acknowledgements

My thanks to the following:

Clint McCown and Jack Driscoll; the faith of masters is never forgotten.

Dr. Robert Stith, who introduced me to the Greeks; they were with me all the way.

The eagle eyes, Patty Zion and Michele McGovern.

Jonathan Scott, for his patience and generosity.

Ben Moyer, Charles Fergus and Dave Drakula; writers never know whom they inspire.

Mark Stoltz, who gave me the big question asked here.

Rick States, for getting me into that troubled mind.

The Henry Ford, which helped me find the key.

The Pennsylvania Council on the Arts.

The Pennsylvania Humanities Council.

All my fellow natives of St. Marys, Pennsylvania, who, as a matter of course and to our great fortune, keep true the culture. I hope they'll forgive the liberties.

My grandfathers—Joe Piccirillo and Philip Charles Edward PC Fish Herzing, S.B.D, P.P.—for all the stories.

And lastly, Fred Herzing, whom I still remember holding me in his big logger's hands when I was yet a baby. My greatest distinction is that I am descended from a woodhick.

Made in the USA
Middletown, DE
12 July 2022

69079185R00187